CARSON

PROMISE

— ⊹ —

KC WARDELL

Second Printing: 2023

ISBN 979 8 9881357 0 8 Ebook

ISBN 979-8-9881357-6-0 Paperback

ISBN 979-8-9881357-2-2 Hardback

Cover design by RDH Book Cover Designs

Formatting design by Carlette Whitlock

CONTENTS

To My Readers

These thank yous could go forever if I am not careful. Just remember, I appreciate all of you.

The fact that *Carson Promise* is finally published is my sister's fault. I started this novel when I was twelve years old and I'm in my forties now. She insisted it was time to make this happen. Thanks, Ash.

Dorrance Publishing, thank you for taking a chance on me, I had dreams of a wall full of rejection letters from publishing companies; that never happened,

All those years ago, it was a tutor I had that showed me how fun writing could be. I still have the cassette tape and the finished project. Yes, I'm that old. Thank you, Mrs. Lowe.

Mr. Carter, YVHS Choir Members, you are the best! I remember late night talks with the girls, being carried on and off the bus by the guys, and the time we spent on stage and behind. The inspiration came from here.

To my Readers:

I hope you enjoyed the characters' relationships with one another. I wanted to write something that is rarely discussed, and that is blatantly ignored. Boys and men can be raped. The studies talked about in Lechner's office are real. The stats that Lechner gave were accurate at that time, they may have changed. The laws that Atlas spoke of were true in California at that time. But it still happens. Boys and men still get sexually assaulted. If this is you, **I believe you**. Please reach out. Take some of that power back and find an individual or a group you feel safe confiding in. If someone confides in you that they were raped or sexually assaulted, **Believe them**. Help them find the resources they need.

One resource that is available is Rainn's National Sexual Assault at RAIN.org.

Their hotline is (800) 656-HOPE (4673).

This here is a Trigger Warning. In this book, you will find sexual assault, language, and ideas of suicide.

Again, read the above.

Take of yourselves and each other. I love you all.

KC Wardell

PROLOGUE

The plaza on Glazier Drive was where stuff got done in Pacific Heights. Local grocery stores and an ice cream shop filled peoples' refrigerators and stomachs. A helpful staff at the local post office timely sent out and received packages. The gas station had its tiny shop filled with maps, transmission fluid, and a good deal of snacks for those who drove by on their way to various destinations. The bank, of course. And the best fish place in the city was smack in the middle of it all: Leroy's Fish and Chips.

Kevin Meyers, one of the city's finest, loved the joint. His favorite spot, rain or shine, was the verandah, with its small Bistro-type tables and its canopy. Leroy was always good about serving him a couple of fish tacos and a large, cold drink when he was on one of his breaks. Most people thought that as an officer he would desire a cup of coffee with a donut or bear claw drizzled in icing. But Leroy's fish tacos with their lettuce, avocado, and sour cream always hit the spot.

With a pen in hand and a pad of paper in front of him, Kevin would scribble out figures and then eventually scratch them out. He had been at it for almost an hour. But this kid with a camera kept breaking his concentration. Kevin picked up his glass and swirled his drink around, the ice clinking as he did so. He looked down again and tried to reconsider his options. There seemed to be enough money to pay for the mortgage on the new house and the car insurance. But his son Chris needed new cleats for football and his six-year-old daughter Cindy had just signed up for ballet lessons. His wife had picked up the annoying habit of scrapbooking, which cost at least eighty dollars per book. She had already finished three and was working on another. The only way to pay for all of it was to take extra shifts at the station, which he did, even though it meant he missed out on time with his family.

"Honey." Kevin raised his head at the sound of a woman's voice. He turned the paper over and laid his cell phone on top before he stood up. His wife, Beth, came toward him with a beautiful smile on her face; his children pushed past her to reach him first, his daughter to get hugs, his son to get away from any PDA his parents would no doubt show.

"Watch for cars." Kevin warned them. Chris grabbed Cindy's hand and the two of them were soon by his side. "Hey, sport." He stood up and handed his son his last ten-dollar bill. "Get you and your sister an ice cream cone."

"Daddy, where's the pretty lady with the yellow hair?" his daughter squealed. Cindy loved seeing the stations dispatcher; the lady always brought her a treat.

"Her name's Nicole, sweetie. She works with Daddy at the police station, remember?" Kevin kissed the little girl on the head. "Now, go get your ice cream." He watched his children disappear into the ice cream parlor, then turned and wrapped his arms around his wife.

"How's your shift been going? Caught any perps?"

"Just one. Mostly shuffled paperwork."

"Jeff's coming to dinner tonight, right?"

A sudden tension came to Kevin's bones. Something didn't feel right. He looked around. His spine grew cold. Kevin pulled his gun from the holster and carefully tucked it into his coat. " Bennett and Sara. Yeah. Tonight." Chris and Cindy ran out of the parlor. He saw the tears that streamed down the little girl's face.

"I want chocolate chip ice cream." Cindy threw her arms around her daddy's waist.

"Cindy started crying," Chris said. "He told us to get the hell out."

"This is important, Chris. How many?" The wind picked up as Kevin grabbed his cell. The forgotten stress of unpaid bills flew away, both literally and figuratively. He passed the cell to Beth.

"Just one, Dad." Chris slid both hands into his back pockets.

Kevin felt divided on protecting his family or upholding his sworn duty. *It's just one guy,* he passed his trembling daughter to his son. "Get in the car and go home," he told Beth. "Call the station. Tell them I'm going after him."

He watched as the robbery suspect ran out of the store clutching three bags of cash in his muscular hands. Kevin pulled his gun from his coat and followed at a dead run. "Stop! You're under arrest!" He realized he had no backup, no cuffs, nothing. He darted past the kid with the expensive camera that was still clicking away aimlessly; the suspect dropped one bag. Kevin grabbed it before he continued his pursuit.

The suspect rounded a corner and disappeared behind a dumpster. Kevin followed and was introduced to a nine-millimeter handgun. "I remember you." The criminal grabbed a handful of cold hard cash and stuffed it into Kevin's jacket. "Long time no see."

"Oscar." Kevin had arrested Oscar for the sexual assault of a young woman not even six months ago. It had taken months to get the arrest, and here the scumbag was, back on the streets.

"You still fucking that bitch of yours?" The criminal paused. "Kid, we ran past had a camera." Kevin had hoped Oscar hadn't noticed the boy. Oscar snarled as he gathered the bags.

"Oscar, I'm warning you." Kevin brought his gun up nice and steady.

"No. Find him. We have evidence to get rid of. Bring Nicole with you." Oscar paused with a smirk on his face. "Maybe we can do it at your place."

Pull the fucking trigger. But something stopped him. "Oscar, no. There has to be another way." Yes, Nicole was his mistress. But Kevin loved his wife, and he didn't want to hurt her. *If I make it out of this, I swear I'll break it off with Nicole. Hell, I'll switch partners.* Kevin looked over his shoulder. *Where are they?*

"There is no other way. Don't worry, Kev. This'll be fun." Oscar again paused, as sirens closed in. "And remember, I know where you live. Don't give your little girl a reason to fear me."

Kevin's legs buckled. His gun clattered to the ground. Oscar was gone. With his head in his hands, he wondered what to do. If he took the money, and it was discovered, they could consider it a bribe. Two cop cars pulled behind the building, lights flashing, sirens screeching. He got to his feet and zipped up his jacket. He shook his head, "Sorry guys, he got away."

After a quick word with one officer, Kevin jogged over to a beige sedan, where Beth was still waiting, sitting behind the wheel. "Go on home." In the backseat, Cindy sat in her booster seat. He blew her a kiss. "Everything's fine. I'll be home in a couple of hours." After he kissed his wife, the car sped away.

Kevin joined his fellow officers in a squad car and made his way back to the station to make a report. He leaned back in the front passenger's seat and closed his eyes. Sure, he had thrown out the evidence against Oscar when he had assaulted that woman. The man's rap sheet seemed a mile long. The convictions he had were all petty crimes. There were a couple of felonies on the list; they had never convicted him of those. But this was different. Because of this stupid kid with a camera, it would force Kevin to go from merely tampering with evidence to murder. His young daughter's life was at risk.

CHAPTER 1

ANOTHER BUSY DAY

The winter sky was gray and dismal. San Francisco wouldn't see a patch of sun until April the following year. But people who lived in the city enjoyed things most people never experienced, like hot dog stands on the corner of every street, and artists chalking beautiful drawings right in the middle of Main Street. Tourists came from all over the country to admire the striking arches of the Golden Gate Bridge and laugh at the antics of lazy sea lions sunbathing on the docks of Pier 39.

In a complex in the Tenderloin close to Hastings University, a twenty-four-year-old young man walked into the Hundred Acre Woods. The walls covered with blue skies, trees, and of course Pooh, Piglet, and the rest of the gang. The brown crib filled with pillows and blankets, the mobile a montage of Pooh characters was now gone. But the room still smelled of baby spit and Johnson's baby powder.

In place of the crib was a toddler bed, in the shape of a honey pot, in the middle of the Hundred Acre Wood. They had bought the bed two weeks before, the box picture side up. Ashley would read Brenna a bedtime story and then Atlas would remind the little girl that in a short time, she wouldn't need her crib. She would sleep in her very own 'big girl' bed. According to all the psychology books, this was supposed to make transition easier for the child. Whoever came up with this idea had never dealt with his daughter.

They moved the last piece of the crib out. Atlas found Brenna in the corner. Tears the size of heffalumps rolled down her little face. "Honey, you're a big girl." Atlas got down on the floor and pulled Brenna into his lap.

"Bwenna sad." She laid her head on his shoulder.

"I know." Atlas smiled, running a hand through her soft hair.

"It's seven-thirty. I'm off." Ashley came into the room dressed in pale blue scrubs, ready for her third day back at work since Brenna was born.

"Remember, we're eating at my dad's tonight."

"I'll meet you there, okay?" Atlas nodded. Ashley held out her arms and Brenna dove into them with fresh tears. "I love you, Brenna. Be good for Daddy."

"Honey, you're going to be late if you don't head out the door right now." Atlas got up from the floor and reached for Brenna. "Come here, you little monkey." With his daughter in his arms, he leaned over and kissed Ashley. "Don't let Old Mr. Meyers grab your—you know." he teased.

"Sure," Ashley answered from the doorway. "Senile, Mr. Meyers won't grab me if you can promise me you'll keep Brenna in that same outfit all day." Their daughter hadn't quite mastered potty training. She was also prone to putting on many fashion shows, which, on a good day, were five outfits at the least. Both Ashley and Atlas were going to lose their bet, and they both knew it.

Atlas walked out the front door an hour later. With Brenna in her car seat, he pulled out on to the street and felt the day's weight on his shoulders. He tutored three days a week, took care of Brenna daily, and studied for the Bar exam whenever he could fit it in. It was hard to find time to enjoy being a father and husband. His own mother had died when he was ten. His dad had to raise him and his three brothers with little support. Sure, when the accident had happened, he was old enough to take care of himself; but Jensen was four at the time and the twins were two. Atlas had always admired his father for his ability to put his family, his children, first. So, when he had gotten married, he wanted to put all the attention, love, and consideration he could into his relationship with Ashley. Later, he had wanted to put in the same effort when Brenna was born. But things hadn't been that simple. They hardly ever were.

Atlas had met Ashley the summer he turned twelve, just a month after he graduated high school. The boy was already girl crazy and his father, Robert, knew that if he didn't do something soon, problems would arise. The concerned father did some research and then sent his son to St. Isabella School for a month. It was a camp, not a school, and along with s'mores, campfires, and canoes, the morning hours were comprised of etiquette classes. After breakfast, the next three hours spent learning to associate with the opposite sex, how to set a table, as well as other lessons in etiquette.

One evening Ashley's marshmallow fell into the flames and Atlas got her another one. They went to the dance together the following night. And throughout the next six months, while she finished high school and he learned whatever languages were available, the two of them kept contact through letters, and phone calls, later through Facebook.

Robert had immediately seen a change in Atlas when he returned from camp. He was more studious (not that he needed to be), and all the girls that used to come by, stopped. The phone no longer rang off the hook. Robert wondered if the relationship might be a little too over the top for kids their age, but since they lived several hours from each other, it wasn't that big of a deal. When they got together, it was a couple hours spent at a museum or at the park, with Robert or Ashley's mom Harriet, nearby.

Atlas and Ashley slowly grew into adults. The supervised outings turned into actual dates, the movies or quiet walks on the beach. While they both saw eye to eye on politics and child rearing, the arts were something neither of them could find common ground on. Ashley liked the boldness of most pieces, colors, and shapes that jumped out at her. Atlas preferred sculptures and paintings that had to be studied and scrutinized. The couple had spent a lot of enjoyable hours at the city's museums.

Two years after they started dated, on Ashley's twentieth birthday, Atlas had proposed. She accepted. The wedding itself had been small, nothing elegant. Jensen, Zack, and Rustin were there, as were Robert and both of Ashley's parents. There was a cake, and then life went on as normal, until Ashley got pregnant two months later.

College was always seen in Atlas's future; he was too smart not to. At eight, they often found him in his father's office with an enormous book of penal codes in his lap. When he was ten, he held a thirty-minute debate with his father's associates over the eleventh amendment, where he cited cases and other amendments that pertained to the issue. Another couple of years would have to pass before they would allow him into Hastings, and so he spent the next twenty-four months at San Francisco Junior College completing his requirements. His dad had encouraged him to try for a scholarship at Harvard Law School. He even offered to move the family all the way to Connecticut. But Atlas hadn't wanted to move; he hardly got to see Ashley as it was; moving out of state would have made visiting even more impossible. So, he had enrolled at Hastings University, where he graduated with his degree. Maybe in a couple of years he could get a more serious job, but right now, this worked for his family.

Atlas parked the car in front of Scrappy's Diner and took Brenna from the back seat. "You ready, Brenna?" He slung his backpack over his shoulder and closed the door.

"Jesnin!" Brenna called as they approached the entrance. The door opened, and a pair of hands relieved him of his daughter.

Atlas said hello to his rescuer, a server who was also his brother, Jensen. "Hey, Squirt." Jensen tickled Brenna and started toward the kitchen. He called over his shoulder, "Back table. Most of the group's already there."

"Thanks, JC." Atlas's phone rang and quickly he answered it. "What's up, Zack?" He paused as he listened for a moment, then laughed. "No, your homework, your responsibility. Don't even try. You know that's not how it's supposed to be used. I must get to work. Get to class." At the back of the restaurant, a bunch of tables were forced together, a rocky mountain of notebooks, pens, and penal code books scattered the area.

With a quick glance toward the back of the restaurant, Atlas saw his daughter talking up a stream with Joel, the restaurant's owner, her hands and mouth going a mile a minute. "Se', cookie, amabo. Crustulum comederunt Elmo con leche!" Joel looked confused.

Atlas laughed, "Brenna." His daughter looked up at him with wide eyes. "Sweetie, Uncle Joel doesn't know sign language. Use your words."

Joel laughed. "And English, please."

"Okay!"

Jensen walked around the group, taking everyone's drink orders. Atlas cleared his throat to get his students' attention. "This is our last session before your final. Are there any questions?"

Silence. For several seconds, nobody said a word. Atlas heard what sounded like someone getting kicked under the table. Then one of his gutsier students cracked his knuckles. "What's your real name?"

"Alasdair."

"Then why do we call you Atlas?"

Atlas paused, then took a deep breath. "I was a prodigy kid. The globe was my specialty."

"What was your GPA?"

"4.0." The answer was automatic. Atlas grimaced when he heard Jensen laugh.

The students all turned to look at Jensen. "When other kids were reading 'Encyclopedia Brown,' Atlas read that." Jensen pointed to a worn copy of the Penal Code. "Twenty-four, seven. His GPA was 4.0. His I.Q. is 215."

"An IQ of two hundred - considered a genius," one student replied in awe.

He saw Jensen glance at him. Atlas shook his head. *Don't you dare.*

Jensen laughed again. "And he was fluent in Latin by the age of four."

"I-way oke-spay ig-pay atin-lay ith-way ay-may other-bray I-way as-way even-say. Ig-bay eal-day."

Before Atlas could say a word, Jensen said, "Ad astra porcus in alis. Non amico, no latino. Carpe diem. Come saper scegliere un armadio?"

Everyone's mouth dropped. They looked at Atlas, who smiled and translated. "To the stars on the wings of a pig. No, my friend, not pig Latin. Seize the day. Would you like food with your drink?"

A student half raised her hand. "Your kid...."

"Is fluent in ASL and English. She mixes in Spanish and Latin." The group fell silent. Atlas laughed. "With my educational background out of the way, are there questions regarding your final?"

He watched as one of his better students, a Chinese man named

Dirk, looked up from his book. "PC 261, rape."

Another student raised her hand. "I don't get this section at all. I mean, it talks about penetration, and arousal, and male rape. That's impossible. Rape is something that happens to a woman, and.the law is making some big joke out of it."

Atlas flipped through the study guide as Jensen brought the drinks to the table; everyone reached for straws and napkins. Once everything had calmed down, he spoke, "You're right, rape's not funny. Let's get some definitions down first. Penetration. All you need for this is skin against skin. If someone lays themselves on someone who is protesting, that's penetration. Arousal is unnecessary to commit the crime. This is all in your study guides."

Another student raised his hand. "Men are stronger than women. That means men are raping men, right?"

Atlas remembered a time when the same questions were going through his head. "No. you must have two physical parts to commit rape. One of them was a penis, the other a vagina. There is a crime of men sexually assaulting men, but that's called sodomy. Men are usually stronger than women. How would a woman succeed at raping a man?"

Everyone was silent for over a minute. Atlas could see them struggling with the concept at hand. Dirk shifted in his seat. "Accomplices, maybe? Drugs?"

"Accomplices, drugs, absolutely. Remember folks, rape is about power, not just sex. Both psychologically and legally." Atlas was about to change the subject when he noticed the puzzled expression on a newer student's face. The young woman had bright green eyes. "Lacey, what's on your mind?"

The eighteen-year-old woman wrinkled her brow. "Arousal isn't necessary to commit the crime. Sex is just touch. So actual sexual intercourse doesn't happen...." She trailed off, not sure how to continue.

"Sometimes it does," Atlas said. "There are cases where, under psychological stress, men have had an erection. If they threatened you with a gun or they threatened to injure a loved one, most likely you would give what they wanted, right?" He watched his students nod. "In other cases, men, having been sexually battered, caused the erection. Even if he physically wants it, and he says 'no' but she persists, that is rape." He saw several frowns. "Sexual battery is the physical touch of the anus, vagina, or sexual organs without consent."

"But Atlas, who would rape a man?"

"Why would a man rape a woman?" Again, the awkward silence. Rape was one of those subjects that no one really wanted to think about, let alone discuss why it occurred. "Ignoring possible malfunctions in the brain, why would one gender rape another?"

The new student scribbled down a note. "In abnormal psychology, they say that serial killers have an immense hatred toward woman. They were abused as children. No one protected them." She appeared to be grasping at straws.

"Hatred of the opposite gender, abuse, that's good. What else?" Atlas leaned back in his seat and watched a couple of students stir their drinks; they all seemed to wind down. "Come on, you guys, we've got twenty minutes left. Let's make them productive."

Dirk cracked his knuckles. "Pay back. Say someone saw something they shouldn't have seen. Like a drug exchange or a robbery."

Atlas nodded. "Good, good. How could someone debate rape?" For the next several minutes, they continued the topic, where the discussion turned to the request by the victim to the use of a condom and the potential crime of a husband raping his wife. As the hour ended, Atlas stuck around as backpacks slung over shoulders and dollar bills tossed on the table.

With the group dispersed, he put the tables back in their proper places and pushed in several chairs that were blocking the walkway. Atlas gathered the mound of dollar bills and approached the cash register and his brother. His daughter was sitting at the counter with a crayon and paper in front of her. "I take orders like Jesnin," Brenna told him with a big smile on her face.

Atlas ruffled Brenna's hair. "You must love Mondays and Saturdays," he told Jensen. "They don't seem to understand that drinks are only a buck twenty-five. They all gave you three dollars. It can't be your service. I've seen enough of it at home."

"Nah. It's my sparkling personality." Atlas watched Jensen put the money in the cash register and another mound of it in his pocket. "You and Ashley coming by tonight?"

"Yes, Dad wanted to discuss some case he thinks I might be interested in researching. It'll be late though. The Bar Exam is coming up, and I have a lot of studying I need to do." Atlas saw the look of disbelief on Jensen's face. "Trust me, I have to study." Atlas headed for the exit, his daughter back in his arms. He turned at the last second and looked his brother straight in the eye. "Don't let the weight of that tip go to your head."

The seventeen-year-old shook his head, laughing. "How can I, when I've got a brother who's twenty-four, yet acts like he's forty?"

CHAPTER 2

THE SECRET CRUSH

Rustin Carson was a fifteen-year-old who was born and raised in San Francisco's upper class Pacific Heights District. His mom died when he was two. Along with his older brother, Atlas, who lived in Nob Hill, Rustin lived with his father, another older brother named Jensen, and his identical twin brother, Zack. They lived on Green Street and the house was huge. It had six bedrooms, four baths, a library, a family room, den, two guest rooms, and even a solarium. The front yard boasted a circular driveway, with tall black gates in front of it. There was an umbrella like tree in the center. In the backyard, a large swimming pool stretched out behind a protective fence and several fruit trees that gardeners tended to all year round. A tree house hid in a large oak tree. The back door of the solarium led to an extensive deck with everything from a grill to several lawn chairs.

As he walked past the tree and put his house key into the front lock. It was a relief for Rustin that winter break was just around the corner, just two more days. No Latin verbs to congregate or English papers to worry about for two entire weeks, just a photography project that was more of an enjoyment than a chore. When he arrived home that afternoon, it was almost five. Jensen wouldn't be home for another hour. Atlas would visit later that night, and he did not know where

Zack was. Rustin walked up the path to his door feeling relaxed. Who knew when he would get another opportunity like it? It wasn't unusual for his dad to bring client's home, or on good nights, his business associates, like Keisha. He grabbed his keys from his pocket.

Rustin liked it when Keisha came because she brought her daughter, Natalie. He often dreamed of the day when he would find the courage to ask her out. When he realized he had feelings for Natalie, he did the exceptionally stupid thing in the world and began a relationship with a girl from South San Francisco, a seedy area known as the Castro District. The girl did nothing but use him for his upper-class status. That was last summer. Now rumor had it she landed a boy from North Beach.

In the house, Rustin slammed the door shut behind him and dropped his backpack in the front den beside the couch. He strolled towards the kitchen when the phone rang. He picked up the receiver on the coffee table. "Hello, Carson residence."

"Rustin, I need you to do me a favor." Rustin knew his father's voice. "Can you start dinner tonight? The Spencer's are coming and so are your brother, Ashley, and Brenna. Do you think you're up to the task? Get Zack to help you."

"Sure, Dad." After he reassured his father that he was capable of the task, Rustin got off the phone and headed to the kitchen. The fifteen-year-old could cook two things: meatloaf and pasta. He decided on pasta (just in case anyone else should show up) and began pulling out the ingredients from the pantry. As the water boiled, he prepared some hamburger. He was in the middle of draining the oil when he heard the front door open. "Zack, in here."

Rustin's mirror image walked toward him, dressed exactly like him, but in opposite colors. Zack knew him better than anyone, knew his strengths, his weaknesses, and his emotions. He knew when something was up, even when it was just a tiny thing like dinner with a crush. Therefore, it was no surprise to Rustin when Zack said, "Natalie's coming over tonight, huh? You want me to finish making dinner so you can get ready for your date?" He lifted his eyes suggestively.

Seeing the expression on his brother's face, Rustin laughed. "It's a family dinner, not a date. Dad said you had to help. But you're not touching my noodles. You never cook them long enough. Go set the table." Rustin turned and opened three packages of dried spaghetti. He broke each one in half before dropping it in the pot of bubbling water.

"Demanding, aren't we, little brother?" His twin brother was always the one to point out that he was older. Even though it was only by one minute, that small amount of time meant everything with privileges and who should get them first. According to Zack, he had been justified in his anger at six-years-old, when Rustin had his training wheels removed before Zack did. Both boys were going for their driver's license in another year, and Zack would not see it happen again. He would drive before Rustin or die trying.

Zack left the kitchen. Rustin could soon hear the clattering of good china being set in the formal dining room. His family had dinners like this all the time. It was nothing new. At least once a week, everyone came together and had dinner. Keisha Spencer, her husband Nathan and daughter Natalie were like family; Rustin could never figure out why their father insisted on the use of the good china, probably for the same reason Rustin and his brothers always had to wear a tie and jacket to school. Yes, it was a private school. But it wasn't as if the school had a uniform. A heated discussion on the issue had once gotten Zack grounded for two weeks, and Rustin wasn't about to make the same mistake. After he drained the noodles and mixed in the tomato sauce, Rustin pulled a head of lettuce and the other ingredients out of the refrigerator for a salad before he turned his attention to making garlic bread.

It was six forty-five when the breadsticks were placed on the table and the doorbell rang. Rustin walked into the living room in time to see Zack taking Keisha, Nathan, and Natalie's coats. Jensen, who had showed up at six-thirty with Julia and Travis, came from the solarium. Atlas walked in minutes later, with the baby in his arms, Ashley right behind him. Twelve people surrounded the table, chair to chair, and elbow to elbow, but nobody seemed to mind.

The entire dining room permeated with the delicious smells of spaghetti and garlic bread. A large bowl of salad was in the center of the table. One by one, they gave each person the opportunity to express a thanks or concern for the day. After fifteen minutes of catching up, everyone broke into their own conversations.

Jensen and Zack were again discussing the merits of basketball, a topic Jensen could never seem to understand. The five adults were having some sort of debate. This time, it seemed to be about President Bush's position on terrorist attacks. Just Rustin and Natalie remained silent as they ate their meal, each alone in their own thoughts.

Natalie's hair was long and a lighter shade of brown than his. She always wore it pulled back in a ponytail, but not tonight. Tonight, it hung down over her shoulders, and at the moment, Rustin wanted nothing more than to run his hands through her hair. But that was out of the question. Even if they weren't sitting at the dinner table, her parents were right there. What if she told him to get lost? He was chicken. *But I want to ask her to the dance.* The dance was formal, and the only one he had ever gone to was with Claire, the money sucking cow. *Natalie's not Claire. Ask her out. Quit being a wimp.*

Just as Rustin was about to open his mouth, Zack kicked him under the table. "Who is better, Rus? The King's or the Laker's?"

And the next thing he knew, he was in his own debate with Zack, with the argument that it didn't matter who was better. The Sacramento Kings had Jason Kidd, and the Lakers had Kobe Bryant. It all equaled out. The discussion switched constantly, Zack always controlling the flow of the conversation. First it was professional sports, then it was high school sports, and then the usefulness of learning another language. It lasted until ten that night, when Keisha, Nathan, and Natalie headed out the door.

The moment the door shut, however, Rustin realized he blew his chance to ask Natalie out again. Once the door closed, he threw himself at Zack, who had headed toward the stairs. "I hate you!" Both boys lay tangled at the bottom of the stairway, Rustin punching his brother in the hip and arm. "Why can't you mind your own business?" He felt someone pull him back from behind.

"Not again," Jensen muttered, as he got a better grip on his brother. "Rus, come on."

Robert, who had seen the whole thing, sighed. As Zack got to his feet and trudged upstairs, along with Jensen, Rustin was about to follow when he heard his name called. "Rustin, you're on restriction to attacking your brother."

"Dad, it was his fault." Rustin turned to face his dad as he ran his hand through his hair. "He keeps invading my head. He won't leave me the hell alone."

"That's another week, Rustin. Sit down."

Rustin shuffled to the couch and sat down, wondering what was going to happen. He had surprised even himself; Zack was the one who went all out of control, not him. Rustin got to his feet. "Dad, I'm sorry."

"I'm not the one you need to apologize to and you know that." Robert sat down across from him, looking stern and tired. "I will not have my son's going at each other's throats, especially over a girl. Even Natalie." Rustin watched his father shake his head. "You're on restriction for two weeks. No TV, no basketball after school, you will come straight home. And you will write a five-page paper on the Nazi camps and their experiments done on twins, plus a work cited page. Due Friday night." Robert paused. "Go to bed."

"Yes, sir." Holding in a sigh, Rustin stood and started up the stairs. He turned when his father called to him.

"I'm calling Coach Felix. You will sit on the bench at the game on Friday."

Rustin nodded. In his room, he found Zack ready for bed. As he stepped out of his shoes and pulled on a pair of pajamas, he realized he had to sit out a game and turn in a five-page paper the same night. Then again, the last time one of them had gotten into trouble, Zack had to write a ten-page paper on some weird topic neither of them had heard of before. Rustin had lucked out. Once in bed, he apologized to his brother. Zack didn't say a word, but Rustin knew he was smiling.

CHAPTER 3

SCHOOL, AGAIN

Zack woke up the next morning to the sounds of water running in the bathroom next to his room. The smell of coffee drifted from the kitchen downstairs. "Zack, are you out of bed?" he heard his father call.

"Yes, Dad." For several minutes, he stayed beneath the covers. His eyes browsed the room he shared with Rustin. Strangers always expected that since the boys were identical twins that they shared everything in common. But they were different as night and day. While Zack enjoyed loud parties and basketball, Rustin was interested in photography and, whether he admitted it or not, Natalie. His own side of the room had walls covered with pro basketball stars while Rustin had only one picture on his side, an enlarged canvas of a photo he had taken himself, a picture from the top of Mount Shasta where they had gone camping just last year.

Zack got out of bed as he heard his father's footsteps as they padded upwards. The door opened without so much as a knock. "Get a move on it, Zack. If you end up with one more truancy, you'll get grounded for a month. I mean it." Zack nodded. His father left the room.

Zack groaned. *Damn, I hate school.*

San Francisco University High School, where all the Carson boys attended, was known for their academic and student-teacher ratio and had only fourteen young people in a classroom. Along with regular classes, each student was required to complete eighty-four hours of community service to graduate. Zack didn't mind the requirement. In fact, once he started and got the routine down, he enjoyed it. What bothered him most was the foreign language that they forced him to take. When Zack and Rustin started their freshmen year, their dad had clarified that they could take any electives they wanted, if they concentrated on their core classes first. Three years of a foreign language, Spanish, Italian, or Latin. Their father had insisted that all his sons take Latin. The course wasn't hard, but what was the point of taking something he would never use? He would not be a lawyer like Atlas and his dad, and there was no way he was going to go through who knows how many more years of school to be a doctor. *Stupid, archaic language.*

Like most mornings, Rustin made it to the shower before him, and so Zack spent several minutes getting his clothes together. He pulled out a pair of black khakis and a black dress shirt from his side of the closet. He threw a pair of socks onto his unmade bed. With his arms full of school clothes, he made his way to the bathroom door and pounded with a loud whoop. "It's Tuesday, Rusi. Last day before winter break." he said.

"No. There's school tomorrow." Rustin stepped out of the bathroom, a towel around his middle. "Are you ever going to clean your side of the room?"

There was a knock on the bedroom door. "Hurry, you two." He could hear Jensen from the hallway. "I'm leaving in five minutes."

"We're walking this morning." Zack could barely hear Rustin over the water pressure. Rustin closed the door that his brother refused to close; Zack was already nude from the waist down. "I don't need to see that."

With a glob of shampoo on his head, Zack enjoyed several minutes of quiet before Rustin pounded on the door. "Come on, it's bad enough we have to walk. I don't want to be late. Mrs. Cho's probably going to give everyone a surprise quiz."

Zack could hear the frustration in his brother's voice. He rinsed off and stepped out of the shower. "Think car, Rus. A two thousand and two blue convertible. You, me, Natalie, and maybe that girl from JC's Camerata class." Zack pulled on a pair of slacks, and he wondered for the millionth time why their father made such a big deal about the clothes they wore. It wasn't like their school had uniforms. Zack stepped out of the steamy bathroom and found yet again that the two of them were wearing the same thing. The only difference between the outfits was the color of the boys' ties. Zack's tie was red, Rustin's purple. "You know, the one who talks like she's from England."

"She is from England." Zack watched Rustin head out into the hallway. "And there's no way Dad would let you date her. She's seventeen."

Zack slipped on shoes and followed his brother into the kitchen, where they each grabbed an apple and finally headed out the door. "Hey, you've got Natalie."

"I don't have anyone," Rustin insisted, as usual. "Natalie and I are just friends."

"Sure, Rus. I have a picture of you and Natalie in the bath. You were sharing your rubber ducky, if I remember correctly." Zack grinned. Both boys had seen the picture in question; Rustin and Natalie had been two years old when it was taken. What Zack failed to mention was that he, too, was in the photo, standing right outside the bathtub, naked as a jaybird. "Besides, you two will be making out in the backseat while I'm driving our convertible."

The two boys walked side by side, passing several homes that were just as large and posh as their own. Rustin walked along in silence, and then paused at a corner before he crossed. A moment later, he realized what Zack had said. "You're not trying to pull what you did when we were six?"

Zack laughed at the memory of the two boys, both eager to get their training wheels off. Zack had promised Rustin he would wait so the two of them could ride down the street together. But six-year-old Zack had the same problem with patience as he does now. That would probably never change. Zack had pedaled off just as soon as the transformed big kids' bike was handed to him. He left behind a bewildered and upset twin. When Rustin had caught up with him to ask why he had gone on without him, Zack had simply shrugged. He declared in a boisterous voice that since he was the older of the two; it was his given right to ride without training wheels first. "All I said was that I was older than you. That means I get to do stuff first, like riding a bike and driving."

"You're only older than me by a minute, Zack," Zack heard the incredulous in Rustin's voice.   "One minute older, a lifetime wiser," Zack paused. "Damn it!" He pulled his cell phone from his pocket and called his oldest brother, Atlas. "Hey, I forgot my report. Oh, come on, Atlas. Carson Promise." There was a slight hesitation and then grumbling; Zack put the phone away.

"I wonder what type of paper you'll get from Dad." Rustin was smiling.

"Shut up."

They walked up to the school grounds located two blocks from their home on a street called Jackson. The school had several two-story brick buildings surrounded by basketball courts, a track field, and a huge auditorium. As they walked up the stairs to one building, Zack watched Rustin shake his head in disbelief. But he was surprised a moment later when Rustin looked at him and grinned. "Just remember, big brother. Brains before birth order."

The bell rang just as they stepped to the front of the big brick building; Zack and Rustin touched fingertips before they ran off in different directions. Zack entered his Latin class with a shake of his head. Not that he would ever admit it, but Rustin had laid a good slam.

As he sat down, the teacher clapped her hands. "Bonum mane classis. Venite carpe diem. Obsecro, manus tua in Duis congue sem." Backpacks opened. Papers handed toward the front of the classroom. "Zachary, duis conue ubi est? (Where is your homework?)"

"Domus (home)," Zack answered.

The woman tsked, shaking her head. "Post genus videret (See me after class)."

But Zack wasn't paying attention to any of that. *Carpe diem. Exactly!* Zack spent the rest of the hour forming a sure-fire plan to make sure Rustin and Natalie never got together, rubber ducky or no rubber ducky. One page after another, he scribbled down one idea after another, followed by how he expected the evening to end. Before he knew it, the bell rang and class ended. Zack went up to the teacher's desk and apologized for his lateness and lack of responsibility. After he was reprimanded and given a handful of demerits, he went back to his desk to gather his things. He was in such a hurry to avoid a tardy for his next class, he never saw one of those sure-fire plans flutter to the floor.

CHAPTER 4

MEMORIES

Robert entered the office at nine-thirty that morning. He placed a trañscript tape in his secretary's in-basket. He had an easier time getting his thoughts in order, alone in the car on the way to work. It was also the most efficient way to handle his routine correspondence.

With a glance at the clock on his desk, Robert sat down, going through case files; which ones needed to stay on file and which ones could he put in the archive. Being a defense attorney put him in the often-tricky situation, and it was his own father who had warned him about the complexity of law. Robert had an obligation to defend a person, even if the individual had committed the crime someone accused them of.

Lauren, his love, had been on her way to watch Atlas play a game of baseball. The twins were in their car seats in the back of the car. There had been an accident. Both Zack and Rustin had nightmares for months afterward. Zack had even broken a leg. Jacob, the driver responsible, had made it through the accident, paralyzed and riddled with guilt. Months after he recovered, he drowned himself in his backyard pool, wheelchair and all. And Lauren? Lauren had died on her way to the hospital.

It was funny, in a non-funny way, that they had had the talk just two weeks earlier. The talk where they decided what they should do if one, or both, of them were to pass unexpectantly. They had discussed who would take care of the children, how their assets were to be divided up. Both of them had wanted the other to move on and love again. Altruistic as always, Lauren wanted to donate whatever organs she could. She had made quite clear, in fact, that she wanted her healthy organs to be used to save others who were near death. When that horrible day occurred, he almost couldn't do it. He had wanted to remember her as a whole person. But it was Lauren's choice, and he had allowed it for her as his last gift to his beloved sweetheart.

That Jacob had killed himself was a bonus, Robert was told. That karma, that God, had leveled the playing field. What playing field? This wasn't soccer. Yes, he had lost his wife, his children had lost their mom. But Jacob's parents and his sisters were also drowned in their own grief and guilt. Robert wouldn't have wished that on anyone. And it didn't bring Lauren back.

Robert was reading case files two or three times and getting nowhere. Still distracted, he turned on his computer and opened his daily calendar. Seeing the date, he realized why he couldn't concentrate, how hard today was going to be. It was the anniversary of Lauren's death. "I can't do this." After turning off the computer, Robert gathered his coat and poked his head into his associate's office. "Keisha. I'm taking the day off. Make sure that confession gets dealt with, okay?"

"Sure." He watched the recognition flicker in the woman's eyes. "We all miss her, Robert."

Swallowing the lump in his throat, Robert backed out of the room and took the elevator to the first floor. The memories came back out of nowhere, like memories in quicksand filling his mind. It was thirteen years ago today.

Robert walked into the house and pulled off his coat, aware of the unusual silence in the house. Listening more carefully, he could hear faded squeals coming from the back of the house. "Lauren, do you need any help?"

"Grab the twins' clothes; they're set on the table in their room. We have to be at Alasdair's baseball game in an hour."

"Where's Jensen?" Robert felt a tug on the back of his slacks. When he looked down, the four-year-old was right by his side. "Never mind." He knelt down and gave the little boy a hug. "I need to help Mommy with Rustin and Zack, ok? How about some special TV time? Do you want to watch Barney the Dinosaur?"

"Daddy. My feet squish." The little boy paused for only a second. "What's status fender?"

"That's when kids don't follow the rules and get into big trouble with the police. Sit down." Robert took both shoes off and switched them from one foot to the other. Then he pulled Jensen to his feet. "Why don't you go play with your blocks, okay?"

He watched Jensen run down the hall. Then he went to the twins' room where he found the two stacks of clothing, each contained a t-shirt and a pair of overalls, one set green, the other set purple. Lauren had chosen the colors before they were even born. Grabbing what was on the table, Robert made his way into the living room and arranged everything. Finally, he headed to the bathroom.

The bathroom had water covering the floor. Lauren herself was just as wet as the boys, not that she cared. Robert knew that for her it was just one of the many perks of being a mom, and the reason they were trying again to have another child. "Hey, Mr. Space Cadet." Lauren's voice broke Robert's train of thought. "You want to grab Rustin out of the tub?" Grabbing Zack in a dry towel, the mother left the room quickly.

"You ready to get out of there?" The two-year-old stood up in the bathtub and shivered. Pulling him out of the tub and into a warm towel, Robert dried him off, rubbing the towel through his tousled hair and then down his little body. Carrying him to the carpeted hallway, set the little boy on his feet. "Go see Mommy and Zack in the living room, Rusi. Daddy will be there in a minute."

Taking a few minutes, Robert mopped the bathroom floor, cleaned out a potty seat, and gathered the wet towels. After depositing them into the washing machine down the hall, he found Lauren sitting in the middle of the living room. He watched silently as she diapered and dressed Zack. As she dressed him, mother and toddler discussed the pillow fight that Bert and Ernie had that morning. "What happened on Sesame Street today?" Lauren pulled the tot into her lap, the boy fully dressed in his red overalls.

"Bert was mad at Ernie." Zack grew excited and began squirming in his mother's arms. Lauren let him get up.

"Why do you think Bert was angry at Ernie?"

"Ernie snore like Daddy." The little boy hesitated. "I want Nuffy camp with me," he said, speaking of the big elephant-type creature on the program.

"Honey, our tent's not big enough for Snuffalumpagus. Where would he sleep?" Lauren smiled gently. "You don't want Big Bird to be lonely, do you?" Robert watched as Zack shook his head and then eased his way back into her lap. Lauren ran her fingers through Zack's hair. "How about we find Mr. Teddy? I bet he would like to go camping with Zack." Lauren got to her feet and almost tripped when the little boy dragged her toward his bedroom.

Robert laughed out loud. The chattering of teeth and a trembling body in the corner caught his attention. People, strangers, were always asking him how he could tell the two toddlers apart. While they looked *identical, their personalities were complete opposites. There was no way in the world Zack would have stood there quietly, shivering. When Zack was uncomfortable, everyone knew. But not Rustin.* "Rustin, are you ready to get dressed and go watch Atlas play ball?" *The phone rang and Robert grabbed the landline on the coffee table.* "Hello? Keisha, yes. The Martinez case goes to trial next Wednesday; he's pleading not guilty to attempted murder. His alibi is cut and dry. Let them try to pull something." *Robert laughed.* "We'll be there. Don't forget the marshmallows. Bye."

As he put the headpiece on the receiver, Lauren returned with Zack by her side, the teddy bear held tightly in the little boy's arms. "I'm going to change my clothes. You can handle the boys?"

"Yeah. Come here, Rustin." *Zack spoke what should have been nothing more than gibberish at Rustin, and the next thing Robert knew, the two of them began running around the room in opposite circles. Robert knew that if he captured one twin, the other twin would stop running. The challenge was grabbing Rustin, who was still running around naked. Robert waited patiently and then stepped in front of Rustin and grabbed him under the arms.* "Gotcha!"

Everything was good until Robert tried to put a diaper on him. Rustin threw a fit, kicking his little legs. "No ditty. Rusi big boy."

"Yes, Rustin is a big boy. But even big boys have accidents on long car rides. How about we put some pretties on?" *Rustin nodded; the crisis was averted. Robert sprinkled a bit of sweet-smelling baby powder on him before fastening the diaper on. Lauren walked back into the room, dressed in shorts and a t-shirt.* "Did we pack b-l-a-n-k-e-t-s?"

As his wife nodded, Jensen ran into the room crying, a wet spot dribbled down his leg. "I'm sorry. I didn't mean to!"

Exchanging glances with Lauren, Robert pulled the four-year-old close to him. "Jensen, it's okay. We'll get you cleaned up and then we *can meet Mommy and your brothers at the park. Sound good?" Lauren nodded and five minutes later, with Robert's help, was backing out the driveway.*

Leading his young son into the bathroom, Robert turned on the water and then watched as Jensen undressed. The rinse off that should have lasted five minutes turned into a bath that lasted twenty; the little boy had insisted on having time to play with his rubber ducky and to have his hair washed. Robert indulged. Since the little ones were born, Jensen had been given the backseat more often than he would have liked. The phone rang once more, and Robert pulled Jensen out of the tub. "Go to your room. I'll be right there." He watched his son head for his room and then ran into the kitchen and grabbed the phone. "Hello?"

"Robert, it's Nate." Robert heard his associate's husband and his best friend on the other line. His voice sounded too firm, deliberately steady. "Who has your car?"

The question was ridiculous. Nate knew Robert and Lauren had never loaned out their car. Robert could hear Jensen calling to him from the bedroom. The TV suddenly turned on too high. "Lauren has the car." Robert felt a chill run down his spine. "We're supposed to meet at the park. Why?"

"Daddy!"

"Wait a minute, Jensen. Daddy's on the phone. Why, Nate?"

"There's an accident on Van Ness. A car swung out in front of her." Nate paused. "Where are the boys, Robert?"

And at that moment, his world had ceased. Nothing could have ever helped him deal with so much loss. He had to I.D. Lauren; that was the hardest part, seeing that she had indeed died. Going through with her wish to have her organs donated, her body cremated. Her memorial. Helping Rustin and Zack through nightmares, a broken leg. Trying to explain death to three toddlers. Consoling an inconsolable ten-year-old who wanted nothing more than to have both his parents watch him hit a homerun.

Robert wiped the tears from his eyes. He started the engine and backed away from the tall building. At a local store, he picked up a dozen white roses, Lauren's favorite. Robert soon pulled into the cemetery and walked down a dirt path where he found her tombstone. Falling to his knees, Robert let his emotions go; tears fell like a torrent, sobs racked his entire body. It amazed him how much he still missed her, as though it had been only days since she had passed away, when in reality it had been thirteen years. This day got no easier for him.

Under her gravestone was a molded, misshapen rock he had the children to help him make. Robert smiled through his tears. He could still see Jensen and the twins' tiny fingerprints all over the place. He remembered how angry Atlas had been with his younger brothers. The ten-year-old had yelled at them and accused them of destroying the dedication to their mother. Robert had pulled his eldest son aside and explained to him it would only be ruined if not everyone was involved.

But Dad, she's gone. She's really gone. Robert had hugged Atlas close to him, running his fingers through the boy's hair. By the time his attention was again on the little ones, the clay was smashed down on the left side.

Robert stayed a while more, memory after memory flooded through his mind as he stroked the rock; memories where Atlas hugged his mom after he aced a test that he had stressed over; how Rustin had, until she died, preferred her rather than Robert when it was time for bed or bath. Jensen, even though he never really got to know her, was just as talented in music as Lauren was, if not more so. Zack's temperament was exactly like his moms with the injustices they saw in the world. "They're great boys, Lauren. They really are."

Robert left the cemetery moments later with a smile on his face.

CHAPTER 5

THE POWER TO TWEAK

"Sopranos quit pushing so hard." Jensen's music teacher tried to keep time by pounding on top of the piano, yet as a lover of music, he wanted to play the piece as well. He failed. "All right, stop. Grace, show them how it's done." The girl sang through the verse and stopped when instructed to. "Good job, Ms. Barnes. All right, let's try that again." The shrill sound of the school bell rang. Fourth period ended. Every student sat still for a moment while the instructor gathered his notes. "You're dismissed. Jensen, I want a word with you."

Students gathered their backpacks, sheet music slipped into black portfolios before they walked down risers. Jensen waited as most of the class headed out. He saw his girlfriend Julia Jacobs cornered by her best friend Grace Barnes, an English girl who had come to the states a mere six months before. With a smile on his face, Jensen almost laughed. He saw that once again Julia was trying to explain American customs to Grace. "Mr. Carson," Jensen looked up at his instructor. "Once you have finished ogling at the young women, would you care to join me at the piano?"

Jensen had Camerata, his high school honor choir, right before lunch. Juniors and seniors auditioned to be a part of this elite group that comprised just thirteen students, eight girls, and five guys. Broken down, there were three altos, three second sopranos, two first sopranos, two tenors, two baritones, and a bass. They competed in national competitions and spent an entire week on tour, visiting different high schools to San Diego and back. Those five days were spent on a tour bus, four nights in different motels, and a long nine-hour drive back home. Jensen loved the early morning prank calls that started with a four AM phone call to select members of Camerata, and an extra early breakfast at some restaurant nearby.

The choir room was built in a circle with high ceilings; back walls aligned with closets that contained the choirs many robes that were worn during performances. The risers, elevated tiled floors, were movie theater type chairs that were positioned in a half circle around an old piano. The banged up old instrument, despite its age, still was in tune. But even with the not so glamorous appearance, the acoustics in the room were outstanding.

Walking to the center of the room, Jensen approached Mr. Delaney, a short, even-tempered man who always dressed in slacks and a cardigan. In past years, they had accused him of his expectations being too high for a bunch of teenagers, especially considering the expectations of the school all ready. Summer participation was mandatory. Every performance was half a quarter's grade. But parents complained when the instructor handed his directing duties over to one student; they felt it had denied their own child a chance at something that would jump out on a college transcript. But Mr. Delaney knew his students well, prided himself on knowing their strengths and weaknesses, all one hundred and thirty of them. Adults, even the principal of San Francisco University High School, wondered how any human could know his students so well. It helped that most students were repeats, kids who had been in his class since their freshman year. But there were plenty of occasions when he saw them outside of class, at dances, at his house, and on the mandatory camping trips in the summer before a new school year even began. It took time, and a lot of patience, but for Mr. Delaney, it was all part of the job.

Jensen stepped up to the piano. "Yes, sir."

"You are the leader of *Just the Five of Us*. It is your responsibility to find an appropriate piece of music that your group will excel at." Mr. Delaney watched Jensen as he approached one of three two-inch binders and opened it. "Pick something too easy. You fail. Pick something too hard, your group collapses, and you fail. If you don't get it to work, you put next year's group in jeopardy, understand? This is half your grade, Jensen."

Just The Five of Us was the male members of Camerata, who pulled away as an independent group. The group was always directed by a senior, one whom Mr. Delaney thought could run a group on his own. Jensen had been a prospect for the teacher since his freshman year.

Jensen nodded. "Yes, sir. Not a problem." Last year's group had done an a cappella version of 'It's Alright' that had brought everyone to their feet. *What could measure up?* He took several minutes going through all three binders before he ended up picking something that he felt had a lot of potential. With the sheet music in one hand, he shrugged his backpack up on his shoulder. Then he followed Julia and Grace across the quad area and to the cafeteria. They joined the usual group, which consisted of all the members of *Just the Five of Us* and their girlfriends, most of whom were in the honor choir.

As Jensen sat down, the girls got up to do whatever it was they did every afternoon when they made a detour to the lady's room before heading for the lunch line. He heard Grace say something about chips and bubbles. The guys were left alone momentarily. "What took you so long, Carson?" Miguel Sanchez asked.

"Delaney had me pick music for the spring," Jensen said as he pulled a sandwich from his lunch bag. He looked at the young man across from him. "You realize, Steve, you're going to be the only one left in the group come next fall? Delaney will probably have you taken over as leader."

"I'd make a better leader than you any day," Steve O'Connor scoffed.

The lunchroom was crowded and moist. Students bumped into one another and tripped over backpacks that were strewn on the floor. From the other side of the room, he could smell the overcooked baked lasagna they liked to serve in the cold months. He couldn't wait until the weather warmed up and they could eat outside.

Jensen stood as the girls returned with trays of food in hand. Before Julia could sit down, he gave her a big hug and, after a glance around the room, a quick peck on the cheek.

"Don't make me sick, JC," Travis warned. "That's my sister you're kissin' in front of me." Travis Jacobs was Julia's older brother. He and Steve were tenors; Travis sang first, Steve second. He was the only one besides Jensen, who really took music seriously.

"Don't threaten me, Jacobs, 'cause I can tweak this thing any way I want," Jensen warned with the hint of a smile. "And I can have both you and Steve singing on top of your heads." He laughed out loud as most of the group acted like their lives had been threatened.

"So what are we singing, oh powerful one?" Tyrese Bannister was a black young man and a baritone like Jensen. The two of them were always up for the same solos. "Anything over played?"

"Try 'Lean on me.'" Jensen saw Steve roll his eyes. "I suppose you could come up with a better song?"

"Anything's better than 'Lean on Me'. That song's been out for decades."

"It doesn't have to be that bad," Travis told Steve. He looked at

Jensen. "Just think of all the options we have with it. An all-male vocal rendition of 'Lean on me'. JC, we can tweak it however we like."

"Exactly," Jensen nodded. "Come on over after school. Bring your sister with you." He felt Julia slug him in the arm. He paid her back with a quick kiss.

"Would anyone like some chips?" Grace asked as she held out an open container of food.

"Chips?" Tyrese looked confused. "Who calls them chips?"

"What do you call them?" the girl asked.

"French fries." Steve reached over and grabbed a fry.

"And this is not 'bubbles'" Miguel picked up the can and gave it a little shake. "It's called soda. Pick up the lingo, girl."

Grace had only been in the States for just over three months. She was doing well. But Tyrese, Steve, and Miguel would never let her live it down.

CHAPTER 6

SWEET, SWEET THUNDER

Lunch, of course, was lasagna. No garlic bread and no extra sauce, so it was dry. For all the money his dad put into the school, one would think the lunches could be decent. Rustin choked down his lunch and, as he did, he kept getting all these slide remarks and pats on the back from older students. "Great job," they would whisper. "Heard you hit a home run. Keep it up" "The Spencer girl got lucky." That last one made Rustin's blood boil. He knew it was Zack who had started the rumor.

The bell ending lunch had rung before Rustin could track Zack down. He had barely concentrated in history class; he would have to get notes from one of his classmates. But finally it was the last class of the year. Winter break was fifty minutes away. And it was photography, his favorite class.

They spent the period going over old material. Ms. Juska talked about lighting and the use of shadow. She also talked a lot about texture. The clock read two forty-five.

On a stool near the front of the class, Rustin watched with interest as his photography teacher, Ms. Juska, brought out a bunch of weathered portfolios that former students had put together over the years. "Look through them all and get some ideas. Your portfolio is due a week after winter break. I want your topic emailed to me by Friday."

Papers crinkled, stool legs scratched the floor, and voices muttered throughout the classroom. Rustin grabbed the stack of books handed to him and took the book on top. The book clunked on the table. Rustin then passed the other books to his left.

Beside Rustin, Eric sighed. "Isn't it enough we have to study for a Latin quiz right after break? And that fucking government paper?"

"Eric!" Both boys looked up and saw Ms. Juska standing over them with a scowl on her face. "Code of conduct violation. Don't have me remind you again."

Rubbing his chin with his thumb, Eric looked up at the teacher. "No, Ma'am. Sorry."

After a pointed stare in Eric's direction, Ms. Juska turned to Rustin. "Mr. Carson. To my desk, please."

Rustin pushed his stool back and followed her to her desk. "Yes, Ma'am."

With wrinkled, bony hands, the woman smiled as she retrieved a sturdy picture box out from beneath her desk. "You are my most talented photographer in all my classes." Rustin felt his cheeks grow warm. The woman continued. "I wanted you to have the first opportunity to choose this as your subject. Go ahead."

Rustin pulled the box toward him and slowly lifted the lid. Inside was a book withered by the passing years, yet still well kept. He took the book in his hands and his teacher pushed the box aside. Laid out in front of him, Rustin opened the book and turned the page, ignoring the title. His mouth dropped open. The pictures were amazing; snapshots of a sandy beach blending into the sky and others, where the particles of each grain of sand could be seen. The guard towers looked as if they belonged in a medieval style masterpiece. The sun started high in the sky, and as the pictures progressed, the sun sank low on the horizon, until nothing but the moon showed.

"Your style is quite similar to this photographer." She nodded toward the book. "Her cover was absolutely breathtaking."

Closing the book, Rustin stared hard at the cover and his heart stopped. A moment later, it restarted like a hurricane. "Lauren Antonelli." Rustin cleared his throat. "My Mom went to school here. Dad said there wasn't anything left. She died when I was two."

Ms. Juska paused only to take a breath and smile. "Keep it."

"Really?" The woman nodded. "Wow. Thanks."

A shrill bell rang. Students gathered their books and packs. Rustin, with his mom's book in his hands, went back to his desk. As he collected his belongings, he was barely listening as Eric was going on and on about the portfolio he had looked through. "This idiot went here?" Eric said, shoving the sample book toward him. "I could take better pictures with my eyes closed."

Rustin pulled on his pack. "Look, there's no point in me going to practice."

"Rus, just because you and Natalie did the deed?"

The two boys headed out the door and into the hallway. Rustin sighed, "Not you, too."

Eric was smiling like a Cheshire cat. "I can't believe it. Even before Jensen, I thought it would be Zack first. I can only imagine."

"Argh!" Rustin lowered his voice. "I did not have sex with Natalie."

"Why not?"

Rustin let Eric led him to their lockers. "I'm not Zack." With his locker door opened, he piled several books into his backpack, his binder, and his digital camera on top. "I swear, people think we're like." Rustin fumbled for the right comparison. "A package of Twinkies."

Eric laughed, "So, you're telling me you're not filled with a creamy white center?"

"I don't pretend to be interested in a girl and then spread rumors around like wildfire."

"But you haven't gone out with anyone since Claire." His friend refused to be distracted. "Why not Natalie?"

Rustin huffed, pulling his backpack to his shoulder. He slammed the locker door shut. "It's not because of that." As they made their way off school grounds, Rustin paused to scruff his shoes along the cement edge. "Just drop it, okay? You don't date a girl who's practically your sister." A car turned the corner, and after a slight pause, both boys crossed from Jackson on to Pacific Avenue.

Eric fist bumped Rustin as they reached his block. "All right, man. You're probably right. I'll see you later."

The boys went their separate ways as Eric headed to his home. Rustin was still seething as he took his key out and opened the front door. Zack's eyes had followed him home. He could feel it. Wanting to avoid his brother, Rustin made a quick peanut butter and banana sandwich and devoured it, leaving behind crumbs and a dirty knife. Then he ran upstairs.

Rustin pulled off his tie and loosened his collar; he changed his shoes. Finally, everything from his bag was unceremoniously thrown onto his bed, his camera, school books, and binder. He removed the book Ms. Juska had given him with gentle hands. Then, finally, he picked up his school binder.

Every break he had gotten at school over the past day or so, he had spent in the library. The paper was finished this morning after he printed it in the library. Rustin pulled out the fresh copy 'Nazi Experiments on Twins' from his binder and set it on his desk. He then took his Mom's book and knelt down beside the bed. He removed a small rug and pulled up a loose floorboard. Beneath it were several hidden items, a report card, a picture of Natalie, and his very first, very broken camera. Nobody knew about the secret area except Zack. This was where both boys had hidden a detention slip or a love note from some girl. Rustin took the casing off his pillow and wrapped the book inside before placing it in the space. The rug once again covered the floorboard. He would ask his dad about the book later.

Finally, he grabbed his camera. He noticed the picture count was off, way too high. Slowly, he went through the newest shots. "Argh!" Exasperated, Rustin found a bunch of shoddy and unfocused pictures. He didn't have time to go through and delete each individual shot. He took out one SD card and replaced it with a new one. He placed the used one on top of his paper; he'd print those pictures out tonight.

Half an hour later, Rustin was down on Baker Beach with his camera around his neck and both hands on the handles of his bike. The ride down had taken half an hour. There was still plenty of great sunlight. He ditched his bike at the end of a rack and headed for the sand.

His camera poised before his eyes, he took pictures of a father giving his daughter a piggyback ride, and of an older couple exchanging kisses. After taking a few more shots of the populated beach, he dodged noisy, preying seagulls that fought over pieces of food found on the sand. The squawking in his ears seemed to follow him up a steep incline to a cliff that revealed a glimpse of the entire beach with the ocean beyond it. In an isolated area, several wooden posts with red paint warned about getting too close to the edge. *Stand back,* one read. *Watch out!* Read another. Like many times before, he ignored the signs. What he couldn't ignore was the penetrating stare he felt at his back. "Damn it, Zack," he muttered.

Rustin decided right then that when he got home, he would remind his brother that any relationship he may or may not have with Natalie, or any other girl, was none of his business. He would hate sitting on the bleachers on Friday night. But Rustin had, of course, not wasted any time on writing the paper. He would give the paper to his dad and sit the game. Then he would come home and spend the rest of the night curled up with his mom's book.

By five o'clock, the sun was already setting. Rustin waited for the shots that would show the beauty of the world; the eagerness of a tree's falling leaves, the playfulness of water chasing seashells on to the shore, the teasing wings of seagulls touching the wind. It all waited for him impatiently as the sun went down. In the night's black sky, the moon shone with ambivalent grace, reflecting beams of light off the ocean. "Beautiful night, isn't it?"

Rustin turned around. He found a police officer who was walking up the steep incline. "Yes, sir. It is."

"That's a nice camera you have there." The stranger walked up to Rustin. "My wife's into photography; she's always asking for a camera like yours. Can I look at it?"

"Sure." Rustin handed his camera over and past the officer saw a man and a woman approaching. His attention diverted yet again at the sound of his camera being thrown to the ground, and a shoe stomping on it once, twice, three times. "Hey, why did you do that?" He watched the officer pull the gun out of his holster and point it at Rustin. A firm hand grabbed him by the arm and yanked him from the ledge.

"You got any other film that needs to be destroyed?"

"What are you talking about?" Rustin's voice shook. The once magnificent dark skies seemed intimidating, like crashing symbols intruding upon sleeping newborn babies. The only witness there to protect him was the moon; Rustin doubted it would be enough to save him from a beating. "The pictures," he choked, "Haven't been developed yet. This project's worth half my grade. What are you do-ing?" The officer turned and kicked the mangled camera from the cliff top into the crashing waves below. Rustin turned to run.

Rustin made three strides toward safety before the second man he had seen continued to come forward. He caught Rustin around the waist, dragging him back towards the cliff's edge. The stranger had a chunky belly, was about fifty years old, and wore a plaid shirt, jeans, and thick cowboy boots. He stepped around Rustin and, without hesitating, kicked him in the groin. "Let's get a little action going here." Rustin had doubled over; the pain was so bad he couldn't see straight. When the second kick caught him in the hip, he went down. He tried to get up. He grabbed at the stranger's clothing and dug his toes into the ground, but to no avail. The man broke Rustin's grasp and twisted his whole body until he lay flat on his back. "Nicole, are you ready to have some fun?"

You can't do this. Rustin tried to get himself out of the grasp of a man who looked big enough to fight an enraged gorilla. He quit struggling when a woman appeared on the cliff's edge. "Please," he said as she approached him. "I don't know what film they're talking about."

Nicole was a woman in her early twenties, a slim blond drenched with too much perfume. As she stepped forward, a strong floral scent drifted up his nose and down the back of his throat, nearly choking him. The woman crouched above his hips; her bright pink blouse opened enough to reveal a set of over developed breasts. Rustin kicked as Nicole found the zipper on his jeans. *No, no. She can't do this.* His throat caught. He couldn't say anything to protect himself. His body tensed as she laid her head on his chest and panted in his ear.

"Look at how excited he is. Is this your first time, you little bastard?" Rustin could hear a sudden annoyance in the woman's whiny voice.

"Please make him stop, Oscar. I want to have some fun." He froze when Oscar knelt his bulky self-beside the boy and pressed the muzzle of a gun against his head. "That's more like it."

Rustin's heart pounded, and everything went white. His fingers tingled. "Get up," he ordered. Rustin got to his feet. "Drop your pants. Now."

With a gasp, Rustin said, "I don't want to."

"Do you want a bullet in your head?"

Looking over at the police officer, Rustin begged for help with his eyes. All he saw was a set of eyes staring back at him, a pair of arms crossed. With tears streaming from his eyes, Rustin removed his jeans.

"I don't have all night. One... two...."

Quickly, Rustin pulled off his underwear. Oscar threw him to the ground, and the woman was on top of him; the fondling began. Her icy fingertips touched his most private parts. She moved her hand down his rib cage and hip. Rustin's body trembled. The next thing he knew, she was on top of him with her knees on his upper thighs, his legs forced apart like a wishbone about to snap. She took what Rustin refused to give willingly, and as she did, all he could do was panic, without words, without sound. The tingling moved from his fingers, to his hands, and then his teeth. "*Please, please! I'll give you whatever you want! Don't! Don't!*" But words failed him. It was as if he wanted it to happen; his body screamed, his brain screamed, but nobody heard it but him. Even though he refused to give his consent, his body reacted anyway; the more he struggled to stop, the more his body gave in. In a short time, sex went from something that filled his daydreams and fantasies to something he would never think of doing again.

Finally, they seemed to relent. All three adults backed away from the body and in hushed tones, discussed the situation. Rustin wanted to run; everything in his conscious demanded that he stand up to them, to fight them with every bit of strength he had left. But he lay still, afraid any movement on his part would quicken the bullet to his brain. He tried to ignore the fact that he had succumbed to weakness. Listening to the voices above him, Rustin tried to steady his shaking body as the wind kicked up and the water pounded on the shores below. "Oscar, let's get the hell out of here." It was a man's voice speaking. Rustin could tell it was the cop.

"No. The boy needs to be fucked with first." The reply was a muttered a stream of curses. "If you have a problem with that, tough shit. You're going to help me get rid of the body." Oscar paused. "I lost a lot of money with that robbery you botched. Your son plays soccer at Golden Gate Park, doesn't he?" The threat was obvious. "What about your little girl?"

"Come on, they have no part in this."

"We don't know how much this bastard," Oscar kicked Rustin in the groin again and the boy moaned, "Has on his fucking camera. If I go down, I'm taking you with me." Tense moments passed. The cop took a step back and lowered his weapon.

Rustin was still laying in the same position Nicole had left him in, legs spread eagle, his arms stretched out as if he were about to be arrested. Oscar started the attack again by taking his gun and pointing it at the boy's head, "Our young friend here has yet to pay for his crime. Stand up, *cobarde*."

Rustin got to his feet, trying to keep his feet together, as if to hide the pain between his legs. He watched Nicole step back into her skirt. He saw the police officer going through his pants then pulled taken out of the wallet. "Aww, look at this. Our little bastard has a girlfriend. Doesn't she look sweet? Oscar, you might be interested to know that our friend here has a twin brother."

Not Zack, please, Not Natalie. Don't hurt them. What are they going to do to me? "Please," Rustin said. His half naked body shook with cold and absolute terror. "I won't tell anybody. Please."

"Look at the little boy, beg." Rustin could hear the threat in Oscar's voice. "This is going to be fun, kid, I promise. Deb, give me your underwear." The man laughed. He took a bandana from his back pocket and stepped behind Rustin, tying the piece of cloth over his eyes. Fingers entangled a fistful of hair and yanked his head back, jamming Nicole's silk panties into his mouth. "On the ground, bastard, face in the dirt." Kicked in the back on the legs, Rustin fell forward on to the hard ground. "Hands out in front of you. Now!"

Rustin was finding it difficult to breathe, as dirt found its way into his nose. With trepidation, he moved his hands from beneath his stomach to above his head. *Don't kill me. Please don't kill me.* He heard something about first aid kit. A moment later hear the unmistakable sound of latex snapping against skin. A large hand rubbed the inside of Rustin's thigh, his muscles tightened. Oscar laughed as his fingers dug deep into Rustin's rear. The skin tore like little slivers of glass being dragged against bare and tender skin. The pain was immeasurable. With the gag in his mouth, Rustin let out a stifled scream. Hearing Oscar laugh, Rustin was sure they were going to put a bullet in his brain. It startled him when the big man's bare leg brushed his. "What would your wife say if she saw you having so much fun?"

The officer hesitated and then managed a grin. "Hell, Oscar, she'd want to join in."

Rustin could sense Oscar kneeling above him. He placed his disgusting, bloodied hands on Rustin's shoulders and invaded his body repeatedly.

The brutal attack lasted over forty-five minutes. When Oscar decided he'd had enough, they forced Rustin on to his feet, down the slope, and toward a police van. Nicole got into the front seat as they shoved Rustin in the back of the vehicle, half naked, bruised and bloodied. The police officer looked at him with a sadistic smile on his face. "Oscar's going to keep you company. I hope you don't have any problems with that." The back door slammed shut and moments later, the car moved.

Oscar licked his upper lip and laughed. The man moved like a hyena on his hands and knees, stalking his prey. The creep situated himself opposite Rustin, his feet angled right between Rustin's legs. "Have you ever played soccer using someone else's balls, kid?" His dirty boot came toward Rustin, who tried to fight back by kicking out. "So, you want to play it that way? All right, then." The first kick to his genitals caused Rustin to scream out in pain. The second kick came, and he black out.

The games never stopped with Oscar. When Rustin regained consciousness, they started again, from taunting him with water to oral sex. The car drove for an hour, and the paved roads turned bumpy. *Where are they taking me?* Rustin's panic grew as the doors opened and they dragged him out. He stood there, still blindfolded and gagged. He was aware of the dirt road beneath his feet, the sound of running water beside him.

"Which one should I use?" Oscar walked around Rustin, debated the issue as if he was deciding whether to add caramel or hot fudge to his sundae. "Gun or baton? If I use the gun, you'll definitely be dead. If I use the baton, you'll suffer more. In three or four days, you'll be dead, anyway."

"Decide, damn it. I've got other stuff to do." The police officer was getting short-tempered. "That kid over by Baker Beach. I should've run him down."

Oscar took the gun and put the muzzle to his head again. "Knees, bastard." *"Oh no, please no. I can't go through that again."* Rustin tried his hardest to stay on his feet for as long as he could.

But Oscar would have none of that. "I said knees. You god damn fucking bastard." Oscar kneed him, and Rustin was on the ground curled up in a ball. Rustin choked on the underwear as they pulled his head back, his face spit on.

With his eyes still covered with a blindfold, Rustin brought his hands forward to cover himself. Laughter erupted around him. His chest pounded in his ears. He became lightheaded. *Please, don't kill me. Please.* Fear overwhelmed him, and Rustin felt tears fall. A moment later, a frustrated Oscar threw his gun to the ground. Instead, he took the officer's baton and brought Rustin up to his knees.

Unable to protect himself, Rustin took a sharp blow to his head and crumbled to the ground.

CHAPTER 7

THE BIRDS AND THE BEES

"I want a gwilled cheese." Brenna looked down at the plate in front of her with all the disgust a two-year-old could manage. It wasn't a horrible lunch, like sardines on rye bread. The plate was occupied by the standard peanut butter and jelly sandwich and three orange wedges. Atlas had even remembered to cut the crust off the sandwich.

"Honey, Daddy doesn't know how to make a grilled cheese." Graduate law student that he was, the man did not know how to make a grilled cheese sandwich. "Brenna, your friends will be here soon. You need to eat your lunch, or you can't play with them." *There, show her you're the authority figure.*

"Okay, Daddy." Brenna took a bite of her sandwich, smearing jelly all over her face. "Daddy?"

"Yes, Brenna."

"You take cooking lesson, okay?"

Minutes later, Atlas was wiping off the mess from his daughter's face and hands when the doorbell rang.

"I do it. I do it." Brenna ran to the door and jumped up and down.

"What do you say, Brenna?"

"Pease?"

Atlas shook his head. "What do you say when someone's at the door?"

"Who dare?" Atlas nodded. Brenna's hand grasped the doorknob and pulled it open. "Who dare?" she squealed.

Laughing along with everyone on the porch, Atlas opened the screen to allow three women into his home, each with a child in their arms. "Come on in." He felt a tug on his sleeve and looked down: Brenna was doing her little march.

"Pee-pee, Daddy. Pee-pee."

Atlas grinned and rolled his eyes. "The playroom's down the hall to the left. Excuse me."

Brenna made it to the potty chair in time. Atlas helped her clean up and then washed his own hands. He sent her on back to the playroom while he went into the kitchen to prepare refreshments.

"So, I'm right in the middle of a PAP smear," The storyteller had the other two women listening with wide eyes. "My feet are in those blasted stir-ups, and his cell phone rings."

"You're kidding" a soft voice exclaimed.

Atlas, carrying a tray of ice-cold drinks, could hear this as he walked down the hall.

"He didn't answer it, did he?" another voice asked, mortified.

"He had the phone to his ear before he even left the room." The storyteller told them.

Atlas could feel his face turn hot. He took a deep breath, counted to ten, and then once he felt his cheeks cool, he cleared his throat. The room fell silent as Atlas entered. "How about some iced tea, ladies?"

"Sounds great." one woman said a little too cheerfully. "Here, let me help you with that."

Both Ashley and Atlas had decided that with toys, the less, the better. They wanted their child to understand what privilege was, and that they had it. They wanted her to understand that not every child was as lucky as she was. But since Brenna was the first grandchild on both sides, the request had been ignored. From the doorway, it looked like a toy store; a rocking horse was in one corner of the room, and an entire wall of shelves with labeled plastic containers faced the east side. The shelves on top held the toys Brenna had outgrown or was still too young to play with. There was also a play kitchen, a shopping cart, and a princess tea set, complete with a pink crown.

The crown was in the hands of a little boy Brenna's age. But not for long. Brenna stomped over and grabbed the tiara. "Mine."

"Brenna. Brenna, look at me." Atlas waited until his daughter's eyes were on his. "Share." Brenna made a pouty face, but Atlas wasn't buying it. "You share, Brenna. Or you go on timeout." He waited until the toy was returned and then smiled at the woman nearest him and waved. "Hi, I'm Atlas. Ashley's husband."

"Samantha." The woman had short blonde hair and an athletic build. She pointed to the same little boy who now had the crown around his tummy. "And that's PJ."

"Hey, Rachael." Atlas had met her years ago; she was Ashley's best friend.

"So, how's the stay-at-home thing going?" Rachael asked.

"Not bad." Atlas glanced around the room; Brenna had a baby doll in her arms.

"I'm Miko." Atlas looked down and found a woman with a swelling belly sitting cross-legged on the floor. A one-year-old lay asleep in her arms. "And this is Cassie."

"Nice to meet you." *Great, now what?* Atlas cleared his throat.

"I saw the bags by the door," Rachael said. "Ashley never said you guys were going on vacation."

"I'm taking a weekend up to the cabin. My aunt owns the woods surrounding it." Again, the adults fell silent.

Brenna, PJ, and Cassie had soon taken over the room. They ran from one end of to the other. It was at a point where the squealing had temporarily ceased that Miko cleared her throat with some uncertainty. "What is it, Meek?" Samantha asked.

"When I went to the doctor's yesterday," Miko hesitated. She glanced at Atlas, and her face paled. Atlas was about to excuse himself from the room. When she spoke the words they were almost inaudible, "I'm having twins."

Samantha and Rachael shrieked with excitement. Atlas laughed. "You are going to have your hands full."

"Do you know the sex?" Rachael squealed.

"Not for a few weeks." Miko looked up at Atlas. "You're a twin, right?"

"No. My baby brothers are twins." Atlas paused and shook his head. "Babies. They're fifteen now."

Atlas spent several minutes with Miko as they discussed the ins and outs of raising twins. He could tell how nervous she was. "Miko, you're gonna do great."

"I want one."

Atlas sighed and got to his feet. He found Brenna standing over Sean, a six-month-old. The baby was in the middle of a diaper change.

"Brenna."

"I want one, Daddy! Seannie won't share."

Atlas glanced at Rachael. "His little boy part. I'm sorry."

"No, don't be. Come here, baby girl." Atlas took Brenna in his arms and sat down on the floor. "Honey. You can't have one of those."

"What's that?" she asked, pointing.

"It's a penis, Brenna. Only boys have them."

"Like Daddy?" Atlas nodded. Brenna's eyes filled with tears.

Atlas hugged her tight for a moment. "Honey, it's okay." *Well, now that you've introduced physical anatomy to her vocabulary...* "You have something you can't share with Sean." *If only that were true.* "You have a vagina. Just like Mommy." Atlas watched his young daughter's eyes widen. The smile came back to her face.

"Where?"

"It's a secret. I'll show you at bath time, okay?"

"Tell Mommy?" Brenna whispered.

"Yes." *Please, yes.* "Now, go play nicely with PJ."

From the floor, Miko applauded. "That was good. Maybe I should hire you to give the talk to Cassie when she's older."

"The talk? Oh, hell no. Ashley's giving her the talk. That was just a lesson in anatomy." Atlas laughed. "Besides, that was easy. Does anyone here know how to make a grilled cheese sandwich?"

Chapter 8

Oblivious

Robert had been on the phone with a potential client for over an hour, and by now had determined that there was no way he could take on the case. It involved a DUI that had killed two people, the drunk driver and the victim in the other car. The person on the other end of the phone was a relative of the victim, who was now in tears because she wanted someone to pay, in this case, the bar that had sold the alcohol. He understood more than he could say. But he couldn't take the case, even if he wanted to. The defense would object. They would say he was too close to the situation, and they would be right. "Mrs. Nunez, I'm sorry for your loss. If you give me a minute, I'll transfer you to a qualified lawyer who can take your case." After he got off the phone, he stared at the clock, amazed at the hour. Shaking his head, he told his secretary that he would be gone for a few hours, and to take down any messages that might come in.

Grabbing his coat off the rack, Robert was about to run off and get some take out when Keisha and Nathan appeared in his doorway. "Hello, Robert. How are you?"

"Nathan, everything's going well. Are you two off to lunch?"

"We were wondering if you'd like to come with us? We're going to that seafood place up the street." Robert had met Keisha at Harvard years and years ago, not long after he had married Lauren. Nathan had been his friend for years. Robert and Lauren had been responsible for the two of them getting together. At their wedding, Robert had been Nathan's best man, and Lauren had been Keisha's maid of honor. Both Keisha and Nathan had been very supportive when his wife had died, taking the kids to school and lending a shoulder when needed. They even had allowed him and the boys a place to stay with them after the accident. Taking a moment, he looked through his planner and at his calendar, he told them he would meet them at Tommy Toy's, an expensive restaurant down on Montgomery Street. His boys had a basketball game at six, but that was a couple of hours from now.

At Tommy Toy's, Robert noticed, not for the first time, the restaurant's delicate porcelain lamps placed on dining tables and waist high vases at every corner of the room. The three adults were seated beneath a beautiful chandelier that sparkled like it was encrusted with diamonds. They were given menus. "This is where Nathan proposed to me. Gosh, everything looks so good." Robert watched as Keisha skimmed over the menu and then looked up at the server. "I think I'll have the seafood bisque."

Robert caught Nathan looking at him. "Lobster, please, with peanuts in a peppercorn sauce." After his best friend ordered his own meal and a bottle of champagne, Robert asked the couple how their daughter was.

"Oh, Natalie's fine." Keisha watched as the server poured champagne into her glass. Taking a sip, she continued. "She's looking at colleges all ready. It's like it was only yesterday that she was playing hide-and-seek with Rustin, Zack, and Jensen. How are the boys?"

Robert smiled. He tried to only mention only one or two of his children; it embarrassed him to have the attention all to himself. But when he tried to keep the dialogue open for everyone, Keisha always asked about the children he had left out. "I came across one of Rustin's notebooks." He took a sip of the sweet yet bitter drink and laughed. "He wants so badly to ask Natalie out. Zack goes through girlfriends like they were on sale, but Rustin's more selective. He had one major girlfriend who broke up with him, I think. I don't know. I probably shouldn't worry about it."

Lunch was served. The adults took a moment to put napkins into their laps and taste a first bite of their meal. "Mmm, this is delicious!" Keisha exclaimed, after digging into her pastry topped soup. Robert watched as she offered a spoonful to her husband. After he swallowed, Nathan gave Keisha a peck on the cheek.

"Atlas is the best college assistant we've ever had. I only have to give him directions once, and he's not intimidated by any of it," Keisha said a moment later, as if to prove Robert's earlier thoughts. "Did you teach him how to interview potential clients?"

Robert nodded, "Twice. Once when he was thirteen and then again when he started working with us. The second time he was insulted." He laughed. "I'll never forget. He was eight when he walked into the living room dressed in a red flannel pajama and the Incredible Hulk slippers. He said, Dad, I'm going to be the best lawyer in the world. Can we build a jet powered submarine?" Robert shook his head, laughing. He went to take a bite of lobster, when he his cell phone rang. He cleared his throat and stood up. "Excuse me."

Pulling his phone from his jacket pocket, Robert stepped to the back of the restaurant right outside the men's bathroom. "Hello?"

"Dad, it's me." Zack sounded stressed, which was unlike him. "The basketball game was canceled, and I really screwed up this time." Robert could hear his son take in a quick breath. "Have you heard from Rustin?"

"No, I haven't." Robert was not in the mood to hear Zack's excuses.

"It's Friday, Zack. With the game canceled, I want you home by eight, got it?" Robert couldn't count the number of times Zack had missed curfew, and it didn't seem to matter how many times he put the boy on restriction or took away privileges. "You miss curfew again, you'll owe me a five-page paper on child labor laws, complete with a work cited page. Do you understand?"

"Yes, sir," Zack said. "But Dad. Something's wrong. He's sick, he's hurt."

What does he think he's trying to pull? Robert shook his head, amused and agitated at the same time. "No. Zack, home by eight P.M. sharp. End of discussion." Robert hung up the phone without another word.

Back at the table, he found Keisha and Nathan engaged in a heated debate. Both of them were at the edge of their seats, their voices quiet yet confident. Their body language spoke volumes, though. "What's the topic?" Robert asked, taking his seat.

Keisha looked up. Her eyes were intense, as if she were in the courtroom in a struggle to convince the jury of a major detail. "Did Bush win the election fairly? I think President Bush is doing the best he can. Does it really matter?" Now, Robert had heard Keisha complain about the actions the current president had been taking since he began his term. This was merely an exercise in argument.

"The idiot has family working in the government. It's not like he's making all these monumental decisions by himself," Nathan's voice was loaded with sarcasm. "He probably has his father on speed dial."

Robert stepped in. "I'm going with Nathan on this one, sorry Keish. In some of the voting locations, people had to be carried down in order to vote. Access to the elderly and those with physical limitations was hampered. Would you go through all that trouble to voice your opinion? And what about all those votes at sea that weren't counted? You really believe they did not screw the system in the Bush's attempt to gain more control over the country?"

The discussion went on until almost five, when Robert realized he had errands to run before he went home; with the game canceled, they decided that they would have a family movie night. Like always, the Spencer's were invited. Paying the bill only took longer than it should have because the debate topic changed. The three adults decided that they'd get together that weekend to go sailing and continue it then.

CHAPTER 9

BAKER BEACHES SECRETS

When the school bell had rung and Zack found out that the game was canceled, he cleared out his locker and prepared to go home, a long overdue history paper waited to be written, as well as Latin proverbs needing translation, three pages of algebraic form, a book report, and a short story that had to be written and revised. Overwhelmed, Zack walked off school grounds and took the scenic route down Glacier Drive.

Half an hour later, he passed by the Plaza shopping center. The bank within the center had been robbed a couple of weeks ago. But Zack remembered it like it was yesterday. He had come out of the Tasty Freeze with a double-decker sundae in one hand and Rustin's camera clicking away with the other. Two adults had knocked the plastic cup out of his hand, rushing past him. "Hey!" One culprit had turned around. His arms carried a couple of weighted pillowcases, and it was then that Zack got a good look at his face. An instant later, the man was gone. Why Zack had insisted on leaving right away, he couldn't recall why he left before the police got there. But the way he saw it, the problem wasn't his. It was someone else's.

Zack shook his head at the memory. *Why in the hell am I thinking about that? Now, that girl in Camerata, that's who I should think about.*

Passed the Plaza, he headed towards Fisherman's Wharf, where there was nowhere to hide from the smell of fish and the sounds of the ocean beating against the docks. He approached one of Annie's hot dog and pretzel carts, with its white and blue stripes and large red umbrella, and bought a warm, salted pretzel.

As he took a bite, he walked by the Aquarium by the Bay a place where he had taken several field trips. Water surrounded the tunnels inside. Seven gill sharks would swim over head as would river otters and octopuses. Rustin hated the tunnels, fearing they would collapse around him. But Zack thought it was cool, almost like scuba diving, which he had a certificate for. The touch pools were something they both enjoyed. The sea stars were prickly, as were the sea cucumbers.

The one store Zack did drift into was called Puppets on the Pier. When they were younger, Jensen, Rustin, and Zack would sit on the floor in front of a long table covered with some sort of tablecloth. Sometimes the tablecloth was white, showing a snowy area. A blue cloth meant a water voyage, and if the cloth was green, they were in some sort of grassy field. Atlas used the puppets they bought here to put on puppet shows that would entertain the younger boys on rainy days.

There were different puppets all throughout the bright store. Marionette puppets hung from the ceiling, dressed like a farmer or princess, or even the exotic Burmese. There were glove puppets that were made to look like Sesame Street characters or Bernard and Max from Where the Wind Things Are. The most intriguing puppets, though, were the ones that made sound. Tigers would roar, the white duck would quack, and the cow, complete with horns, would moo.

Zack left the store and headed home. He and Rustin had been at odds the entire week. Zack hadn't known why until this morning in English, where one of his friends had made some smart aleck remark about Rustin being the first to bed a girl, that they had all expected it to be Zack. *Don't worry,* they said, *you'll catch up soon.* With the realization of what had caused Rustin's anger, Zack wanted to go home and sort things out, fight if they had to, even if it meant he had to admit he used up space on his brother's SD card.

It took an extra four blocks to get home. The longer the walk became, the more irrational Zack's thoughts became. He entered the house and found Rustin had already been home and left again. There were dishes in the sink and breadcrumbs on the counter. *Fine. If he doesn't want to deal with this crap, neither do I.* Several minutes were spent slamming cupboard doors, looking for something to eat. For some unknown reason, he ended up with a peanut butter and banana sandwich. Zack hated peanut butter and banana sandwiches. But somehow, he choked the whole thing down with the help of a glass of milk. Once the sandwich was consumed, he washed the dishes and then wiped the counters clean. *There's no way I'm getting in trouble for Rustin's screw up.*

With everything in the kitchen as it should be, Zack went to his room. At his desk, he tried to start his homework. He opened his backpack, pulled out his second-year Latin book, and tried to decipher what was on the pages. His mind refused to cooperate, and he spent most of the next thirty minutes trying to get himself to concentrate. He couldn't do homework; he couldn't even watch television. Two hours passed as if he was waiting to have a root canal. He wanted to get this fight over with, and all he could do was wait for his brother to get home. He ended up in the front yard. Zack would dribble a ball half a dozen times, shoot, and watch as the ball would skate around the rim of the basket before it fell to the ground.

It was half-past five when Zack felt a headache coming on. His heart pounded and a slow intense heat seemed to rise from his feet to his hips. *Rustin, where are you?* Rubbing his shoulders, Zack went inside to the downstairs bathroom with his backpack. He poured the contents onto the floor. He paused a moment to swallow back the bile that rose in his throat, leaving behind a heated electrical sensation. Opening the medicine cabinet, he threw in everything, from band-aids to stomach tablets. The gauze pads went in next, as did a tube of ointment and the peroxide. It had happened before, years ago, only it was Zack who had broken his leg at the roller rink, and Rustin, who had showed up before the ambulance had left for the hospital.

Now, as he turned to leave, he felt his legs give out underneath him. A sharp pain penetrated his head. Zack stumbled to his feet. A moment later, he grabbed his pack, got to his feet, and headed out the door. He knew his brother liked to spend time at the cable barn. He half walked, half ran up the hills of Van Ness, passed Vallejo, Broadway, Pacific, Jackson, and Washington as he ignored the awful pains that continued to overtake his body. Zack had become exhausted, and there was no reason for it. It wasn't the exhaustion he got when he ran the mile; he had been running these hills since junior high. The sport itself left him feeling happy and awake, but at the moment, his brain seemed to shut down; all he wanted to do was sleep. But he couldn't sleep, not until he found Rustin. He saw the cable barn. Rustin wasn't there. Zack sat on the ground with his head in his hands. *Rustin, where are you?*

Zack wasn't sure how long he sat there. The sun had already gone down. But he didn't want to waste any more time; he had an entire city to search. To tell someone about his gut reaction was pointless. There was no proof that Rustin was missing, let alone injured. Zack thought about calling his dad, because if anyone would believe that Rustin was hurt, he knew Robert would. But as he was about to go to the nearest payphone, he felt a wave of shock that almost threw him off balance. Rustin wasn't just kicked in the groin. It was something more, something he didn't want to think about. *They put their hands on him. He wanted them to stop.* "Why didn't they stop?" Zack was surprised he had spoken aloud, as were several passersby.

Zack went and checked several of the beaches, including Baker Beach, where he almost got ran over by a police van. *I wonder where they're off to in such a hurry. If they had been going a little slower, I would have asked them for help.* Baker Beach was a place Rustin had once told him had the most exceptional cliffs. But he couldn't find his brother anywhere.

Finally, he stopped at a payphone, and with a shaky hand, put several coins into the slot. Rubbing his sweaty hands on his jeans, Zack dialed his father's cell phone. He told his dad about the game being canceled and had just mentioned that he had screwed up when Robert had cut him off, threatening him with a paper if he missed curfew. Zack was about to plead with him when he was reminded about family night, and then the line went dead. He put the receiver back into place. *How are we supposed to have a family night if I can't find Rusi?*

Zack started back to the school, then ran all the way to his father's office before he turned around and went in the other direction. It didn't matter where he went if he kept moving. That Zack could run meant that Rustin, although injured, was not dead yet. *Just keep going.* The message kept at him, flashing in his mind, and he obliged as if his own life depended on it. He spent the next couple of hours running, sometimes full speed, other times just a jog. He always tried to connect with his twin brother, because while it annoyed the crap out of him, he was being replaced by a girl. Rustin was still his twin, his rock.

Zack stopped at the park, out of breath and with a cramp in his side. He sank down onto the grass. For the first time in his life, he felt completely lost.

CHAPTER 10

CALM BEFORE THE STORM

Scrappy's was a small hole in the wall restaurant that had been in the neighborhood for a couple of years, when a twenty-something year old man was trying to start his career as a defense attorney. He would study for hours after school, going over the constitution and the penal codes. Robert would hole up in a back corner until the sun went down before he would go home to his pregnant wife and son. That was eighteen years ago. These days, his second eldest son was a server at the very place where he had passed time with his head always buried in a penal code book.

Old Joel still owned the place, and the educated man considered Jensen his most prized employee. When he needed ideas on how to get younger customers to come in, since the younger ones usually spent more, the seventeen-year-old suggested a night when only teens were allowed in. He also convinced Joel that the place needed a jukebox. And when Scrappy's needed a makeover, Jensen saw that the colors of brown and tan were switched to more vivid colors.

Walls splashed with red and yellow and green. The chairs were a magnificent royal blue. The first few weeks, customers would pour in and everyone was excited about the changes. But now, the steady streams of people came in at noon and after school, which was when

Jensen came to work.

One of Jensen's favorite customers was a lady who had been coming to Scrappy's for as long as his father had. She was an older woman in her late sixties who loved to tell stories of how she grew up on a farm in the South. So, when she came in that evening, he immediately showed her to her favorite spot to eat, a table that looked over on to Glazier Street where cable cars strolled by on long winding tracks. "Here you go, Mrs. Kennedy. Will you be having your usual?"

"Yes, my dear. Could you put a little more whipped cream over the fruit this time? A girl my age needs to have a little fun now and again. Don't you agree, Jensen?"

He watched as Mrs. Kennedy delicately placed a napkin in her lap. "Absolutely," he said with a laugh. "I'll bring your meal shortly."

After he brought the woman her fruit, toast, and iced tea, Jensen busied himself clearing and wiping down tables, and of course taking orders from other patrons. Before he knew it, it was time to clock out. As soon as his last customers had left, he grabbed a bucket from behind the counter and cleared the last table for the night. "Hey, Joel. It's seven-thirty, I'm off," he called to the man who sat in a back booth, going over receipts. Once Joel was behind the cash register, Jensen took his apron off and put on his coat. Handfuls of change and one-dollar bills found their way into his pocket. He could hear his stomach growl at the enticing smells coming from the kitchen.

"All right. See you tomorrow." Joel paused, then said, "JC." Jensen looked up at his boss. "Grab a burger on your way out."

"See ya, Joel." The teenager walked into the kitchen where he fist bumped with the cook, Danielle. "Don't forget, Mr. Everly's burger. Mayo first."

"And a little mustard mixed in." It was a grouchy customer's routine order. The man always knew when it wasn't done his way.

Danielle and Jensen both laughed. "I'll see you tomorrow, kid." As the cook handed him a bag of fresh food, Jensen slipped her a five.

Jensen sat in the front seat of his car for several minutes. There was no point in letting the good food go cold, and Jensen was hungry. In the bag was one of Danielle's famous western burgers, complete with crispy onion rings and barbeque sauce that would drip everywhere if he wasn't careful. In between bites, he stole a couple of fries from the bag. The food didn't last long.

Crumpling up the wrapper of his now ingested burger, he threw both the wrapper and the bag into the back seat of his car. Then he pulled out onto the street and to a stoplight. He debated on whether to do his fourth-year Latin essay, or his trig, both of which he considered the easiest classes he had ever taken. Down Gough Street and turning on to Pine, Jensen saw one of his twin brothers running in Lafayette Park, several blocks from home. Getting out of the car, he raced across a field of grass and grabbed Zack by the shoulder. "Hey, I heard they canceled the game. Do you think it's true? Is mono running rapid on their team?" When Zack didn't give his usual retort, he knew something wasn't right. "Never could understand the point of the game, it's too simple." Jensen paused. He remembered all the times his brother had tried to explain that the game was about territory; the team who had the ball had the power. Jensen tried again. "It's just basketball, it's not like your life depends on it." It shocked him when Zack scoffed. Without another word, Zack threw Jensen his backpack and got into the backseat of the car.

Jensen assumed his brothers were in another fight and said nothing. He put the pack on the floor of the passenger's side, next to his guitar, and then started for home. Putting on a New Age CD, he turned it up. He was determined not to get into the middle of the latest quarrel, probably about the rumor floating among campus that Rustin had done the deed, so to speak. *If Zack's being given the silent treatment, he deserves it.* But he couldn't not get involved. They were family. "Zack, what's going on?" He looked into the rearview mirror and could see his younger brother kicking the crumpled-up paper bag between his feet. There was a pause. A moment later, in a soft voice, the subject changed so abruptly that it caused Jensen to do a double take; he expected it to be one of those rare instances where the twins tried to mess with his head. Zack was fond of using it. But it was without a doubt Zack who sat there staring out the window with vacant eyes. Not Rustin. Turning down the stereo, he pulled off to the side of the road. Jensen shifted in his seat and looked into Zack's eyes. "What did you say?"

"I want to see Mom." Jensen noticed his brother's drawn face and wondered what else could have happened between Zack and Rustin that would make Zack want to visit the gravesite. The last time he had heard Zack mention their mother was when he was eight. He had asked what she had looked like, because their father had still not taken her pictures out of hiding. "Sure, Zack." Once again on the road, he made the drive in silence, first to the flower shop and then to the cemetery, where he parked right outside the graveyard. Walking onto the grounds, he followed Zack along the concrete pathway and then onto the grass toward the marked headstone. Jensen watched his little brother kneel in front of a homemade headstone. Jensen never took his eyes off the fifteen-year-old as Zack picked up the clay rock with both hands. One molded not long after her death. The rock had five handprints embedded on it; his father's handprint was in the center surrounded by four smaller handprints. He remembered nothing about his mother, but he knew the basics; that her name was Lauren, and that she had died at twenty-eight in a head on collision with a drunk driver. His older brother, ten at the time of her death, had once told him about the closed casket service. About fifty people had gathered to pay their last respects, not just family but friends, too. A lot of them were lawyers, paralegals, and even a few judges. Not for the first time, he remembered a stuffed bear that his mother had made for him when he was three. It had gone with him everywhere. He had thrown it away when he was nine. Big boys didn't have stuffed animals; but even though he would never admit it, he still wished he had it.

Jensen's attention refocused on his younger brother, who had laid the single white rose beneath her name. Again, he realized something wasn't right. *Zack was two when she died,* he thought. Jensen looked at his watch. "Hey, it's getting close to eight. We should head home."

"Was Mom in any pain?"

Jensen made sure Zack was with him as he headed back to the car. "I don't know. You'll have to ask Dad."

Ten minutes later, Jensen pulled into the circular drive, right behind Travis's green station wagon. He entered the house to find the living room empty. "Rustin, Dad, Atlas, Travis. Anyone home?" Jensen pulled off his coat and laid it on the couch. He watched as Zack sat down, slouched, with his legs spread wide apart.

Travis came out of the bathroom. "Your dad let me in; he just left. He said it was family movie night, girls' choice, and he's picking up Chinese food." He took a breath. "Your dad said Zack was supposed to be home an hour ago, and Atlas went to the cabin. Where's Rustin?"

Jensen pulled Travis aside. He told his best friend about their visit to the graveyard. "You know, Zack," Travis said. "That rumor about Rustin wasn't cool." It surprised both young men when the fifteen-year-old got to his feet and went upstairs without saying a word.

Travis left to pick up his sister from cheerleading practice, and over the next fifty minutes, Jensen checked on Zack several times. He would always find him sitting at Rustin's desk with his head in his hands. Every time Jensen would ask him if he wanted anything to eat or drink and every time he was met with silence. Jensen wondered what in the world could have happened that would change his exuberant, happy-go-lucky brother into a person who seemed to be nothing but a muted, angry kid.

— · —

CHAPTER 11

SILENCE

After mommy's group was over, Atlas had taken Brenna to his in-laws before heading to his dad's office. They spent several hours in the office and in the courtroom. It had been a long day, one case lost, another two cases won. A good day. But as he pulled into the driveway of his home, Atlas wanted nothing more than to get away from it all. He unlocked the front door and headed for the bedroom to change. Just being able to get out of his suit and into a pair of jeans and a pullover felt good, like shedding off the stress of the day.

Atlas was lacing up his boots when he heard the front door open. "Babe?" a feminine voice called.

"Back here." Little footsteps could be heard running down the hallway. As Atlas stood up, Brenna ran into the room and wrapped her legs around his. Atlas swung Brenna up into his arms as Ashley appeared in the doorway.

"You're heading out?"

"Just about. Do you need anything before I go?"

"Nope. All's good." Atlas had to only look at her face to know what she was going to say next. Still, she hesitated. "Try reading a chapter or two of the book, okay? It's not that bad."

Atlas laughed and shook his head. "Sure." Brenna grabbed his cheeks with two chubby hands. "Yes, Brenna?"

"Te amo, Daddy."

"I love you too, honey." A horn honked outside, just a little too long, and Atlas laughed; it was deliberate on Ryan's part. Atlas knew he could feel the vibration of the horn throughout the car even though he couldn't hear it. "Be good for Mommy, okay?"

Atlas put Brenna down and watched Ashley take her by the hand. "Let's go make some cookies."

Atlas gave his wife a quick kiss on the cheek and then headed out the door, grabbing his duffle as he did. At the curb, Ryan stood outside his truck. With his index and middle fingers on both hands crossed, Atlas flung them outward in the air. "Ready?"

Yes, he had been proficient at Latin by the age of four and French at seven. He also spoke Italian, German, Spanish, of course, and Greek. Portuguese, a language he had started six months ago, was more of a challenge than the others had been. But when he was twenty-two, he stepped into his first ASL class. As easy as it was to learn the signs, being able to interpret them was another challenge. But it was in this class that he met Ryan, who had been a T.A. for the class.

Ryan repeated the sign, a huge grin on his face, and the two young men got in the car ready for a long four drive to Lake Tahoe. As they began the long drive, the sounds of the city, blaring car alarms, the hiss from a city bus, and the steady chirp of different crosswalks ceased. The voices of those who begged for something more all vanished for a time. The fog disappeared.

Crowded neighborhoods were no more.

Atlas sighed as the sun vanished. It wasn't long after this that Ryan pulled the truck in front of Aunt Charlotte's ranch. He watched as she and Uncle Leo rounded the cattle. They could feel the vibration of the stampeding animals inside the car. Both Charlotte and Leo sat astride a horse as they worked to get the cattle corralled into the pen for the night.

The repetitive echo of hooves aground was graceful. Clouds of dust kicked up because of the herd of cows. The powdery dirt grasped on to clothes, skin, hair, even the animals.

He got out of the truck and slammed the door shut. Charlotte turned and waved at him. He waved back. "You need help?" he asked, even though he already knew what the answer would be.

"We're almost done!" She shouted. "Give us five minutes!"

The ranch had been in the Antonelli family for generations; the land being passed down to the oldest child. At one time, the land included one hundred acres; it was now down to sixty. The depression in the 1930s had taken a significant chunk of the land. They also lost an acre or two when the cattle prices became too steep and they could not make sales. A stable and paddock stood a yard from the house; the cattle roamed several yards further out. Beyond that, five miles out, was the forest, dense with trees. This is where the cabin stood.

The Antonelli's owned four horses; two that helped steer the cattle, and two they rented out in the spring and summer. Stomp and Striker both were admired for their strength, not necessarily their temperament. Stomp would never think twice of breaking someone's toes if approached on the wrong side, and Striker was fond of chomping down apples and anyone's fingers that got in the way. The other two horses were of a different breed. Capriccio was easy going, loved to have children ride him, and whinnied in excitement whenever he was steered toward the vast forest at the back of the property. Twilight was of a similar temperament. The only Appaloosa on the ranch, she loved to break out at a gallop. Her legs moved as if she was a ballerina. When reined in, her gait would change without hesitation, and when offered an apple or sugar cube, took it with such delicate grace that if Striker was watching, he would roll his eyes in agitation.

As promised, five minutes later, Charlotte had her powerful arms around him and gave him a peck on the cheek. She did the same to Ryan. Leo then stepped forward and shook their hands.

"You need to ride hard." Charlotte warned them. "Storm's heading in."

"Dinner's in the refrigerator," Leo said, as Atlas interpreted for Ryan.

Thunder snarled in the surrounding air, lightning blazed overhead, and sheets of hail pounded down from the now black sky. The horses were saddled and both young men soon had their horses in a gallop as they crossed the fields. The hail pelted them like ice swords across their face, neck and hands. Once they reached the trail into the dense forest, they were protected.

Squirrels chattered. In a panic, they would dart from one tree to another. The branches of tall pine trees rustled as they fought to be heard over the thunder.

It took almost half an hour to ride into the clearing. By then, hail had turned to snow. The weather worn cabin came into view at last, with smoke that billowed from the chimney. Icicles had already formed along the railing of the verandah. The fire pit was accented by a circle of stones; log benches framed the surrounding area. But yummy, gooey s'mores would have to be enjoyed another time. They were not on the agenda this trip.

Atlas swung down from the saddle as they neared the cabin. With the rein in one hand, he guided the horse into the lean to. It took some time to settle both horses in; saddles were removed, and they draped heavy horse blankets over their strong backs. The trough was filled with water from a nearby barrel. They then gave each horse a bucket of oats. Finally, Atlas grabbed his duffle bag and followed Ryan into the cabin.

Someone had been here. There was a low fire in the fireplace and the tantalizing smell of teriyaki chicken came from the kitchen. To the left of the entrance, tucked in a corner, was a desk with a laptop. Atlas watched Ryan pull off his jacket. The man then cracked his knuckles, pulled a memory stick from his pocket, and sat down to write another article about the deaf community.

Atlas wouldn't disturb him until dinner.

After he put his belongings in the bathroom, Atlas went into the kitchen to fix dinner, knowing his friend would fix breakfast in the morning. He set the table, and a mere twenty minutes later, Atlas removed a pan of golden brown cornbread from the oven and set it on the table. Atlas stomped on the floor to get Ryan's attention. When his friend looked up, Atlas signed, 'eat.'

Around the wooden table, both young men sat down and filled a plate, a square of buttery cornbread, a serving each of macaroni salad, baked beans, and a large portion of Aunt Charlotte's famous teriyaki chicken. They spent the next half hour with forks and knives clinking against plates, Ryan's heedless sounds of edible delight, and the scraping of the bottom of the crock-pot.

With the dishes done and his belly full, Atlas stepped into the bathroom. Not small and not exactly large, the room had the same redwood floors and walls as the rest of the cabin. A nice sized Indian style rug lay between the sink and the spa; the counter held two sets of fluffy towels. With the push of a few buttons on the wall, the spa came alive with a *whoosh!* And then a steady hum. Bubbles infiltrated the spa, and after he stripped down, Atlas submerged himself.

When he finally came up for air, the jets pulsed against his shoulders and lower back. This was worth the long drive, and he planned on doing it again the following night.

Thirty minutes later, the bubbles shut off. Atlas lathered, washed his hair, and rinsed off. He got out of the spa and pulled on a pair of long johns. The bed was calling to him, as was a beer.

With his hair still wet and tousled, Atlas grabbed a can of beer from the fridge before he made his way upstairs into the loft. The small cozy area had a bed, a nightstand, and a wood-burning stove. After he put a few logs into the stove, the surrounding air turned nice and warm. Sitting back on the queen-sized bed, his legs crossed, Atlas popped open the can and took a swig. But it wasn't long though before the book on the table yelled at him, *'Pick me up. Read me. You know you want to.'*

And so, the question came to mind again as he picked up the thick paperback, entitled *Eclipse*. Was all fair in love and war? War, sure, without a doubt. He had watched his father fight war after war in the courtroom. Nothing was off limits. The question remained, however, was all fair in love? Doubts had crept in. *Yes, what is mine is hers and vice versa. I have no problem with that.* But with movies, his wife had dragged him into plenty of theaters against his will to a fair number of what could only be called 'chick flicks'. Ashley's latest obsession was a movie called 'Twilight', based on a book of the same title. It had been sort of interesting to see a love story from a girl's perspective. Sure, Brenna was two now. But she would be a teenager one day. After they had seen the film, Atlas and Ashley had spent several hours in the living room, each with a glass of wine, as they discussed the characters, especially Edward, whom Atlas thought was a little wimpy for being over a hundred years old. Ashley had insisted the character was forever stuck in the mind of a seventeen-year-old. She thought he was emotionally secure. Whatever. She had insisted they read the books, all four of them, together.

With the patience of a saint, Ashley waited for him to get to the middle of the first book where the lead female, Bella, meets her boyfriend's vampire family. And, of course, Atlas hemmed and hawed, as expected of him. But the truth of the matter? He was well into the third book in the series. Could he have lived without reading all the whining that went on for pages and pages in 'New Moon'? Absolutely. Was he enthralled by Stephanie Meyer's series? Yes. Did Ashley suspect? Probably. So, was all fair in love? Absolutely not. Still, Atlas read 'til almost midnight before he went to bed., with the sounds of Ryan typing like a madman downstairs.

Atlas woke up early the next morning and looked down from the window. The storm had blown itself out. But first it left behind a thick frosting of snow. *Something's wrong. I need to go home right now.* He took a deep breath and rubbed his hands together. *Knock it off, Alasdair.* He made his way downstairs. *Maybe I can finish the book or maybe I'll go for a ride.* He pulled a set of clothes on over his thermals. As Atlas went to throw another log in the fireplace, he found Ryan asleep on the couch; he must have been up late. He hadn't even pulled out the couch.

Behind the cabin, Atlas cut enough wood for the day. He then went into the lean to. He patted Twilight's neck and then went over to Capriccio. A few moments before the ride, he rubbed the horse down and cleaned the muck. "You ready, boy?" he asked. The horse neighed in response. "That's what I thought. You give me a pleasant ride this morning, and I'll give you an apple when we get back."

The ride was wonderful. They raced through the trees at a gallop. Atlas could see nothing but streaks of color. But it wasn't long before he pulled the horse in, slowed down, and caught his breath. One would think it would be silent in a deserted wood; and for a while it seemed that way. But the wood had plenty of voices of its own. Squirrels peaked from the naked trees, their mouths full of nuts they had gathered. A wild hare hopped by, almost camouflaged by the snow and dark shadows. A doe and her fawn walked with absolute grace toward the frozen pond to find a drink of water. For a while he just sat there, taking it all in. He would have stayed longer, but his stomach cussed at him, using very vulgar sounds.

Back at the lean to, Atlas found two more horses had joined Twilight. And so, after he gave Capriccio the apple he had promised, he went inside, not surprised to see his aunt and uncle.

Charlotte was at the stove frying bacon; a large stack of pancakes was already on the table. A fresh pot of coffee was also brewing. But that feeling of dread seized him again, and this time it wouldn't let go. Atlas saw his uncle and Ryan leaning over a notebook. Leo scribbled something down and then handed his pen to Ryan, who nodded and wrote a response.

Atlas stomped his foot; Ryan looked up, startled. "What?" Atlas asked with both his voice and his hands. There was a long moment's hesitation. The tension grew. Atlas wanted to bolt for the door. But he still didn't know why. He looked at Ryan and stomped his foot, harder this time.

"Now," he signed. "What?"

He watched Ryan take a deep breath and slowly bring up his left hand. R-u-s-t-i-n, "What about Rustin?" Atlas spoke and signed, not sure who would end up answering him.

Leo looked him straight in the eye. "Atlas. He's missing. He's been missing since last night." |

"Dammit!" Atlas turned and grabbed his coat. "I knew something was wrong."

His uncle stepped around Ryan. He took a firm grasp of Atlas's arm, trying to get his attention. "There's nothing we can do right now."

"What do you mean?"

"The roads are blocked, Atlas." Charlotte had finally spoken. "We're snowed in."

It was all Atlas heard. His mind went back to a time not all that long ago, when all four boys still lived under the same roof. *Atlas was sixteen when he found Rustin in his room, pulling off the birthday cone hat covered in animated Transformers. Optimus Prime was the seven-year-old's favorite. Atlas watched his brother throw the hat across the room. A tear fell from the child's eye. "That Furby was kind of lame..." Atlas sighed. He took a seat on Zack's bed across from Rustin. "Rus, come on."*

"You're never around anymore."

"That's why you're up here crying?"

"I'm not crying." Rustin brushed the tear from his face. The boy was silent for a long minute.

"What was Mom like?"

"Mom?"

"Everyone down there has a mom but us. It's not fair."

What was he supposed to say? We had a mom. She's dead. How was stating the obvious going to help? More tense moments passed as both boys tried to ignore the falling tears. Atlas jumped as there was a knock on the door frame. He looked up. "Hey, Dad."

"Rustin, you're being rude." Robert saw the tears. "What's wrong?"

And in an instant, everything just kind of clicked for Atlas. "Dad, I quit."

"What?" Robert was confused.

"I quit. I want to be here with Rus, Zack, and Jay. After school, I can pick them up."

Atlas looked at Rustin and knelt, looking him directly in the eyes. "Carson Promise."

"What are you talking about?' Robert asked.

"I mean...," Atlas continued to speak to Rustin, "if you need me. Or Zack or Jensen does, I'm going to be there."

"Wait a minute, Alasdair. Your Criminal Procedures class is at three when the boys get out."

"Dad, I read that book three times. I can take any test they throw at me with my eyes closed.

It's the same with calculus and Shakespeare."

"What about Greek?"

"It's in the morning." Atlas looked at his little brother.

"You want to drop three classes?"

"I'll take them this summer, online. That way, I can be here for the boys."

"Nathan's family..."

"I know. But I want to do this." He looked at Rustin again. "I can show you her pictures."

"I know what she looked like," Rustin said.

"No. Not pictures of her. Pictures she took. Stills, black and whites, you name it."

"This is about Lauren?" Robert looked from Atlas to Rustin and back again. "One semester,

Alasdair. We'll discuss details later. We still have some candles to blow out."

Atlas stood up as his dad and little brother headed downstairs. "Dad, can I get a camera like Mom's?"

Atlas shook his head, trying to clear it. He could feel everyone's eyes on him as he tried his cell phone first, and then the landline. Neither worked. He took a deep breath. "So, what do we do now?"

Charlotte and Leo glanced at each other, and it was Leo who answered. "We wait."

CHAPTER 12

THE TORNADO

It was after six when Robert walked through the front door, his arms full of plastic bags, files, and a suitcase. "Jensen, Rustin, Zachary. Family night. Let's get a move on it."

Robert set the bags on the kitchen counter and began pulling out the little white boxes. The entire floor soon smelled of chow mien, fried rice, and several fragrant kinds of chicken. Robert's stomach growled. As he set out the plates and silverware, Jensen walked into the room, Travis right behind him. "Jensen, take out the garbage, or I'm going to have to dock your car privileges. Rustin! Zack!" He passed by the front door that was still open. "Julia, Travis. Come on in."

"Hi, Mr. Carson," Travis had a couple of two liters in his arms.

"Are we too early?" Julia asked. The girl was still dressed in her cheerleading uniform.

Robert smiled as a silver Cadillac pulled into the horseshoe shaped driveway; the Spencer's had arrived. "No, Julia. Not at all. Food's on the table. Go fix yourselves a plate." Robert turned around and found Jensen was practically on his heels. "Jensen." He saw his son's hands twitching by his sides. "What's wrong, son?"

"Rusi isn't home, Dad." Jensen glanced at the Spencer's who had walked up to the door. He then looked Robert in the eye. "Zack had us go to Mom's grave."

"Where is Zack?" Robert remembered Zack's phone call earlier that afternoon. He watched Jensen shift his feet once, them twice, "Jensen?"

"Upstairs."

Robert patted his son on the shoulder, then looked around at everyone. "Girl's night." He looked from Keisha to Natalie, and then at Julia. "Pick something good. Jensen, garbage."

Robert went upstairs and knocked on the twins' door. He found Zack curled up on his bed, which was covered with Rustin's scrapbooks; the boy had one open in front of him. Something was wrong. "Did you have a hard day?" Robert perched himself next to his son. He pointed to one photo that had Zack wrestling with his uncle, Craig, Lauren's brother. Rustin had gotten a new lens for the camera that year. "Wasn't that when you and Rustin went camping in Shasta?" The boys had been thirteen. Zack continued to stare at the picture. A moment passed, and Robert took the book and closed it. "Where's your brother?" Lifting Zack's chin, Robert repeated, "Where's Rustin?"

But Zack would not look him in the eye. "I don't know."

Again, something was off. Robert tried to figure it out. He knew there was some sort of jealousy that involved Natalie. He also knew that hide and seek never worked well for the twins; it was like the boys cheated because one could always visualize where the other one was. But Zack wasn't Rustin's keeper. "Alright, Zack. Let's go downstairs."

Robert followed Zack downstairs and watched as the boy went into the kitchen. In the living room, he found Julia and Natalie on the floor sitting Indian style, a plate balanced on their legs. Everyone else was spread out, sitting on a couple of recliners and the couch. "So. What are we watching tonight?"

"Ghost," Julia announced.

"Patrick Swayze's kind of hot for an old guy," Natalie piped up.

"Natalie." Nathan exclaimed in shock.

Robert grinned as Keisha elbowed Nathan. "She's right."

"You should see him in 'The Outsiders'," Julia added.

"Oh my god," Travis said in a hushed voice.

Zack walked in with a plate piled high with noodles, peppers, and instead of his usual Szechwan chicken, his plate held a large serving of sweet and sour chicken. Robert wrinkled his brow, confused. Zack always ate the spicy stuff. It was Rustin who craved the sweet. He looked at the clock on the wall and continued to do so every ten to fifteen minutes. Forty-five minutes into the movie, Zack disappeared upstairs again.

By nine o'clock, the movie was over. Several bags of eaten popcorn were scattered on the floor, as were plates, empty soda bottles, and a couple glasses. Robert peered out the window.

"Where is he?"

"Wasn't there some big photo project that was given?" Travis asked. "I have art with Ms. Juska fifth period, and she gave us our semester project today."

"Eric's in that class," Robert muttered. Everyone's eyes were on him as he pulled his phone from his pocket and pushed speed dial. "Maria, this is Robert Carson. I know it's late, but can I speak with Eric, please?" Moments later, he hung up the phone and kind of spaced out. "Where in the hell is he?"

"Robert." Keisha laid a hand on his arm. "Robert, what do you want us to do?"

"Do you want us to call the police?" Nathan asked.

Robert took a deep breath and blew it out. "Wait. Let me think." A moment later, his head seemed to clear. "Keisha, can you take Jensen and check the hospitals? Use Jensen's car."

"Sure." Immediately, she grabbed her coat and after Jensen grabbed his, they were gone.

"Nathan, take Travis and go to his hangouts, the mall, Scrappy's, any other place you can think of."

"Mr. Carson, we want to help." Julia nodded. "But can you call our parent's first?"

"Yes. And if for some reason you can't, I'll have Nathan drop you two at home. Natalie, I hate to ask. But can you help with the clean up? Julia, I need you to make calls."

Everyone parted to their designated task. The first thing Robert did was clear things with the Jacobs. He left Julia in the living room with a pad of paper, a pen, and the second half of the family's phone book. Natalie was in the kitchen with the water running. So, Robert went into the guest bedroom, sat at the oak desk, and began making phone calls on his cell phone.

The first was a call to Atlas, but the connection was broken; now that was two sons he couldn't get a hold of. Robert tapped his pen on the pad in front of him. He dialed Charlotte's number and got the same result. *What in the hell is going on?* Robert dialed Craig's number and finally someone picked up.

"Hello?"

"Finally." His next words came out in all one breath, as if he couldn't say them fast enough. "Rustin's missing. And I can't get a hold of Atlas or Charlotte."

"Wait a minute, hold on. What do you mean Rustin's missing?"

"He's missing, Craig. He's not home, it's almost ten o'clock and I do not know where one of my fifteen-year-olds is."

"Rob, slow down." Craig's deep voice was soothing. "I will take the next flight out of San Diego. Call the police. There's a big storm in the

Shasta area. I wouldn't be surprised if the lines were down. Go take a shower, try to relax. I'll be there as soon as I can."

The next hour passed with incredible slowness. Once the cleanup was done and all the phone calls had been made, Robert showed both girls to a guestroom; he wasn't sure when the others would be back. Then he did as Craig suggested and took a hot shower.

Robert was still in the shower when he heard the front door open and shut. He could only hear muffled voices. Stepping out of the bathroom five minutes later, he found Keisha in the kitchen with Natalie. "Anything?" he asked.

Keisha shook her head. "Nathan's taking Julia and Travis home. I think Jensen went upstairs."

Not knowing what else he could do on his own, Robert picked up the phone and called the police.

CHAPTER 13

DETAILS

I t was five after midnight when Robert invited the officers in, and everyone arranged themselves in the living room. Lieutenant Bennett was tall and angular with broad shoulders. Sergeant Meyers was short and lanky, his large hands seemed out of place. Robert introduced himself, Atlas, and Jensen. "Jensen, could you get Zack, please." The questions began all too soon, catapulted at him, one right after the other. They acted like it was possible to catch a thousand balls flying toward him at once. Meyers seemed more than a little skeptical. Robert attributed it to the many runaway, throwaways, and kidnap cases he had processed over the years.

As for himself, Robert should have known what to expect; after all, he had defended several people accused of these crimes. But for some reason, even though he knew what to expect, it didn't make it any easier. It was still tedious and traumatic. The questions started out simple enough, name, age, nicknames, hangouts, physical description, that wasn't the hard part. The details stumped him. "What was he wearing this morning?" Meyers had a notepad and pen in hand.

Robert wracked his brain for what seemed like an endless amount of time. He was relieved when he heard Jensen's footsteps as they receded the staircase. Robert repeated the question once his son was in the doorway. "Black khakis, a purple dress shirt, and a black tie," Jensen answered without hesitation. The answer was so obvious once Robert heard the answer. "But he always comes home and changes into a purple t-shirt, jeans, and a flannel. Black tennis shoes. Always. Zack needs you, Dad."

Excusing himself, Robert went upstairs. As he headed for the boys' bedroom, he heard a retching sound coming from beyond the wall. "Zack?" He entered the bathroom. He found Zack on his knees in front of the toilet, his head resting on the rim. Robert knelt beside his son and placed a hand on Zack's forehead. He pulled away when the retching started again.

Robert grabbed the washcloth on the counter and ran it under the faucet with cool water. After he wrung it out, he again approached Zack. The boy looked like he was about to fall over. "Let me see your hands, son." He cleaned his son's hands first and then Robert rinsed the cloth in cold water and wiped Zack's face. After his son rinsed his mouth out and spit in the toilet, Robert took Zack underneath the arms. Feet scuffed the floor several times before Zack's legs were strong enough to hold him. "Take it easy." The two of them made it into the bedroom; Robert let go of his son to pull the sheets down. When he turned back to help his son, Zack's legs had collapsed underneath him. "I've got you." He again grabbed Zack, this time helping him into bed. "Just relax, try to get some sleep." Robert grabbed an empty wash basin from the bathroom and put it on the floor beside the bed. He remembered a time when his twins were five and playing hide-and-go-seek. The game never worked well for them because one twin always knew where the other twin was. Robert was afraid that he might sound accusatory, but if Zack knew where Rustin might be, the better it would be for both boys. "Zack. Do you know where Rustin is?"

"There's water." Robert watched Zack struggle to keep his emotions from erupting. The boy's body curled into a ball, his knees up to his chest. "He's hot, he hurts all over the place. His head, his stomach, his chest, all over." Zack's voice broke and he cried. "I don't know where he is, he's cutting me off." Robert watched as the boy's body suddenly jerked.

"Zack?"

"His camera's broken."

Robert sat next to his son and for a while all he could do was hold his son close, hold the bucket when needed, and whisper reassurances in his ear. He ran his fingers through the boy's hair. *I will not tell the officers anything. I mean, there's no basis for it, and Zack's dealing with enough crap in his head right now. Maybe I'll ask him again tomorrow.* Once Zack drifted off to sleep, he pulled a blanket over him and headed back to the living room where questions were still being asked.

"Might he have run away?" Meyers asked. "Does he have maybe a hideout or a stash of money hidden somewhere?"

Robert noticed Jensen was scowling. "Rustin was mad at Zack for spreading some stupid rumor. That's all."

"What rumor?" the same officer asked.

Jensen sighed. "Just that Rustin had sex with Natalie. But he didn't run away. Rustin takes nothing off of Zack, he can't."

"Why not?" Meyers wouldn't drop the line of questioning.

Robert stepped in, rubbing his son's curls. "It's alright, Jensen." He looked at both officers. "Zack and Rustin are identical twins. They're pretty close. I don't think there's a stash anywhere. And we checked all of his hideouts."

Bennett spoke up then, "Can you give us a list of those, just in case?" Robert nodded.

"We should really question everyone," Meyers said once the list had been completed. "Can you have him come down?"

"Tomorrow." Robert was adamant; he remembered how ill Zack had become and he didn't want to have it start up again. "I think he's come down with the flu. What else can we do to find Rustin?"

During the next several hours, they went over everything imaginable. The coffee table was soon covered with identification sheets. At one point, they pulled together a list of people Robert wanted to call for supportive purposes. The list included Craig, of course, and his own parents.

Keisha and Nathan were there as the officers headed for the door. "Hey, thanks for coming." The process had exhausted him, yet he knew if he tried to, sleep would be impossible. "I don't know what I'm going to do. I should check on Zack." Keisha nodded. He was about to go upstairs when he found Zack on the bottom stair with a vacant look in his eyes. He pulled the boy to his feet and was relieved to see he had gotten his strength back. With his hands on the boy's shoulders, Robert led Zack into the kitchen. He watched as his fifteen-year-old son lowered himself into a chair at the table. Pulling milk from the fridge, he filled it to the brim and stuck it in the microwave for one minute. "Warm milk used to put you to sleep faster than anything when you were a baby." The little oven beeped, and Robert set the steaming cup of white liquid on the table.

Zack grasped the cup with both hands; his eyes never left the rim of the mug. "What about Rustin?"

Robert smiled at a memory. "Rustin always took longer. He wouldn't take his bottle until we held him for half an hour." He noticed Zack's pale face. "Zack, we will- "

"Was Mom in any pain?"

More memories flashed through the forty-three-year old's mind. He remembered how he had walked into the emergency room a whole person, and moments later it was like his life had shattered. He had been left broken, a widower who had to raise their four boys on his own. Four boys who would never truly understand what an amazing woman their mother had been. "No, Zack. She died before she even got to the hospital."

Sometime later, the father led his son to his bedroom on the second floor. He watched Zack climb back into bed, and then pulled the blankets up to his chin, just like he had done when the boys were younger. "Try to get some sleep, okay? Craig's on his way here and so are your grandparents. So, if you hear the door, that's who it is." Robert didn't want Zack to suffer a false hope just by the sound of the front door opening. "I'll be sleeping in the living room tonight if you need me." In the hallway, Robert flipped off the light switch and left the door ajar.

In the living room, Keisha was seated on the couch, leaning over the coffee table. Jensen was seated next to her and the two of them were trying to construct an appropriate, detailed missing person's poster. In a moment of surprise, Robert watched Jensen seize a picture from Keisha's hand. "You can't use that." They both stared at the teenager. "That's Zack." The tension broke, everyone laughed.

Robert smiled as he cleared his throat. "We're tired. Let's call it a night."

Keisha woke Natalie and Robert showed them to the door. "You call if you need anything," Keisha told him. "We'll be back first thing tomorrow."

As he closed the door, he heard a clatter upstairs. Robert took the stairs two at a time. He burst into the bedroom. The bedside lamp was on the floor, the light bulb shattered. Putting the lamp back on the table, he made sure to pick up every shard of glass. It was after that when Robert noticed how pale Zack looked, especially with the white pillowcase beneath his head. With a glance around the room, he realized he would have to systematically go through it all, see if there might be some clue where Rustin was. If he wasn't so tired, he'd do go through the desk now. But he didn't want to miss anything, any clues what might have happened to his son or where he might be.

Instead, he focused on Zack. He placed a fallen limb back on the sheets. When the boy moaned, Robert ran a hand through his hair. "Go to sleep, tiger."

Robert spent the rest of the early morning hours fixing up the two guest rooms. He made several dozen sandwiches for the next day. He attempted to clear his head. Sleep was impossible. So was watching tv or reading a book.

It was six o'clock in the morning when Robert nearly fell from the chair. He had finally fallen asleep just an hour before; even in that short amount of rest, Robert could feel a crick in his lower back. It was the sound of a car pulling up in front of the house that woke him. He stood up and began making a strong pot of coffee. When the door opened, he called out, "Craig, in here."

A short man with sandy hair walked into the kitchen. He carried a box full of scrumptious muffins that would no doubt wake his boys up. "You need to sleep." Robert shook his head. "Well, at least go take a shower." Craig smiled, "You stink."

An hour later, Robert came back downstairs, his hair slicked back. Just as he had predicted, both Jensen and Zack were gathered around the table, each with a blueberry or chocolate chip muffin in hand. "I'm going to go look around some more. Jensen, I want you to pick up your grandparents at eleven. Craig, monitor Zack." With a full thermos of coffee in his possession, Robert made his way out the front door.

In his car, Robert took a moment to pull himself together. He rubbed the sleep from his eyes. He yawned. Then he took a large swig of coffee before he started the engine and made his way to the nearest hospital.

Entering one of the several emergency rooms in the city, he approached the intake desk. He flipped through his wallet and showed a photo to the woman seated there. "This is my son. Has he been brought in? Maybe within the last twelve to twenty-four hours?"

"Let me see." Robert pulled the picture from his wallet and handed it to her. "Hmm. I've only been here a couple hours. Let me go ask." The woman left with the picture in hand. Moments later, she returned, shaking her head. "No, I'm sorry." She handed the picture back. "We haven't seen him."

Robert would get the same answer at all seven hospitals on the west side of San Francisco. He also checked the park and alleyways; he spoke with the homeless and the beat cops. Coolbirth Park was his last stop. He spoke to several groups of people. The very last person he spoke to was an older woman whose thin hair was matted and oily; her clothes were too big to fit her, yet the rain that had poured, made them cling to her thin frame. "Excuse me, ma'am. Have you seen a fifteen-year-old kid around here, he might be carrying a camera?"

"What are you going to give me, young man," the woman's voice croaked. The rain was saturating both of them, the only difference was that Robert had a way to get dry. "I can't give you any free tidbits now, can I?"

Robert knelt and took her scrawny, wrinkled hand. "I need to find my son. I will give you ten dollars, regardless. If you can give me any idea where he might be, I'll give you twenty." He watched as she took her hand back and slowly went to unfasten the top of her blouse. Robert held up his hands and stepped back. "No. Your answer is all I want."

Huge tears mixed with the rain. The poor woman's body shook. "But I don't have one."

"Hey, that's okay." Robert reached into his wallet and without giving it a second thought, handed the woman a twenty-dollar bill. "There's a shelter up the street. Get yourself some food, then go to the shelter. It'll be dry and warm there."

Robert then stood up and walked away. He hated to seem so heartless. But he needed to find his son.

CHAPTER 14

REALITY BITES

To sit down with the penal code book and a study guide or even finish the last hundred pages of 'Eclipse' would have been nice. It would have been nice to take Ashley and Brenna to the mall. Brenna did need a new pair of shoes. But instead of doing either of those things, he was stressing, stuck in Shasta, snowed in. The phones were working again, at least. Between his dad and Uncle Craig, he got updates every three or four hours.

They were a long couple of hours. Especially considering he was too far away to be involved with the search for his brother. When he did talk to his dad, the man would not stop apologizing for interrupting his weekend, which was ridiculous since finding Rustin was a hundred times more important than some stupid weekend trip he could take any time.

If fact, Atlas had just gotten off the phone with his dad. They had searched the hospitals, the parks, he had even asked the homeless. Nothing. He knew the quicker they found Rustin, the most likely they would find him alive. Even with all the dedicated searches, it might already be too late. It certainly was too late to think that Rustin had just lost track of time. He wasn't the type of kid who missed curfew. Also, if they were having snowstorms up in Shasta, who knew what the weather was like in the Bay Area, especially San Francisco.

While phone lines were again working, the area was still snowed in. Atlas put his cell in his back pocket. Then he rubbed his eyes using his thumb and index finger.

"Still nothing?" Charlotte asked.

Atlas shook his head. "This is driving me nuts. I have to do something!" He started pacing, from one end of the cabin to the other.

"Try to relax," Leo said. "There's nothing we can do right now."

"You already said that," Atlas grumbled under his breath as he continued to pace. Ten minutes crawled by like an infant stuck rocking on all fours. Finally, a hand touched his arm. Atlas looked up.

Ryan raised both of his hands and signed. Atlas nodded. He went to the kitchen and grabbed a pad and pen. He began writing lists, lists of hangouts, lists of friends, lists of hobbies. Hell, a list of groceries to pick up when he got back in town. Anything to keep his mind occupied. When he finished with every list he could think of, he cleaned.

Atlas was scrubbing the inside of a kitchen cabinet when Leo's phone rang. Everyone stopped what they were doing as the phone was answered. "Antonelli Ranch, this is Leo. Yes, yes. Thank you. Glad to hear. Bye." Leo slipped the phone back in his pocket. Without hesitating for even a second, he grabbed Ryan's car keys.

"Leo?" Charlotte asked.

"You." Leo pointed to Ryan and then tossed his keys to him. Then he turned to Atlas. "The roads are open. It's still slick. Drive slowly, use chains. Tell him." Leo again pointed at Ryan. Atlas translated, and Ryan nodded. "You let him drive, do you hear me?" Atlas nodded. "If I somehow find out you were driving, I will come down there and kick your ass. And I will find out."

Atlas felt his heart beating fast. "Yes, sir."

"I'll pack you boys some sandwiches," Charlotte whispered.

Usually when they made the drive back home, they would start noticing familiar landmarks and it would make the ride seem like it was going faster than it had on the way to the cabin. This time was different. Atlas couldn't talk with Ryan or even drive to keep his mind busy. He kept shifting in his seat; the seatbelt pulled at his waist uncomfortably. Half an hour later, he turned the radio on and the volume cranked up. Rock music was soon blaring, causing the car to vibrate. He tapped his foot to the music and sang the songs at the top of his lungs. It relieved some of the stress.

Just as the sun was going down, right around five, Atlas barely waved a goodbye to Ryan as he got out of the car and slammed the door. With his duffle bag in hand, he ran up the walkway and burst inside. In the living room, along with his wife whom he had called twenty minutes before, was a police officer who was standing in front of Zack.

Robert, who had been sitting next to Zack, stood when Atlas entered. His father blew out a large lung full of air. "This is my eldest son, Alasdair. Alasdair, this is Officer Bennett."

Atlas stepped forward and extended his hand, "Hello, sir."

A moment or so later, the officer was again trying to talk to Zack, who was kicked back on the couch with his eyes closed. "I don't know where he is." Atlas could hear the slight tremor in his voice. "I told you... Atlas...."

"What do you need, Zack?" Atlas asked.

"I don't want to be here. Please." Zack's voice was soft, his face pale.

It was obvious he was having a bad time. *Maybe he feels guilty.* Atlas drew a blank. However, he was sure that if they wanted direct answers from him, it wouldn't be in the house where there were reminders of Rustin everywhere. "Let's go for a ride. Just you and me." Atlas glanced at his father and then the officer; both men nodded. "Come on, Zack." Atlas grabbed his brother's coat from the coat rack and tossed it to Zack. A random thought came to mind. He looked at Bennett, "Aren't two officers usually in charge of a case?"

Robert blinked and looked at Bennett. "Where is Meyers?"

"He had some family issues come up. He's officially off the case." Bennett looked at Atlas as Zack headed out the door. "Try to get some information, okay? I want to find this child."

With a nod, Atlas approached his wife and gave her a kiss on the cheek. After a word or two, she handed him the keys to the car, then he followed his brother outside. Zack was sitting on the curb, his head in his hands, his body shaking. Atlas could hear his little brother's quiet sobs. Atlas unlocked the front door and held it open. He watched his brother stumble as he got to his feet and into the car.

In the driver's seat a minute later, he started the engine, backed out of the driveway, and pulled onto Van Ness. As Atlas drove in silence, he left the radio off in case Zack wanted to talk, maybe get his thoughts in order. It was easy to talk with Rustin, because after a while he would open up and tell him what was on his mind. But as had been said more than once over the years, Rustin and Zack were two different people. Atlas allowed Zack enough time to get himself under control. When the boy stopped shaking, Atlas drove to the school.

Atlas grabbed a basketball from his trunk; he beckoned his brother onto the blacktop. "Come on." He bounced the ball twice before he threw it into the basket. Then he tossed it to Zack. "Jensen said the game was canceled last night. You should really think about going for a basketball scholarship. Word is, you're the best player on the team."

"He can't get a scholarship if he's truant. Why weren't you in class today, Mr. Carson?" The voice surprised Atlas. When he turned around, he was face to face with his former sophomore English teacher. The woman now instructed Rustin and Zack during different hours. "Alasdair Carson! What are you doing here?"

"The police haven't called you yet?" Atlas was shocked. Quickly, he explained the situation. He noticed Zack had stopped playing ball and was propped against the pole. "Did Rustin say he was going anywhere after school yesterday?"

The two young men followed the teacher into the school's main office where Atlas was given a copy of Rustin's class schedule and teachers. As he was about to leave, he waved to Grace who he had met several times before.

"Wotcher, Rustin," she said, her accent thick. "Are you going to the dance next month?"

When his brother didn't answer, Atlas said, "Grace, it's Zack. Have you seen Rustin?"

The girl laughed nervously, "That's Rustin, isn't it? Jensen said Rustin wears purple." The girl pointed to the boy who stood next to Atlas. "He's wearing that there purple shirt. Zack wears red, does he not?"

Atlas did know that. He also knew his brothers so well that he could tell them apart without focusing on what color they wore. In fact, he knew them so well, that he forgot they were identical twins. "He pulled a trick on both of us, Grace. Have you seen Rustin?" When she shook her head, Atlas took Zack by the arm and led him back to the car. "You're going to change your clothes, Zack." He shouldn't have expected a normal, sarcastic remark, but he did. When his brother said nothing, it reminded him again of the situation at hand. "We're going to find him, Zack. I promise."

Atlas turned the car around and went home. Once inside the house, Atlas told his brother to change his clothes. "No," Zack shook his head. "I don't have to."

"Yes, you do, Zack." Atlas could feel his father's eyes on him, and for a moment he wondered if he had gone too far. His father was in charge, not him. But he had to have some reason to get Zack out of the living room.

"Atlas-" Robert had stepped forward, ready to take control of the situation.

But Atlas stepped in front of his dad and frog-marched Zack up the stairs. "Change your damn clothes, Zack. Now." Once he heard the bedroom door close, Atlas came back down. It was only then that he addressed Bennett. "Why didn't you call the school?"

Atlas watched Bennett's face turn bright red as he told his father about his run in with the English teacher. Once he finished speaking, Bennett apologized, "I didn't know. I'm sorry. Meyers had given me a list of what was in the file. The list verified that the school had been called. It won't happen again, and I'll report this incident to headquarters."

That his father insisted on making a report himself, did not surprise Atlas. He dropped his head for when his father's eyes turned to him. He took a deep breath and looked at Robert. "I wasn't trying to assert authority over you. I'm sorry. But I had to get Zack out of the room." He paused for a moment, getting his thoughts in order. "It's like he's trying to play switch." Atlas had a hard time finding the right words. "It's like he's in shock. He doesn't know what to do."

Bennett looked at him. "Do you think Zack has anything to do with Rustin's disappearance?"

The front doors opened. Jensen walked in with Craig and an elderly couple, Robert's parents. Both Jensen and Craig were carrying luggage.

Atlas shook his, "No, absolutely not." He answered without hesitation. "Zack wouldn't hurt Rustin for the world. If he did, he'd hurt himself."

—·—

CHAPTER 15

THE TRUTH

W hen Zack had heard Grace call him by the wrong name, he wanted nothing more than to play the part. If he could just become Rustin, all the threats would go away. The most important things he owned he wouldn't have to worry about losing, like his father's respect, or his own conscious, his self-esteem and his self-worth. Zack knew Rustin was hurt; in places he couldn't tell his father about; he wouldn't humiliate his brother like that. It was something no one would understand, the pain, the guilt, especially the guilt, it was something Zack had to keep to himself. Atlas thought it was all about playing switch; Zack could see it in his eyes. Playing was something you did for fun, and this wasn't about having fun. This was about surviving. Just because one breathes air, walks the turbulent road, and feeds on rations doesn't mean a damn thing. Surviving was more than that, surviving was all about living with oneself after tragedy. Another thing he knew for sure was that tragedy was lurking about, timing itself, before it ambushed all of them with shock and pain.

Zack had no intention of changing his shirt. But it wasn't long before he heard his grandparents arrive. It meant going through all the questions again, and his grandfather was ex-military, refusing to give a straight answer was not an option. He would dig and dig and dig, and

Zack could not deal with that. It wasn't long before he heard footsteps heading toward him. Zack quickly grabbed a pair of shorts and a towel and headed for the bathroom and locked the door.

Soon he was under the showerhead, tears coursed down his face and mixed with the bath water. Trying to clear his head, he lathered his whole body with shampoo and let the cold water run down his chest and legs; it soon cooled his overheated body. Zack hoped it would have the same effect on Rustin. Still, there was always this grimy vestige that stuck to him like cement wax, and although he repeatedly scrubbed and rinsed, he could never get as clean as he wanted. He scrubbed his skin until the area around his thighs was raw. Almost an hour later, Zack got out of the shower, shivering fiercely, before he stepped into a pair of boxer shorts. When he entered his room, he found his father waiting for him. "I don't want to go down there, Dad."

"I know. Sit down, Zack."

Zack sat down, expecting a lecture of some sort. He shouldn't have yelled at Atlas, he was being rude to his grandparents, or a laundry list of other topics sure to get him grounded.

"How'd you sleep last night?" Zack was puzzled. "I just want to make sure you're okay. I called the school and told them you won't be attending next semester."

"I can't do this!" Zack just about cracked. Everything was all jumbled up in his head, his sensations versus Rustin's, and his dad's calm demeanor versus Atlas's desire to know the truth. *I need something to drink. I'm so dry. Please.* Zack bolted for the door, down the stairs, and into the kitchen. Zack threw the refrigerator door open. He grabbed whatever was closest, a pitcher of raspberry lemonade, and gulped until the container was empty.

As he threw the container into the sink, Robert was beside him. "You alright?"

Zack turned around and walked into the dining room. He put his head in his hands. "Nothing's right, Dad. It's never going to be right again."

He could hear his grandparents talking over his head. "You need to get him to church, Robert. The Lord can heal all of this," Mr. Carson bellowed.

"He's right, you know. God wouldn't give you something you couldn't handle." Mrs. Carson went over to the sink, took the dishes out of the rack, and washed them again. "You really should use a dish washer, Robert. You don't want to give the family dysentery."

Zack felt a burning heat rise to his waist, a sensation he knew wasn't his; the sensation came from Rustin. When his dad and Atlas approached him, he sniffled. The tingle persisted and he rubbed his sleeve across his nose, trying not to cry again. But Zack didn't know what to do anymore. Rustin's body was his own, everything his twin went through, Zack endured as well. "He's thirsty, he's cold." The responsibility he felt was more than he could handle on his own; it gnawed at him until he felt raw inside. Zack took a deep breath, confused about the right thing to do. "Rustin's naked, Dad. They took his clothes." He felt the back of his throat swell and the tears came whether he wanted them to.

Robert and Atlas exchanged glances. Then Robert pulled out the seat next to Zack and sat down. He laid his hand on his son's arm. "Take it easy. Remember what you told me yesterday? You said Rustin was by the water. Do you know where?"

Taking a deep breath, Zack lowered his head and placed himself beside his brother. He saw Rustin's crumpled body drenched, on the moist ground and once again felt the pain. Specks of dirt blew in the wind and sprinkled bits of grain over his body. Zack could hear water running, not the huge sounds of the ocean, but something smaller. Rustin could no longer stay warm against the bitter cold. To curl himself into a ball was no longer enough. Rustin couldn't move, couldn't think. He struggled just to breathe. But Rustin, wherever he was, denied or could not give Zack any more information than that. He knew Rustin was near death; it seemed hopeless. Zack shook his head. "I don't know."

"Wait a minute," his grandmother pulled off her glasses. She set them on the table and glared at Zack through spider eyes. "We've been worried sick over Rustin missing, and you know where he is? We flew all the way out here from Florida because your brother is supposedly missing-"

Robert cut the woman off. "Mom, back off. It's okay."

"Your sons are playing some stupid game, and you think everything's okay?"

Zack got to his feet and started toward his grandmother, full of emotion and unable to control it. He felt his dad grab him across the chest with one arm and ran a hand through his hair with the other. "Stop. I know it's not your fault, Zack. I believe you."

"It's not a game, Dad. It was never a game." Zack trembled in his father's arms. He could hear Rustin cry out for him. His brother's anguished cries begged and pleaded with him to make the pain stop, to let him go. Zack could feel the cold. It was so bad it was like he was packed in ice. Yet the lower half or Rustin's body was a flaming mass of electrical wires. Rustin had lost control and Zack didn't want his brother remembered like that. "But I can't tell you. I can't tell you. He's hurt. He wants me to let him go, he wants it all to end."

"Shhh. Calm down. Wants all of what to end?" He felt his father's arms grow tighter around him, trying to comfort him. "Zack, talk to me, son. I can help you and Rustin, if you just tell me."

Comfort was supposed to be with family. Comfort was supposed to be a steaming cup of hot cocoa at his lips. Comfort was always found by a crackling warm fireplace, scary stories keeping everyone huddled together, waiting for the climax. But Zack didn't want to hear the climax. He didn't was hot cocoa or to sit in front of a fireplace. Because none of it made a damn bit of difference if Rustin wasn't there.

"Nobody can help, Dad. He wants the pain to end. He wants to die."

CHAPTER 16

DONUTS AND PIZZA

Everyone was wound up tighter than a Jack-in-the-box, about ready to explode. Jensen had watched this phenomenon with interest. At first everyone, the cops, his dad, Atlas, even himself thought Rustin had maybe gone somewhere without telling anyone. But that wasn't like him at all. When all friends and family had been called, and three days had passed, the tension was so high even his grandfather, an unemotional type, was beyond worry. Every time the front door or back door opened, they all held their breath, hoping it was Rustin home, safe and sound.

Robert had pulled Jensen aside only a day after Rustin had disappeared. He had explained that he was spending too much time at the police station and that his parents weren't the ones who should be keeping an eye on Zack. With it being winter break, that had been easy. Jensen became mother hen of the house; he greeted concerned neighbors, answered the phone, and kept a constant eye on Zack. His job was on hold, thanks to Joel's understanding, and the only time he had to himself was the hour he went to the school for practice with Camerata, thank goodness for the holiday practice sessions. People often came by with food, casseroles, enormous pots of stew, and the occasional pizza or take out. With his grandparents always going off to the bakery every morning to buy donuts, their kitchen had never been so full of food.

In the kitchen, Jensen often tried to get his little brother to eat. Since Friday night, Zack had barely eaten enough to keep a bird alive, and every couple of hours, Jensen would set a plate of food in front of him. After the scene in the kitchen, before he went back to the police station, their father had pulled him aside and asked him if he thought he could take Zack out. The suggestion had been to take him to a local restaurant. Jensen had agreed to take him out but didn't agree on the location. Robert grabbed his coat and started toward the front door. He looked at Jensen. "Look, I don't care. Just try to get some food in him." He paused. "If you have any problems, call me."

Jensen took a couple minutes to write a short grocery list and made sure his wallet was in his back pocket. Then he grabbed his coat. "Come on, Zack. We're going to the store."

Zack was again slouched on the couch. "I don't want to."

"Look, I just need to get out of the house." Jensen put his hands in his coat pockets. "I just want company, that's all."

"Hey, where are you two off to?" Atlas asked as he walked into the room. Both older boys watched as Zack headed out the door. Jensen followed. "Jay." Jensen looked at Atlas. "Call me if you need to."

The drive to the store took only a few minutes; it wasn't long before the two young men were heading down the pasta aisle with a shopping cart. Jensen put a packaged pizza crust into the cart along with a jar of tomato sauce. As he headed down another aisle, he spoke over his shoulder to Zack, who followed several paces behind. "What do you want on your pizza, Zack?" The boy was silent. Jensen tried again. "What would Rustin want on his pizza?"

Jensen turned around and looked at his brother. Zack was staring at the floor. "Bacon and sausage." There was no hesitation. When he spoke, his voice was just above a whisper. "With cheddar, jack, and swiss cheese."

Jensen bought the several items and soon was back home in the kitchen, preheating the oven. Zack stood on the opposite side of the breakfast bar. "You take the crust out. I already turned the oven on." He continued to give instructions, and had Zack spread the sauce and garnish the top of the pizza with however much he wanted. Once it was put in the oven and the timer was set, Jensen heard his brother's now familiar denial of food. "Rustin wants you to eat. He doesn't want you to hurt."

"What's that song Rustin likes you to play on the keyboard? The one that deaf guy wrote?"

"That was Beethoven. He didn't go deaf until after he learned to play. The song's called 'Ode to Joy'." Jensen was puzzled by the change in topics but said nothing about it. Minutes later, the timer went off and Jensen pulled a sizzling pizza from the oven. "Eat two pieces of this, and I'll play for you."

"Rustin's hungry."

"I know." Two pieces of pizza were set in front of Zack. Jensen then sat down and began eating a piece of his own. "Everyone's looking for him."

"You don't get it, Jensen. He's dying." The fifteen-year-old got up from his seat and walked to the den. Jensen followed.

"You don't know that. Eat."

"No. I can't do this anymore." Zack turned to Jensen, his hair disheveled. His legs stiffened as if he was trying not to collapse. "I can't pretend everything's okay. It's not, I promise it's not." The role reversal was astonishing. Jensen blinked. Again, there seemed to be some stupid mix up. Rustin he could handle like this. But Zack was an entirely different matter. It was as if he was facing some bizarre mirror, a mirror that reflected Rustin when it was Zack who was holding the handle.

Jensen pulled his brother onto the couch and watched as Zack began rubbing his inner thighs, sobbing. Standing up, he went over to the piano and began playing, first 'Ode to Joy' and then others. Ten minutes later, he stopped. He found Zack asleep, his head laid straight back against the couch. On a whim, he went into the kitchen and grabbed a piece of pizza. Back in the living room, Jensen coaxed Zack awake. "Hey, come on, little brother. I know you're hungry." Jensen shook Zack. "I will not let you sleep until you eat this."

He watched Zack's brown eyes open. "Leave me alone. Please, just leave me alone!?

Jensen tried again. "You feel Rustin's pain, right?" Zack nodded. "Does he feel yours? Is your hunger affecting him?" He was relieved when Zack took the slice of pizza with both hands and devoured it within seconds. "Does Rustin want you to have another slice?" Again, Zack nodded. Jensen took a deep breath. "Let's go get another slice. You and me, okay?" He stepped back from the couch and watched his younger brother amble back towards the kitchen.

"Good job, JC." Jensen was startled. Atlas was standing on the stairs that led to the library; apparently, he had been watching for a while. He walked down the staircase and Jensen finally allowed himself to fall onto the couch.

"What are you still doing here?" Jensen rubbed his hands on his jeans. "He's still not saying anything."

"But you're getting him to eat. Take baby steps with him, JC. You try anything too fast, he'll clam up again."

Zack appeared in the doorway with a lost look on his face. "I can't do this. I really can't do this."

"Yes, you can, Zack." Jensen exchanged a look with Atlas and got to his feet. "We're doing this for Rustin."

Chapter 17

Found!

"Oh my god, oh my god." The woman's name was Linda. She was dressed in a thick tweed coat and boots. Coming to California, let alone San Francisco, had been dream of hers since she was a little girl. She had spent her entire life on the east coast, and had never been to a city, let alone one as huge as San Francisco. The food was wonderful, and the shopping had been so much fun. Her husband, Randy, had treated her to all of this for her fiftieth birthday. Last night, they had even gone to a show. It's why they had gotten up so late and missed their complimentary breakfast and why they were headed out to eat brunch. But first, she had to get a hit off her cigarette.

Linda went behind the motel like she had done the night before; just a quick puff or two is all she needed. She also wanted to get a closer look at the stream she had found. Last night, it had been too dark; she hadn't wanted to leave the security of the lighting from the motel. But this morning, in the brightness of day, she expected to find a beautiful flowing stream that would lead out into the ocean. Instead, she saw the body. Linda pulled out her cell phone; in the cold air, she fumbled and it slipped from her fingers, dropping it with a splash into a watery puddle. "Randy!"

"Lin, what's wrong?" A short, sturdy man in jeans and a plaid shirt walked up behind her. Then, as he stepped forward to block her view, he pulled his cellphone out and dialed.

"9-1-1-, do you have an emergency?"

"Yes." Randy knelt down to get a closer look and then backed away hastily.

"Sir, are you there?"

Randy cleared his throat. "OK, look. There's a kid out here. He's naked, he's soaked. Jesus, it smells and there are flies."

"Is he breathing? Is he conscious?"

Taking a deep breath and placing a hand over his mouth and nose, Randy stepped forward. A moment later, he stepped back and again turned away. "Yes. He's breathing." Randy was a tough guy, he had been working on the family boat for thirty-plus years, gutting fish. He always came home smelling of salmon and albacore, his coveralls stained with fish, blood and guts. But this? This was so much worse. Randy cleared his throat. "He's not awake. What now?"

"Where are you, sir?"

"Uh, we passed San Francisco. Colma, I think. There's a stream, maybe a river. We're behind the Holiday Inn." The man paused. "What do I do?"

"Just stay on the phone with me. Emergency techs are on their way."

The police arrived first, Bennett, with a new partner named Smith. As she began asking the couple questions, he stepped forward to get a closer look at the victim. He swatted a couple flies away. It was then that Bennett gasped; the dingy shirt was a shade of purple, and though the face was smudged with blood and dirt, it was a face he had seen before. Or at least a face that looked very familiar. "Smith, call the station." His partner, Linda and Randy, looked at him. "We've found Rustin Carson."

The ambulance soon arrived with its lights flashing, its siren screaming. The siren cut off abruptly as it came to a stop several feet from the back of the motel. As one paramedic went to grab a stretcher, another paramedic approached Rustin's shivering body. With a pair of latex gloves already on, he removed the blindfold. He flashed a light in both eyes and then checked his pulse. "Twelve beats per minute," he said as his partner approached, rolling a stretcher. He pulled a pair of scissors from his pocket, and he cut off what remained of Rustin's soiled shirt. Moments later, the two of them were rolling him onto a backboard and onto the stretcher. His head in an immobilizer, they straightened out his legs and arms before they covered him with a dry blanket and secured him to the soft mattress.

As the lifeline helicopter circled the area for a place to land, the paramedics pulled an oxygen mask over Rustin's face. They also inserted an IV live that dripped saline. Finally, the helicopter landed and Rustin was loaded. He was on his way to the hospital.

Minutes later, the helicopter landed on the roof of St. Francis Memorial Hospital. Rustin was immediately taken down to the emergency room where the air was chilly, and the smell of antiseptic was strong. The paramedics took hold of their respective corners of the bed sheet and moved Rustin onto a hospital bed. The bag of saline was hung on a pole nearby and the two men left the area.

The head nurse, Ginny, was a woman in her early forties with years of experience in the trauma center. She had tended to countless car crash victims, victims of domestic violence, broken bones, and black eyes; she had seen it all. But victims of sexual assault, those were the worst, woman, child, or man, it didn't matter. She hated that the police were involved; the clicking of the camera was irritating and made it harder for her to do her job. But hey, she did want the bastards caught.

The camera was already clicking away. The sheet that had covered Rustin had been thrown to the side. Nurse Ginny had her gloves on when she opened a rape kit.

Rustin was still unconscious as the examination began. The nurse started the procedure by running a comb through his hair. Once the comb and hairs were collected in a sealed bag, she took a swab to the boy's mouth and sealed the swab into a bag as well.

The examination continued. Ginny noticed the discoloration to his torso and the inflammation to his upper arms. "Bring that camera over here." Taking a clean comb intending to gather pubic hair samples, her peripheral vision caught sight of a foot twitching on the sheets. "Need some help at bed ten," she called out. She put the comb down on the tray and removed her gloves.

Ginny stepped to the head of the bed. She found Rustin's eyes cracked open, his face pale, his teeth chattering behind the oxygen mask. "Rustin, you're in the hospital." There was a shift in the curtain around the bed and she was handed a plastic bracelet. "We're going to take good care of you here." She paused a moment to fasten the ID bracelet around Rustin's wrist. Ginny looked up to see who her co-worker was. It wasn't a nurse or orderly, but someone from the lab. Being so focused on her patient, she hadn't heard the cart being pushed up to the bed. "Hello, Tony."

"Can I help?" the man in red scrubs asked. "They're pretty busy out there." Ginny left and Tony adjusted the oxygen mask. "Rustin, I'm Tony. How are you doing?"

Ginny returned with an armful of leather restraints and laid them at the end of the bed. Exposing his feet, the nurse fastened one end of the restraint to the boy's ankle, pulling it tight. The other end of the restraint was secured to the bed. As the same procedure was repeated with his other foot, Rustin started gasping. His hand came up as he reached for Tony with a shaky hand. "Help-help-help me."

Tony took his hand as Ginny added a strap across his hips. "Rustin, you're okay, bud, I promise." A leather cuff was wrapped around his wrist, the arm with the IV, and secured it to the bed rail. Then Tony let Ginny take the hand he had been holding and finished restraining him.

"Let me finish the kit, okay?" Ginny said, pulling on a sterile pair of gloves. Tony nodded and she started to get samples of pubic hairs.

Tears were streaming down Rustin's cheeks, his body still shivering and clammy as they rolled him onto his stomach. It was then that they saw the back of his head and the condition of his buttocks. "Jesus Christ," Tony muttered.

Leaving the area once more, Ginny soon returned with a doctor who quickly assessed the situation. "Finish the rape kit, complete the blood test, stitch the wound, and get a CAT Scan done. I'm going to find Dr. Salicco."

The doctor left. Ginny looked at the tech and made a motion with her hand, encouraging Tony to start talking to the boy.

Tony brought a calm hand to the back of Rustin's neck. "This is the worst of it, bud. Try to calm down. Take deep breaths. Nobody's going to hurt you here."

Ginny pulled on a new pair of gloves and prepared to take a final sample. As gently as she could, she inserted a slide into his rectum.

Rustin's once raspy voice was gone, his mouth fell open in a silent scream. His hands clenched and unclenched by his sides until Ginny removed the slide and slipped it into the last evidence bag. Finally, the kit was complete.

Tony quickly traded places with Ginny and together they positioned Rustin again on his back. "Rustin, I'm going to get this done real quick, okay?" With practiced hands, Tony tied a rubber tourniquet around the boy's upper arm. A cotton ball soaked in cleaning alcohol was rubbed in the crook of his arm. As the needle was slid into a vein and several vials were filled, Tony kept talking in his soft, reassuring way. Once the last vial was capped and the needle removed, a clean, dry cotton ball was taped into place. "Hang in there, bud." Pushing his cart, Tony left the area. The process of collecting everything needed took over two hours.

The bath that followed was short yet thorough, the stitches administered swiftly. They were about to roll the bed down the hallway when a man in a lab coat approached; it was the prestigious neurosurgeon, Dr. Salicco.

He never addressed Rustin directly. Yet he stepped up to the bed and looked at the head wound. "Prep him for surgery."

"He hasn't had a CAT-"

"I don't care. We have imaging in the O.R." He took another look at Rustin's head, then said, "Ten milligrams of codeine."

Salicco left and it was just Ginny and Rustin who was still gasping. "Rustin, it's okay. Honey, you're going to dry your mouth out. Try to relax." The nurse was at a loss. For the first time ever, she could not console her patient and it bothered her terribly. Her mind raced through years of crisis and for some reason drifted to a time when her granddaughter had found her bird dead at the bottom of its cage. The only thing that had calmed her was her stuffed elephant.

Leaving the side of the bed, she went to a nearby cabinet and looked inside. She pawed through a box that was half full of stuffies. Finding what she was looking for, she brought a teddy bear to the bed and showed it to Rustin.

Just as she tucked it beside him, a man in green scrubs appeared. "Rustin Carson?" Ginny nodded. "Alright, Rustin. Let me pull back the sheet here." The stranger adjusted the blanket and rubbed alcohol roughly along his hip. A moment later, a needle penetrated Rustin's skin and was inserted deep into muscle. Rustin's whole body flinched. "I know. Deep breaths." The needle was removed, and the blanket draped back over his body. The man disposed of the empty syringe and left.

Ginny sat down. She watched Rustin's eyes as they drifted. Several people in head covers and masks arrived and rolled the bed down the hall. Rustin's eyes closed.

CHAPTER 18

TIME STOPS AND BEGINS AGAIN

Three of the longest days of Robert's life ticked by. He had thought it was bad when he was told that his wife was dead and having to decide on whether to have her organs donated like she had asked. They had tried to reassure him that she wasn't in any pain, and it helped him to go along with what she wanted somewhat. But who knew what condition his son was in? If he was still alive. Robert swallowed hard. *Was he in a lot of pain?* He was left with a bunch of questions and no way to get answers.

Friday morning rolled around and along with it, a torrential rain. Robert jumped out of bed, grabbed a pair of slacks and a sweater and got dressed. Going downstairs, he found his parents and Craig going through a portfolio Rustin had put together the year before. "He definitely has his mother's eye for detail," Craig was saying.

Mr. Carson looked up. "There are donuts on the counter. What are you going to do today? Do you need any help?" His father had never been one to show much emotion to anyone, not even his wife. Having been in the military for over twenty years, the man knew how to keep his head in check during a tense time. It was the same thing the day they had arrived; the man made a few adjustments to his clothes and hair and then asked Robert what the plan for the day was. Abrupt and to the point. It certainly helped in this situation.

Mrs. Carson continued going through the photos. "Someone needs to be here in case we get a phone call." His mother was the complete opposite, wouldn't stick her nose into anything. Everybody did their own thing and took care of their own problems. Robert wondered often how they had stayed married for so many years.

"No, I'm alright. Just going to the school."

"I'll go with you." Craig got up, and with his coat in hand, followed Robert out the door.

Robert entered the school's office, Craig at his heels, water dripping from their clothes. He was greeted by the school staff with open arms, and he introduced Craig. Alasdair had already been there of course. Bennett had made a visit, correcting that mistake. "We're all concerned about Rustin, Mr. Carson. Is there anything we can do to help?"

He asked for Rustin's schedule, and he was given a copy. He scanned the paper. "Algebra," he muttered. "PE and photography." Robert stopped there and asked if Ms. Juska was on campus.

Ms. Carol Juska was a tall, slender woman in her early sixties who had been at the school for almost forty years. When the teacher walked into the office, she held out a small, soft hand, the skin wrinkled with age. "What can I do to help?"

The three adults went into a small conference room. Robert watched as Ms. Juska went to the side of the room and began fixing the three of them a cup of hot tea. "It's cold out there." She returned to the table, handing both men a cup before she went back and got her own. She sat down and wasted no more time. "Before break, I had my class go through some old photography portfolios for a project I had assigned. The one Rustin had looked at was from a former student of mine. Her name was Lauren Antonelli."

Robert let out a breath he didn't even know he was holding.

"Lauren was my sister," Craig said, as Robert was at a loss for words. "She went to school here."

"Didn't you?" Robert asked still stunned.

"I was kicked out my freshman year." Craig said with a roll of the eyes. "Can we see the book? Maybe he wanted to recreate some shots."

"Rustin took the book home already. I'm not sure what else I can tell you."

Robert and Craig stood up, both eager to get home with a new angle to look at. Robert could feel Craig's eyes on him as he walked into the house, passed his parents, and upstairs. "Craig, check under the bed." Robert went through Rustin's desk, he set aside an SD card, stacked sheets of paper, and then went through each one of them. The top sheet was titled, *'Nazi's: the abuse of twins'.* Robert flipped through it and found a complete fifteen-page paper with a bibliography that had the usual mistakes, a wrong indentation here, a name not capitalized there. With a sigh, he put the paper back on the desk. *The book. Where's the book?"*

The phone rang. Robert and Craig raced downstairs and found his father on the phone, his expression unreadable. "We'll be right there." Mr. Carson put the phone down. He looked at Zack who was again on the couch. Then he looked at Robert. "They found Rustin. He's at Saint Francis Memorial."

Robert felt like his heart cracked; feelings of shock, relief, terror, an awful sense of denial filled his head. He watched as Zack bolted for the door. "Zack." He watched as Jensen, who had just stepped out of the kitchen reached Zack before he could and wrestled him to the floor. With a quick move, Jensen had pinned his younger brother down. He looked up at his dad. "What's going on?" Jensen asked. Zack escaped from his brother's grasp. Within seconds, Jensen had him pinned again. "Zack, are you okay?"

Running a hand through his hair, Robert could see the fear in Zack's eyes. He approached his son as he would a wounded animal. "Let him go, son. The detectives called. They found Rustin." Robert took Zack by the arms and at once tightened his grip. "You're to stay home, you hear me?" The father watched tears stream down Zack's face. "Hey tiger, relax. I'll call you, okay? But you have to stay by the phone, so you can answer it when I call, all right?" When his son nodded, he smiled and ruffled the boy's hair. "That's my boy. Jensen, call Alasdair and tell him what's going on. He should be at the apartment, if not, call his cell phone. Dad, Mom, I need you to stay here with the boys. Craig, come with me."

After parking the car haphazardly in the lot, Robert dashed into the hospital with Craig at his heals. They approached the information desk. A woman sat behind plexiglass, the black receiver of a phone pressed to her ear. Robert picked up snippets of the conversation, something about an order of bedpans. *I don't give a damn about how many bedpans you ordered.* He tried to suppress a growl at the back of his throat and failed. He felt Craig's calm hand on his arm; Robert took a deep breath. He had to stop himself from pouncing on her as she put the receiver down. "Where is my son?" Robert's voice cracked.

"Your name, sir?"

"Robert Carson. My son's name is Rustin."

She looked at the computer in front of her, typing away. "I'm sorry. The systems running a little slow." Seconds seemed to drag on forever. She looked up. "Yes, he's here. The pediatric ward is on the third floor."

Robert asked Craig to stay and wait for Atlas. He wanted his first visit with Rustin to be private. He would have to bear the initial shock by himself to know how to deal with Zack.

Alone, he entered the elevator and watched as the floors ascended floor one, to two, to floor three. There was a beep and the doors opened.

Officer Bennett was waiting for him. "Mr. Carson?"

"Robert, please."

"Robert. Come with me."

Together, the two men started to the opposite side of the ward. A couple of women were working behind a tall counter; one lady in ducky scrubs was talking on the phone. The other nurse wore pink scrubs. She came around pushing a cart containing a basin, a bar of soap, and several towels.

Robert's mind wondered. He imagined a world where his youngest son didn't exist. He was horrified to think what it would be like to look at, to identify, the body of his dead son. Robert shook his head. *We're in pediatric ward. Not the morgue.*

Without realizing it, both Robert and Bennett had come to a stop. Bennett had to call out to him three times before his voice broke through. "I'm sorry. What?" Looking around, he found the police officer by his side. Standing a few steps in front of him was a man in a white lab coat who had his hand extended. Robert reached out and shook it. "Robert."

"I'm Dr. Todd." The man exuded a sense of calm. He had pale blue eyes and dark, almost black hair. Everything about him, the way he stood, how he spoke, his handshake, reassured Robert that his son was in capable hands.

"Please. Where's my son?"

"Right now, your son is being treated by the best neurosurgeon in California, Dr, Salicco."

"Neuro." Robert felt his face go pale.

"He's had some sort of traumatic brain injury." Dr. Todd paused, giving Robert a chance to process his thoughts. "Dr. Salicco will give you details once Rustin's out of surgery and in the ICU."

Feeling a huge lump in his throat, Robert could not swallow. "What else?" *A broken bone? A blood transfusion?*

"Let's find a place where you can sit down."

"Robert." Bennett was looking directly at him. "I'm going to get back to the station. I'll contact you when something comes up."

Nodding, Robert followed Dr. Todd into an empty hospital room. His chest felt tight. The room felt like it was getting smaller and smaller. He closed his eyes. One deep breath, two, three. *Rusi is alive. It's time to step it up.* Robert opened his eyes once more. "Tell me."

"I'm not going to lie, and I will not sugar coat anything."

"Good. Tell me."

"Like I said before, he has a TBI. A traumatic brain injury," Dr. Todd reminded him. "He has a mild case of hypothermia." Robert could sense the doctor's hesitation.

"*Please. Just tell me all ready.*"

Dr. Todd cleared his throat. "They found your son half naked, blindfolded, and gagged. The police have taken custody of his clothing and a kit was completed in the emergency room." Again, there was a brief pause. "Rustin was raped and sodomized."

Robert flinched. The world seemed to disappear; there was nothing but a dark void with the echo of his thoughts. *What in the hell am I supposed to do? How am I supposed to deal with this? Do I get angry and knock a bunch of stuff over? Do I cry?* Somewhere in the hollow distance between the nightmares of reality and the grim, dark void, there were footsteps and indistinct voices. His knees buckled.

A hand was on his arm, and then his body seemed to move on autopilot; he was helped to his feet and walked a distance before he was eased into a chair. Someone pulled him forward, guiding his head between his legs.

The flurry of movement came when the dark void became brighter and brighter. Sounds became clear. "Dad, are you alright? I got here as soon as I could."

Bringing his head up, Robert found Atlas in front of him: Craig was standing by the door. He ran a hand through his hair and stood up. "Yes, I'm fine." He took a deep breath and then repeated everything he had been told. "How do I tell Zack?" he finished.

"I'm pretty sure Zack knows, Dad. He placed where Rus was when he went missing, remember? What do we do right now?"

Craig looked at the doctor. "You'll let us know when he's out of surgery?" Todd nodded. "Let's get a cup of coffee."

They each grabbed a cup of coffee at the cafeteria and then spent the next couple of hours pacing the hallways. All three men were quiet, each lost in their own thoughts. The tension in the air that followed them was suffocating.

"Robert Carson, to the ICU," the female voice crackled over the PA system. "Robert Carson, to the ICU."

Taking a deep breath, Robert ran a hand through his hair. "Ok, ok, ok. Atlas, I need you to go home and be with Zack. Your grandparents can't handle him on their own."

"All right, Dad." Atlas stepped forward and gave Robert a hug. "Call me if you need anything."

The walk to the ICU seemed long, like going through a dark tunnel, unsure of what he would find on the other side. Robert was grateful for Craig's presence; just being there helped Robert get one foot in front of the other.

Outside the ICU, Dr. Todd introduced Robert to Rustin's surgeon, Dr. Salicco. The Italian doctor wasted no time in telling them all that Rustin had pulled through. "He suffered a fracture to his skull and a blood clot. We'll be observing his condition. Right now, we have him in a drug-induced coma. It'll be a few days before we bring him out of it.

"I want to see him." He watched the two doctors exchange words. Dr. Salicco gave him a nod and then walked away.

"This way." Dr, Todd led him through a door with the label 'Intensive Care Unit' adorned to it.

The first things Robert realized were the constant beep of a monitor and the strong smell of antiseptic. His eyes took in the bare white walls, the emergency equipment on a nearby counter. And then, with absolute horror, a small body lay stretched out, tubes and wires leading to it from various places. The strong face he saw almost four days ago was replaced with one that was almost as white as bones. "Rustin." His eyes were black and blue. The knuckles on both hands were swollen, and one of them clutched a brown teddy bear with light brown paws. Robert looked at Dr. Todd, puzzled.

"Sometimes, kids come in so terrified that it's difficult to treat them. They become aggressive in their need to feel safe. Personnel give the bears to kids who are traumatized, it helps calm them down."

Robert took another step towards the bed and watched his son's chest rise and fall. He reached up rubbed the back of his hand along Rustin's cheek. He saw beauty in the boy's beaten face, in his swollen hands, in a body where he had yet to see the damage. None of it mattered. None of it mattered as long as Rustin survived.

— · —

CHAPTER 19

THE FIRST TWELVE HOURS

D ays passed. Medical personnel at some point began to gradually reduce the pain medication. The fog lifted from Rustin's
brain. He could feel his legs were bare and chilly underneath a hospital
gown and a light sheet. He could feel cool air on his face. His body
shivered once, then twice. It was at this point that his head screamed,
and his hands clenched into tight balls. It was like he fell beneath the
clouds. Sounds seemed way too loud, the beeping monitors, voices.
Lots of voices. The voices he heard were so mumbled at first, that he
wondered if they were real. A large hand caressed his cheek, and everything seemed to pause for a moment. Words separated themselves,
and he recognized two distinct voices. One of which sounded familiar.
Rustin opened his eyes; hope returned.

A fuzzy face smiled down at him. "Hey kiddo, my name's Todd.
You're in the hospital." The face had hands, hands with soft fingertips
that held his wrist for a short time and then laid it back on the bed. The
face repeated itself, "My name's Todd." Like static, there was another
pause. Then, "What's your name?"

*It sounded like a question, but what was the answer? Was there a
right answer?* Rustin's attention focused on the constant beeping of
the monitor and a piece of soft fluff in his hand. A moment passed

before he looked up at the face. *Hospital?* "Don't have the pictures. Please..." His voice trailed off, and the pain hit again, hard. His face grimaced and his body tensed.

A short moment later, the sheet that was covering him was pulled down, revealing a body whose bruises were fading. Rustin shivered again from the cold. "Just a minute, kiddo." A needle punctured his hip. Tears came to his eyes. "Can I take the teddy for a minute?" The fluff disappeared from his hand. "We don't want you getting pressure soars." The face's hands rolled him on to his stomach. The pain drifted away. Rustin's eyes fluttered closed.

He is ten again, and with a little help from his dad, he got on the horse. "Hold on to your brother tight, Rusi."

A loud buzzing noise alerted the staff of a malfunction in the IV.

And he did, he held on so tight that Zack teased him. "Hey, Dad. Rustin's a scary cat." "Cool it, Zack."

A nurse hurried in, adjusted the tube, and the alarm stopped beeping.

The ranch worker walked them around the corral.

His only escape route? A twenty-foot drop off a cliff. "Stand up, coward."

Fingers on his wrist checked his pulse. A slight pause and the removal of sheets,

Halfway around the coral, the horse stumbled, and Rustin lost his hold. The hard, dusty ground rushed up to meet him.

Rattling on a bedside table and a hand carefully spreading his butt cheeks. Rustin cried in his sleep. Time is lost.

"On the ground, bastard. Goddamn fucking bastard."

"Rusi, I'm sorry Rusi."

"Look at the little boy beg. Make him stop, honey."

A thermometer was inserted into his rectum, smooth glass into an open wound. It was like breaking into yet another nightmare. The pain. The invasion, again, of a body that he no longer controlled. Rustin cried out. *Please don't hurt me anymore. Let me wake up. Just let me wake up.*

Brown eyes popped open. Rustin tried to get to his knees, tried to get himself out of the nightmare. Hands pulled his legs out straight and a hand on the small of his back held him still. An unfamiliar voice spoke, "Take it easy, Rustin. We're almost through."

Without warning, Rustin gasped. "No! Don't touch me. Please." The gasping quickened. A moment later, the thermometer was removed.

The familiar voice he had heard earlier that afternoon asked him how he was, realization dawned on him. His breathing slowly came back under control. "Dad." Rustin's voice was dry and hoarse, no louder than a whisper. A chair scrapped along the floor, was pulled up to the bed. A body lowered itself into it. He saw the face of his father. "School. Gotta go to school."

"Not now, honey. It's winter break, remember? Try to go back to sleep." A knock at the door, and Robert got to his feet; it was an oriental man with a cart covered with packages of needles, syringes, and a small army of empty vials. "The lab tech is here, Rus.

Robert helped Rustin roll on to his back as the man pulled on a pair of blue latex gloves. "Hello, Rustin. How are you today?" Rustin didn't say a word. Instead, he watched as the lab worker attached a needle to the syringe. Without a word, the lab worked grasped Rustin's left arm and examined it. Grabbing a cotton ball and moistening it with alcohol, he brushed the cotton against his skin and then the needle was inserted into a vein. Rustin was exhausted; all he could do was watch with half-opened eyes as several vials of his own blood were filled. The needle was removed, and a new cotton ball taped into place.

The lab worker left after having a few hushed words with his father. "I want to go home." The few words drained him. He watched as Robert traded places with the lab tech and took a seat beside the bed. His dad's arm crossed over the bedrail, brushing back Rustin's bangs.

"I know you do." His father's presence was enough to allow Rustin to fall into a restful sleep. While he felt drained, the strong sense of safety the man provided was what he needed to nod off. And finally, he did.

Robert did not rest at all that night. He spent hours just watching Rustin sleep. Every time his son moved, every sound the boy made, caused the father concern. The only time he left the hospital room was when he had to use the restroom. Nurses checked Rustin's vital signs every hour and turned him over every two hours; the last thing the boy needed was bed sores besides everything else. A strong pain killer was administered every four hours. Rustin slept through all of it.

Early Saturday morning Rustin found it to be a great effort just to wake up; it was like coming up for air after a long dive. Everything seemed a hundred times brighter, a hundred times louder, a hundred times more painful. He looked around confused. He was confused about so many things like where he was, or why he was in so much pain. His eyes scanned the entire room, the monitors, the IV pole with its red numbers, and the thin blanket that covered his body.

"Go back to sleep, Rusi."

He may have dropped off back into the deep end. But when he opened he eyes again, a man in a white lab coat stood beside him, a stethoscope around his neck. "Good morning, Rustin. I'm Todd. Do you know where you are?"

The boy struggled for a moment as he tried to turn onto his back, his legs refused to do what he wanted them to. He was too tired to do anything. Even his shoulders rejected his attempt at movement. The doctor helped him turn over onto his back and then pushed a button on the side of the bed. Slowly the head of the bed rose until he was sitting at a slight angle. Rustin looked around, confused how he got to where he was. "In the hospital? Why? Where's Zack?"

"Zack's at home, Rustin." The boy listened as his father told them there had been, Rustin heard him hesitate, an accident. "How's your head?"

He tried not to think about the searing pain in his head; he didn't want to sleep anymore. He was about to lie when someone entered the room. He didn't see the person; his father and the doctor obstructed his view. But the voice was, without a doubt, female. Without understanding what it was, he was in the first stages of a panic attack, with the dizziness and shortness of breath. He froze for a split second and his chest heaved.

Dr. Todd and the woman left the room, and his father tried to pull him close. But Rustin recoiled from the man's hands. Mere touch at that moment was so morbid and scary that Rustin thought he might be about to lose his mind. Or maybe he already had. Maybe that's why he was in the hospital to begin with. Rustin watched as his father grabbed a brown teddy bear from the counter and put it in his hands. "It's okay, honey. No one's going to hurt you, Rusi. Calm down."

With the bear in his possession, he relaxed; he didn't know why. It was almost like a light switch, emotions get out of control, he couldn't breathe, but as soon as the stuffie was placed in his hands, the panic was gone. He took a few quivering breaths and grasped the bear tighter. Rustin looked at his dad. "Why am I here? Why am I really here?"

Robert hesitated again; Rustin knew it. "You don't remember getting hurt?"

Dr. Todd entered the room with a cart filled with toiletries, a basin of water, and several towels. Rustin eyed it with a certain amount of concern. The doctor was quick to reassure him that Robert could help him bathe. "Do you want to give me the bear?" Rustin shook his head. As ridiculous as it may have been, the bear was the only thing he could depend on. "Okay."

Moments later, with the door shut, Rustin watched as his father soaked a cloth and then lathered it with a bar of soap. His father worked around the bear and at first, everything was fine. His face, his stomach, even his aching legs he could deal with. But as the warm sudsy cloth moved southward toward his hips and then groin, he felt regurgitation rise in his throat. The teddy bear fell to the floor. Rustin turned to his side and vomited on the sheets.

He heard his dad go for help, as he tried to get away from the horrible smell. A woman in a nurse's outfit appeared with his father and a gurney. "Let's get you cleaned up, Rustin. Then the doctor can look- "

"No, No." Rustin's mind went somewhere else, some place dark and haunted, somewhere his conscious couldn't reach.

At the house, Zack walked away from Jensen who was trying to get him to eat. Going into the family room, he grabbed a pen and wrote.

The sunset on the beach is sweet like Neapolitan ice cream, and Rustin clicks away with his camera, his lifeline, and every drop he captures is for eternity. Suddenly monsters are all over him. They rip at his clothes. The sound is worse than nails on a chalkboard. Feet and hands explore and assault places they shouldn't. Eternity is set aside while the camera drops to the ground, kicked aside as if it doesn't matter anymore. Ice cream doesn't look so good anymore.

A monster with long blonde hair and green eyes appears out of nowhere. She demands and takes whatever she wishes, chocolate sprinkles, the sunset, M&M's, and virginity. Her hot skin on his, ice cream melts between his legs like fire.

Zack dropped the pen and sobbed.

"Stop!" Rustin began to kick and scream, anything to get the monsters off him. "Please, don't. I don't have the pictures. No."

The doctor rushed into the room. Rustin didn't notice the concerned expression on his face. "Hey kiddo, did you make a mess on the bed?" He saw the cart moved back. An orderly had just finished changing the sheets, the dirty bedding put in a receptacle by the door. Once she left, Dr. Todd again stepped forward. He said, "Let's have a look at your head, kiddo. Just to make sure there's no infection. I'll be right back."

Rustin watched as Robert stepped out into the hallway with the doctor. He wanted nothing more than to move, to demand an answer to why he was so sore, especially in certain private places. With that idea in mind, Rustin ignored the pulsing pain in his temples and the nausea in the pit of his stomach. Throbs of pain grew worse as he got to his knees and crawled to the end of the bed. His bare feet touched cold tile floor, and his knees wobbled. He heard footsteps hurry in. His father asked what he was doing. Rustin's voice shook as he replied. "I can do this." Someone stepped behind him and took him under the arms.

"Kiddo, you're too weak. You need to lie down." Rustin felt the doctor's strong arms around him, one beneath his legs, the other beneath his head. Todd moved as if he was carrying a china doll; he laid Rustin back on the bed and made sure his head was supported by a soft pillow. He pulled a new heated blanket over the boy and then pulled up the bedrail. He called to someone outside the door. "Rustin, this is Noah. He's going to be your new nurse."

Why do I need a new nurse? He wasn't allowed to get up by himself, and now some new person was going to his naked body, his sores and everything that went with it. The pain in his head became excruciating. He couldn't understand why in the past day or so he had felt no urge relieve himself. But at that very moment, Rustin wanted nothing more than to get up out of bed and use the toilet. It didn't matter if there was no pressure on his bladder or the fact that to take a dump was out of the question; the fact was, it hurt too much to do either. "Please," he pleaded. "I gotta pee." He grew nervous when Dr. Todd chuckled.

"Relax, kiddo," he was told. Rustin was pulled into a sitting position, the blanket swung to the side. Looking down, Rustin found a tube between his legs. "See that? It's all taken care of. Once you're stronger, we'll let you use a urinal, okay? But right now, you need to rest. Do you want to wash your mouth out?" Dr. Todd filled a small cup with a nearby pitcher of water.

Rustin swished the water around in his mouth and spit it back in the cup. He laid back down. With his head propped on the soft pillow, he was asked if his head hurt. "What happened?"

"Answer the doctor, Rustin," his father said.

The boy shook his head even though it pained him to do so. "I don't want to sleep anymore." He watched Noah leave and return with a different cart, this one piled high with a lot of bandages, medical tape, and such. "Dad, please."

"I need you to stay awake right now, anyway." Rustin watched Dr. Todd pull on a pair of latex gloves. He removed the gauze from his head. "I'm Todd. What's your name again?"

Rustin winced as the gauze pad was pulled off and the wound was cleaned. He took in a quick breath. "Can I see?" Rustin took the mirror he was handed and looked hard at the abrasion, hoping for answers. But he couldn't remember anything; it was as if the flashback had never occurred. Discouraged, he shook his head. The mirror was taken away.

"Do you have any brothers or sisters?" The doctor applied a new bandage to his head.

"Three brothers." The doctor cleaned the wound site with iodine and then applied a sterilized bandage. He had just finished wrapping his head in gauze when a surge of pain hit that was so strong, Rustin screamed. He brought his forearms to his head and brought his knees up to his chin. The doctor's voice sounded faded, said something about codeine.

The head of the bed moved down until it was flat. Hands pulled his legs down from his chest, and then moved to his thigh and shoulder. Rustin was then turned from his back to his stomach.

His arms were then brought down to his sides. Tears came to his eyes. He wanted something. Control maybe, or answers to the questions he had. He wanted something that wouldn't leave him feeling so desperate and alone. He could not handle all the stress that came at him, all at the same time. "Please. Please, I don't want to sleep." An alcohol pad was rubbed on Rustin's arm, then the boy watched as Dr. Todd took the hypodermic needle from Noah. The cap was removed and the needle tested; liquid spurted out. As the doctor approached him, Rustin's panic escalated, his heartbeat twice as hard. His face started to tingle, first his teeth and then his lips and nose. His palms sweat. Rustin kicked at false villains that accosted him. Both the catheter and IV came out. Rustin tried to escape but was soon surrounded by medical personnel whose strong hands pinned him on his back, his arms down by his sides. A leather strap was pulled tight across his wrists and both legs were secured to separate bed rails. A nervous sweat saturated the sheets. Fractured pictures flashed through his mind, pictures he couldn't put together.

He saw Dr. Todd approach again with the painkiller in hand. "No stop! I said stop, please."

Rustin wasn't sure where the words were coming from, but he felt a sense of overwhelming helplessness that he couldn't conquer. He felt the sharp needle puncture his left hip.

Tears fell from his eyes, his hands clenching and unclenching by his sides as the medication entered his body. His voice cracked, "Please, no." The needle hesitated a moment and was then removed. The painkiller worked within seconds. His body was introduced to a thick fog. It was almost as if his head was detached from his body. Most of the room cleared out. Hands became gentle again. Tight muscles went limp as tension was eased in both body and mind.

"I'm sorry, kiddo." The doctor's voice sounded as if it were moving farther and farther away.

"We're going to take good care of you here." Every remark was followed by static, just as before. "You're safe here, Rustin. I promise." The voice sounded like it was smiling. "Medicine feels good, huh?"

Rustin fought the drug as hard as he could, even to where objects twirled and colors faded. His muscles were worthless; with Noah's help, the doctor removed the restraints. "Home," Rustin whispered. "I wanna go home."

Todd laid a reassuring hand on the boy's arm, for all the good it did. "I know you do, kiddo.

Noah is going to start you on some new medicine and help you relieve your bowels." The doctor hesitated. "But when he's through, I want you to get some sleep."

It was nine-thirty at night when Dr. Todd left. Noah was then by his side. An IV stand with its own monitor was brought close to the bed. "Hey, Rustin. I'm Noah. I'm going to take care of a few things and then make sure you're comfortable. I've seen a lot in the past several years. There's nothing to be embarrassed about. Let's get that IV in now." Noah took Rustin's hand in his and ran his fingertip along

Rustin's arm, searching for a good vein. He turned the hand over and found what he was looking for. "Alright now. Try to relax." Noah rubbed a strong-smelling liquid onto his arm. He prepped the needle and a moment later, was sliding the needle into a vein beneath the skin. Rustin moaned. "You are doing outstanding." Tape secured the needle into place and Noah took a minute to get the monitor working.

"Now what?" Robert asked, stepping up to the bed once more.

Rustin watched with blurry eyes as the nurse injected a clear liquid into his IV line; the drifting was almost immediate. It took him further into oblivion somewhere between wakefulness and slumber, pain and non-existence. "Take out," he slurred, saliva dripping from his mouth. Noah stepped back.

Robert took a hanker chief from his pocket and wiped Rustin's mouth.

"I can't, Rustin. I'm sorry." Noah pulled a new pair of gloves on, and while being careful that the IV didn't pull loose, he rolled Rustin onto his side. Both men could see the boy's eyes roll; Noah chuckled softly as he tinkered with the tray behind him. When he turned back, he had a cotton ball with iodine in his hand.

Robert watched Rustin's face as the boy's behind was cleaned and a laxative was given.

Again, Rustin moaned. Robert rubbed his finger against his son's face. "Can he still..." Robert wasn't sure how to finish his question.

"If we don't, he'll become constipated. There might be a little blood at first, so don't be alarmed."

Minutes after the laxative was given, Rustin, whose eyes had closed, opened. His hands began to clench and unclench as a burning sensation took hold. The sensation grew worse as feces reached the surface of the skin, passed torn tissue. Rustin screamed as spasms racked his insides.

"Oh, my god."

Noah put a restraining hand on his shoulder and another on his leg. "Deep breaths, Rustin."

The spasms are pretty bad, huh? It's almost over. Let's give it a couple minutes. Did I tell you about my dog Tug?" For several minutes, Noah prattled on about his dog Tug who was part Pug and part Chihuahua. She could open bathroom and bedroom doors anytime she wanted; privacy was never guaranteed at his house. "She is quite exasperating sometimes," he said.

After what seemed like an eternity, the nurse cleaned the area and then pressed a warm cloth on his behind. Gradually, the spasms ceased. "It's over, Rustin. We're all done for today." He pulled the blanket back over him.

"No more," Rustin whispered. He was afraid that Noah would have him go through the same routine the next day. He had to tell the nurse he couldn't go through that again, ever.

"Tomorrow Rustin, same time." Noah was looking at him with concern. "Every day, same time. It will get easier. The spasms won't always be so bad." He thought about going into detail of what could happen if they didn't but thought it might be too much for right then. Instead, he said, "Get some sleep. No worries right now." Noah glanced at Robert and then left the room.

"Hey, Rus." Robert wiped up another small puddle of saliva that had found its way down Rustin's chin and on to his pillow. He then took Rustin's hand and gave it a gentle squeeze. "Go to sleep, honey."

Rustin opened his mouth and tried to speak, but no sound came out. He tried again. "They hurt." He gasped. "The needle." Forming a complete sentence at that moment was just too difficult. The teddy bear, his safety net, was placed back in his hands.

"Shhh. No one's going to hurt you here."

Rustin could hear a light clatter on the bedside table behind him. He was then rolled onto his back. Noah was there, putting on a new pair of gloves and spreading his legs.

"Focus on the bear, Rusi." His dad took hold of the bear and brought it up, essentially blocking Rustin's view of Noah who was lubricating a catheter. Robert took a page from the nurse's book and began telling Rustin about an old teddy bear Jensen used to carry around with him everywhere. "Your mom had made it for him. I found it in the trash some years ago. Don't tell your brother, but I have it stashed up at the cabin."

Rustin groaned loudly as a new catheter was inserted, and then groaned again a moment later.

"You did great, Rustin." Latex snapped once more as the gloves were removed. "Just relax. Take nice deep breaths." A blanket covered his body. "We're all done."

Sounds became more and more faded. His eyes grew heavy. As hard as Rustin fought, he was no match for the power of the drug. Against his strength and against his will, slumber took over.

Chapter 20

Bainbridge?

L unch had been uneventful; it had comprised of a cup of milk, a peanut butter sandwich, and a serious discussion about Winnie the Pooh, Tigger, and sharing. Atlas lifted her from her booster seat, took her in his arms, and headed upstairs.

"No nap." The little girl began to scream and kick. "No nap. Bwenna big girl."

Atlas laid his daughter down and covered her with a blanket as she cried. "Brenna, big girls take their naps without crying." He kissed her on the forehead. "Have sweet dreams, sweetie." The phone rang just as he left the room. Skipping down the stairs, he grabbed the phone in the living room. "Hello."

"Alasdair, I need you to do a couple things for me."

"Sure, Dad. What do you need?" He grabbed a piece of scratch paper and a pen.

"I need you to call Grandma Antonelli, tell her to e-mail me a list of the schools on Bainbridge Island. Then, I need you to take your grandparents to the airport. Can you do that?"

"I can do that. Why bother Nana, though?"

"Are you sure?"

"Of course. You thinking about moving up there with Rus and

Zack? Maybe Jensen?"

"It's an idea. Just looking at options. You need to get a move on it. Their flight leaves in two hours."

"On it."

It was early afternoon by the time Atlas had sent several links to his dad on the schools around the entire Washington area and packed Brenna in the car with all her paraphernalia. With Brenna in his arms, he entered his father's house. He found his grandparents packing last-minute things. "George and Patty said to join them for dinner tonight. Maybe we can still join them on that cruise to the Bahamas." He heard Mr. Carson say to his wife, as he put a final pair of slacks into an already stuffed suitcase. The bed was neatly made, even though the sheets would have to be changed, and Atlas knew how things would be arranged when they got around to cleaning the room and its adjoining bathroom. The towels would be on the back of the toilet and the cleaning supplies would be found alphabetized under the sink.

"I'm just happy they found Rustin." His grandmother looked up and saw him in the doorway.

"You don't think we're leaving too early, do you? Robert would never ask us to stay, you know that."

"Of course we can leave. Rustin's fine," his grandfather bellowed. "The Lord brought him back to us, and now he's in a place where the workers of Jesus can get him back on his feet."

Atlas hid his annoyance. Rustin was far from being fine, and they were already planning to leave. They weren't even going home. They were going on vacation. Like Rustin's recovery was a sure thing just because they prayed. It wasn't their belief that made him mad. It was their blatant disregard for their grandson. But Atlas bit his tongue. "We should be heading out the door, traffic's still bad this time of day. I'll be in the car."

Peeking into his brother's room, he found Zack at Rustin's desk, going through more pictures.

"Zack, you want to come with me to take Grandma and Grandpa to the airport?" He watched Zack shake his head. "All right, I'll see you in a couple hours then."

After seeing that Craig was in the kitchen making a sandwich, Atlas headed out the door. He was joined by both grandparents' minutes later. During the ride to the airport, he listened as the couple planned their weekend. Atlas tried to hold his tongue because his daughter was in the car. However, fifteen minutes later, he was at the end of his rope. He glared in the mirror.

"Aren't you the least bit concerned Rustin was raped and nearly murdered?"

"Sonny," Mr. Carson peered at him over his glasses, "You need to watch the road."

"That's right. I'm sure you're just tired." Mrs. Carson laughed. "Rustin, raped! Honey, you know that's impossible?"

Atlas bit his tongue, furious at their ignorance. But he kept his eyes on the road. By the time they got to the airport; he could stand back as they gave Brenna kisses and gave them a civilized goodbye.

After he dropped Brenna off at Ryan and Rachel's, he went to the hospital. He began thinking about secrets. Not stupid things, like reading a book meant for adolescents. Bigger than that.

Like how much longer they would be able to keep the truth of what had happened to Rustin from Rustin. It just seemed wrong.

He stopped at the nurse's station and leaned against the counter. Rustin's room was the first in a long corridor and Atlas found his father with the doctor right outside the door. The doctor was telling Robert that Rustin's condition was on the borderline of critical. As long as the fracture to his skull healed properly, he would be fine. But if the swelling didn't go down soon, it could cause irreversible brain damage.

"He's so confused though," he heard his father say. "And emotional. He's never like that."

"He may be for a while," Dr. Todd answered. "He will not be the same child you've raised for fifteen years. This has changed him."

"And that's why he has a different nurse."

"Exactly. For some reason, just the voice of any adult female, will cause him to have a panic attack." The doctor paused. "He probably won't remember the attack, and you have to be prepared for that. You also need to decide if, what, and how you are going to explain to him what happened."

When do we start talking about this? Together. Not like it's something we can avoid. Clearing his throat, Atlas pushed himself away from the counter and walked up to the two men. "Hey, Dad. Grandma and Grandpa got on the plane safely. They said they want updates on Rus. They'll call you tonight."

He watched his father rub his eyes, an action that had become a habit over the past week.

"How's Zack?"

"Climbing the walls. Kid didn't sleep at all last night." Atlas recalled the night before when he and Jensen took shifts watching their little brother, who had spent most of the night pacing the house. When either of the older boys physically force him to sit down, he would pull away, stand up and continue pacing. "Craig's with him now, said he's staying until Rustin comes home. You're really moving to Washington?" They discussed the situation for several minutes, how Robert wanted to protect both boys from the after effect of the crime. "I'm kind of hungry, you want anything from the cafeteria?"

"No, I'm heading back to the station." Robert rubbed his eyes again. "Something's not right. Can you monitor things here?"

"Sure, not a problem." After he said goodbye, Atlas walked down hallways that were gradually becoming familiar to him, almost as recognizable as his own home. He went to the cafeteria, bought a cup of coffee and a couple sandwiches. On his way back to the ICU, he was surprised to run into his uncle. "Where's Zack?"

"I don't know. He was in his room when I went to the bathroom, when I came out he was gone. I can't get a hold of your dad either." Craig ran his fingers through his hair. "He's not answering his cell."

"Dad just left for the station. I'll tell you about it in the car." Atlas pulled his keys from his back pocket. "We've got to find Zack."

---·---

CHAPTER 21

EMOTIONALLY CRASHED

Zack had watched his uncle go into the bathroom and decided that he had to get out of the house. He grabbed his coat from the hall closet and went outside, where he walked several blocks. He passed houses, a school, and even a liquor store. Sitting in front of the store, he noticed a bank across the street, the one that had been robbed a couple weeks earlier. *Bastards.*

He was about to head toward the hospital when someone came out of the store and handed him a can of beer, "Looks like you could use one." Then the stranger walked away.

He was turning the can over in his hands when there was a sudden flash of pain in his head.

Look at the little boy beg. Zack pulled back the tab and for a moment, he stared at it. He debated on whether to take the first sip, because it smelled like crap. But a moment later, he was taking a sip. The bitter taste was too much and most of it he spit up, the liquid trickling down his shirt. *I don't have the pictures.... three or four.... dead anyway.*

Zack saw the attack again and again. He couldn't forget hearing Meyers's voice from upstairs the first night Rustin went missing. He couldn't look Bennett in the eye and say the allegation that he didn't know more was true. Atlas kept pushing for more. Jensen was wrapped up in everything from playing host to choir management. And his dad was never home.

The boy needs to be fucked with. An arm came out of nowhere. *I'll give you whatever you want.* Without looking up, he began punching the chest and stomach of whoever had grabbed him. And he couldn't stop, because the voices kept coming. *Please, no. On the ground, face in the dirt.*

A foot swept behind his legs and Zack fell to the ground. "What's going on?" the voice paused. "Have you been drinking?" A hand reached out and Zack took it, getting to his feet. "Zack." It was Atlas.

"No, I haven't. What do you care, anyway?"

"You know how Mom died-"

"Yeah, I do. And I haven't been drinking." Zack tried to walk away but was grabbed from behind. "Let go of me, or I'll scream."

"You go right ahead. I'll tell anybody you're drunk."

"I'm not drunk." *On the ground. face in the dirt.* Zack shook his head, trying to get the voice out of his head. "Let go of me. I have to say goodbye to Rusi. I gotta-"

"Zack, I can smell alcohol on you."

"Someone gave me a can. I took a sip, Stuff tasted like piss. I threw it away."

"Zack."

"Dammit. I spit it up, okay?" Zack pulled away from his brother and sat down on the curb.

A couple of people peered out from inside the store, one had a cell phone in hand. Atlas ignored them and sat down beside Zack. "What are you talking about? Rustin's got a long road ahead of him. But there's no reason to think -"

Zack took in a slow deep breath, trying not to break down again. "I have to say goodbye. You can't feel his head, Atlas. It's going to explode, and I can't stop it."

Atlas could think of nothing to say. Instead, he just sat next to his little brother and rubbed his back in circles. Several minutes passed. Atlas then got to his feet, "I'm going to take you home. You need to take a shower and change."

"I didn't drink, dammit."

"Regardless of whether you drank, that smell is on your clothes."

Zack stood up and started toward his brother's car. He could feel Atlas's eyes on him the entire time it took him to walk to the car. The ride home was tense. Zack rocked back and forth. When they pulled into the driveway, he raced from the car to the kitchen sink, where he threw up.

Before he could finish, Craig was right behind him. "Where in the bloody hell were you? I almost called your father, and he has enough on his plate right now."

The boy needs to be fucked with. Help me get rid of the body. Zack shook his head. His knees buckled, and he only stayed up by grabbing the sink.

Craig spun him around and grabbed a fistful of Zack's shirt, smelling it. "Zackary Nathaniel.

My sister, your mother, died because of a drunk driver."

Tears came to Zack's eyes. *They're never going to believe me and Rustin's going to die.*

Atlas came into the kitchen after grabbing a towel from the hall closet. "He says he only had a sip." Zack watched as Atlas grabbed a glass and filled it with water. "Here. Rinse your mouth out."

Zack swished the water in his mouth and spit in the sink. Atlas handed him the towel.

"Downstairs. Go take a shower."

With the towel in hand, Zack slowly backed away from the sink and made his way into the bathroom, a dull yet intense pain attacking his brain. He locked the door, disrobed, and stepped into the shower; he didn't even bother to adjust the water temperature. A powerful stream of cold water pulsed onto his head and down the length of his body. Ten minutes later he stepped out, his muscles tense from the cold but otherwise more relaxed. He found a new toothbrush under the sink and got rid of the aftertaste of something he thought he would never drink again.

Zack found Craig and Atlas still in the kitchen, both with a cup of coffee in hand. "Now what?" he asked.

Craig set his cup down on the counter. "Your father called while you were in the shower. He wants you to come down to the hospital. I told him I wasn't sure that was a good idea." Zack swallowed hard as Craig walked to the opposite side of the huge kitchen. "A sobriety test. If you pass, I'll drive you to the hospital myself. If you fail, there's an AA meeting down the street in an hour."

"I want you to walk to Craig," Atlas glanced at his uncle and then focused again on Zack.

"Hands by your sides, eyes straight ahead, heal to toe."

Zack completed the task with ease and was rewarded with a hug and a pat on the back from Craig. "If you ever get to where you do drink or even if you're thinking about it, call me or your dad or Atlas. Okay?" Zack nodded. "Get your jacket, let's go."

At the hospital, Zack met his father downstairs in the lobby. He watched from a distance as his uncle and dad spoke, and then seconds later, Craig left. His dad approached him slowly. "Hey, Zack."

"Dad." Zack could feel his hands shake and his knees ready to give out. His dad stepped behind him. As Zack's knees gave way, his dad grabbed him under the arms. The two of them made it, step by step, to the couches in the waiting area. He fell onto the nearest couch.

Robert knelt in front of his son. "Talk to me, Zack."

Zack could feel his heart hammering in his chest. "They beat him up, Dad. They had him on the ground, and they kicked him and all this other stuff. He wanted them to stop." He choked for only a moment and then took a deep breath. "He couldn't tell them." Zack curled his hands into tight balls; he knew Rustin was in incredible pain. He could feel it in his temples and throughout his entire body.

"I know you want to see your brother, and you will. Eyes up here, son." Zack looked up and watched as his dad took a deep breath. "Drinking will not solve your problems or help Rustin heal faster. Are you listening to me?" Zack nodded. "A lot of my clients have got into trouble because when they were under the influence, they did something stupid that they normally wouldn't have. And I am not about to lose one of my boys like I lost your mom." Robert took his son's head in both hands, ruffled his hair, and kissed him on the top of the head. The man stood up and pulled Zack to his feet. "Let's go see Rustin."

The elevator they took to the third floor opened in the middle of a short hallway. They were greeted by the words 'Pediatric Ward' which were colorfully displayed opposite the elevator. The words were surrounded by a bright sun and children, one in a wheelchair, one on crutches, and another child was bald and holding onto an IV pole. All of them had smiles on their faces. Passed the short hallway was the ward itself. The ward was built in a circle with the nurse's station in the middle. A gurney and several wheelchairs were scattered throughout the floor. The walls were a pale blue.

Zack watched as Robert walked up to the nurse's station. It was hard to be this close to his twin brother and not be physically able to touch him. It had been three very long, hard days. "Zack." His dad beckoned him forward.

He walked by several rooms, where doors were left wide open. The rooms were small, barely bigger than his dad's walk-in closet at home. Children laid on hospital beds with blue blankets covering them, watching tv or listening to headphones. There was also a little girl, maybe three, in a crib that looked more like a cage. She was standing, holding on to the rails, crying.

"Zack, come on. This way." Zack followed his father down another short hallway and passed a door adorned with the initials 'ICU'.

It was at this exact moment that Zack's senses went into overdrive. The smell alone, concentrated antiseptic, almost made him vomit; he could taste the bile rising in his throat. With great effort, he forced it back down. The otherwise quiet room was assaulted repeatedly with the monotonous pings of several monitors. Zack approached his brother's bed. With his hands clasped behind his back, he spent several minutes just watching the rise and fall of Rustin's chest. *I'm sorry, Rusi. I didn't mean for you to get hurt.* "There's no one to play basketball with. Dad!" The pain went straight to Rustin's head. Zack's knees buckled. He grabbed on to the bedrail to keep himself partially vertical, and not slamming his head on the ground. Zack could only watch from a crouched position as Rustin's back arched and his head tossed from one side to the other. Unsettling noises came from his brother's mouth.

Edging his way to the end of the bed, Zack watched as a doctor and nurse hurried to his brother's bedside. Something was injected into an IV port. A blood pressure cuff was wrapped -around his upper arm. Rustin's body gradually sunk back into the bed sheets. As the doctor brought a hand to his forehead, Rustin opened his eyes. "Hey, kiddo. Are you warm?" Dr. Todd rolled the boy toward him and nodded at the nurse who left and returned with a thermometer. Rustin seemed to shrink more into the sheets as the blanket was removed and his temp taken.

"Too high," Zack heard the doctor mutter moments later. "His breathing is so shallow right now."

"Cold," Rustin's voice was nothing but a whisper. His entire body trembled, his teeth chattering. "Wanna-wanna go home. P-p - please."

Todd pulled Rustin's hands down by his sides. "Robert, I need you to hold Rustin's hands." The nurse left and returned with a machine on wheels. "Rustin, you're not breathing well. I'm going to put a breathing tube in." They all saw Rustin try to pull loose from Robert, his body movements lethargic. "Hey, kiddo. It's okay." The doctor took a neck brace from the nurse and quickly immobilized his head. "I'm going to put this in and then we'll get you a blanket. Hold him tight, Robert."

"I got him."

"All right, kiddo. Look up here, look in my eyes." The heart monitor started beeping like crazy. "I know you're scared." Todd pulled on a pair of gloves on and within seconds was guiding a thin tube down his throat. "Swallow for me. Swallow. There you go. Good job, Rustin." Dr. Todd put a piece of tape at the boy's chin, securing the tube in place.

Zack had watched all of this, shaking at the end of the bed. He again felt overwhelmed with guilt because again he hadn't protected Rustin from terror. But he also knew that if he didn't speak up now, it would be worse for his brother. The shaking stopped. "Don't let go of his hands, Dad." he said from the end of the bed.

Robert turned. Still holding Rustin's hands, he looked at Zack who suddenly had tears running down his face. "Zack?"

"He's gonna pull it out," Zack choked.

Dr. Todd looked at Robert, who nodded. The doctor left and returned with two thick leather straps; he handed one to the nurse.

With slow, gentle hands, the doctor and nurse rolled Rustin onto his stomach, adjusting the oxygen tubing as they did. The arm that would be close to his face otherwise was brought down to his side. His other arm was situated over his head. Each hand was then pulled through a restraint and pulled tight around his wrist. The other end of the restraint was fastened to a bed rail. Huge tears coursed down Rustin's cheek, the heart monitor, with its steady *Ping!* beeped a lot faster.

"He's scared, Dad," Zack's tears were gone. He took a deep breath as he realized the best way to help Rustin, would be to translate. "He thinks they're going to hurt him again. Now. Like before."

As the nurse left the room, Dr. Todd pulled a heated blanket over Rustin's body. "I will not hurt you. Never." The nurse came back with another syringe and handed it to the doctor. "Okay, kiddo. This is the last shot for a while." As the nurse adjusted the blanket, Dr. Todd tested the needle; liquid spurted from the top.

"What are you giving him?" Robert asked.

"This is a mild sedative." The doctor brushed the boy's hip with alcohol, and with no warning, stuck the needle deep into muscle. As the drug was slowly injected, he started counting backwards from ten. At five, he pulled out the needle. At one, Rustin's muscles went limp and his eyes rolled. "Hang in there, kiddo." Todd pulled the blanket back into place.

Zack felt Rustin fight the drug, try to grab onto Zack's thoughts as if they were a lifeline. "Is he gonna be okay?"

"He's going to hurt for a while," Todd answered. "But he's going to be all right."

Reaching over, Zack pressed his fingertips to Rustin's. A moment passed, maybe two. Zack felt his twin let go; Rustin's eyes rolled behind his head. The monitor slowly regained its steady rhythm.

"We'll change his body position every two hours. But he'll spend most of today sleeping," Todd told Robert. "Zack." The boy looked up at the doctor surprised. "You are the best brother I have ever met." Todd gave a nod to Robert and left the area.

"You hungry?" Robert asked, as he led the way out of ICU and back to the elevator.

"Starving."

"Let's grab something at Scrappy's."

— · —

CHAPTER 22

A FATHER'S LOVE

What kind of father was he really, Robert thought as they got in the car. The first time he had seen Rustin suffer through a panic attack, he had wanted nothing more than to reassure him, to make him feel safe. But Robert could do nothing to help his son, the more he tried, the more Rustin pulled away, in fear. *And what just happened probably made it worse.* He pulled away from the nurses, the doctor, even Robert. The only comfort he accepted was from Zack and that teddy bear. Even though it was ridiculous, Robert envied that bear. The only good thing was that when Rustin's blood results came back, they came back negative for any sexually transmitted diseases. Robert started the engine and pulled out of the parking lot.

"How come you never talk about Mom? How come all her pictures are gone?" Zack was staring out the window. "I found one once. Did she always rock me in the living room?"

"Yeah, she did." He remembered the picture. It had been on his dresser for years and then disappeared. He assumed it had accidentally gotten swept up in some junk mail or that one of the boys had found it, his guess was Jensen, maybe Rustin, but never Zack. Lauren was sitting in a rocker surrounded by her younger children. They were playing with those blasted wooden blocks that never seemed to make it back into the toy box. A three-year-old Jensen had been stacking the blocks by color. Rustin was trying to get to his feet, his little butt sticking up in the air. All of this was in the background. The picture focused on Zack who was sitting on his mommy's lap. His finger pointed to something in the book they were looking at together. She had one hand around his stomach, and with her other hand had run her fingers through his hair. "She loved you very much." Robert took a moment at the stop light to glance at his son. Zack was sitting stiffly beside him, his hands in his lap. *A couple of weeks ago, he was running around and getting restriction because he was tardy all the time.* The child next to him was so unlike the child he had raised.

Minutes later he pulled into the parking lot where Scrappy's was located. Getting out of the car and entering the restaurant. Robert gripped Zack's shoulder. "After this, I have to go to the station. I'll drop you off at home. Craig will be there." He paused, "Stay home. I promise we'll visit your brother this evening. Got it?" He watched Zack nod.

"Hey, Dad." Robert turned around. He watched as Jensen grabbed a couple menus. He led them to a table in the back of the restaurant. "I'll tell Joel you're here. What do you want to drink?"

"Coffee please, decaf." Robert answered. "And get Zack a glass of milk." As he looked around the restaurant, he was amazed by the décor his older son had helped create. When he had first started coming here, it had been a place for small gatherings; but since the change last fall, it had been talked about as the city's most inviting diner.

As he was about to engage in conversation with Zack, an older man came up and ruffled Zack's hair. "Hey, kid, Robert. I haven't seen you in a while. Jensen told me about Rustin, I'm sorry. How's he doing?"

Robert looked at Zack. "Go tell Danielle what we're having. Anything you want." He saw Zack's eyes grow big, his lips slightly upturned. "Help Jensen bring it out." Joel sat across from him. He then spent five minutes talking about Rustin and thanking Joel for letting Jensen have the time off. "With Zack so unstable I can't afford to send either one of them back to school, even after the holiday. He deserves a little break during the day."

Joel nodded. "Of course. Take all the time you need." The man got to his feet. "I'll go see what's taking the kid."

Zack, with Jensen carrying a tray behind him, sat down across from his father with a tray of his own. The tray comprised one of Danielle's rodeo burgers, a side of onion rings, and a vanilla milkshake. Off to the side of his plate, were tiny serving bowls filled with ranch dressing.

Setting a tray in front of Robert, Jensen looked at Zack. "Oatmeal to go, right?"

"Yep," Zack grinned as he dipped his onion ring into the dressing. He let it drip twice and then popped it in his mouth.

Robert laughed as Zack spit the ring into a napkin. "Too hot, huh? Slow down, we got time."

Zack blew on the onion ring and pulled the onion out. He blew on the remaining part, dipped it one more time and then ate it. He then turned his attention to the colossal burger.

Meanwhile, Robert began cutting his potato methodically, first vertically and then horizontally. As he applied sour cream and butter to the vegetable, he wondered how to bring up the subject. Without so much as a clue where to begin, he set fork and knife down. He looked at Zack who had barbeque sauce on his fingers. "You've been wanting to talk about your mom a lot lately. What do you want to know?" he asked. Robert cut into his steak and then looked up at his son.

Zack put his burger back on the plate and licked his fingers. Then he looked into his father's eyes. "What was she like?"

Robert set his fork and knife down again. He gave a small smile.

"You boys remind me a lot about her. Atlas's curls, Jensen's blue eyes and dimples. But you and Rustin, your mom was a great photographer, just like Rus."

"What about me?" Zack's voice was soft. His eyes shifted downward to stare vacantly at the burger.

"I think you remind me of her the most. Lauren was always involved in something. If she wasn't taking pictures, she was swimming or taking classes at the junior college. But she always made sure, you guys came first. You meant the world to her."

Robert flashed back to the day when his wife went in for her third ultrasound. *No. go to work, she had insisted. It's just a routine check-up.* An hour after the appointment, she had come to his office and laid a film on his desk. *What's this?* he had asked. Robert had brought the film up into the light. He hadn't been exactly sure what he was supposed to be looking for. However, he did notice that there weren't two arms and legs, but four of each. *Four of each* he had muttered out loud. He had looked up at his expectant wife, who was grinning from ear to ear. *Yes, Baby. We're having twins. Boys.*

Robert took a bite of his steak and a moment later he laughed. "After Jensen was born I said, 'This is it, right?' She said, 'Nope. We're not even halfway through.' She had wanted a whole house full of kids. And I would have given them to her. Your mom was the most beautiful, most caring, most amazing woman I have ever met. No one could ever replace her. Eat up, son."

He watched Zack finish the onion rings and the burger. He had laughed when the boy had even started on his oatmeal while he paid the bill. "You ready to go home?"

"Why am I so tired?" Zack got to his feet and Robert followed him outside.

"It's been a couple of stressful days." The ride home was silent. As they entered the house, both of them hung their jackets on the rack by the door. Craig was waiting in the living room, a book in hand. "Go upstairs and lay down. I'll be up in a couple minutes."

Craig closed his book and set it down beside him. "Your parents called. Said they got back okay." Robert nodded. "How'd it go?"

"Craig, I really appreciate you being..."

"Stop. I called the school district and told them I'm going on sabbatical. You're stuck with me until this is over."

Robert shook his head. "No, I can't."

"You don't have a choice. Lauren's children need you." Craig paused. "Besides, who's going to do the laundry when you're out gallivanting around." He shook his head and then looked toward the staircase. "Go. My nephew needs you."

Robert went to his room and changed out of his suit and into a pair of jeans he hardly wore. He knew he would be at the hospital late, if not all night, and he wanted to be comfortable. After stepping into a pair of sneakers, something else he rarely wore, he crossed the hallway and entered Zack's room.

He was already asleep on Rustin's bed, laying on top of the comforter. Robert adjusted his legs just enough for him to pull off the boy's shoes. The boy moaned softly. Robert brushed back his bangs. "Shh. Get some sleep, honey."

Treading downstairs, Robert went into his office and put his head in his hands. When his wife had died, he had to emotionally support four boys who had just lost their mother. This time, he had to support only two. But their needs were so different. It also didn't help that one of them was confined to a hospital. At that moment, he had to decide who needed one-on-one attention at that very moment.

He found Jensen in the kitchen with an open math book, a sandwich in hand.

CHAPTER 23

ACCUSATIONS

J ensen had his head buried in one book or another for the past hour. He had saved Trig, his best subject, for last. He got up to get a drink and noticed his father entering the room. "Hey, Dad." He took a carton of milk from the refrigerator and poured himself half a glass. "Keisha called when you were out. Said something about 'misattribution of arousal'," Jensen shook his head, still confused by the term. "And some guy named Adam Lechner. How's Zack?"

Dang, he's growing up. "I need to stay home with him tonight." Jensen saw his father linger. "I was wondering if you could spend a couple hours at the hospital with Rustin."

Jensen put both the carton and the half-filled glass in the refrigerator. "Sure, Dad." He was pulling on his coat in the living room, when he was asked about his homework. He laughed. "It's only trig. I'll finish it in the morning." The truth of the matter was, Jensen's brain was fried. The assignment wasn't due until after break, anyway. Jensen was sure *Just the Five of Us* was due for a practice in front of the class once classes started again. But getting together for practices had been put on hold when Rustin went missing. The seventeen-year-old was concerned about his brother and happy for a chance to clear his head.

"Jensen," Jensen looked up at his dad. "They had to intubate him. Just be aware."

Getting off the elevator on the third floor, his guitar in hand, Jensen went to the nurse's station to sign in.

"Dammit!"

Jensen turned around and found a boy his age on crutches, a paperback book at his feet. "Hey, I got it." Jensen grabbed the book with his free hand. "Where you headed?"

"Ahhh, this way. Thanks."

Jensen followed the patient back to his room and watched as the boy backed up to a chair by the door and sat down. "Hey, man. Thanks again." Jensen handed him the book and took the crutches, leaning them up against the wall beside him. "You stuck here?"

Shaking his head, Jensen said, "No. my brother's here. I gotta go. Maybe I'll stop by again. See ya."

The boy's eyes lit up. "Sure."

He entered the ICU and froze. Someone in a suit and tie was by his brother's bed and had him exposed, the blanket lying on the floor on the opposite side of the bed. The man had a camera in his hands and was taking picture after picture. "It's so much easier when they don't squirm," the man muttered. He adjusted his lens and started shooting again. "Now, that'll make a nice shot."

"What are you doing? Get away from my brother." The intruder turned just in time to get a glimpse of Jensen before he was tackled to the floor. The camera crashed to the ground. Jensen kicked it with his left foot and was about to punch him when someone grabbed his arm.

"Jensen, stop." It was Rustin's day nurse, Marc. "I called security. I'll call your dad in a couple minutes." They both watched as two men came in and grabbed the stranger by the arms. "Take that camera," Marc told them, pointing toward the bed. "It's what he came for."

The room cleared out. Marc patted Jensen on the shoulder. "Let's take care of your brother." Marc checked the intubation and then Rustin's vital signs. Rustin was still restrained; each time they had removed the leather straps and the sedative wore off, the boy had gone to grab the tubing in his mouth. He covered Rustin with a new blanket. "Jensen, how're you doing?"

Jensen had just seen his brother's body for the first time in years. There were areas that were smudged with color along his shoulders and the back of his neck. Even lower, he saw the back of Rustin's thighs black and blue and swollen. "What happened?" Jensen whispered.

The nurse explained that the methods of assaulting women were the same as with men. The victim must be immobilized for the criminal to get what he, or she, wants. "Hey, Rustin." The boy's eyes were barely open, but he was conscious. "Your brother is here."

"Hi, Rus." Jensen stepped to the head of the bed. "Can I touch him?"

Marc nodded, "Just be careful. His fever's two degrees higher. I need to get a hold of Dr. Todd."

The nurse left. Jensen grabbed Rustin's hand and told him about an art show that was coming up at the local gallery. "They have an exhibit for amateurs. You should put together a collage of your photographs. The ones you took when you went to Shasta." Jensen rubbed the top of Rustin's hand. He grew nervous when Marc and Dr. Todd didn't return as fast as he thought they would. He laid Rustin's hand down and grabbed his guitar from the end of the bed. He played certain patterns repeatedly, then changed them from major to minor, or played the whole pattern backwards. As he played, Rustin's hands would flinch at his sides, his head seemed to dig into the pillow. Marc and Todd arrived then, along with a stranger.

Jensen stood up and set the guitar aside. "I didn't know what to do.

Who was that?"

"You did fine, Jensen." Marc was standing at the end of the bed, as was the stranger, a big black guy with a calm demeanor. "This is Peter. He's here to guard your brother, make sure this doesn't happen again."

Dr. Todd approached the bed and rechecked Rustin's vital signs. "There's an infection somewhere."

"Septic?" Marc asked.

"What's that?" Jensen looked from Marc to Dr. Todd.

"An infection in his blood," Marc answered. "Doctor, does that look a little red to you?"

Dr. Todd quickly pulled on a pair of gloves and gently ran his finger against the exposed area. The body flinched. "I want another lab done. And put in a rectal cath. If he does test positive for septic, get a surgery scheduled." The doctor paused.

"Surgery?"

"He may need a blood transfusion via dialysis."

Rustin's cheeks were bright pink, his eyes red from the drugs. The nurse was soon painting his behind with iodine and then inserting a lubricated catheter; Rustin's muscles tensed, his heart rate went up. "Try to relax, Rustin. I'm almost done."

Peter, the guard, stepped beyond the curtain, making sure the boy's privacy was in place. He allowed someone from the lab to enter with her cart.

"I heard we need to draw some more blood." As the woman was pulling on gloves and arranging her tools, Marc removed the restraints and rolled Rustin on to his back. The boy appeared to be asleep as his left arm was straightened, a tourniquet tied on his upper arm. She brushed a cotton ball along his inner elbow until the area shined and then inserted a needle into a clear vein.

Rustin's eyes opened, his right hand came up suddenly and clawed at his face. Todd grabbed his wrist and brought it down. "Relax, kiddo. She's almost done." Todd restrained the arm with the strap again and then looked up at Jensen. "I need you to go into the hallway and call your dad. Tell him he needs to get here ASAP."

CHAPTER 24

SWALLOW

After Jensen had left for the hospital, Robert called Adam Lechner, the man his son had said to get a hold of. Within a few minutes, he had found out that Lechner had a doctorate in psychology, his focus pertained to abused males. When the man suggested that the two of them meet in person, Robert had agreed; he would also bring his eldest son with him. The appointment was scheduled for the following Tuesday, an hour after Atlas would have finished the Bar Exam.

Robert went upstairs to check on Zack, who had been sleeping for over an hour now. He found the bed empty. He ran down the stairs. "Zack, where are you?" He found Craig trying to toast a piece of bread in the toaster, that refused to stay down. "Hold it down for a couple seconds. Have you seen Zack?"

The two men first checked the neighborhood; the hope was he hadn't gone far. When that idea fell through, they took separate cars, promising to check in with each other in half an hour. Forty-five minutes later, Robert was searching the high school grounds again when his cell phone rang. Craig hadn't found Zack, he'd keep looking. But the hospital was trying to get a hold of him. There was an emergency.

The drive took a good fifteen minutes, too long for Robert. He bypassed the nurse's station and went straight to the ICU. He approached Jensen and handed him a twenty. "Go get yourself something to eat. Then call your uncle. Zack's missing." He saw his son leave. He grabbed his arm. Jensen looked quizzically at him. "Be safe. Drive slowly. I don't need two of you in the hospital."

"I know, Dad."

Robert watched Jensen leave and then approached the opposite side of the hospital bed. The first thing he saw was a bit of dried blood on Rustin's face. Something caught his eye and Robert looked down. "Another catheter?

"Yes. I want him to relax, and he can't do that if he's having spasms. Also, we're testing his blood to see if he's septic. I don't want to take any chances. The pressure in his brain is too much. I need your consent."

"Todd." Marc was diving for the IV lines that had somehow wound themselves around Rustin's neck. Todd reacted in an instant and cradled the boy's head as Marc pulled the lines away.

Robert never saw Rustin's eyes roll to the back of his head. He did see Rustin's muscles go rigid; his limbs made constant jerking motions. "What's going on?"

Todd looked at Marc, "Twelve and a half grams of Mannitol." Marc left at a run. "Rustin's scared us with a seizure, huh, kiddo." The doctor cradled the boy's head as it shifted toward the bed rails. "One thousand one, one thousand two, one thou-"The seizure stopped. "We have to bring down that swelling." With gentle hands, Todd laid Rustin's head on the pillow. He looked at Marc who had just returned and nodded. Marc stabbed the needle into the boy's thigh. Rustin cried out, his entire body flinched; Todd grabbed his hands, as the needle was removed, Rustin's eyes opened halfway. "Robert." The man up. "I need you to consent for surgery. The forms on the clipboard.

Marc, let's get him started on one hundred and fifty milligrams of Depakote. Tell Dr. Salicco what's going on. Try to get him in within the next hour."

Robert grabbed the clipboard, skimmed the page, and signed. Everything was going too fast. He handed the clipboard to Marc and then walked back to his son's bedside. He watched Rustin's eyes drift. The strength he had always wished for his son was gone, literally non-existent. And there was nothing he could do to help him, comfort him even. Rustin was fighting for his own life.

Marc returned with a cart that held a clear bag of liquid. He disconnected the line from the old bag and replaced it with the new one. The doctor removed the old IV. "That seizure made you kind of sleepy, huh?"

"Depakote?" Robert asked.

"It'll prevent him from suffering another seizure." Todd held his hand steady as Marc cleaned a vein in his hand. The needle slid beneath his skin and the nurse taped it in place. "There you go, kiddo. Restrain him for now, Marc. And trim his fingernails."

Dr. Todd pulled Robert just beyond the curtain. "The swelling needs to come down, or he will not make it. It's putting too much pressure on his brain." He paused. "I'm going to call Dr. Salicco and get surgery scheduled."

As the doctor left, Robert went back behind the curtain. Marc was seated on a stool, clipping the nails on his right hand, speaking to him in a quiet reassuring way. "The waterfalls at Yosemite Park were beautiful. And the hike you take through the Crest of Vernal Falls...There are no words to describe it." Marc finished with his right hand and restrained it before switching to the other side of the bed to trim the left hand.

Robert came forward and squeezed his son's hand lightly. "Rustin went to the Shasta Mountains. You should see some shots he took. He's a photographer, you know."

"You'll have to show me one of your portfolios."

Someone pulled the curtain back and a stretcher was rolled next to the bed. When Rustin caught sight of her, tears fell. "Honey, don't cry."

"They need to give the Chlorpromazine now," Marc said. "I don't want him pulling on anything."

"He's a fighter, huh? That's good." She brought a syringe up and Rustin started tossing his head. "Honey, calm down. I will not prick you." She forced a clear solution into an IV port.

Rustin's head, while still tossing from side to side, was slowing down. Marc walked up with a tissue and gently wiped the tears from Rustin's face. A moment passed. The boy's eyes went glassy. "He's ready."

Marc pulled the leather straps loose and grabbed the top corners of the bed sheet, the woman grabbed the corners at the bottom. Together, they moved him on to the stretcher. Before Robert was ready, they were pushing the gurney out into the hallway. Dr. Todd walked with them.

They stopped in front of two large doors labeled 'OR'. The orderlies stepped back and gave Robert a moment. Taking a deep breath, he looked down at his son. He went to speak and his throat was caught. He searched for words but couldn't find any. Taking another breath, he cleared his throat. "I love you, Rusi. Your head's going to feel so much better. Teddy and I will be there when you wake up." Robert bent down and kissed his son's forehead. Then he stepped back.

Despite his ability to remain in control in front of his son, when Rustin disappeared behind the unfamiliar white doors, Robert lost it. "I don't know if I can do this. Can I make them take him out?" Robert paced the floor. "What if he doesn't make it? What if I lose him?"

"Yes, of course you may have him brought back to his room." Dr. Todd laid a hand on his arm and looked him in the eye. He said, "If he doesn't have this operation, if we don't get his fever and the swelling in his brain down, he will die. I cannot promise that he will make it through this. But he will not survive if he doesn't." A tall gruff looking man dressed in scrubs strutted into the operating room. "That's Dr. Salicco. He's the best pediatric neurosurgeon in California. Your son's in good hands."

—·—

CHAPTER 25

THE THREAT

Z ack had awoken with the desperate need for all the guilt and fear being over. Rustin had been in tremendous pain. Still was. And it was all Zack's fault. It was Zack's fault that nothing had been done to stop the attack from happening. He treaded down the stairs with light foot falls, making his way out the front door without Craig noticing. Jogging down the front steps and on to the street, Zack made his way down Powell, toward Baker Beach and the Aquatic Park.

He stepped across the sandy floor and onto the weathered dock. Sitting on the dock with his legs hanging off the edge, Zack looked out at the ocean. The stars could still be seen; the fog had yet to roll in. The smell of salt and fish filled his nostrils. Again and again, he could see those bastards dragging Rustin onto the cliff and beating the crap out of him. He remembered the look on Meyers's face when he pulled that picture from Rustin's wallet, when he discovered that their crime might not be hidden. That there was another set of eyes, a set of eyes that knew everything. Zack came to Jefferson Beach to be with his brother one more time. Either Meyers would find him here and kill him, or he would jump in the ocean at high tide. It didn't matter which.

He knew what he needed; he needed a way out; he needed to end all of it. Not just the guilt and fear, but the responsibility. *Everyone thinks it's cool to have a twin. How'd they like to be responsible for someone else's life? Someone's death?* Zack had thought about using a knife in order to make the pain go away, there were plenty of them in the kitchen, but he didn't want to leave all that blood and guilt all over the floor. He was also sure his uncle would find him before the task was complete. What he needed was a gun. Something fast, something sure. Tilt the head back, aim it under the chin, and pull the trigger. Guilt gone.

The next couple of hours were spent in that exact spot, his feet swinging back and forth off the edge of the dock. Thoughts crowded his mind, everything from his relationship with Rustin, to basketball and the season's playoffs, to other mundane topics. It was when he couldn't avoid the inevitable thoughts of guilt, that he seriously thought about just leaning forward and letting the surf take him.

As he stood up to take the final step, Zack felt a strong grip on his shoulder. When he turned, he was face to face with Bennett. "I'm not going home." He tried to pull loose but couldn't. The police officer pulled him away from the edge of the dock. "What are you doing?" Zack almost passed out when Bennett brought a pair of handcuffs into view and secured them to his left wrist with ease. His face went pale. He hyperventilated as both hands were brought behind his back and restrained, "They're gonna kill both of us."

Bennett took a moment and turned Zack to face him. "Relax, Zack. I don't know what's going through that head of yours right now. But jumping into the water will not solve your problems. Come on, now." Taking a hold of Zack's arm, the police officer walked him off the dock and across the deserted beach to a parked police car. Bennett protected the boy's head as he eased him into the backseat then knelt for a minute. "Try to calm down. A suicidal threat gets you admitted to a psych ward. That's where I'm taking you." Bennett watched him for another moment and then stood up, closing the door.

As the car moved through the city, he tried to get himself freed from the cuffs. He knew he was being punished; he would be paying for this crime for the rest of his life. He felt powerless. He wanted to be the one to issue the punishment. He wanted to be sure he got what he deserved. But more than that, he just wanted it to be over.

The car stopped near a back entrance of Saint Francis Memorial Hospital. "Please. Just take me back. They don't have to know." Two men dressed in white jumpsuits, one of them black the other white, both burly, came out of the hospital and towards the car. "I just want to die!" he screamed. "Can't anyone understand that?" The back door opened. Zack was pulled out, grabbed by the arms. The attendants yanked harder as Zack tried to escape, his feet sliding along the cement. They pulled him past a security gate that opened automatically and then locked once they had gone through. "Let me go."

The next thing he knew, he was being slammed against a wall, his cheek rubbed against the abrasive concrete. A hand at the back of his neck and a knee put pressure at the base of his spine to immobilize him. "You need to calm down. I can go a lot easier on you if you quit fighting me." Zack continued his struggle to escape. He kicked and pulled any which way he could. "He's not cooperating. Think he's high on something?"

"Let's hope not, we've got enough addicts in this city. We don't need more." A leg tripped him, deliberately. Zack lost his footing and crashed to the floor. The same hands restrained him at the neck and waist, but this time it felt like they were about to separate his shoulders from the rest of his body.

Zack lay panting, his body tingling with nerves. His muscles tight-ened as his pants were yanked down off his hips. The surrounding air was frigid. "You can't do this." He gasped. "You can't-stop." His eyes grew wide with terror. *You deserve it, you bastard. Take it like a man.* He never saw the red-haired woman come up behind him with a syringe in hand. Cold fingers pressed hard against bare skin and before he was ready, a sharp object was jabbed into his buttocks. A high-pitched noise came from Zack as the injection was made. Within moments, he couldn't lift a muscle to save himself.

The same two attendants approached him once the drug kicked in. "I'll grab his legs," one of them said.

Lifted from the cold hard linoleum, Zack's eyes feverishly scanned the room. There was no one else. The woman with the red hair had left through a door, a door that had been left ajar. She walked up to Robert and shook his hand. In a loud voice, she said, "My name is Carol Hastings. I'm the head nurse on this ward." She stopped speaking for a moment. When she spoke again, she said, "No, I don't think visitation is in his best interest right now. George and Malakai have taken the patient into an examination room where they are handling the admittance. We need to get a couple signatures from you and then it's best if you leave." Robert walked up to a counter with his head in his hands. A moment later, he picked up a pen, signed something and then disappeared.

Dad, please. Please don't go. Get me out of here! George and Malakai had moved Zack onto a gurney with railings, one raised the other not raised. One of them held him upright while the other pulled his shirt off over his head, because Zack was nothing but a rag doll. They laid him down flat without a pillow and brought the other railing up into place. His wrists were then secured to the rails. Zack could do nothing as they removed first his shoes, and then his pants and underwear. Stripped naked, thick straps were pulled tight across his legs, hips, chest, and right arm. His left arm was still fastened with a leather cuff. He watched as his clothes were put in a brown paper bag with his name on it, an ID number scrawled underneath. A plastic bracelet was clipped around his wrist.

Zack's eyes shifted around the room. George left with his clothes and Malakai was taking notes on a clipboard. Nobody was paying him any attention. A clock somewhere in the room was ticking. The smell of coffee and antiseptic. An overwhelming sense of despair. A set of shoes clicked their way to his bedside along with the sound of squeaky wheels. A Filipino man popped up over his head.

The man glanced at his bracelet and scanned it. The tray he had with him had several empty vials, vials with his name on them. Zack could do nothing but watch as the stranger in a lab coat prepped a needle and then tied a rubber tourniquet around his upper arm. A cotton ball was then saturated with cleaning alcohol. He brushed the area roughly with the cotton ball, one vial tucked between his middle finger and index finger. Zack moaned as the needle was slid into a vein. One vial was filled, then another. Three vials later, the needle was removed, a clean cotton ball taped into place.

The tech was about to cover him with a sheet when the woman named Hastings entered the area with a group of young adults dressed in scrubs. They each carried a clipboard and were copying down Hastings every word. "Thank you, Mohinder. We won't be needing the sheet."

The students circled around the bed where Zack was laying. "Just the normal procedure here," she said in a loud and clear voice. "The lab just collected blood samples, they'll test it for drug use and nutritional needs. All patients are started on medication immediately upon arrival, and we keep a constant check on their vital signs while they are here. Suicidal patients like this one go through a cavity search before being started on their medication. The hospital now requires all incoming psychiatric patients in ten-point restraints. We had an incident last year that involved an intern breaking her ankle."

Zack felt the interns staring at him. They judged not only the woman's performance, but they judged his as well. *I don't take medication.* "I wanna see Rustin," he said, barely audible. *What is she doing? Make her go away.*

One student looked up from his clipboard. "Are they permitted to see family, Ms. Hastings?"

"Not in the first week. And then only if they earn enough points. The award system we have here involves the opinions of the medical staff and the psychiatrists who work with the patients."

Zack watched as Malakai came back into the room, pushing an IV pole and metal cart. "Carol, they found painkillers with his belongings."

Painkillers? What painkillers?

Ms. Hastings nodded. "Make sure that it's noted. This is Malakai, he's been with the hospital for over a year now."

"What's the IV for?" a voice at the foot of the bed asked.

"The IV is for nutritional purposes. He'll stay on it until we are confident the patient will eat on his own." The IV pole was rolled up to the bed. Hastings grabbed Zack's hand and turned it over. "He's got a good vein right here, Malakai." As Hastings went back to answering questions, Malakai swabbed the inside of Zack's wrist with alcohol. Zack screamed as the needle was forced deep into a vein and taped down. "You need to be able to ignore their discomfort. What we do here is done in their best interest." She turned to the orderly, "Please get Zack situated, Malakai."

Situated? What's she talking about? Gotta get the needle? His right arm was released. Zack tried to reach over, tried to get the damn thing out. He moved about an inch before his arm was grabbed and he was pulled over on to his side. Both wrists were now secured to the same bed rail. Zack's heart was racing as his right leg was restrained to the same railing. Zack couldn't move if he wanted to.

On the other side of the room, he could hear water running from a nearby faucet and latex snapping against wet skin. "The cavity search is new to the ward. We found it necessary when patients smuggled in various drugs and paraphernalia." Measured footsteps walked behind him. "Yes, Mr. McCormick?"

"Two questions, actually. One, why would patients bring drugs in? And second, what about the patient here? Is he aware of what is going on?"

"Money, self-medication. It's not that hard to figure out why they would bring in outside drugs. As for Zack Carson here, his mental state is really no concern of yours. Make sure he's stabilized, Malakai."

The male orderly stepped in front of him. He took a firm grasp of Zack's thigh and shoulder as the group of students debated anyway. The head nurse waited a mere two seconds before she interrupted them. "We have a patient to deal with here," she said, raising her voice. Zack could feel everyone's eyes back on him. He could see nothing but Malakai's black belt.

No. This isn't happening. Zack drew back his hand slightly, the movement causing the bedrail to rattle. He was rewarded with a thump on the back of his leg. Tears fell; his breath came out in harsh gasps. He laid on his side, his cheeks burning with humiliation, as his legs were adjusted and the cavity search began. The gasping increased to where his entire body tingled. *Please stop. I didn't mean to.* Zack groaned again as his bowels were cleaned out. Sweat poured from his body in exaggerated amounts. Malakai tightened his grip on Zack's leg and moved his other hand to pin his head in place. To escape was impossible, so he laid there trying not to fall apart, trying to keep his dignity. But they had already taken that. All he could do was wait for the procedure to be over. He heard latex snapping again and then the sound of a water faucet.

Malakai adjusted the restraints and rolled Zack onto his back. In a soft voice, the orderly said, "The worst of it's over."

Hastings was back, pulling on a clean pair of gloves. "Restrain his head." She flicked Zack on the leg again as the orderly placed his hands on both sides of Zack's face. "Quit crying." With a flashlight in hand, she tilted his head back and checked both nostrils. Once she was satisfied, she turned his headfirst to the left and then to the right, looking into both ear canals. The head nurse turned to put the otoscope down and grabbed a cotton swab. She forced Zack's mouth open, her fingers digging into his cheeks. Then she brushed the swab along his gums and beneath his tongue. A second swab went further into his mouth, causing him to choke and gag.

The group of students had been watching in shock. "Does it hurt them?" a young woman asked.

"Of course not." Hastings laid the swab on the metal tray and removed the latex gloves which were thrown in a tan basin. Her voice raised, "Now that you've all seen how we intake a suicidal patient, if there's no other questions. We'll observe another patient. This next one exhibits the signs of schizophrenia." She led her students to the middle of the ward. She turned and looked at Malakai. "I want Zack Carson medicated promptly. Ten milligrams of Xanax. Nothing else until we get the blood results back." The woman left, her entourage following her like a bunch of monkeys on parade.

Two minutes slowly passed. Malakai spent that time with his back turned toward Zack. He then left the area, going in the same direction Hastings had. When he returned, another man in scrubs was with him. "Yeah, let me get Zack here ready for bed. Then I'll meet you at the cafeteria."

"Let me give you a hand." The stranger went to the other side of the room and opened the upper cupboard near the sink. He pulled out a washcloth, a towel, and a hospital gown. Then he pulled a curtain around the bed where Zack laid.

Meanwhile, Malakai filled a basin with water and brought it to the side of the bed. "Alright, Zack. Try to calm down." He took the washcloth from his coworker and soaked it in the basin before wringing it out. The sponge bath that followed was humiliating and invasive, but never cruel. His heavy arms were raised from the bed sheet and slid through the short sleeves of a hospital gown. A hospital gown that made an attempt, real or not, to assure him a bit of dignity.

Zack watched everything, his heart still beating a mile a minute. The constant gasping was drying out his mouth. He saw the stranger pick up a little glass bottle with a black rubber top. He took a syringe in the other hand. "I heard Hastings, she said she planted some pills on a patient." He stuck the needle in the cap and slowly withdrew the prescribed dose.

"Yeah. She does it once or twice a week. Then she charges more for treatment. Watch the IV there." Malakai once more put Zack in ten-point restraints. He then brought his hand up and brushed Zack's cheek with his thumb. Zack flinched, still breathing hard; there was a pallor to his face. "It's time to relax, Zack. Time for bed." Malakai nodded at his coworker and continued to stroke his cheek.

No more needles. Too early for bed. Zack cried out as the drug was injected into his hip. Moments later, he was given a heated blanket and the bed moved. It wasn't long before his breathing slowed. His eyes grew heavy. He was asleep before the bed arrived at the observation area of the psych ward.

Somewhere in a dream, Zack's bladder felt like a water balloon about to burst. Time isn't measured by the ticking of a clock, but by a high pitched, sweet song from childhood. *"It's time to go potty in the big boy's potty seat. It's time to sit on our tushies if we want a real treat. Wait and watch the pee-pee come, wait and see, wait and see. Wait and see the pee-pee come, here it comes. I'm proud of me!* Nurse Hastings, Malakai, and the unknown coworker, all three of his brothers, and both his parents are standing around him, singing, as he stands in front of a tiny child's potty seat. They all watched and waited. And when he can't do as he's supposed to, there's a price to pay. There's always a price to pay.

Zack did not know how much time had passed, but he woke up groggy and not rested at all. He wanted to go back to sleep, into a real sleep where stupid little songs did not intrude his mind. But the head nurse was determined on getting his vital signs. His arm was adjusted, a blood pressure cuff secured around his bicep. Once his blood pressure was recorded, he was rolled onto his side, his temperature taken with a lubricated thermometer to his buttocks. Zack moaned in discomfort. He was rewarded with a thump to the back of his thigh. "Knock it off."

He could barely open his eyes as he was rolled onto his back. Hastings was standing over him, a syringe sticking up out of her bra. Going to a locked cabinet beside the bed, the head nurse used a key to open it. She retrieved a set of restraints and took them to the end of the bed. She turned and handed the key to her student. "Lock it." The young student stepped forward and complied. After the key was back in her hand, Hastings went to the end of the bed. With rough yet quick hands, she yanked Zack's frame to the end of the bed and used the ankle cuffs to secure both legs to opposite rails. Then she tore the blanket off of him, just managing not to throw it on the floor. "Why did they bother to put a gown on him?" she muttered. She pulled the gown from his body and threw it to the end of the bed. Zack again lay exposed. "Come here," she beckoned to the girl. "I want you to feel this."

The girl, with short curly hair pulled back by barrettes, stepped forward, her hands shaking. "Why can't he wear a gown?"

"He's a level zero. Clothes pose a suicidal threat. He's lucky I'll let him have a blanket." Hastings grabbed her by the hand and pulled her up to the bed. She laid the girl's hand on Zack's lower abdomen. "You cannot be shy, Katrina. This is what a full bladder feels like."

"Wow," Katrina sounded amazed. "Is he allowed to use the restroom?"

"Of course not," Hastings scolded as she slipped on another pair of latex gloves. "With uncontrollable patients like this one, we put in what is called an indwelling catheter. You've studied this in class?" The girl nodded. "Good. This is also our chance to finish the cavity search. Put a pair of gloves on and I'll walk you through it."

Zack, medicated and exhausted, had every desire in the world to make himself invisible. He did not know what an indwelling catheter was, and he was pretty sure he didn't want to find out. His eyes shifted to the ceiling. A moment later, with trembling hands, Katrina started cleaning the area with iodine. She took the catheter from Hastings.

His heart pounded, and at first, he thought it was because of the situation he was in. But then the world seemed to grow cold. Rustin's heart had stopped. Zack bawled. He could sense the urgent action around his brother, felt the currents of electricity they sent through his body. Zack's body jerked several times. And then he sensed a heartbeat. The air grew warm again.

The young woman backed away, intimidated. Afraid he really was crazy. Hastings sighed in frustration. "It's just the medication. Now watch, you'll have to do this with the next intake." With no hesitation at all, she grabbed hold of his penis and stuck the catheter in. Zack groaned, tossing his head from left to right and back again. Grabbing a syringe, she injected water into the port and then tugged on the tubing; the catheter didn't come out. "See, there's nothing to it. Once the instrument is in, you apply pressure to the abdomen to make sure the bladder is empty." Her gloved hand pressed hard on his stomach for several seconds and then let go. "Questions?" Zack saw the girl shake her head. "Let's go. Malakai." The tall black man came toward her, a questioning look on his face. "I want more liquids on him for the next forty-eight hours. Remember, he's still unstable. Leave him in ten-point restraints until further notice." Hastings paused. "And no gown. Not until he's out of isolation."

Zack felt a piece of rubber tied around his leg, the bag for the urine positioned between his legs. Straps were adjusted, and Malakai covered him with a thin sheet before he crossed the room to the nurse's station. When he returned, he had a pink plastic pitcher and a medium-sized cup that matched. Using a remote, the assistant brought the head of the bed up to a slight angle. Zack's eyes closed. "Zack." A hand gently slapped his cheek. "Come on, kid. Wake up." He heard liquid being poured into a cup. When he felt a straw against his lips, he drank, his dry mouth eager to be wet again. He finished the first cup and Malakai poured him a second. But when the straw hit his lips this time, he refused. "Come on, now. As soon as you drink what's required, I can let you go to sleep."

"Is he causing problems again?" Before Malakai could answer, Hastings was back, walking up to the other side of the bed. "Give me that." Hastings took the cup and flicked Zack on the arm. "Drink, now." Again, he was flicked. Too tired to fight anymore, Zack knew he was fighting a losing battle. He gave in and sucked on the straw. Quickly at first and then slower and slower until he had to stop; he was too full. Hastings flicked him yet again as he cried. "You will not sleep until this cup is empty. You will do as you're told, or I'll put in a second IV." When Zack finished what was in the cup, he felt like he was going to explode. "You will have the cleanest urine on this ward. Don't make me come back."

Malakai's smile looked forced, "Have a good night, Carol. See you tomorrow." The woman gave a curt nod and walked to the elevator. Moments later, she was gone. "All right, Zack. I know you're tired." Malakai laid the bed flat once more, removed the restraints and rolled him onto his stomach. He took a moment to adjust the restraints and when he turned back, Zack was curled in a ball.

Zack just wanted it all to end. He felt the assistant nurse pull his legs out straight and put the ankle straps back on. Gradually his body became one with the mattress as he was slowly put back in ten-point restraints. Straps soon ran across his lower legs, and his hips. Malakai came to the head of the bed and removed the pillow beneath Zack's head. "Arms up." He helped the boy straighten his arms out above his head. The restraints for his wrists fit like a glove, then were strapped to the bed railing. A final strap was secured across his chest.

Malakai gave Zack another dose of Xanax, a quick injection to the back of his thigh. Even with the restraints in place, the man could see his body flinch. Malakai took a moment to dispose of the syringe and when he looked, the boy's eyes were fluttering. He brushed back Zack's bangs. "Do not bite yourself, or I will be forced to put you in headgear. Okay? And I really don't enjoy doing that. Get some sleep now."

Zack's eyes rolled to the back of his head, where once more, he was surrounded by loved ones, strangers, and a small child's potty seat.

CHAPTER 26

RESPONSIBILITY

Atlas opened his eyes. The morning sun shone bright through the bedroom window. Turning onto his side, he could see Ashley sitting at her vanity, brushing her long hair, her eyeliner and eye shadow lay off to one side. Several shades of lipstick were lined up in front of the mirror. Atlas couldn't count the number of times he had told her she didn't need to wear any of it; she was beautiful the way she was. "Morning, babe." It was Ashley's day off. They had talked about their plans the night before, how she was going to take Brenna to the mall; the little girl was growing like a weed and needed a few things. Atlas was supposed to go to the library to study; the exam was right around the corner. But he just wasn't feeling it. The bedroom door swung open and Brenna ran in, flopping herself on the bed beside him. "Ashley, how about the three of us go out for breakfast this morning?"

"You mean fast food? You've been stressing the exam." She turned and looked at him curiously. "What about your brother?

"We'll get Brenna dressed and go. Two hours will not ensure a failing grade on the Bar Exam. And the sooner I pass this test, the sooner I can help the family" *Yeah. Like Jensen said, it's not like I haven't been studying this stuff since I was ten.* With the decision made, Atlas got up, kissed his wife, and then swung his daughter up in the air.

An hour later, they were being seated at a table at Scrappy's. Atlas slid Brenna into a highchair. "Think she'll always let me do this?"

Ashley smiled. "What? Put her in a highchair?" Atlas laughed. "No, she won't. But I'm sure she'll hate my guts before she hates yours."

"Why's that?"

"Girls always love their daddies longer. I'll be giving her the speech about the birds and the bees, and she'll probably go to you when she has problems with a boy. I always did." Ashley took a drink from her glass. "But then, who knows, she might do the opposite."

Breakfast at Scrappy's was pancakes, bacon, and eggs. The couple spent time addressing issues they hadn't touched in weeks because of the exam and Rustin's care. They kept Brenna entertained with paper and crayons, and they both got to hear how Big Bird gave one of the adults a high five for sharing that morning on Sesame Street.

After he paid the bill, Atlas followed Ashley outside and lingered a few paces behind, watching her walk, the toddler balanced on her hip. Ashley turned around and shook her head, smiling. She knew exactly what he was up to. She admonished him, laughing. "Atlas Christopher Carson." She laughed out loud, and Atlas was again reminded of why he loved her; she was lighthearted and knew the score, just like his mother had. The two women who had made his life complete never had to guess what was on his mind or how he felt about anything. Lauren would have loved Ashley, without a doubt.

Atlas cleared his throat like he did whenever he had been caught and then laughed. "Where do you want to go?"

They had reached the car. Ashley was putting Brenna in her car seat. "Go McDonalds?"

"No Brenna. You have Jazzercise in an hour." Ashley pulled the safety bar down and snapped it into place. Closing the back door, she got into the passenger seat and put her seatbelt on as Atlas started the engine. "When do they plan on releasing Rustin? Do you think the authorities are close to finding the bad guys?"

"I don't know, I'm hoping I'll find out after I drop you and the baby off." He paused. "You don't mind, do you?"

"Of course not." Ashley looked into the rearview mirror to check on their daughter; Brenna had pulled off her shoe. "Remember, you and Ryan are supposed to go to the ranch a day or two after you take the exam. You still plan on going?"

"No. I talked to him last night," Atlas turned on the blinkers and switched lanes. "We're going to wait until court is complete."

Late that night, his father called to tell him that he planned to move the boys to Washington after the trial. He had found a great piece of property, right on the river. The bastards who had traumatized both of his fifteen-year-olds would go to prison indefinitely. But Robert doubted Rustin and Zack would feel safe in the Bay Area again. Bastards. That's what his father had said. Atlas said he understood, but the truth of the matter was, the cops and the detectives who Robert had hired still did not know who had committed the crime.

Atlas had entered his dad's house pulling off his coat. His cell phone fell to the floor. He hoped to take an hour break; he had been studying ever since he dropped Ashley and Brenna off at Jazzercise. He went into the kitchen to make himself a sandwich. On the refrigerator door, however, he found a scribbled note in his uncle's handwriting. *Rustin's condition worsened, we're at the hospital.* Making a beeline for the door, Atlas left without either his coat or cell phone.

Once at the hospital, he found his father and uncle downstairs in the lobby. His dad, who was on his cell phone, had his back toward him. Atlas watched Craig tap his dad on the back. Robert hung up the phone and turned around. "What's going on?"?"

"Someone came out a while ago. Rustin's heart had stopped twice." Atlas was shocked. But before he could ask the obvious horrible question, Robert said, "They did get it restarted, yes." Atlas watched his father shake his head. "How have your studies been going? Did I tell you about Adam Lechner? You have an appointment with him at three o'clock on Tuesday." He got his thoughts in order, and Atlas followed his gaze toward the entrance of the hospital. "There's Eric and Natalie. Can you go talk to them, please? The other kids are in the cafeteria."

His father was incapable of handling social affairs at the moment; Atlas called out to the two teenagers and took them to the cafeteria to join the others. He found Jensen, Julia, and Travis seated near the window. Atlas handed Natalie a few dollars and told the two of them to get something to drink. Then he joined the others. "Hey guys, where's Zack?"

Atlas listened as Jensen told him about the seizure Rustin had and that Zack had been admitted to a psychiatric ward. The older brother saw piles of sheet music on the table. "You're working on an original piece?"

"A rendition of '*Lean on Me*', Travis said, when Jensen didn't answer. "Just trying to pass the time, you know?"

Atlas nodded. Natalie and Eric came back with cups of hot cocoa in their hands. Natalie was quiet like usual, but the way Eric was talking, you'd think they were in a pizza parlor instead of a hospital cafeteria.

Eric laughed. "I took a picture of this kid; he had his whole butt sticking up in the air. What was really a crack up was that he fell over and landed in a sand box. I can't wait to show Rus-"

"Rustin's in surgery right now," Atlas told them. Eric's unyielding dialogue ceased without recrimination. "They have to get the swelling down in his brain, or he will not make it." He had seen nothing silence

Eric faster. After a second, Natalie sobbed.

"He never asked me to go to the spring dance with him." Natalie's long mousy hair fell over her shoulders as she rested her elbows on the table, her head in her hands.

Eric stood up; his chair flipped backwards. People were watching the commotion, but he didn't seem to care. "Everything's not about you, Natalie! What if he doesn't make it? Who's going to ask you to the dance then, huh?" The teenager stormed out, a full cup of cocoa spilled, dripping from the table to the floor.

"Travis, can you go after him?" After Travis was gone, Atlas turned and found Julia's hand on Natalie's. "He's just upset, Nat." He ran a hand through the sobbing girl's hair. Several minutes were spent calming the girl down. Jensen even went and bought her a bottle of water, which the girl gulped down. Someone who worked for the hospital approached with a mop in her hands and cleaned up the sticky mess. Atlas nodded his thanks before the woman left and then focused on Natalie.

The girl was taking a few quivering breaths. Natalie asked, her voice barely audible, "Should I go pray?"

"Sure, if it'll make you feel better." Atlas stood up. He left Jensen and Julia behind, took Natalie out into the hall and checked the directory on the wall. At the hospital's chapel, he watched her walk to the front of the small room and kneel. For several minutes, he stood there feeling somewhat awkward. He didn't belong here. He understood people came here to pray to a divine spirit, that it may guide them toward helping others; to help themselves get through a hard time. But for Atlas, people should help those around them because they were all equals, because everyone deserved to be treated with dignity and respect. And whatever happened, happened. Rustin was going to make it because of his physical strength and doctor's care, or he would die because of the strength and care that he lacked. His little brother had lived through so much already; he couldn't see Rustin pulling out now. Softly, Atlas cleared his throat and pushed the awkward feeling away.

As Atlas watched, Eric entered the chapel and walked down the aisle and stopped beside Natalie. The boy's voice said a soft prayer. Atlas could then hear both of them say a soft, "Amen." Both teenagers came back up the aisle and Natalie gave him a hug. "He's going to make it, you know." Atlas could hear the slight tremble in her voice.

"I hope so." They walked back out into the hallway. Travis stood there leaning against a wall. Atlas stepped forward and shook his hand; he could see the awkwardness on the boy's face, the awkwardness of a fellow free thinker. "Let's get back to the cafeteria." Atlas wanted nothing more than to believe, as Natalie did, that Rustin was going to pull through surgery and recovery with no repercussions. But nobody could go through a traumatic assault of any kind and be left without scars of some sort. It wouldn't be fair to Rustin to expect otherwise.

CHAPTER 27

TICK. TICK. BOOM!

The waiting room was a small rectangular area. Its pieces of furniture, two couches and three chairs were unused by the two families who waited to hear about the outcome of their child's operation. While Craig found comfort in exchanging pictures with the mother, both fathers wondered off in opposite sides of the room; the floor became more and more worn as the hours went by.

It was around seven o'clock when a tall doctor entered the room. "Mr. and Mrs. Ramirez." The tired couple approached him at the same time. He broke into a smile, "Your daughter's doing well. She's in recovery. If you'll follow me."

Once the couple left and the two men were alone, Craig sat down across from Robert. "Their daughter's beautiful. She looks like her mother." He paused and then said, "Rob, you and I have always been able to talk about anything."

"I had Zack admitted," Robert snapped, as he tried to avoid a subject that no parent ever wants to think about. "You know nothing about having kids."

Craig could see the exhaustion on Robert's face, the circles under his eyes, the tired wrinkles beginning to set in. He dismissed the shortness in temper and continued. "You're right. You're absolutely right, and I'm not judging you. You did what was right for Zack." Craig paused. "I'm talking about Rustin. If, for some reason, Rustin doesn't make it through surgery, decide what to do with his remains. Now." Robert couldn't know it but Craig set aside his own feelings to help his brother-in-law deal with his. "What do you want? What would Lauren want?"

Flashing back, Robert remembered a talk he had with Lauren in bed one night, about how to prepare for their future and their children's future, especially if one of them were to die. He had been ready to tell her how much he loved her. But she had stopped him, told him she wanted her eyes to help someone see, and her heart and lungs to help someone breathe. She had said, *Cremate me so our children can hold on to me.* And he had done everything she had asked him to do. After thirteen years, he couldn't get it out of his head, the image of her beautiful face turning to nothing but ash. He knew Lauren would have wanted Rustin to help other children live the life he had lost. But he couldn't go through that pain again. He couldn't go through the thoughts of someone else's loved one living while his had to die. Maybe he was selfish, he didn't care. "No!" Robert exclaimed with a shake of his head. Lowering his voice, he looked at Craig. "Rustin's going to make it. The longer the operation takes the better his odds. That's what the nurse told us." He closed his eyes and a moment later, reopened them. "I cannot go through another loss like I did with Lauren. I can't." A big lump formed in his throat, not for the first time, and he had a hard time swallowing it. Without further disagreement, Robert checked the change in his pockets. He cleared his throat. "I'm going down to the cafeteria, do you want anything?" He watched Craig shake his head. Standing up, he went down the hallway toward the cafeteria. He passed exam rooms and a pharmacy. He let himself wander into the gift shop, to pass some time. Candy was up front by the cashier. There were little flags proclaiming, 'It's a Girl!', and balloons with little children in wheelchairs, 'Get Well Soon'. Robert navigated toward a bunch of stuffed animals on a shelf in the back of the store. A teddy bear wearing a blue hat and scarf reminded him of a stuffed animal Jensen had played with when he was little. It had gone with him everywhere until one day he was caught with it at school and then teased for it. It also reminded him of the bear the paramedics had given Rustin when they had first found him. He wanted to be sure it was one of the first things Rustin saw when he came out of surgery.

Robert exited the shop. He stopped by Rustin's hospital room and grabbed the teddy bear. It was only then that he went to the cafeteria where he bought himself a cup of decaffeinated coffee. Slowly, he made it back toward the waiting room, cup in one hand, teddy in the other. In a brightly lit hallway, he found the Ramirez couple was outside an open door. Mrs. Ramirez was sobbing in her husband's arms, the man was whispering soft words in her ear, something about a long hospital stay, chemotherapy, and losing hair. "*If Rustin has to go, I don't want him to go through any pain.*"

Back in the waiting room, Robert was apologizing to Craig when Keisha and Nathan showed up. "Any word on Rus?" Nathan asked. Robert shook his head. "You up for a debate?"

"Nathan," Robert heard the warning in Keisha's voice.

"Yes." Robert needed a distraction, something to keep his mind off what was going on. "What's our topic?"

"Twins," Nathan answered without hesitation. "Do they have ESP? I say no way. I finish Keisha's sentences all the time. That does not mean I have ESP."

"What about Cryptophasia?" Keisha interjected. "Twins develop their own language all the time. What about the research where one twin is injured and the other knows it instinctively?"

"That's happened between Rustin and Zack. The Cryptophasia, too." When Craig asked for more, Robert continued. "Cryptophasia, most of the time, is just screwed up English." He said that while single children have their parents and older siblings as their language role models, the main role model a twin has, is his own twin. And his English is just as bad as his brother's. "There's something so deep between them. It's like you're looking at them, looking at each other, and even though you should all be seeing the same thing, you're not. You, as the outsider, are missing something so intense." Robert paused, as he tried to remember. "They may have been ten, maybe. But Zack was at the roller rink with some friends. Rustin was at a friend's house. I got a call that Zack was being taken to the emergency room for a broken leg. I don't know if the traffic was a mess or what, but Rustin got there before me. Nobody had called the house, the parents in charge knew where I was. And then come to find out, Rustin got to the rink before the ambulance showed up."

Keisha and Nathan stayed a while longer, always eager to change the debate topic or walk with him to the cafeteria for another cup of coffee. They would have stayed with him the whole night if he had needed them to, but Robert insisted they go home. He didn't want Natalie home alone; she didn't deserve to be dragged into this. Craig left and returned after he dropped all the kids off at their own homes; Jensen had gone home with the Spencer's for a while, everything fell to an eerie silence.

Both men spent the next three hours waiting for the suspense to end, like the cliché of climbing walls. The walls seemed as if they were made of sand, where even if the whole castle didn't cave in, they were pretty sure a part of it already had. They spent their time doing anything to take their minds off the wait; they walked the hospital grounds, visited the playroom, or stopped by the nursery. They talked constantly about anything and everything, from sports and the news to Robert's last case and the young kids in Craig's history class.

It was at a quarter past eleven, when Dr. Todd and the surgeon Dr. Salicco, entered the waiting room. Both wore an expression that neither brother could read. Pulling the chairs near the couch, the four adults took seats in the far corner of the room. "The blood clot is gone," Dr. Salicco announced. "We'll do several CAT scans to make sure it doesn't come back."

"The next forty-eight hours are crucial," Dr. Todd added. "His fever has dropped slightly, but we've yet to see if it's done any damage to his brain." He hesitated for a moment. "Robert. Your son is in a coma. We've listed him in critical condition, He's not breathing on his own."

Coma? Critical Robert coughed. "What are his chances?"

"We don't give chances," Dr. Salicco answered. "Too many people could get hurt."

Robert didn't like the surgeon's attitude, and apparently neither did Todd, who spoke up with a small smile on his face. "Hey, he's taken the first big step, he made it through surgery. Would you like to see him?"

Craig announced then that he would be going back to the house with the offer to pick him up in the morning. "Thanks, Craig." Tossing his stack of empty coffee cups into the wastebasket, Robert grabbed the teddy bear. He followed the doctors down a different hallway and into a small room where beds aligned a single wall. Robert watched while a nurse took Rustin's vital signs. It was a moment later, when the nurse moved away, that he took in the surroundings. The plastic line still attached to his son's arm, the oxygen tube taped to his mouth, the thick gauze around his head.

Robert took a deep breath and tried not to cry, but the tears came anyway. He wanted to do more than give his son this stupid little bear;

he wanted to make Rustin's pain go away like he had been able to when he was younger. But he couldn't. He couldn't make the pain go away. Clinging on to the bear, Robert wiped his tears away. "You hung in there, Rusi." His voice faltered. A moment later, he tried again. "Come out of that coma as soon as you can, okay? I want you to tell me what you think of Natalie, and any photography projects you have coming up." He paused again, then put the bear in his son's hands. "Zack's in the hospital, too. He misses you a lot." Robert talked to his son for a few more minutes and then went to talk to the nurses about getting a cot for the room. Tonight, was going to be a long night.

CHAPTER 28

THE LAWS OF MUSIC AND THE HEART

J ensen had come home after convincing the Spencer's that he just
needed some time alone. After clearing it with his dad, he went up
to his room and found he couldn't sleep. Along with the responsibility
of *Just the Five of Us'*, he still did not know what he wanted to do
with his life. Not to mention this overwhelming sense of guilt. He had
never been that into playing big brother, he had always considered that
Atlas's job, seeing as how he was the oldest. Maybe if he had taken the
role more seriously, Rustin and Zack wouldn't be in so much pain.

Walking into the kitchen Saturday morning, he was surprised to
find Ashley and Brenna sitting in the living room. After saying hello
to his sister-in-law and exchanging a high five with Brenna, he went
into the kitchen where he found Atlas putting a jar of mayonnaise into
the refrigerator. "When do you see that guy Keisha put you in touch
with?" Jensen sat at the table and waited for his brother to join him.
"I want to go with you."

Jensen watched as Atlas sat down with two sandwiches and shoved
one over to him. "JC, it's going to be long and boring. Half the
stuff we're saying is going to be about process anyway." Atlas paused.
"You're not responsible for any of this, you know that, right?"

Taking a deep breath and a bite of his sandwich, Jensen nodded.

Head wise he knew that what had happened had nothing to do with his actions, or lack thereof. But his head kept playing games with him, and he wondered if mind games had gotten Zack hospitalized. "I just want to make sure that Rustin and Zack will be..." Jensen wasn't sure how to finish his thought.

"I know. I haven't even met this guy yet, and I have my own doubts." Jensen saw Atlas thinking to himself as he got up to put his dishes in the sink. "Let me take care of this, okay? I don't want either of us jumping to conclusions this early. He may be the only contact we prove that male rape happens. Most of society likes to pretend it doesn't happen at all." Both of them heard a car door slam. Atlas peaked out the window. "Your friends are here. Go have some fun, okay? I'll be in Dad's office."

Jensen opened the door just as Julia and the guys from *Just the Five of Us* got to the doorstep. "Hey, come on in. Let's go to the solarium."

The solarium was a room in the back of the house with a door that led to the backyard. The area was meant for social gatherings, which at the Carson house was few. Most of the time they kept Jensen's keyboard, guitar, and violin in here, since Robert still didn't like the idea of Jensen having girls in his room. He remembered when his father had laid down the law, so to speak, and he had laughed. Like Travis would let his little sister stay alone in a room with any guy, even him.

Jensen joined everyone at the nook along the glass wall, his head bent down. Minutes passed before he realized everyone was staring at him. Clearing his throat, he went into the kitchen and came back with his backpack. Rejoining his friends, he pulled out several sheets of music and passed them around. "It starts off with a bass solo. Miguel, that's you."

"Maybe we could start it off a Capella," Travis said, glancing at

Miguel and then Jensen. "Measure in some clapping, and then have Miguel come in on the fourth count."

Jensen looked at his best friend and nodded. "Get a baritone to harmonize on the eighth count as a jump off point. Then bring everyone else in. Tyrese, you take it."

"Leaders are required to take solos, JC."

"It's a lead in, Tyrese. I'll take the solo later." Jensen got up and started walking around the room. When he sat down again, everything was silent. "I haven't figured out my solo, but Tyrese has to take the lead in. My voice has more range that his, we should use that to our advantage." Nobody argued, they all knew it was true.

Jensen felt Julia take his hand. "Take your solo. Then lead into the next verse and have Travis backing you up. Your voices harmonize well together."

An idea was slowly forming in Jensen's head. He kept thinking about the words to the song and what was going on in his own life. How everybody was pulling together to help his family get through the most traumatic event that had happened to them since their mom had died. "What if we brought in Chorus? What if we got all of us together, we could bring in an extra verse at the end?"

Steve nodded. "What about our dress? Are we going to wear our robes? Or do we wear suits?"

"If we're trying to express a sort of camaraderie, we shouldn't wear dress robes," Miguel said, glancing at everyone." And we need to ask Mr. Delaney before we get everyone involved."

Jensen rubbed his hands together, trying to keep his mind on topic, trying not to think about the last time he had seen his brother's body, damaged and riddled with pain. "I'll do it when I can get away from the house. Miguel's right, though. We need to wear something that shows we're united. Black slacks or skirts and shoes. Any ideas for a shirt?"

"What if we assigned a shirt color to each vocal range?" Julia looked at her boyfriend. "Jensen?"

He saw her try to reach out to him, to console him. But all he wanted to do was quit thinking about the attack and the fact that his dad had decided they were moving out of state; he had overheard his father telling Atlas. He didn't want to move; he didn't want to lose any of his friends or family. But it had to be. "Let's just deal with the music, okay?" He stood up, went to the other side of the room and began playing the song on the keyboard. He got through the first verse before the keyboard wouldn't make any sound at all. Looking up, he saw Travis standing by the wall. Jensen sighed. "What are you doing, Travis?"

"We can't concentrate on the music if your head's somewhere else. So, what's going on, is Rustin still in a coma? How's Zack?"

"Knock it off, man." Jensen stepped away from the keyboard and came at his best friend threateningly; he even drew back his fist before the entire world stopped. He took a deep breath and brought his hand back down. "Oh, damn."

Travis laughed. "Relax, JC. It's not like you've never thrown a punch at me before." Jensen joined in uneasily. "So, what's going on?"

Shaking his head, Jensen stepped back. "No, I can't do this right now." His voice broke for a split second. When he spoke again, however, his voice was steady. "We have to work on this. The concert's right around the corner."

"Whatever you want, JC."

"It's Jensen." The seventeen-year-old was adamant.

Travis looked confused for a minute, maybe concerned. Jensen couldn't be bothered with trying to figure out his friend's mental clarity. "Music's great at getting us on track. But if we don't deal with this now, it's going to affect the entire group." Travis paused, then tried again. "Jensen-"

"I know." Jensen's voice was soft. He knew the camaraderie of the group would help him if he let them. But he wasn't ready for that yet, he had to handle it on his own. "Later. Music, first. We have a concert to get ready for."

CHAPTER 29

A NEW DAY

Zack opened his eyes. The nurse's station lay out before him. Chatty women dressed in scrubs were discussing the latest plot twists on their favorite soap operas. They ignored him. Zack's hip still throbbed, the injections from the night before reassured him, or not, that the nightmare he had lived through had indeed happened. He found his wrists tied to the bedrails with leather straps that seemed to get tighter every time he tried to pull loose. *Oh, damn. They're going to find us. They're going to kill us.* Zack's head pounded like metal against bass, a crescendo and a climax at the same time; he struggled to gain control of the torrents of emotion, his heart striking as if he was being pummeled against a snare drum.

Zack took in the light blue walls that surrounded him; a green door down one hallway seemed out of place. There were no beeping monitors or hissing machines. Everything was silent. Half a dozen beds were aligned against a wall, half of them occupied by patients. From where he lay, he could see a room off to the left with a single toilet, sink, and shower head. The room had no stalls and see through walls. A padded removable screen provided the only availability of privacy.

He watched as the nurses behind the counter divided pills into small plastic cups and placed them on a tray. The woman with red hair turned and brought a syringe up to eye level, and then measured out a prescribed dose of medication. As she set it down on the counter, he could have sworn he heard her say his name. *Please, not again. Just let me go. Rusi needs me.*

The green door opened at the end of the hallway and a wheelchair was pushed out. In it sat a young man with dirty blonde hair; he wore nothing more than a thin hospital gown. The stranger had his head bent down. His legs were spread; his feet dangled on either side of the chair, and his arms rested against the metal frame of the wheels. Thick straps were pulled secure over his shoulders as if he would collapse without them.

The blonde nurse approached the patient with a bucket; Zack pulled against the restraints when the young man's head jerked back. He vomited three times before the nurse could take a washcloth to his face. She put the bucket down. Then the nurse took a moment to place his bare feet onto the footrest, both hands in his lap. She brought his head up with her palm and said a few soft words. Zack saw a pale face and a bright red mark on the patient's temple.

Zack came close to throwing up himself. Some time when he slept, they had put a similar gown on him; one slight breeze and his entire body would be exposed to the entire world. Or so it would seem. Zack had no desire to undertake the same treatment the nameless boy had. His wrists stung as he continued to pull on the restraints. The straps became moist and sticky.

Someone dressed in a white uniform came into the unit through the elevator. She pushed a tall cart that smelled of nothing more than grease and fat. Zack watched as the black woman took a tray from the cart and spoke to one nurse. He could do nothing but stare as the tray was directed to yet another patient on the ward. This young man had a shaved head. He was secured to the bed like he was, with straps pulled tight across his shoulders, arms, legs and feet. When one nurse approached, the patient screamed incoherently. The nurse spent several minutes with him to calm him down, but to no avail. The woman left for a short time. Once she returned, there was no hesitation as she made an injection in his thigh. A moment passed, then another. The patient's breathing slowed down, his face slacked, and his body became still. "There you go, sweetheart. Let's have some applesauce now."

Breakfast seemed to take forever for the boy to consume. Zack wondered if he would be fed just like his fellow patient, a bowl of applesauce, another bowl of oatmeal, and a small carton of milk, complete with straw. For every spoonful that went into the young man's mouth, another landed on the towel below his chin. Once the meal was completed, the tray was removed. A curtain was pulled around the bed. Zack did not want to know what was going on behind it.

On the opposite side of Zack's bed lay the only other patient in the room, a boy that looked younger than him. He had been through the routine already this morning. He slept as if he were in some other bed, where it was warm. Dreams involved him being a hero, or perhaps he scored the winning touchdown at the Super Bowl. No straps held him to the bed. He laid there with his eyes closed, his long eyelashes fluttered like a bird about to take flight. His arms rested on top of the blanket, both wrists protected by iodine, a pad, and gauze wrapping. The boy could not have been any older than ten. Zack didn't remember him being there the night before.

One nurse approached the young boy with a small metal cart pushed out in front of her. The woman's footsteps were crisp and authoritative. As she neared, Zack took in her angular face and thin lips. She pulled on a pair of latex gloves and then drew the boy up against her chest. "Come on, Jeremy. It's time for your meds." The boy's blue eyes had just opened when she placed a pill in his mouth and brought a cup of water to his mouth. The nurse then inserted her finger into his mouth and searched his gums and the area around his tongue. She laid him back down and covered him with a blanket. "All right, Jeremy. You can go back to sleep now."

A phone rang. Zack turned his head as the red-haired nurse moved to answer it. Again, he heard his name, along with the words medicine, hallucinations, and bowels. She raised her voice at whomever she spoke to. Just as suddenly as she picked up the phone, she slammed it back down on the receiver. She grabbed the prepared needle and started toward him. She thumped the vial of the syringe and tested it. Liquid spurted from the tip. But just as she was about to approach his bedside, the elevator opened with a light *bing*. A man in a white lab coat beckoned to her. After a moment of hushed conversation, the woman went back behind the counter. Her expression was more than one of resignation, she was pissed off. The doctor soon approached Zack. The syringe was nowhere in sight.

"Good morning, Zack. How are you feeling this morning?" Zack didn't respond. "My name's Dr. Veksler and I'll be the one who watches over your physical well -being while you're here." The head restraint was removed, a pillow placed beneath his head. "Do you want to ask me anything before I go?"

Zack hesitated. "How's Rustin? When do I get to leave? Did the cops find us? Where-"

"Slow down, Zack. Just take a couple deep breaths. Do as you're told, son." Zack did what the doctor asked and tried to calm down. He didn't want to give them any reason to force anymore drugs on him; Zack's eyes were still red from the medication he was given the night before. "You'll go home as soon as we know you're ready not to hurt yourself. He's all yours, Patti."

The doctor left and a tiny woman with jet black hair came rolling a blood pressure machine. She peeked beneath the sheets and clicked her tongue. "Not drinking enough," she said in a quiet tone. She made a note on her clipboard. She checked his blood pressure and made another note. His temperature was taken with a thermometer she stuck in his ear.

Zack watched as she traded the machine for a breakfast tray. She brought the head of the bed up so that he was sitting almost vertical. Then she removed the cover from the tray to reveal a bowl of oatmeal and a bran muffin. Zack shook his head. "I'm not hungry."

"This is no big deal unless you make it one, Mr. Carson. Food is not an enemy here." He watched as Patti prepared the food, cutting the bran muffin into two pieces. Then she poured milk into a bowl of oatmeal. She took the muffin in hand and brought it up to his mouth. "Big bite let's go." She paused, "I'm not leaving until this plate is empty, and if you want to get out of those restraints, you'd better eat." Zack took a small bite of the muffin and almost gagged, the thing tasted like cardboard. "Chew. Good job. Now swallow. Let's take a bigger bite this time."

Breakfast took twenty minutes to consume. She forced a quart of water on him and by the time he was through, Zack was overwhelmed and cried. All he could think about was Rustin, how his twin brother was unconscious, unable to eat and breathe on his own. Zack just wanted to curl up and die. Minutes after Patti left, the woman returned with a prepared needle in hand. "Please, no," he begged, his voice cracking. "I did nothing. I'll do whatever you say."

"Zack, this isn't a punishment. You must take your medication properly. Once we're sure your system can handle this, we'll change to pill form. Let me see your arm, Mr. Carson." She used a wet wipe saturated in alcohol to clean his arm. The needle sliced into his arm.

All Zack could do was squeeze his eyes shut and wait for the pain to be over.

"Dr. Westlake will be here in a few minutes," she said as she withdrew the needle. "We're going to change position now. We don't need you getting bed sores." With icy cold hands, Patti turned Zack on to his side, adjusting the bag of urine as she did so. The drug kicked in fast, leaving him unable to move, even if he tried. She lifted his arms one at a time, fitting the restraints and securing both to the bedrail. "We have to keep these on for your protection." Patti grabbed a pillow from an empty bed and placed it between his legs. She then pulled the blanket up to his mid-section. "Get some rest, Zack."

The next forty-five minutes passed incredibly slow. Zack laid there unable to move and unable to think clearly. A small puddle of saliva collected beneath his jowl. He nodded off only to be awaken minutes later by the sound of curtains being pulled around his bed. Opening his eyes, he was greeted by a man dressed in khakis and a dress shirt. "Hello, Zackary. My name's Dr. Westlake." The man paused as Zack's eyes rolled into his head. "I know it's hard right now. I need you to open your eyes, Zackary."

"Zzzzzack." Zack slurred. He felt a handkerchief brushed against his mouth and chin. Zack struggled to open his eyes.

"Alright, Zack." Dr. Westlake smiled. "I'll keep it short. I wanted to introduce myself. Today, we're going to take it easy, get your body used to the medication. You'll have injections three times a day and you'll be here at least a week."

Zack's eyes rolled again as the IV machine beeped. "Excuse me, Dr. Westlake." Patti said as she walked through the curtain, an IV bag in hand.

"We're finished for today, Patti. Take good care of our patient here." Westlake stood up. "See you tomorrow, Zack."

Patti stepped up to the head of the bed and replaced the empty bag with a full one. As she checked the line, Zack mumbled. "Shhh." She took hold of his wrist and looked at her watch, counting. She made a note on the clipboard.

"Nmd, nnnmd." Zack's eyes went glassy, yet he still tried to communicate. Saliva flooded from his mouth to the sheets below. His hands began to clench and unclench in their restraints. "Nnnma nnnnda."

Patti turned her back to him and pulled the curtain back. Nobody would recognize him as Zack or Rustin's twin. Zack's new world comprised of blurred objects and cold air. As Patti walked away, Zack's mutterings grew softer as his world grew dimmer and dimmer. The potty song returned.

CHAPTER 30

THE TRUTH WILL BE HEARD

Atlas had a lot on his mind when he first sat down to take the exam that Monday morning. Rustin was still in a coma. He had an appointment with someone named Adam Lechner, someone he had never met, that was supposed to help him understand what his brother had gone through. He didn't know how. *Maybe it'll help the prosecution.'* To top all that off, Brenna came down with a cold and kept both Atlas and Ashley up all night.

The exam hall had been silent. It took all the control Atlas had to concentrate on the paper in front of him. What he really wanted to do was put the control back in the hands of those who deserved it. *You've been studying this forever! Take the damn test.* Atlas took a deep breath, picked up his pen and looked down at question number one. "Yes." He realized his voice may have carried a little too far; he glanced around. He found the test proctor glaring at him. Atlas gave an apologetic smile, cleared his throat, and bent his head over the paper. With pen to paper, he wrote.

After he finished the exam, Atlas went to the men's restroom and looked in the mirror. His hair stuck out in a thousand different directions. His face was pale. Atlas felt as if he stood on the very edge of a mountain, and he doubted the stress would go away until he knew whether he had passed the Bar. He turned on the water; he cupped his hands full of the cold liquid and splashed his face. A little color returned to his cheeks. *I either passed or I failed. Move on.* After combing his hair, Atlas looked at his watch. He had an hour and a half to get himself to Concord for the conference with Adam Lechner.

In the drive-thru of a Jack-In-The-Box, Atlas ordered a Jumbo Jack, fries, three egg rolls, and a chocolate milkshake. Off to the side of the restaurant, he devoured both the burger and egg rolls before he allowed himself to get on the freeway. He had filled the tank the night before. And so, while watching for the nearest exit, Atlas munched on fries.

Atlas entered the office building, scanned the list of mental health workers, and then walked down the hall to the correct door. Inside he found a man with short spikey hair who was focused on a file in front of him. "Adam Lechner?"

The man looked up, smiled, and held out his hand. "You must be Alasdair Carson. Take a seat." Lechner turned away and put the file into a cabinet. "A defeated soldier used to be the right of the winner, historically, and the winning soldier often raped the losing enemy who was then denied the ability to be a warrior or ruler. Sexually penetrated by force, he had lost his manhood, permanently." Lechner stopped to take a breath. He looked at Atlas with an expression he couldn't pin down. "Did you know, most children abused and murdered are boys? Males account for eighty percent of completed suicides and seventy-five percent of assault victims."

Atlas was blown away by the rapidly given facts and was unsure of what to say. Several seconds passed as he absorbed the information he was given. He cleared his throat. "You take your research seriously."

"You bet I do. If you don't see the deep injustice on how we treat males, I think you'd better leave." Lechner's eyes bore into Atlas's; this was a test. A test more important that the one he finished taking two hours ago. Atlas knew if he blew it, he'd have to scurry to find someone else to explain the whole physical process of male rape to him.

"Rustin's on life supports right now, and Zack's falling apart. That didn't happen because of some lame ass fight or some stupid game." Atlas stopped to get himself under control. He took that moment to look around the office walls. While most psychologists had plaques on their walls, Lechner's walls were covered with pictures of battered bodies, presumably all males. "We need your help to prove it happened. No one believes in male rape. They say males can't get aroused if they're scared. That it's physically impossible."

The psychologist leaned back in his leather chair. "And what do you think?"

The casual manner the man seemed to give him, was pissing Atlas off. He would look up male rape on his own, if he had to. "It happened. I know it happened. This isn't a joke!" Atlas headed for the door.

"Wait." Atlas turned and watched Lechner get up from his chair. As the psychologist stepped around his desk to the wall full of photographs, Atlas walked up next to the man. "In 1982, Sarrel and Masters studied nineteen victims of male rape. All of them had erections and six of them ejaculated. It was Alfred Kinsey who first listed other emotional states that could trigger a sexual reaction. These emotions include fright, anger, and pain as well." Atlas watched as he carefully removed the tacks and pulled down several graphic pictures. Lechner took his seat again and gestured for Atlas to do the same. Once Atlas had taken his seat, the psychologist handed one picture to him. "This is a young man who was attacked from behind." In the photo was a man's nude body, curled up against a brick wall; Atlas assumed it was some alleyway anywhere in the country. "He was found dead. An autopsy never could figure out how he died. All they knew for sure was that he had something to do with some drug bust in the South Beach area.

Atlas was handed another photograph; it almost made him physically ill. All he could see was a crumpled body with black and blue marks covered in dried blood. The picture placed the victim on a tile floor. He took a deep breath, "What is that?" he asked, pointing.

"That is a young man's buttocks," Lechner answered in a quiet voice. "The victim was sodomized. The lining of this young man's anus was torn, the pain had to be immeasurable. This one survived, they found him huddled in a motel bathroom."

"Í know all the legal reasons they take pictures of the crime scene and the victim." Atlas paused, not sure where he was going with this line of thought. He continued to speak out loud. "But they let this person, this human being, continue to suffer just so they could get pictures for the prosecution? This guy's life and integrity is one hundred times more important than that." Atlas paused again. "They found Rustin blindfolded, gagged, and naked. They let Rustin suffer more, just so they could get more evidence?" Atlas was worked up; he did not know when it had become so personal. He had come for information, that's all.

"Yes. And then they did blood tests and a rectal slide when they got him to the hospital. The humiliation is sometimes necessary in order to get a conviction."

"Screw the conviction." *Get control, man. You need him.* Atlas looked at Lechner who tilted his head to the side.

The man paused a moment to look at his hands. Then he met Atlas's eyes. "Tell me about your brother. What type of assault are we talking about? Molestation? Obviously rape, otherwise you wouldn't be here talking to me." Atlas told the psychologist what they knew about the attack and about Rustin's present condition. Lechner nodded. "That's unusual. More often, an assault does not involve stimulation of the victim's penis. Usually the attacker will penetrate a victim only anally or orally. I've only met a handful of victims who lived through all three. I'm sorry." Lechner paused. "Go home. Absorb what I've told you, I'll get back with you in a couple days." Atlas tried to hand the pictures back. Lechner shook his head. "Keep them. Always remember, your brother is not the first victim of male rape, and sadly, he won't be the last."

CHAPTER 31

ONE STEP FORWARD, TWO STEPS BACK

Zack had not seen Hastings since the night he was brought in. He was out of isolation and in the general population. People took time to talk to him. After lunch, before his mandatory rest period, all the young adults on the ward joined for group therapy. It helped Zack to know that he wasn't the only kid who had ever thought of killing himself. Some problems discussed in the group were more serious than his own. Two therapists were always there during these sessions, one of them Dr. Westlake, the other a woman named Dr. Travers. If one patient fell apart emotionally while in the circle, one psychologist would take them into another room for some one-on-one counseling. Zack had not experienced a meltdown.

He did have some minor complaints; his room was small, with nothing in it but a bed, a nightstand, and a barred window. Since he was started on medication, he was tired all the time and sluggish; he had no appetite whatsoever. But other than that, everything seemed okay.

Zack had been awake in bed for the past twenty minutes, his eyes focused on the camera up in the room's corner. He heard a key in the lock. A nurse appeared in the doorway. "It's time to get up," she said in a cheerful tone. The woman took the clipboard from its position on the wall and made several notations, as he stood up.

Remembering what Rustin had showed him the night before, Zack realized that with him in the hospital, Meyers had every opportunity to get Rustin out of the way. Zack's voice shook, "They want to kill us."

The long hallway that he walked down had a dozen rooms, six on each side. It opened to the living quarters where a huge TV hung high on the wall behind fiberglass. Off to the side was a small dining area, no kitchen. On the other side of the room was the bathroom, like the one in isolation, a toilet and a shower head enclosed behind glass walls.

"We'll get those voices down with a little medication," the nurse said as she led him into the bathroom. "But first you have to see Dr. Veksler."

He watched and listened as Dr. Veksler took the clip board from the nurse who took a few moments to get his vitals and check his weight. They also discussed Zack's failure to relieve his bowels for the past two days. The doctor looked at Zack with stern determination. "Son, you are going to show me some stool, right now. Get undressed, please." Zack couldn't move, wasn't allowed to move. It was all a part of the punishment he made himself suffer through, because he truly felt that he deserved to suffer. He deserved whatever pain and humiliation that came his way, even if he had to die. Zack's eyes turned glassy as Dr. Veksler approached, his large hands grabbed the elastic around his sweatpants and then pulled his underwear down to his ankles. He felt a tap on the back of his shins. "Leg up, son."

Stepping out of his clothes, Zack was naked from the waist down. "I don't have to go," he lied. "I'm not mental, I have to save Rustin. The cops want to kill him." He could feel the tension in his muscles grow worse.

"Yes, you do. And you will." Dr. Veksler walked him to the back of the room and placed Zack's hands on the cold tile wall. Zack felt like a criminal as he stared at the wall; he heard latex snap against skin. A moment later, the doctor spread his legs apart.

Zack tried to get away, to fight what felt like an assault; his breathing became erratic. He twisted his body and tried to push the doctor away. Before he could even plan an escape, two burly men had him pinned to the wall. "No, please."

"Relax, Zack," Dr. Veksler wedged his foot between his patient's feet. "Let's just get this done."

Just as a suppository was inserted into his rectum, he heard a voice from his not-so-distant past that he wished he would never hear again. "He still hasn't gone?" Zack could feel the blood drain from his face. "Get me an eight-ounce glass of prune juice." He wanted nothing more than to just die when Nurse Hastings frog marched him back to the front of the bathroom. She forced him to sit down on the toilet. "Keep your hands up where I can see them," she ordered him. One of the burly attendants handed Hastings a clear plastic cup with a straw. "No," she said when Zack reached for the cup. "Hands stay on your head." She directed the straw into his mouth. "I want it gone in sixty seconds. There will be major repercussions if you don't."

Zack, having never had prune juice before, took a sip and instantly spit it back out. Hastings shook her head. "I want him in ten-point restraints. I'm going to have to administer an enema."

"Can I try?" The attendant glanced at Zack and then looked directly at Hastings.

"You've got ten minutes to get him to give us a bowel movement or I will go in manually." The nurse could obviously see the panic came to Zack's eyes. She gave a stiff nod. Then she left the area after handing the cup to the attendant.

The attendant turned to watch the head nurse leave the area. Then he turned toward Zack and knelt in front of him. "Relax, man. You will not have any issues if you drink half of this." Zack shook his head. "I don't want to see her do that to you. Come on, man. Just give us a B.M., I'll get you a bowl of ice cream." Again, he offered Zack the straw.

Zack took the straw between his lips. He swallowed quickly, once, twice, three times. And then he almost gagged. The attendant pulled the cup away and set it on a nearby counter. "I'll be back in a minute."

The attendant walked past the room divider. Zack could only sit there, exposed to anyone who came by. His stomach felt like a load of bricks. A breath later, the attendant returned with Dr. Veksler by his side. It was at that moment when Zack's body started making embarrassing noises. Zack's cheeks turned red as he felt his bowels drop, thick like a milkshake. Humiliated, he sat there, with a desire to run, yet he also feared retaliation by the staff.

Zack watched as the doctor spoke with the nurse. "Be sure to add prunes to Zack Carson's diet." Dr. Veksler glanced at his patient and caught his tired arms slip into his lap. "Watch those hands, son. We don't want to lose any points, do we? Are you done?" Zack nodded. A single tear fell from his eye.

The shower that followed was quick and to the point, Zack could shower without help, though he was still monitored. As he finished dressing, he heard the squeaky medicine cart roll up behind him. Zack once again felt the sense of power lost. "There are no voices," he tried to tell them again. "I promise. They want to kill him. I have to save my brother."

Dr. Veksler left and the nurse handed him a paper cup with several pills in it. Zack took each of them with a sip of water and then let the nurse check his mouth. She patted him on the back. "Good job, Zack."

An hour in his room passed as other patients were taken to use the shower and given their medication. At nine o'clock, everyone was marched down to the small dining area. Zack took a seat at one of the small round tables. A plate was set in front of him, a plate that contained scrambled eggs, greasy ham, and a small lump of red mush, probably a fruit. A carton of milk was already at the center of the table. Zack picked up his spork and started moving the red stuff around his plate.

"The food sucks, huh?" Zack looked up and found a thin Mexican girl beside him. She had beautiful almond-colored eyes and shoulder length jet black hair. "I'm Isabelle."

A nurse stepped between the two teenagers and admonished them both. "There is no leaving this table until your plates are clean. And if you take too long about it, I'm going to have to deduct some points. Zack, you've only eaten half of your eggs and you haven't touched your prunes. I want them gone when I come back." Zack watched the nurse turn to the girl. "Isabelle, I'm glad to see you've made yourself acquainted with Zack. Five points." The nurse marked something on her clipboard and then left to check patients at another table.

Zack picked up his spork and gathered a bite of prunes. They were absolutely disgusting. He even tried mixing them with the eggs and ham. Knowing that the nurse could return at any moment, he gathered the last in a final huge bite and swallowed it. *I will not throw up, I will not throw up.* He grabbed a carton of milk and chugged it down, trying to get rid of the taste. *Hell. Even brushing my teeth will not get rid of that taste.*

After breakfast, Zack wanted nothing more than to go to sleep; the guilt he suffered from made the desire to sleep bad enough, but the pills made it especially difficult to stay awake. But personnel wouldn't allow it. Outside in the recreation area, patients were encouraged to play basketball, a game Zack use to play with vigorous enthusiasm. As far as basketball went, Zack would have nothing to do with the other patients or even the sport itself. Basketball was just too painful for him.

Two hours outside and then sand art caused the time to tick by. Zack did the bare minimum, just to get past the radar. He made tiny rivers in the sand, dried rivers, in case anyone asked. Dried rivers that contained nothing more than skeletons and secrets. And maybe a gun or two. The little boy with blond hair tried to engage him. But Zack just couldn't deal.

Dr. Westlake approached a medicated and exhausted Zack in the art room around eleven o'clock. Zack was found slumped in a chair. He knelt down in front of Zack, concerned. "You ready to go to your room?" Westlake pulled Zack to his feet and walked him back to his room.

Zack climbed into bed as the doctor left the room, locking the door behind him. This was his mid- morning rest period. Zack knew the drugs would knock him out. He would sleep for two hours. Lunch was next, usually a grilled cheese sandwich, the only piece of food they seemed to cook right, and it came with another pill. An hour would be spent in a group session where patients talked about life's pressures. The next hour involved board games. Then another nap.

As his head rested on a thin and worthless pillow, he listened to the sound of a struggle in the hallway right outside his door. Soft-soled shoes ran along a tile floor. There was the sound of a physical struggle, and the urgent call for a sedative. It would probably subdue the patient for the rest of the next day and a half. Zack held his breath, as he waited for the loud cry. When it finally came, tears coursed down his cheeks like fire.

CHAPTER 32

AWAKENING

Throughout the next three weeks, Rustin's fever would bounce between one hundred and four to a hundred and six degrees. Seizures had overtaken his body twice. It was then that he was packed in ice for several hours. The doctor had gone over the option of taking him off life supports; although Robert wanted his son not to be in any pain, he couldn't take the life of his own child. Even if Rustin became a vegetable.

Someone was always there during the day, talking to Rustin, telling him how much he was loved. At first, he had been intimidated when the doctor had suggested that Rustin would benefit from laying his head on Robert's chest; he had, in fact thought the idea ludicrous. But Robert grew to enjoy sitting in a rocking chair with his son in his arms, tubes, and all. He felt pride when he would walk into the hospital room after a break in the afternoon to find Jensen playing his guitar, the sound of the heart monitor would fade into the background. Atlas was intent on his studies, even after taking the Bar Exam. Probably for a distraction. Robert knew his eldest son had never seen the physical condition Rustin was in; he was pretty sure Jensen had.

Robert had also seen Zack several times; he too, appeared to be doing better. His face had more color. He had even gained some weight. The staff had concern when he made a naked doll out of clay, complete with a penis. But Westlake thought they might finally be able to break through the wall Zack had put up. It was the psychiatrist's opinion that the boy still had issues with control; he worried Zack would withdraw again. Staff did allow him a visitor, with Robert's permission of course, a female patient whose name he was not given.

Twenty-two days after Rustin went into the coma, Robert and Craig were in the ICU once more discussing the love the two of them had shared with Lauren. "I remember when we first got married and Atlas was born; she was a neat freak. If something got spilt on the floor, the whole house was vacuumed and shampooed. If the baby spit up a little, he got a bath and a new outfit. By the time the twins were born, she was a lot better."

"She wasn't always so wonderful, you know." Craig laughed. "When she was younger, she'd take my action figures and flush them down the toilet. *I just wanted to see if they could swim the rapids,* she'd say." Robert watched as Craig got up and stretched. "I'm going to get a cup of coffee. Do you want anything?"

Craig left. Robert went down the hall to the restroom. After he relieved himself, he went to the sink and turned on the water. "If Rustin doesn't make it, I want him buried by his mom." Surprised he spoke aloud, he caught a man in his twenties looking at him, a diaper bag slung on his shoulder. Robert smiled, "Kids are great, aren't they?"

Robert had not expected the man to respond, but he did. "I don't know, man. She's so small and helpless. It's like she's gonna break, ya know?"

"They get bigger with time," Robert smiled. "And then you wish they were small so you can hold them close again. You'll love every moment."

With his hands washed and feeling a little more relaxed, Robert made his way back to the pediatric ICU. He accepted another cup of coffee from his brother-in-law. And then he waited. He waited like he had been doing for the past three weeks. So, when Robert saw Rustin's hand move, he thought he had jostled the bed. But when he stepped back, the hand moved again. Afraid of another seizure, he looked at the nurse's station. "Get the doctor."

When he looked at his son again, the boy's body was thrashing about, like electricity was forcing its way through his body. The spastic movements in no way resembled the seizures he had grown used to seeing where his muscles jerked so hard, they looked like they would break. This time, though, Rustin's arms and legs moved more slowly, as if he was agitated. It was as if Rustin was trying to fight his way back into the conscious world. Medical personnel rushed past him. Robert found himself pushed to the other side of the room. Dr. Todd arrived and squeezed through the crowd around the bed. "All right, now." Rustin's entire body shifted toward the rails. "Watch his head." One nurse lifted his shoulders while Dr. Todd cradled the boy's head and laid it back on the pillow. Robert watched in shock as several nurses struggled to bring down Rustin's arms; he wondered if he had endured as much when he was raped. "Relax, kiddo." Moments later, Noah was there. The nurse spoke in a quiet tone as he tightened his grip on the boy's wrists. "Fifty mailgrams of Chlorpromazine," Robert heard the doctor order. Todd brought out his light and checked his pupils. "Hey, Rustin, it's Todd. I'm glad you've come back to us." He watched the boy's legs kicked 'til the sheets were on the floor. To Robert's amazement, the doctor chuckled. "Where's that Chlorpromazine?" A nurse entered the room, a prepared syringe in hand.

The injection was made in Rustin's hip; everyone watched the boy's legs as his reflexes slowed and then ceased. Robert saw Dr. Todd's eyes close for a moment as he said a short thank you, and then began giving orders. "Let's get his vitals."

"Rustin." Robert felt overwhelmed. He wanted nothing more than to hold his son. Rustin was going to make it, and the doctor took him away again. He knew the feeling was ludicrous, but that didn't stop the golf ball sized lump that formed in his throat. As he cleared his throat, he saw the sympathetic doctor wait for him to voice his concern. "He was coming out of it. Why'd you-"

Robert's voice got stuck and he couldn't go any further.

"He is coming out of the coma." Todd looked at the nurse and was informed that his patient's temperature was at a hundred and three degrees. "Let's do an alcohol bath, get that fever down more." Todd turned his attention back to Robert. "Coma patients are a little restless as they first come out of it. To prevent Rustin from hurting himself and pulling loose from any IVs or tubing, we'll keep him sedated 'til he's not so restless. Right now, he's incoherent and unaware of any pain." It sounded like a reassurance. "It'll be a couple of days before he's fully aware. Both men looked at the bed as Noah brought the bedrail down and undressed him. Dr. Todd put a hand on Robert's shoulder. Then he left.

Over the next day and a half, Robert had Craig call their family and tell them that Rustin had come out of the coma. They declined several offers of homemade food because no one was home. When they told Atlas, the young man had shouted with happiness, then insisted he get off the phone. He had research to do with Lechner. Time passed slowly. The nurse bathed him every other hour; his temperature was taken every thirty minutes.

On one trip to the restroom, Robert stopped a nurse and asked her about Dr. Todd's involvement with his son. She had smiled. "Dr. Ravenwood is always involved with his patients. He has a niece who suffers with a head injury. It's been twenty years. He visits her at the

group home whenever he can. He understands what they go through."
Robert was confused. "His full name is Dr. Todd Ravenwood."

Early that evening, Robert was reading the newspaper when he heard Craig's soft voice. "Hey, Rus. Rob, look who's up."

On his feet in an instant, Robert ran his fingers through his messed-up hair. He glanced at Craig. "Could you find Dr. Todd?" Approaching the bed, he grasped Rustin's hand and took notice of Rustin's swollen eyes. "You feeling better, honey?" He felt a small amount of pressure on his hand. He smiled as the doctor entered the room.

—·—

CHAPTER 33

SHOCK, DESIRE AND PAIN

Rustin had laid there for a while, as he listened to the sounds of the hospital, the beeping monitors, the hissing machines, and the soft murmur of footsteps nearby. His brown eyes opened. He let them wander around the room. His blurry vision made it difficult for him to recognize not just objects but faces, too. "Hey, Rus." One thousand one...one thousand two...one thousand three...The face refused to come into focus. "Rob, look who's up."

Zack.... Zack...

Before he could figure out the first face, it disappeared. A second face came into view. This one floated above him, a balloon without a string. A strong hand grasped his. "You feel better, honey?"

No. Rustin squeezed his father's hand. *Make it stop. I want to sleep.*

Footsteps could be heard as they echoed in the hall. They grew louder and louder. And then they stopped. A warm, gentle hand cupped his face, and a bright light was flashed in his eyes. He heard the doctor's soft voice at the same time the pain hit. The pain resembled a lightning rod being driven through his head. Rustin's head jerked sideways. An uncoordinated hand came up to his face. Todd grabbed it and pinned it down. "Robert." Robert placed a firm hand on Rustin's wrist. "We're going to get you off that respirator, kiddo."

Rustin watched the doctor turn a couple of knobs on one machine. "All right, Rustin. Take a deep breath and blow, just like you're going to blow out your birthday candles."

That first breath took forever. Christmas would come again before he was ready to take on the task of breathing on his own. *I can't do it.* Rustin wanted to be left alone. He wanted to be left on the respirator and just be allowed to drift off, to drift back to where the nightmares and the pain was non-existent. *I don't want to.* The nightmares made his muscles stiffen, his mind race with no memory at all. But the breath came anyway, and the intubation fell from his mouth.

The tube was removed. "Take nice, even breaths. How are you feeling, kiddo?"

Rustin opened his mouth to speak, no sound came out. His throat was too parched. He tried again. "Thirsty," he choked out.

"I know. In a minute. You can let go, Robert." Rustin felt the physical restraint lifted. "Can you move your hands for me? Reach up and grab my hands, kiddo."

The doctor's hand hovered over Rustin's. Both Todd and Robert watched his hand flinch, his eyes squeezed shut; it was obvious how hard he was trying. "It's alright." Todd laid his hand on Rustin's, then brushed his finger against his skin gently. "Rustin, stop. Stop. I'm going to get you some ice chips. Tomorrow you'll start your therapy. But today I want you to relax. I'll be back in a little while to check his skin." Todd left.

A short time later, Noah came in with a paper cup half full of ice chips. He showed Rustin how to bring the bed up to an angle. The nurse held the cup to Rustin's lips. "Suck on the ice." He poured a little into the boy's mouth.

"When will he be able to drink water?" Robert asked.

"If he handles this well today, he might have a light breakfast tomorrow."

Rustin moved the ice around in his mouth; it slowly melted. He wanted more. He wanted to drink a whole gallon of water and eat at an all you can eat buffet. *Where's Zack?* Rustin looked up at his dad. The boy's eyes grew big, his breathing came out fast.

"Rustin." The boy let his eyes followed the voice. "You're in the hospital. I'm Noah, and I'm your nurse. It's ten o'clock in the morning."

Rustin looked around, his eyes shifting from one side of the ward to the other. The small room was crowded with machines, including a TV. A small window looked out onto a green lawn with several trees. There was also a dry erase board that hung near the door with several things scribbled on it with bright green ink.

"Rusi." Rustin looked at his dad who was on the other side of the bed. "Zack's in the hospital, too. Both of you are going to be fine."

Where is he? I want my brother. Pain shot through his head. His whole body tensed. His head pressed hard against the pillow. Rustin groaned. His voice was raspy when he finally spoke, "Make it stop." Rustin coughed. "Not Zack's fault." Noah left. Rustin tried again to move. It took a lot of concentration and physical strength for him just to roll onto his side. His right arm pinned down by his body, he found he couldn't move his left arm either; it lay limp draped behind him.

Robert took his son's arm and laid it on the sheet in front of him. "Honey, nobody blames Zack." He brushed back Rustin's bangs. "Shhh. Calm down.

Noah returned, pushing a metal cart. He took the syringe and injected the drug into an IV port. "Alright, Rustin." Rustin's eyes rolled as the medication hit. "Try to focus. Here." Noah gave him a few more ice chips. While he waited for the ice to melt, Noah rearranged the cart, a couple towels and a washcloth were up beside a bucket half full of water. Once he had finished setting up, he leveled the bed so Rustin was laying down. "The doctor switched him to a painkiller. Todd wants him bathed early. Did you turn over by yourself, Rustin?"

Robert smiled, something he hadn't done in a while. "He sure did."

Rolling Rustin onto his back, Noah soaked the washcloth and lathered it. "Tell me about school. What grade are you in?" The nurse washed his arms.

"Tenth," he croaked. "Christmas?"

"Christmas was a few weeks ago. It's January second, two thousand and two. One o'clock in the afternoon." Noah rinsed Rustin's arms off and started on his trunk.

"Wanna go to sleep."

"Soon, okay? You're going to lie on your stomach now, so I can wash your back."

Dr. Todd returned just as Noah was finishing. The two men traded places so that Rustin could see the doctor. "We are going to work on getting you out of here. But Rustin, if we're going too fast, you let us know."

"Go home." Rustin whispered.

"That's what we're working towards. Tomorrow, if you can handle a light breakfast, we'll get that IV out before you have any therapy." Todd paused. "I'm going to check your skin now." The sheet covering his lower body was adjusted, Rustin could feel the cold air in the hospital.

"Dad." Rustin's voice shook. Something didn't feel right.

Robert came up next to Todd. As the doctor lightly ran his fingers over the boy's skin, Robert said, "I love you, Rusi. It shouldn't take long. Take nice deep breaths."

Less than five minutes passed as an ointment applied to his damaged skin; but for Rustin, it was too long. His eyes were getting heavier. As

Dr. Todd covered him with a blanket, his cheek pressed against a soft pillow. "Why here?" he asked, drowsily.

Todd glanced at Robert. Then he looked back at Rustin. "Later, okay. Quit talking so much. Get some rest." Both Todd and Noah left the area.

"I want food Dad."

"I know, Rustin."

"I want bacon, I want pizza, and a burger." Rustin felt lost. He failed to figure out why they would not allow him to shower, but they refused him food as well. He had seen the grey trays being served from the hallway. *Did I do something wrong?* "Not Zack's fault." Rustin's leg kicked out beneath the sheet. His face grimaced as his foot hit the bed rail. "Wanna...wanna play basket-basket balllll." It was becoming increasingly difficult to speak. Rustin's eyes rolled again. "Please."

He watched his father try to smile. "I know you want to play basketball. Soon, okay?" He paused, adjusting the blankets, tucking them in. "You need to sleep, honey."

"Why does it hurt?" His eyes closed, his father's voice grew more and more distant; words seemed to float in the air, words about being safe, vague words about the pain not lasting forever. *Safe from what?* But Rustin was asleep before his lips could form the words.

CHAPTER 34

FACTS

A tlas had tried several times during the past several weeks to meet up with Lechner, but conflicts of time on both sides prevented this from happening until after the new year. His own family had spent the Christmas holiday crowded around Rustin's bed, as they waited for him to awaken.

As Atheists they celebrated Christmas as a tribute to Saint Nicholas, a man who had given to others. They exchanged gifts the night before, and on Christmas Day they volunteered at a homeless shelter. They brought gifts, helped serve food, and socialized with those less fortunate.

This year, with both younger boys in the hospital, they did not take part in the tradition. Instead, they went around the halls of the hospital singing carols with anyone who would join them. Even with the religious stories behind most of the songs, it really didn't matter; music was music.

On January second, Lechner had arranged for the two of them to continue their discussion at an amusement park. Atlas was surprised by this location. That afternoon, Atlas found Lechner by the entryway. "Hello. How are you?"

Lechner paid the fair to get in, even though Atlas tried to pay his own way. Inside the park, he led them to a long line at a roller coaster. Half an hour later, they got on. Atlas sat beside the psychologist as the safety bar was pulled down. "What are we doing here?" Atlas asked as the ride began to move.

"It's an experience." Lechner answered as the ride took off.

When he was younger, riding the roller coaster was a way to get his little brothers to do his chores for him. He remembered one instance when he had dared Jensen to ride the contraption half a dozen times. Atlas laughed at the memory. His seven-year-old brother had thrown up the third time around and Atlas had been grounded for a week and given a two-hundred-word essay to write.

The same feelings went through him as the ride started. The slow incline wasn't too bad; it was the slight pause at the top that gave him a desire to vacate. But, it was too late for that; Atlas screamed as the loop turned him upside-down, and then went through the whole process again before the ride came to a screeching halt. Atlas took a deep breath. When he got off the ride a little off balance, he had to sit down for a minute. Lechner joined him, asking him how he liked it. "Never again," he replied with a laugh.

First, they stopped by the man's car where he pulled a folder from the passenger's seat. Once the car was locked, Atlas followed the psychologist outside the park and across the street to a diner much like Scrappy's. Inside, a server escorted them to a table and both men sat down. Atlas ordered fries and a root beer; it was the most he could handle after the thrilling ride. "That was a blast." Lechner shook his head and Atlas grew nervous. He cleared his throat. "I guess I don't get the connection. I didn't mean to offend you."

"You didn't." The food was set on the table, and after the server left, he continued. "Think back to when we got to the top of the coaster and came down, when we went through the loop. Your heart was pounding, like it was being knocked up against your chest, right? Were you scared?" Atlas shook his head, confused. "What if I suddenly started driving toward you at a high speed, and for whatever reason, you couldn't move. You would panic, right? Your heart would be doing the same thing." The folder Lechner had retrieved from the car had been laying on the table. He opened it and pulled the contents, shoving a stack of paper toward Atlas. "It's called 'misattribution of arousal'."

Atlas read about several male rapes that were studied by a couple of psychologists by the names of Sarrel and Masters. There was one description of a twenty-seven-year-old that had been tied to the bed and blindfolded. He was forced to have sex with three women who threatened him with a knife at his scrotum. "How do they do it? How do they get guys to perform if they're so scared?"

"What happened when you were on that roller coaster is the same thing. It's nothing more than your body reacting to stress. It's a physiological response, there's no control over it, regardless of what most people believe. Little boys have erections all the time. Do we think they have a desire for sex?" Atlas shook his head; it was starting to make sense to him. "Males have had an erection while under attack, and much like female rape victims who have orgasm, males have also ejaculated when raped. It was Alfred Kinsey who first acknowledged that fright, anger, and pain can trigger a sexual response." Lechner took a sip of his drink. "How's your brother? Is he out of the coma yet?"

Atlas nodded. "I talked to my father before I saw you. He's worried. From what he said, Rustin's more worried about Zack. Did I tell you they are identical twins?" Lechner nodded. "I mean, how are we supposed to know the difference between repressed memory and the effects of the head injury?"

"If it's alright with your father, I'd like to be there when they decide it's time to break the news." Atlas watched as Lechner reached for the phone. "What's your father's number again?" He listened while Lechner set a date with Robert on when he should talk to Rustin. Setting down the phone moments later, the psychologist looked at Atlas. "You have something on your mind?"

"Last time we talked, you said my brother wasn't the only one." Lechner nodded, and Atlas was encouraged to continue. "How many guys are we talking about?"

"We're really not all that sure," Lechner answered. "Legislature never considered statutory rape of males' illegal until 1993. We've always known that males make up the majority of physical assault victims, regardless of if the perp is male or female." He took a breath. "Women are assaulted once every fifteen seconds, yet men are seventy-five percent of assault victims. That's every five seconds a man in assaulted; twelve in one minute as compared to four women in the same time span. In 1994, there were approximately four thousand, eight hundred and ninety cases of male rape reported. We also don't look at all the men who are raped in prison each year. I mean. Look at the under reporting that goes on for women, only one in fifty report that they've been raped. Can you imagine what the numbers really are for men? Men are always supposed to be in control, right?"

"Damn," Atlas said in a quiet voice. He spoke louder, "Most of the public only sees that most of the assaults that occur against men, are by other men. That there's a difference when a man hits a woman. I'm not saying that's not important. But do you think people would think differently if women were sexually assaulting other women with blunt objects?"

"I don't know." Lechner looked at his watch and then signaled the server for the checks. "I have a client to see. Just keep your phone on."

He stood up, leaving money on the table. Atlas did the same. "I'll call you with our next meeting."

CHAPTER 35

A MISSING PUZZLE PIECE

J ensen had found his father in the twins' room the next morning; almost a month had passed since they found Rustin. When school had started a week after Christmas, Robert had asked if he would mind staying home until Rustin was released from the hospital; there was still too much going on for Robert to handle everything, even with Craig there. He needed someone on hand if he needed to tend to Zack or any new information that might come in. "Hey, Dad. Is it okay if I go to the school for a couple hours? I want to get this week's assignments, maybe do a practice with Camerata."

He watched his father stack a bunch of paper that was scattered on the desk. Then Robert handed Jensen an SD card. "Yes, of course. Here. Drop this off at the hour photo place before you go, alright? I'm going to see about visiting Zack, and then I'll be there with Rustin."

After Jensen dropped the film off, he pulled into the high school parking lot, and made his way to the office. There was the usual crowd of four or five people behind the desk; students and teachers who were set on finishing their designated task. But when he entered the room, all work ceased and all the attention was then focused on him. It made Jensen nervous. Sure, he could get up and sing in front of over hundred people. Singing, performing, that was easy. The entire audience wasn't just focused on him the whole time. He traded one stack of papers for another with the secretary he had assisted his freshman year. "How is Rustin?" she asked.

And there it was. All that pressure in three little words. Jensen wasn't sure if they really wanted the answer; what they wanted, was hope. "He's doing better," he told them. "Should be starting therapy in a day or two." They wanted to know everything, like when Zack might return to school, and how soon they would be going to court. *We can't go to court until we find them,* Jensen thought. Instead, he smiled and said, "I really don't know. I'm sorry." He was relieved when he could escape the questions that engulfed him every week.

Jensen waved to several acquaintances as he walked down the corridor and across the quad. As he neared the room, he could hear his teacher giving out orders. The piano began and voices soon entered the piece. They sounded almost angelic. *The sopranos actually hit it right this time.* Jensen waited until the music cut off before he entered the room. "Hey guys. Mr. Delaney, sir."

The next forty minutes were spent in the emersion of music and the rhythmic interpretations of voice. Five minutes upon his arrival, the pressures Jensen was under, faded away. Nothing in the world made him feel more at peace than this group that surrounded him; the camaraderie was so real, so intense. And it didn't end with just the members of Camerata, but also those in Chorus. "Are you ready to give us a performance? I want *Just the Five of Us* up front. Jensen, I especially want to hear your solo."

Jensen let Miguel pass him as he retrieved the music from his backpack. He exchanged high fives with Steve as he made it to the front of the classroom, and he grinned at Adrian who was still in the back of the room kissing his girlfriend. "Hey, Nicholson. Stick a cliff note in it." The class laughed as Adrian broke away and joined the rest of them. Without being asked, Julia took the sheet music from Jensen and sat down at the piano.

After the boys completed a couple of warm-up exercises, they snapped their fingers, and on the fourth count Miguel sang. "*Some-times in our lives...*" Julia did a little transition solo on the piano and the five of them came in to sing the main verse. "*Lean on me, when you're not strong...*"

Jensen stepped forward, feeling the music in his blood, and all the tension that was his life, evaporated. He took a deep breath and counted off the beats in his head. Then he sang. *Just call on me, brother-*

Jensen felt Travis step behind him, the tenor's voice high and confident, *Yeah.* He turned to face his best friend and grinned.

The two of them ended the verse in unison. *We all need somebody to lean on.*

The harmony was all there, Julia was right. "All right, stop," Delaney directed. "I like it. Keep working at it." Just then, the bell rang. Jensen was more than a little disappointed that class was over. "Class dismissed."

Jensen grinned and shook hands with the other guys. He waited until the room had cleared out before he went up to talk to the instructor. "Mr. Delaney, sir, can I speak with you for a moment?"

"Sure, Jensen. I wanted to talk to you as well." Mr. Delaney must have seen the puzzled expression on Jensen's face. "I was wondering if you were handling the group okay, considering what's going on at home."

Jensen took a deep breath. "Honestly, sir?" The man nodded. "It's kind of holding me together. I need this." Delaney nodded again, understanding. "I wanted to talk to you about something." Jensen filled the teacher in on the ideas he, Julia, and the guys had discussed.

"If you think you can handle the responsibility of shaping a group of a hundred and thirty singers, go for it."

Jensen was pretty sure the teacher was trying to scare him. He knew there were over a hundred kids within the two groups, but it only made him more determined to make the project work.

He entered the drug store around eleven; Jensen went up to the photo counter and minutes later was handed a yellow envelope. He took out the photos and flipped through them. There were several pictures of the high school basketball team and one of a baby walking toward her mother at the park. As he turned away and put the photos back in the envelope, a child about the age of eight ran up behind him, knocking every picture out of his hand and onto the floor.

"Taylor, I told you not to run in the store." A woman, presumably the girl's mother, apologized. "I'm so sorry, she doesn't think sometimes. Let me help you pick those up."

"Hey, no prob-"Jensen picked up the last picture. In the center of the picture was a large thumb print. Quickly, he laid out all the pictures on the counter and went through them, one by one. More than half the stack were expert photos; those he paid no attention to. No, the ones he focused on, the photos that caught his attention were the photos that were angled wrong. One of them appeared to be a smeared face. Jensen set aside the one picture and went through the whole stack again. A side view of the bank on Polk Street, black sleeves with hands that clutched a moneybag, and a clear mug shot of Officer Meyers dressed in regular day clothes, a revolver in hand. Without another word, Jensen grabbed everything and ran to the car with nothing on his mind except getting to the hospital.

‒ ⋅ ‒

CHAPTER 36

CHECKERS

Having gained special privileges for good behavior, Zack could go outside in the hospitals garden for recreation. When he had asked the staff if he could take a board game outside and play it with another patient, he was awarded five points for taking an initiative.

"What are you going to do when you get home?" Zack had spent a lot of time with Isabelle over the past week. They sat together at meals and spent their free time talking about life's pressures, school, and family. The girl didn't have much of anything, family or support group of any kind. She had spent most of her youth in the foster care system. He realized that, yes life sometimes got bad, but he did have a lot to back him up when he needed it. Zack set up a game of checkers. He let Isabelle make the first move.

"I'm not sure." Isabelle moved her red piece to the safer outer edges. "I want to get back to drama at school. Maybe take up piano again."

Zack looked the girl in the eyes, then made his move. "I have a brother who plays piano, guitar, too. He's so mathematical about the whole thing, it makes me wonder how he has any fun." He heard the door open behind him. His name was called. Zack turned around in his seat and found Malakai looking at him. "Yeah?" *Please don't say it's time to pee.*

"Your dad is here."

Zack slowly rose to his feet and walked to the attendant. "It's only Tuesday." He could hear the tremor in his own voice.

"You're going to deal with things as they come," Malakai told him. "Don't jump to conclusions." Zack took a deep breath. He followed the man through a security door and walked with him to the end of a bright corridor. One of his therapists met with him and led him into a small conference room. Zack took a moment to look around; the wooden table in the center of the room was surrounded by four chairs. Only one of them was occupied. But not for long. Robert stood up and for several minutes Zack refused to meet his father's gaze.

"It wasn't your fault. Look at me, Zack." Slowly, Zack brought his head up. "Did you know it was Meyers?"

"I heard his voice," Zack replied in a soft voice. His hands balled into fists. "Rusi, was on a cliff. He said, *the boy needs to be fucked with.*'

"If he's still hearing voices- "Concerned, the attendant stepped forward.

"Just shut up." Robert shook his head. "Sorry." He sat back down and beckoned to his son to take a seat. As Zack sat down across from his dad, Robert pulled an envelope from inside his coat pocket.

"How's Rusi?" Zack was asking about his brother, but his eyes never left the envelope. Pictures were something his dad and Rustin spent time going over. "What's with the envelope?"

"He's doing better," Robert answered. "Tell me, did you use Rustin's camera?" Zack nodded, the hairs on the back of his neck stood on end. He had taken the camera several weeks before the attack; he wanted to figure out what attracted Rustin to photography. Zack had gotten bored after only a few minutes. He didn't even realize that he was still clicking aimlessly with the camera. That's when the bank robbers had shoved him. Zack grew pale. His head swam. "Tiger, are you okay?"

Shaking his head clear, Zack took the envelope from his father. His fingers trembled as he pulled out the photos. On top, was a picture that was clearly angled wrong, and the top of the officer's head had been cut off. But clearly, it was Meyers with his gun. "Oh, damn." Zack took several deep breaths as he tried to calm his nerves. But the bile rose anyway. "He knew," Zack sputtered as he threw up on the table. "He knew I saw the robbery." Zack got to his feet and paced. "Rusi, did get hurt because of me."

Malakai left the room as Robert approached Zack; he laid a hand on the boy's arm. "You're safe now. Both of you are safe."

The attendant returned with a paper bag that had his name on it, the same one that had disappeared the night they admitted him. He put it at the opposite end of the table. Malakai looked at Robert, "Are you sure you want him released?"

"Get dressed, Zack. We have to leave soon." Zack changed his clothes. "Remember, tiger. You and Rustin are identical twins. Very few people can tell the two of you apart without hesitating. And these assholes didn't know there were two of you until Bennett walked into the house several days after the initial missing person's report was made."

Zack pulled on his socks and tied his shoelaces. "It was supposed to be me, Dad. They wanted to kill me, and they tried to kill Rusi instead." He sat back in the chair and slouched. He remembered the connection from that night, the connection he shared with his twin brother. He remembered how ill he had gotten when the attack first happened. "I knew it was Meyers. Ask them, Dad. I even told them it was Meyers." Zack paused. The next time he spoke, the words came out as if he were remembering an event from long ago. "There were three of them. Meyers and a woman and another guy. The one who got on his back." He looked up at Robert. "He said, *He's gonna have to get us a little more than that.* It wasn't Bennett, Dad. It wasn't."

Malakai was listening to the exchange with a puzzled look on his face. "Have you always given into his delusions?" he asked Robert.

"They aren't delusions. It's hard to explain." Robert grabbed his cell phone. But he made sure he addressed Zack first. "I believe you, Zack. We're getting you and Rustin out of here." He pushed speed dial. "Craig, it's me." Robert reached out for the clipboard Malakai handed him and signed his son out. "I'm not sure. Maybe a vanilla milkshake." He looked at Zack again. "What do you want to eat?"

"Fast food?" Robert nodded. "A burger and onion rings. Chocolate milkshake. And a sundae?"

Robert laughed out loud as he repeated the order to Craig. "I'm going to go by the department store on Sutter. I'll meet you at the airport in an hour."

"The airport?" Zack asked after his father hung up the phone. They started outside and to his dad's Cadillac. "Where are we going?"

At the department store, Robert explained that the boys, the twins, would be going somewhere with Craig. He wouldn't say anymore. Robert grabbed two matching pairs of blue jeans, a bag of black socks, and a bag of boxers. He had sent Zack to the other side of the men's section to grab a couple shirts. But when Robert went to track him down, he found Zack focused on a collection of rings that were on display. "What's going on, Zack? We're kind of in a hurry."

A smiling woman in a business suit came behind the counter. "Can I interest you in anything?"

"I need something. I need a ring. I need a promise ring." Zack's eyes scanned the display. "The kind that are two rings in one."

"We are having a sale on our couple's rings," The woman said, smiling. She pulled out a variety of rings.

Okay, okay. Robert's eyes scanned the area and grabbed two flannels of different colors, a couple long-sleeved shirts and matching hoodies. "Zack. You take the last of your meds and I'll get you a ring. But we have to hurry." Robert took a bottle of pills from his pocket and gave a capsule to his son who swallowed the pill without water.

Zack's eyes scanned the rings and a moment later he pointed. "That one."

—•—

CHAPTER 37

SHOCK, SHOCK, AND MORE SHOCK

Rustin woke up that morning to the sound of squeaky carts being rolled down the hall; breakfast would be served soon. He turned on the television and flipped through the stations, an infomercial on some miracle product, way too many soap operas, and a Jerry Springer type show about a cross-dressing cultist who wanted to have Brad Pitt's baby. Rustin groaned as he turned the TV off. Instead, he laid back and tried to remember what happened. *Why am I even here?*

Taking in his surroundings, Rustin took a moment to read the dry erase board that hung on the wall. The board listed the day of the week, the date, his medications, and the names of his nurse and doctor. It listed medical treatments, like IV fluids, fever control, and wound care. The board also listed two goals. The first goal was to manage pain. The second goal stated that all medical attendants be male. Robert and Atlas's phone numbers were also posted.

A moment later, Noah walked into the room. "How's your head?" The nurse took hold of his wrist and looked at his watch.

"It's fine. Why am I here?"

Noah stuck a thermometer in his mouth. "You're at Saint Francis Memorial Hospital." The nurse refused to answer the question. A moment later, he was recording the boy's temperature. Noah must have sensed that Rustin was upset. "Relax, okay? Look, your breakfast is here." Noah took the tray of food from the cafeteria worker, laid it on the bedside table, and removed the cover. The table was rolled up to the bed. "Eat up, Rustin. You have therapy in an hour."

Rustin stared hard at the nurse as he headed for the door. He could feel tears of unwanted emotion well up behind his eyes. Rustin felt helpless and was angry. He shoved the tray of food off the table and screamed as it clattered to the floor. "Tell me why it hurts. Tell me why I'm here!"

The nurse went over to the intercom to page the doctor. When he was finished, he stepped up to the bed. Noah grabbed a napkin; he wiped up a bit of food that had stained Rustin's hospital gown. "You need to calm down, Rustin. Dr. Todd will be here in a minute, he'll decide what's best. Tell me what hurts."

Rustin shifted in his bed as he tried to hide his flushed cheeks; he wasn't about to tell Noah or even his dad about the pain; the embarrassment just wasn't worth it. "No. It's not fair." Dr. Todd walked into the room, and as the nurse stepped back, he approached the bed. With him was a stranger introduced as Adam Lechner. Rustin refused to let the adults off the hook, if he did, they would continue to keep secrets from him. "It's my life. I hate you. All you do is lie to me. Why won't you tell me anything. I want to go home." Rustin felt his throat tighten.

The doctor never raised his voice. "Kiddo, you need to calm down." Rustin, about to burst out again, stopped as Todd laid a hand on his arm. "Rustin. You came in with a head injury and extensive wounds because of an attack." Todd told him how he had been missing for three days and how he had been found by a river in Colma.

Lechner stepped up to the bed. The man was tall, his voice steady and full of confidence. Whatever he came for, there would not be an effort on his part to avoid truth or responsibility. "Rustin, do you remember being attacked?"

Rustin tried to remember, tried his hardest, but all he could recall was a fight he had had with Zack. "Was Zack there? Did someone hurt Zack?" Rustin's breath quickened. He struggled to get out of bed and got a leg over the railing before he was stopped. Dr. Todd pushed him back. He took hold of both Rustin's wrists and squeezed them until the boy's eyes were on his.

"Relax, kiddo. Your dad is with Zack, right now." The doctor paused. "I want you to eat breakfast and have your therapy. Then I'll tell you the rest. No lies, I promise."

Another tray of food was put on the bed tray, and once the cover was removed Rustin was shocked; the plate held two eggs, toast and jam, and a small carton of apple juice. "I don't want this crap!" Rustin was exhausted. All the emotion that came out seemed to drain him; he felt as if he were going to cry at any second. "Please. I want real food. I want pancakes and sausage, and those potato thingies. Zack got to have a burger, please. I'll cook it if you want me to, and I'll make extra," Rustin didn't want to lay there anymore. He even made another attempt at getting out of bed. The doctor again restrained him. "Please."

Breakfast was high caloric Dr. Todd explained. It was an attempt to get Rustin's body weight back up to what it was supposed to be. "We'll bring you another tray in two hours." The doctor took a moment to check the bandage on the boy's head. "Eat up, kiddo. You have therapy in fifteen minutes." The doctor and Lechner left the room.

Noah took his time. He removed the lid from the tray of food first and then grabbed the remote that was laid on the edge of the bed. He allowed the head of the bed to rise to an angle and then stopped. He then brought the tray closer to the bed.

Rustin watched as the nurse took the plastic knife in his hand and cut his eggs into several pieces. Then Noah brought a spoonful of egg to the boy's mouth. The first bite was delicious; sure, it was hospital food, but it seemed like he hadn't eaten in ages. The nutrition that came from the IV just didn't cut it. Rustin wanted nothing more than to devour everything on his plate and then demand more. But after only two bites, he was pleading with his stomach not to regurgitate what he had just consumed. Noah could see it in his eyes.

"How're those first bites, Rustin? Do you want some more?" Rustin nodded and Noah prepared another bite. "Your stomach's getting used to processing food again, so we're going to take it slow." Noah stopped for a moment. He grabbed a bucket from the corner of the room and placed it at the end of the bed. The nurse then opened the sample of strawberry jam and spread the contents on a piece of toast. "Let's try some of this now."

Rustin had finished half of what was on his tray when a man knocked on his door and entered. "Hello, I'm Nat. Do you remember me?" Rustin nodded. "Are you ready to work those muscles?"

Noah was watching him with an inordinate amount of concern, Rustin could sense it. But he couldn't understand why. It was as if both men expected him to snap at any moment. *They promised me they would tell me what happened. So, what's the big deal?* Rustin took a deep breath. "What do I have to do?"

Several minutes were spent testing Rustin's strength; Nat had him push against the palms of the therapist's hands with his feet. It was a good ten minutes later when the sheets were pulled to the end of the bed. "How about we try to get you to your feet?"

Rustin turned on to his stomach as the bed rail was let down. Subconsciously, his mind was aware of where the man's hands were, more like hyper-aware. But he thought and felt nothing as Nat's hands grasped him under the arms. It felt great to have the ground beneath his feet. "Rustin, you alright?" Rustin nodded. "Okay. Let me know if you get lightheaded." He turned around, the therapist's hands still supported him.

Rustin faced Noah. The distance between the two of them may have only been a couple feet. But to Rustin, it seemed like miles. "Come on, Rus. The first step is always the hardest," he heard the nurse encourage. That first step was like his first breath without the ventilator. His body would not cooperate; it would not do as he asked it to. His leg felt like a totem pole, something buried beneath the linoleum floor.

The therapist's hands moved down his trunk, to his hips, and then to the back of his leg. "Put all your weight on your -"

Rustin gasped. His legs folded and if it weren't for Nat, he would have face planted. The room turned black and cold. The air was suffocating. *Give me the camera, you little bastard. He's gonna have to give us a little more than that.* "Please no, please. I'm sorry, please." Rustin's breath continued to come out in harsh gasps. Cruel hands, real or not, disappeared from his leg. Like a light switch, the darkness was gone.

Light seemed to filter back into the room. "I got you, Rustin."

"Ease him to the floor," Noah said as he took a step backwards. "I'll get the doctor."

The words of reassurance were muffled. "Deep breaths. Take it easy."

For a while, Rustin thought he heard other voices, somewhere in the background. His eyes, having glazed over, closed. But when he opened his eyes again, he found himself crumpled on the floor; Lechner and his nurse were by his side. Nat was nowhere to be seen. "What happened?" Rustin's voice quivered; his mind raced. "I'm not-I'm not gay." He grasped Lechner's wrist with his fingers and brought his shaky legs beneath him. Rustin pulled himself to his feet. A more important issue came to mind. But with his head swimming strokes that left him blinded, the issue was carried away by the tides. Rustin fell forward into Lechner's chest.

The two men helped Rustin over to a chair in the room's corner. Noah knelt in front of him, his strong hands on the boy's arms. "Bring your head down between your knees. That's it. Now, take slow even breaths." Everything fell silent for a while, just the beating sound of Rustin's heart filled his ears; it beat quickly then tapered off to a steady rhythm. "When your head stops pounding, when the black dots go away, you can bring your head up." Several more minutes passed in silence. Noah was about to call for the doctor when Rustin raised his head. "You feeling okay?"

Rustin looked at Lechner who was standing by the nurse. "Am I?"

"What, Rustin?"

"Am I gay?" Confused, Rustin looked at Noah and then back to Lechner. "Is that why you're guys?"

Lechner shook his head. "This is not now, nor has it ever been, about whether you're gay."

Rustin's brow came closer together; Noah cleared his throat. "I heard your dad talking to you while you were in a coma. He talked about a girl you liked. Someone named Natalie."

Shaking his head, Rustin brought the palms of his hands to his temples. He remembered Natalie, could see her face in his mind. "Why?"

He saw Noah glance at Lechner and then approached Rustin. He started removing the IV from his wrist. "Can you ask me again? I don't understand what you're asking."

Rustin winced as the needle was removed, a cotton ball taped into place. "Aren't nurses supposed to be girls?"

Noah looked at Lechner and nodded. "Most of us are. Rustin,

do you remember any part of what just happened?" The boy looked puzzled. "We just got you off the floor. Do you remember why you were on the floor?"

Rustin's brow crinkled. A moment passed, and he shook his head. "It was dark. That's all. He said it wasn't about being gay.... What was it about? What was it?"

The room went silent. "You just had a panic attack." Lechner took a deep breath. "Some part of you remembers. It's why those of us who surround you are all males. It's why touch and restraint of any kind cause you to react. It's why the sound of a woman's voice causes you to have an attack. Rustin, look at me." Rustin brought his eyes to Lechner and saw both clarity and nervousness. "Someone raped you."

Rustin shook his head. "Guys can't get raped."

"Rustin. Someone beat the crap out of you. Someone hit you over the head with something, probably a gun. And someone, maybe more than someone, assaulted you sexually." Lechner paused for a moment, trying to let it sink in. "Your body hurts. Doesn't it?"

It was at that moment that Robert, Dr. Todd, and Officer Bennett entered the room. Rustin tried to bolt from his seat. Noah put a hand lightly on his shoulder, preventing him from getting to his feet. "Dad, you're a lawyer. Tell them. Tell them guys can't get raped. I just fell."

"Oh, boy," Robert muttered. Taking a deep breath, he approached his son. "We can discuss legality later, okay? We must get you dressed and then we'll go to the airport."

"Why?" Rustin asked as Robert handed a stack of clothes to the nurse. Noah laid out each piece of clothing and then moved to shut the door.

"Because it's in your best interests."

"Is Zack okay?" His father nodded and then turned his attention toward Todd and Bennett.

A moment passed and then another. "Let's get this hospital gown off of you." Noah slipped the gown from Rustin's arms. He then pulled a long-sleeved shirt over the boy's head. "Where's your arms, bud? There you go. Let's get your pants now."

Too tired to lift them on his own, Rustin watched the nurse take one leg and then the other. He was then helped to his feet, his pants pulled up into place. It was then that exhaustion fell over Rustin's body like a sudden downpour of sleet. His face paled, his head fell forward. His body crumpled. "Too tired. Head hurts."

As Dr. Todd left, Noah grabbed him under the arms. "I've got you."

Moments later, Todd was back carrying a box of supplies With him were two attendants pushing a stretcher. Noah picked Rustin up using the firefighter's carry and laid him down. Both side rails were pulled up. The nurse took a moment to put socks on the boy's feet before covering him with a blanket.

Robert was at the back of the room with Bennett. "If you have anything to do with the attack on my son, if I find out that you are informing Meyers on the location of where my boys will be, I will legally hunt you down and make you pay for this." Rustin had never heard his father threaten anyone before in his life. "Zack trusts you. That is the only reason I have not insisted you be removed from this case."

Rustin's attention turned to Dr. Todd who had removed the gauze from his head. "It's healing nicely, kiddo." After the incision site was cleaned and again bandaged, the doctor looked at Rustin. "You need to have someone help you change the bandage twice a day. You need to take it easy. If you ever get those headaches where you can't see straight, where the pain is so bad you can't sit up, or you throw up, get to the hospital." Todd looked at Robert and handed him the box. This is so he has enough supplies to last a week. Mild pain killers are also there.

Use them accordingly."

Robert nodded. "I'll let his uncle know."

"Hang in there, kiddo." Dr. Todd looked at the attendants. "I'm going to send him with a compress for his head. I'll be right back."

Noah was standing by the stretcher. He helped Rustin to sit up and then leaned him against his chest. "You come see us when this is all over, okay? Try to relax now. Just go with it."

Todd returned with a tray holding three items. The tray was set at the end of the stretcher. "This is a painkiller." A small paper cup of water and a pill were handed to the boy. "It'll take a little while for it to kick in. Let's lie you down now." Todd helped Noah to secured Rustin to the stretcher. Todd laid the compress on the boy's right temple. Noah lifted Rustin's heavy arm and laid the teddy bear beneath it.

"I don't need the bear," he murmured. Fifteen-year-olds weren't supposed to have stuffed animals.

Everyone in the room insisted that he take the bear with him. "It'll help you through the hard times, Rustin. Keep a hold on it." Todd squeezed his hand.

Determined to speak with Zack, Rustin fought the painkiller's side effect as he was rolled out in the hallway and then into the bitter cold off outside before being lifted, into an ambulance. It took a good twenty minutes to get to the airport. The ambulance came to a stop just a couple feet from the helicopter.

The medication was just about to drag him under when the doors of the ambulance opened. Suddenly, the air got even cooler as the stretcher was loaded into aircraft. Robert ruffled Zack's hair, shook Craig's hand, and then leaned over and kissed Rustin on the forehead.

"You're not coming?" he heard Zack ask.

"I'll be in contact with Craig, okay? I need to stay in San Francisco right now." The noise of the helicopter cut off the rest of the man's words. Robert tucked the blanket around Rustin a little tighter and then stepped back. The door shut, and the aircraft lifted into the air.

Laying down, Rustin tried to remember the last time he had seen any of his closest friends, Eric and Natalie. Especially Natalie. *Maybe Eric was right. Maybe it didn't matter that they had shared a bathtub together when they were three. Hell, even Zack had been there. Zack would have asked Natalie out by now if his brother wasn't so different from him.* Embarrassing pictures of Zack and Natalie started going through his head. Rustin laughed them off. *It was bad, man. But not that bad.* A fuzzy scene started going through his head. He wasn't sure if it was real or not. *I'm in a photography class. We were looking at old photo books from past students. 'I could've taken better pictures with my eyes closed.'* "Zack." Rustin tried again, louder. "Zack." He saw his brother look at him. "What did you think about Mom's old photo book?" The struggle to form complete sentences was becoming intense. "The one from high school?" He watched as Zack took a sip from a large paper cup, from a fast-food place.

"What are you talking about?" Zack went to hand the drink over and found Rustin unable to lift his hand. He held the cup up to his brother's lips and waited for him to swallow. "Dad said we don't have any."

"Zack, let him sleep." Craig thought the discussion had gone on long enough. Rustin was clearly struggling to even have this conversation.

Zack tried to do as his uncle asked. Rustin, however, was determined to go on. "We found it in old school projects she had us look at. Mom's was there." Rustin went back in his mind. He could place himself in the classroom, could hear the bell ring. He watched himself put the book in his backpack. He left to find Zack. *Because no way in the world*, the fuzzy picture froze with Rustin obviously mad about something and heading into the school's hallway.

"Rustin, please. You need to stop." Craig shifted the compress to the other side of Rustin's head.

"I was mad." Rustin's eyes rolled. Again, he struggled. He tried desperately not to allow the drugs to grab him, take control of him anymore than they already had. His head pressed back against the pillow. Tears came to his eyes, and it wasn't long before a hand wiped his face dry. When he looked up one last time, he saw Craig gazing down at him. "Not his fault."

"I know, Rus. Go to sleep now, okay?"

Rustin felt Zack press his fingers against his own. His eyes finally closed. The pain was no more.

CHAPTER 38

RESPOND

Robert stood back and watched as the helicopter rose into the sky and took off. Stations on the radio and TV were broadcasting an urgent story about the child who had been attacked and left for dead in Colma several weeks ago. He was transported from Saint Francis Memorial Hospital to an undisclosed location earlier that morning. The news reported that the boy was being moved somewhere in the state of Texas, near relatives. Evidence had turned up that had led to the decision to hospitalize the child elsewhere; police were doing all they could but were having difficulty. The father refused to comment.

Of course he refused to comment. But apparently radio talk show thought different. They knew, obviously, what they would do in the same situation. Responsibility was the issue that was brought up time and time again, Robert's, the family structure the criminals, and society. "This is KR72, the station where your voice counts," the disc jockey bellowed the stations call numbers. "This is Rick Diamonds, we're back, and we want to hear more of your opinions on this whole rape case involving Justin Carson, a young man from Pacific Heights. Caller, you're on."

"Hi, Rick. I'm Andrea Scott. I listen to your station all the time."

"Thanks, Andrea."

"I think the father's in on it. Don't feed me any lines about male rape, the whole thing's ludicrous." Robert could hear the venom in the woman's voice, determined to make her point clear. "He took part in a sexual encounter and deserves to pay for the consequences of his actions. And I want to know where the mother is in all this? We wonder why our kids are ending up in prison, and it's because kids aren't made to face the consequences of their actions. If he got the girl pregnant, he should be paying her child support."

"Well, now. That statement has conservative written all over it. When we come back, terrori-"

The idiots couldn't even get his name right. Robert turned off the stereo and tried to get his thoughts in order. Jensen had called him after he had discovered the incriminating photos. Robert then had a long talk with Keisha, trying to find the best way to protect his sons. His associate had pointed out that once Rustin and Zack were out of the city, the assailants would probably follow them. Robert still wasn't sure if those involved in the crime knew that they had attacked a twin; if they did, they wouldn't let something as trivial as travel put them at risk for incarceration. Which brought up the question, why had they attacked Rustin to begin with. The photos discovered on his son's SD card had solved that question. So, Robert had asked Craig to take the boys to San Diego until the criminals were caught. He wanted to stay in the city to make sure everything was being done correctly. He still had his doubts about Bennett's lack of involvement in the attack.

In the driveway of his gated home, Robert turned off the engine and stepped out, slamming the door shut behind him. Atlas was on the front porch. He stood up as his father made his way to the front door. "Your grandparents?" Robert asked.

"They got off safely."

He noticed two other cars besides theirs in front of the house; one of them he recognized. "Keisha's here. Who else?"

Atlas nodded as both men headed in doors. "Adam Lechner. They're in the living room. Do you want me to take them up to the library?"

Wanting to speak freely and feel secure while doing so, Robert nodded. "Please. I'll be there in a minute."

Robert had a tray of coffee in his hands a while later and carefully set it down on the table. He poured a cup for each of them. Straightening himself up, Robert looked at the man he had seen in Rustin's hospital room. He had a bald head and intense blue eyes. Robert stuck his hand out. "I'm Robert Carson. Atlas, Jensen, Rustin, and Zack's father. You must be Adam Lechner."

After shaking hands, everyone sat down around the large table in the middle of a room surrounded by mahogany bookshelves. Robert had kept every law book he read in college and still bought the thick, overweight penal code book every year they published. He'd been doing that since the late nineteen sixties, and the bookshelves proved it. Also, on the shelves were many books written by John Grisham. Occasionally, Atlas liked to read them and pick out all the flaws, and then he and his dad, sometimes Keisha and Nathan too, would debate the matter. Of course, there hadn't been time for that lately, with everything that was going on.

For a while, the discussion revolved around the attack. They talked about everything from the two crime scenes, the rape, and the involvement of Bennett. Robert mentioned what Zack had said about the officer. Atlas nodded. "He was the one who acknowledged Meyers's failure of informing the school. He even tried to make things right by making a call to his superior. And didn't Zack say he didn't see Bennett there?"

"That doesn't mean he's not involved, Atlas, you know that. And as connected as I know the twins are." Robert shook his head. "Zack may have good judgement of character, but he's only fifteen years old. He's never dealt with criminals until now." The phone rang as he poured himself another cup of coffee. "I would give anything-" He was cut off when Jensen came into the room and handed him the phone. "Excuse me. Hello?"

"Mr. Carson, or should I call you Robbie?" The male voice was deep and throaty, like someone trying to disguise his real voice. "I know the boys in San Diego. Two of them I do believe." Robert's face went as white as a sheet of cake. Everyone in the room had their eyes on Robert. "Not like I'm trying to throw it in your face or anything, but I wonder what it's like to fuck twins. Have you ever fucked twins, Robbie?" He pointed to Keisha, *Call cops now* he mouthed. As Keisha rushed out of the room, he took a deep breath. He knew he had to keep the suspect on the line as long as possible.

The other line was full of static, which probably meant he was calling from a cell phone. *Damn.*

"I could be outside your home right now. I could be working for the police or against them." The voice paused. When he spoke again, Robert could tell he was smiling. "These shots I got of your boy in the hospital. My friend got some beauties. Should I keep them? Maybe I'll post them."

"They're already charging you with rape and attempted murder. Don't think you can — "

"Get away with what, Robbie?" The laugh that followed made Robert's blood sting like fire. The voice, the threat, everything inside him told him it was Meyers on the other line. "Robbie, come on now. Both you and I know it's impossible for me to rape your boys, as much as I would like to. But go ahead. Keep moving them. They won't stay hidden for long. Besides, the chase makes it so fun." There was another laugh, and the line went dead.

A silent moment passed and then another. Robert took several deep breaths as he put the phone down on the table. *Think. He said it was impossible for me to rape.* He knew the man was right, legally. At least in the state of California. Rape had to be between a male and a female, a male forcing himself on another male would be the crime of sodomy. *Zack had said there were three culprits. Was Meyers the one who had sodomized his son?*

Keisha walked in with Bennett. The officer confirmed that the call could not be traced. Robert reiterated the conversation. "There's more than one suspect, and one of them is a female. We thought so." Bennett cleared his throat. "Before I get to that, there's another problem. I went to the evidence locker to take the clothing down to the lab for another round of testing. It's empty, the entire shelf is empty and there's no record on who took it out."

Robert looked at the cop as another piece seemed to fall into place. "You should have heard his voice. He was going through the pictures that were taken at the hospital. He threatened to post them. *Bennett must know. How can he not know?* "Bennett, where is Meyers?"

"No one has seen him in the past week." Bennett paused, his eyes falling across the room, on to Keisha and then Atlas. He cleared his throat, looking Robert directly in the eye. "When we checked his house, his wife said he was doing research on some bogus case. She said he had even missed his daughter's ballet recital." Again, he paused. Then he tried to smile. "On a better note, we did find out who the other two suspects are. Nicole Taylor-" Robert heard the change in Bennett' voice.

"You know her?" Were Robert's fears about to be confirmed?

Bennett nodded and sighed. "She's one of our dispatchers and apparently Meyers's mistress. Oscar Hernandez has also been found. It's only a matter of time before we find Sergeant Meyers and Nicole."

CHAPTER 39

CAMARADERIE PREVAILS

Jensen took a deep breath. After he had showed his dad the developed pictures, Jensen had been encouraged to blow off some steam. When there was something that Robert thought he should know, then he would call; it was like waiting for an inevitable explosion. But he had decided to do as his father suggested. He called the guys and suggested they meet at the mall.

Before going to the mall, he went by and picked up Julia. Travis had said he'd take his car, that way he and Julia could just go straight home later. The ride was short and silent; there was a tension in the car. Jensen hoped hanging with his friends would help ease it. He pulled into a parking space in the mall's underground lot. "Damn, we've got a lot to do before the concert," he muttered. He pulled the keys out of the ignition, and after stuffing them in his pocket, ran both hands through his hair. "I don't know why I didn't just have you and the other girls take care of this."

"Jensen, you're directing this." Julia's tone was sharp. He remembered their first fight six months ago, and he didn't want to have another, especially now, considering everything that was going on. "It's your vision."

He leaned over and kissed his girlfriend on the cheek. "I know. I'm sorry." Jensen blew out a breath of air he didn't know he had been holding.

"What's going on? You're never snappy, not even when Rustin was missing."

He laughed, "Yeah, I was." Jensen paused. "You can only tell Travis, okay?" Julia nodded. "Dad sent Rustin and Zack somewhere with my uncle. I just..." He was surprised when his voice broke. He took a deep breath as he tried to get his emotions under control. But the tears came anyway. "I can't do this anymore, Jul...I can't." Jensen wanted to say more but couldn't find the words. He gripped the steering wheel with both hands. He remembered the stress of the past couple months. He was the one who greeted concerned people when Rustin was first missing, he looked after Zack when his father and uncle were busy, and he had spent hours in Rustin's hospital room. It was as if everything bombarded him at once. No matter how hard he tried, the tears would not stop.

Jensen felt Julia's hand stroked the back of his head. "If your dad had them go someplace that probably means they're close to finding whoever did this."

"We gotta go, Julia. The guys are waiting." Jensen tried to get out of the car, but Julia grabbed him by the arm. "Tyrese said to meet them in front of Burger King."

"No, stop. They can wait." Julia again pulled on his arm. "Jensen, it's not your fault."

"Dammit, it's not about fault." Jensen pulled away from his girl-friend and got out of the car. "You didn't see him, Julia. You didn't see what they did to him."

Julia got out of the car and shut the door. She looked at Jensen over the hood of the car. "Tell me, then. Tell me everything." Julia went around to the other side of the car and, getting on her tip toes, put her arms around his neck, kissing him. "Come on." She took hold of his hand and the two of them walked across the street and into the mall. She took him into the nearest fast-food place, not Burger King, and went up to the counter.

Jensen shook his head. He pulled his wallet from his back pocket, and it was then that he realized how bad his hands were shaking. "Help me," he whispered. "Please." Swallowing a lump in his throat, he allowed himself to let go of some of the control he had been forced to endure; he handed his wallet to Julia.

After buying a couple of drinks, Julia led them to a table in the back of the restaurant; she sat down as he put his wallet back in his pocket. "Talk to me," she said.

Jensen took a sip from his straw and looked into Julia's eyes. "It was the nastiest wound I had ever seen, Jules. They literally tore him open. And when he had that seizure, I was so sure he was going to die." He took another swallow from his cup. "I don't want to talk anymore, okay?" Julia nodded. Jensen paused and looked down at the floor. "It's just-It seems like no one's really taking this seriously enough."

"What about your dad?"

This is what Jensen had needed all along, and he knew it. "Dad always takes us seriously. When he's not making sure Zack's okay, he's spending time with Rustin. But the cops, especially Meyers, are just making me mad." He led Julia out into the middle of the mall and started toward Burger King. A small group of teenagers soon surrounded them.

"Hey Carson, you're late." Miguel had his arms around Elizabeth who fought to get away.

"You sodding wanker, let go." The girl was laughing.

Jensen fist bumped Tyrese, Travis, and Steve. "What's up?"

Miguel released Elizabeth, looking somewhat confused. He glanced at Julia. "Translation, please."

Julia looked over at Elizabeth who shook her head, smiling. "She called you a sodomizing masturbator. In American terms, 'fucking asshole'."

Miguel scoffed, his hand clutching his chest. "And I thought girls from Britain were supposed to be all polite and whatnot." Everyone laughed.

Steve rubbed his hands together. "Let's do this fast. The last thing I need is for my sister to find me here. Black slacks and shoes, right? Are we going casual? I mean, it would be easy to buy a bunch of hooded sweatshirts...or a flannel?"

Travis shook his head. "SFUHS choirs have never been about casual. You know Delaney, he'd never go for that."

Tyrese looked at Jensen. "That leaves dress shirts in bold colors, right?"

Jensen nodded. *What the hell are we doing?* He rubbed his hands together and laughed. "Maybe not all bold colors. We'll have to see what they have."

The entire experience was almost comical, and in the end, it would have probably been simpler if they had shopped the way Jensen had suggested in the car. The girls could have figured out everything with the guys not even there. The problem was, there was too much clothing to look at, and every time they came close to deciding, someone would have an objection, especially Miguel who was always worried about the expression of his manhood.

It was Julia who picked a dress shirt off a rack in a popular department store. "Look at this. It's a button down, it has the collar. They've got several colors here."

Jensen looked at the shirt and nodded. "How many ranges? Three, right? Baritone, bass and tenor. There's no point in breaking the tenors down, there's only six of them." Everyone nodded. He looked at the purple shirt Julia was holding, then pulled off the rack a blue and green shirt in the same style. "Any ideas for the girls?"

"Wait a minute, you're not done yet," Julia said. "*Just the Five of Us* is a group in its own right. You guys are leading everyone else. Shouldn't that be expressed?"

The debate started up again. What were they trying to say through the music? How could they express the camaraderie they shared? With *Just the Five of Us* leading, how could they show the group coming together on stage? As Miguel said more than once during the rift, the guys of Camerata ended up spending just as much on their outfits as the girls did when they performed. It was in this time frame of several hours, that the Americans learned to appreciate British slang.

CHAPTER 40

ASHLEY'S SURPRISE

"B renna, dinner." Atlas used a ladle with teeth to scoop a small serving of spaghetti onto a plastic plate. The child's plate was divided into four sections. He added a piece of garlic bread, a scoop of buttered green beans. He finished the plate off with half a peach cut into sections. He brought the plate to the table. Silverware that matched the princess plate were set to the right side along with a napkin. "Brenna!"

Atlas could hear his little girl's feet padding quickly down the hall. "Here I am."

"Put your dolly down. It's time to eat." He watched her drop the doll to the floor. Then he swung her up, gave her a kiss, and sat her in her booster seat at the table.

"Bwenna thirsty." She looked down at her plate and scrunched up her nose. "Beans yucky."

Atlas brought his plate to the table and sat next to her. "No drink until you eat your dinner. Green beans first. Then you can eat whatever you want."

"Peachies?" she asked. Atlas nodded. Brenna gave a little sigh as she picked up her fork and speared a bean. Bringing the vegetable up to eye level, her nose wrinkled as she put it in her mouth. She gagged once but then ate the beans that were left on her plate.

"Good girl. If you finish what's on your plate, you can have ice cream for dessert."

"Banilla?" Atlas nodded. He watched as the little girl ate her garlic bread.

Dinner lasted another fifteen minutes; another five was spent eating a small portion of the single scoop of vanilla ice cream. "Time to clean the table. Can you bring your plate to the sink, please?"

Atlas put the last dish in the rack and turned off the water. Something small agitated his pant leg, and when he looked down, he found Brenna beside him, tomato sauce and noodles entangled in her hair. She was trying to hand him a dish rag. "Thank you, Brenna."

"I clean the table."

Looking at the dining room table, Atlas saw crumbs spread at one end and another pile of crumbs on the floor, along with a sippy cup. But the area around Brenna's booster seat seemed spotless. "Good job, honey. Let's have a bath now."

"Daddy," Brenna whispered.

"What?" Atlas knelt in front of his daughter, curious what secret she had to tell. *Maybe Piglet had a thing for Pooh. Or Bert hit Ernie over the head. Or Barney. Barney is a fictitious purple dinosaur; he is not real.*

Brenna's chubby little hands came up to his cheeks; she had to make sure she had his undivided attention. "Da secret, you promise."

Oh damn.

"'Member?"

"Yes, Brenna. Go get your jammies now." Atlas stood up and watched his daughter run down to her room. The little incident with Seannie had happened weeks ago; he had forgotten about it, to be honest. His two-year-old, however, had not. *Dammit.*

In the bathroom, Brenna was on the floor naked from the waist down. The little girl was struggling to get her head and arms out of her shirt; she looked like a pretzel. "Help!"

Soon, the tub was full of bubbles and warm water. Atlas took his time shampooing and rinsing Brenna's hair until all the tomato sauce was gone. Not being able to put it off any longer, he helped her stand up. Bubbles floated down from her body. "Remember when you used to wear a diaper?"

Brenna stomped her foot in the tub, making a small splash. "Bwenna big girl."

"Yes." *Keep it short, man, she's two.* Atlas pointed, "That's your vagina."

"Like Seannie's penis?"

"Yes." Seconds ticked by as his little girl sat again in the water, contemplating things. *Ashley's gonna kill me.*

Brenna sat down once more and kicked the bubbles. "Piglet yellow."

Atlas let out his breath. He sprayed the soap from her body. He took his shivering daughter into his arms and set her on her feet. "Piglet's pink, remember?" With a warm towel, he rubbed her dry and pulled a blue velour nightgown over her head. "Go to your room. Give Daddy a minute and I'll be there to tuck you in."

After mopping the floor and letting the water out of the tub, Atlas took time with his daughter. He tucked her in and read to her; her favorite book was 'Goodnight Moon'. "Alright, sweetie. Good night. See you in the morning." He leaned over and kissed her on the forehead.

"Good night, Daddy."

Atlas turned on the Cinderella nightlight and exited the room. He left the door slightly ajar. In the hallway, he could hear noises coming from the living room. *Ashley shouldn't be home for another hour?* In the dark, Atlas felt something under foot. "What in the hell?" He reached for the light switch. Down the hall, placed there with obvious care, was a line of silver wrapped Hershey's kisses. They led all the way to the bedroom. Atlas followed the trail and then paused for a moment, his hand on the doorknob. A light scent of vanilla raspberry drifted through the cracks of the door. The smell grew stronger as he stepped into the bedroom. "Ashley?"

The room was dark. But candles allowed a bit of light throughout the room. In the middle of their queen-size bed, her curly dark hair still wet from the shower, Ashley lay with her legs tucked behind her. Her chin was propped up with her left hand. She wore a lingerie Atlas had never seen before, a sheer black lace baby doll night gown with long, gorgeous caplet sleeves with matching panties. She wore nothing else. "I was thinking if we had another girl, we were going to name her Jessica but what if it's a boy?"

Atlas broke into the widest grin. "We're having another baby?" Ashley nodded. Atlas laughed and then pulled his shirt off over his head. And then, with a tap from his heel, the door gently closed behind him.

CHAPTER 41

ECHOES

Zack had watched his brother lay back on the gurney, his eyes close. That was fifty minutes ago. "He fought them as hard as he could. I think he even caught one of them in the balls." He looked at his uncle. "Do you miss teaching? All those kids looking up to you?"

Craig's face appeared puzzled. "I don't know that they look up to me. Why the sudden change in topics?" Zack shrugged. "Teachings great. I give them as much information as I can and let them draw their own conclusions." Craig seemed surprised when his cell phone rang. "Hello?" After a few minutes of hushed conversation, he put the phone back in his pocket. He leaned toward the pilot. They needed to change direction of the flight. Robert would double the payment if he would take them in the opposite direction.

"Where are we going?" Zack asked, not for the first time. "Are we going to stay with Grandma and Grandpa Antonelli?" He could feel his leg muscles growing tighter and tighter; he wanted nothing more than to stand up and stretch, but there was no room in the helicopter. He was seated on one side of a rectangular space surrounded by suitcases he didn't remember packing. His uncle was beside him, and Rustin lay in between the two of them. His brother had been asleep for almost the entire time.

"No, Zack." That was all that was said the rest of the flight. The next thirty minutes passed just as slow as the first hour. Half the time, with his ears popping a great deal, it felt like they were making big figure eights in the sky. The tension in the aircraft was almost unbearable. *Are we being followed? Where are we going? To another hospital?*

Uncle Craig had his eyes on Rustin when he asked, "Did you take that medicine like you're supposed to?"

Zack nodded. "Yeah. Dad said he'd buy the ring if I did."

"What ring?" Craig looked puzzled, but Zack said nothing. The ride continued in silence.

The helicopter landed some time later. The large door opened. The stretcher was pulled out. By the time Zack got out, Craig had Rustin in his arms. As the stretcher was pushed back in and the helicopter lifted into the air again, they walked toward a chauffeured car with tinted windows. A woman wearing a black suit with gold buttons down her coat stood by a green Lexus. She opened the back door. Craig told him to get in and scoot to the other end. Rustin's head was then laid in his brother's lap. A moment later, his uncle and the driver were in the front seats and the car moved. Zack looked down at his brother's face. He wondered how those jerks that had attacked Rustin could get the two of them confused. Their family didn't confuse them. Zack smiled. *Rustin always joked that my ears were twice the size of his.*

The trip from the small airport to the hotel took no time at all. When they did arrive, they didn't pull up under the awning at the front of the building. They drove to a door in the back. His uncle and the chauffer exited the car first. The woman headed straight to the hotel. When she returned, she was pushing a luggage cart and in the presence of another woman. Zack's soft tone shook ever so slightly, "Uncle Craig?"

Craig, who had Rustin in his arms again, turned to see what was making his nephew nervous. "I'm sure she's just the manager of the hotel. Grab the bags, Zack."

"I've got it, sir." The chauffer began piling their belongings on to a cart.

"Mr. Antonelli, I am Keri Macias, the manager here at..." She saw Craig shake his head ever so slightly. "...this hotel. Your suite is prepared, on the first floor, just as was requested. If you'll follow me, we'll get inside before it rains."

"Go on, Zack," his uncle reassured him.

Zack followed Carol inside, Craig was behind him, and the chauffer took up the rear. It wasn't long before they stopped outside a door. Carol handed Zack a key. Before leaving, she said, "If you have any need at all, just call my office, the number is by the phone."

Zack opened the door. After Craig entered the suite, Zack stepped back to allow the chauffer to roll the luggage cart in. He turned to ask his uncle about the tip and realized he wasn't there. Craig had taken Rustin into a back room. "Umm."

The woman smiled at his uneasiness. "Don't you worry about it; your father has already paid me well. Good day, young man."

Zack gave the woman a nod and after she stepped away, he closed the door and turned the lock. He shook his head, confused. *The chauffeured car, the luxury suite, his dad had gone all out. But why?* Zack turned around, taking in his new home away from home. Zack laughed. *Forget why. This is sic.*

The walls of the front room were painted cranberry at the top and cream a third of the way down. To his right was a large screen television with speakers on either side. A couch and recliner were arranged before the TV. Walking further into the room, Zack found a couple game controllers resting on the coffee table. "Oh, wow!" He bent down to find several video games that he had back home and another couple that he had asked for.

Setting the games down for the moment, he walked past a warm electric fireplace. Zack's stomach growled as he walked into the small kitchen. On the right side of the sink near the fridge, was a state-of-the-art coffee maker. On the left, a toaster. The cupboards contained his favorite cereals, ingredients for pasta, peanut butter, and a dozen cans of food. His fingers brushed the tile counter tops. In the fridge, he found mayo, mustard, cheese, and lunch meats. Zack wondered what the room service was like.

Zack made his way to the other side of the kitchen; he took a seat at the nook. He peaked through the blinds just as the gray skies had opened up. First there was thunder, and then lightning zig-zagged through the sky. Other guests splashed through puddles, trying not to get soaked; but they did not have the same personal service Zack had been treated to. Instead, these other hotel guests carried their own luggage in one hand, while trying to keep a hat from flying away or using a soaking wet newspaper to keep their head dry.

"Hey, away from the window." Craig came into the main area and then toward the kitchen. "You want anything?"

"Coffee." Zack was surprised that Craig never questioned his request. Without hesitation, he put a pot of coffee on.

The room was relatively quiet, aside from the steady drop of the coffee percolating. His uncle opened the freezer, moved things around, and then pull out a large bag of french fries. From the cupboard, he took out several cans of chili and from the refrigerator he found a bag of shredded cheddar cheese. It wasn't long before he was sliding a chili fry dish into the oven. Craig took a moment to prep two cups of coffee. He handed one to Zack and then took a seat across from him.

"Zack. It's important that you not look out the windows or open the front door. If the phone rings, let me answer it."

"Where are we?" Zack took a sip of coffee and made a face. Looking around, he saw no brightly colored advertisements of fun things to do in the area. No 'Welcome Here' signs. No phone books with the area code displayed on the front. "Why did we leave so fast?" Zack finished the entire cup of coffee, then rested his folded hands on the table with his head down.

"There's a lot I can't tell you. I'm sorry. Your dad and I are just trying to keep the two of you safe." Zack could feel his uncle's eyes on him. A silence fell between them that lasted way too long. Finally, a hand reach over and squeezed his arm. "Don't shut down on me, Zack. Keep talking."

"There's more coming. Something happened that night," Zack paused. "Rusi and I talk to each other all the time." Craig nodded, waiting for him to go on. "I couldn't get him to talk to me that day." Zack had never felt so disconnected. A part of the chain Rustin and Zack shared had been broken that night, and neither boy could fill in the gap. Zack knew whatever was missing was going to challenge them once they figured out what it was. The boy's stomach made a rude noise. "How long 'til the fries are ready?

Craig laughed as he got up to check their lunch. A moment after opening the oven, he put on a set of oven mitts, and pulled out a steaming casserole dish. The delicious smell permeated the entire room. "Go grab a couple glasses, would you? Soda's in the fridge."

Zack went into the kitchen and opened several cabinets. He grabbed three glasses, one of which he left on the counter. He checked the freezer, found the ice, and prepared two glasses. Walking back to the table he handed one glass to his uncle who had already set a plate down for each of them. "Thank you," Craig said after wiping his mouth.

"No problem." Zack sat in his seat and inhaled. This wasn't his uncle's first crack at the dish; all the Carson boys begged him to fix it whenever they got together. Zack wasted no time as he picked up a fry that was drenched in both chili and cheese. He paused a moment to watch the thick cheese drip heavily onto his plate. When his watering mouth couldn't take the wait any longer, the fry was folded into his mouth and savored. Zack moaned. He soon went onto the next fry, only to hear his uncle laughing at him.

CHAPTER 42

EMOTIONS ARISE

Jensen didn't like that Rustin and Zack were out of sight. He understood his father wanted to keep them safe. But why did he have to have them flown somewhere? The entire time they were hospitalized, Jensen had stayed ahead with his schoolwork. Now, though, now all he could do was sit and ponder. *What happened? Why did my brothers suddenly go into hiding?* Frustrated, he picked up the phone and dialed.

"Hello?" Jensen recognized his friend's voice.

"Hey. Do you think there's any chance of getting everyone together for a practice?"

"Can't take the wait, huh?" Jensen wasn't surprised when Travis didn't wait for a reply. "Sure. Julia and I'll call everyone. We'll be there in an hour."

Setting the receiver down, he was surprised when the phone rang. Again, he picked up the receiver. "Hello, Carson residence."

"Jensen, how are you my dear? It's Grandma Carson. Grandpa and I just wanted to check up on everything. How's Rustin?"

"He's fine." Jensen wanted to avoid any disagreements. "They're looking for Sgt Meyers."

"Well, that's good. You don't worry about a thing. Our church has started a prayer circle out here. He'll be getting a lot of—"

His grandparent's denial of the entire situation caused the seventeen-year-old to lose it. "Of crap," Jensen said. *So much for avoiding conflict.* "Your stupid book was written by a human being over four thousand years ago, there's no way it's accurate. You idiots claim your god is loving, but he enforces racial discrimination and sexism, and—, "Jensen was cut off by the phone being yanked out of his hand by his father.

"That's enough." Robert was standing beside him with a look of disappointment on his face. "Go wait for me downstairs."

Running his hand through his hair, Jensen pushed himself off the wall and went downstairs to the solarium. He turned on his keyboard; he played a Beethoven classic, trying to clear his head. Music had always been a way to reflect and digest a stressful situation. But for some reason, right now, it failed him entirely. As he played, he remembered the condition of Rustin's legs not that long ago. The song stumbled. Jensen hollered with frustration. He paced the perimeter of the room, his fists clenched by his sides.

Ten minutes later he heard his father in the doorway. "That was unacceptable, son."

"I'll go call and apologize later. Everyone will be here in a couple of minutes." Jensen headed for the door but stopped when Robert laid a hand on his shoulder. "Dad, I can't deal with this right now."

"You're going to have to. In the living room, son." Jensen followed his father and took a seat on the couch. "You have been handed a lot of responsibility for someone your age. We're all under a lot of stress right now." The seventeen-year-old watched his dad pause. "The thing is, we're Atheist because we don't like the way religion judges others. Do you understand?"

"Dad, I know. But they can't go around placing all this crap on

Rustin. It isn't fair to him." He saw his father's confused expression. "No one's doing anything, Dad. The cops don't care, they have done nothing to get those bastards."

"Jensen. They have Oscar in custody. They are looking for Nicole and Meyers. I wouldn't stand back and allow them to neglect their responsibilities. And they wouldn't. They know I'm a lawyer," he paused. "You will apologize to your grandparents," Robert insisted. The doorbell rang.

Jensen went and opened the front door where he found Julia and Travis on the porch. Everybody else was crowded on the lawn and in cars parked all the way down the street. Jensen tried to smile. "Go through the gate to the backyard, you guys. I'll be there in a minute."

"Jensen, what's going on?" Travis had the words out before he closed the door. "How's Rustin and Zack?" Apparently, Julia had not told her brother about his break down in front of the mall.

Jensen glanced at his father who was still standing there. "They're gone. Let's go set the group up. How many are here?"

"Maybe sixty," Travis answered. "Everyone's studying for exams, I guess. JC, I need to talk to you."

Jensen was puzzled as Julia kissed him on the cheek; she left to join the others outside. "What's up?" He followed his best friend into the kitchen. He took the lead as he grabbed a couple of bottled waters from the fridge and tossed one to Travis.

"You're the leader, okay? You and I bounce ideas off each other, but you're the leader of this whole thing. This song is what it is. Just..." Travis paused, twisting the bottle in his hands. "Live in it okay?"

Jensen remembered how he had met Julia when he was a sopho-more, at that point he was only in the running for the leadership role of *Just the Five of Us*; he had yet to audition for Camerata and was in Chorus, as was Julia and Travis. Mr. Delaney had asked him to accompany her on the piano for her solo at *Carols by Candlelight*, the high school's Christmas concert, and it was during that time they got to know one another. He and Travis weren't exactly friends at that point; hell, they couldn't stand each other. When Jensen had started dating Julia, everything came to a head and the two young men fought it out on school grounds. Both young men should have been suspended; it would have left Julia without a piano player and both Chorus and Camerata without a soloist for the school's version of 'Silent Night'. But Delaney got involved, and for punishment, required the two of them to perform a song together. In the beginning, they argued about everything, the song, the octave, even the pitch of the piano. It took them almost a month to work through all the bull shit, but in the end, they realized that music meant everything to both of them. It was easier and more productive for them to work together at it, than be separated by it. As for his relationship with Julia, the love affair didn't take off until that summer, when Jensen spent most of his time with Travis.

Jensen and Travis took a little time to discuss the rehearsal and then headed outside. Travis fist bumped Jensen and then jumped off the deck to join everyone else. Jensen cleared his throat as he stepped in front of all his friends. His head cleared as he ran a hand through his hair. "Thank you for coming. There's no border for this song. By that, I mean we are not separate choirs, we are one. So, I want rows of ten, in the grass, guys up front. Tenors to my left, baritones, and then basses to my right. Ladies, stand behind them. Same structure as we are in class." Jensen directed everyone with his hands. "From my left, altos, then second and first sopranos. Members of *Just the Five of Us*, up here with me."

It took several minutes for everyone to get rearranged and for the remaining members of *Just the Five of Us* to disentangle themselves from the larger group. He smiled and shook their hands as they came on to the deck. "Intro, that's you, Miguel, just like before. Watch me, I'll count off three seconds for the piano transition, and I'll bring in *The Five of Us* for the main verse." Jensen turned to Travis who was on his right side. "Then we come in, let's try bringing it up an octave. Okay?" Travis nodded. Jensen took a deep breath. "All right, let's do this."

Jensen took the guys through the music twice and grinned as everyone else applauded. Once the noise died down, he addressed the entire group. "After my solo, we do the main verse again, that's where we all come in. We want to break up the lines. Ladies first, 'Lean on me' through 'I'll help you carry on'. Then the guys all the way through 'someone to lean on'. And we do it one more time after that as a total group with the cut ins and drop offs, sung by those in Camerata. The only thing I haven't figured out is the ending. Probably a solo. So if anyone has any ideas, come talk to me after practice. "Let's start—" Jensen broke off as someone pounded on the gate that was on the other side of the large yard. "Come on back!" he hollered, thinking it was another choir member.

"Carson, show your face, you asshole." The gate had opened and a young man of about fourteen entered. He was dragging a six-year-old little girl behind him.

Stepping off the deck, Jensen approached the teenager. "First, it's Jensen. Second, do not cuss me out in front of a little kid. It's not cool.

The little girl looked up at her brother, "Why does he want to hurt Daddy? Why, Chris?"

"Shut up, Cindy." Chris took a step forward. "You tell your damn father to back off. Unlike yours, my father would never touch or threaten anyone. Your brother had sex, and your brother paid for the consequences. Leave my dad out of it."

Jensen almost felt sorry for the guy, how would he have handled it if his own father were accused of such a crime? But he couldn't take the dismissal of the actions taken against his brother. People had sodomized and raped Rustin, and one of the criminals was Kevin Meyers, a crooked, low down, dirty cop. To compare what had happened to Rustin with something similar happening to Cindy was one way to handle this kid. But he didn't want to scare the child; she already looked like she was going to cry. He felt Travis step up beside him. "Get her out of here, this is not about her." He saw the little girl back up behind her brother.

The back door slid open. "The singing stopped," he heard his father say. "Is everything okay?"

Jensen took a deep breath and let it out. "Yeah, Dad. Everything's fine. Chris needed some ideas for a humanities project, he's heading out now." Jensen took a step back. Everything seemed to be in slow motion; Chris left the way he came, leaving his sister behind. Travis and Steve jumped off the porch and followed him, as Julia approached the little girl who had started crying. Moments later, he could hear tires squealing.

"Jensen? What's going on?"

After he told his father what had happened, Jensen watched his father go inside to call the police. "Hey guys, I'm sorry. Let's call it quits. I'll try to set up something more organized in a couple days. Good practice, everyone." Jensen paused, "Julia, bring Cindy in."

Jensen went into the kitchen, Julia coming up behind him, holding the little girl's hand. They found Robert on the phone already. "Yes, his boy came through the backyard and threatened Jensen. Left his daughter behind." Robert listened and then said, "Yes, she's here."

Jensen watched Julia go to the pantry and grab a box of graham crackers. Taking his lead from her, he poured a half glass of milk and set it at the breakfast bar.

"Can I lift you?" Julia asked the little girl who nodded. She put Cindy on a stool and wiped her tears. "It's okay, we'll get you back home. Do you like graham crackers?"

Officer Bennett showed up not long after taking a statement from Jensen; Robert led him into the kitchen.

"Uncle Jeff!" The little girl jumped down from the stool and ran into Bennett' arms.

"Hey, Cindy." The officer smiled as he greeted the child. "I have to talk to some people here and then I'll take you home." Bennett looked up at Robert who took the little girl's hand and coaxed her into the living room. "Alright, Jensen. What happened?" Jensen was glad his girlfriend was there; it amazed him how many details he had forgotten already.

Jensen was still talking when his dad's cell phone, laying on the counter, let out a shrill ring. Bennett pointed to it, silently asking him to answer it.

"Hello," Jensen said into the receiver. "Robert Carson's line."

"J.C, is that you?" It was Travis on the other line. "Steve and I are downtown, he took back roads, near Colma. Didn't they find Rus in Colma?" Not waiting for a response, he went on. "There are a couple of motels down here, we lost the car that kid was driving." The phone started breaking up. "Look ... there." The line went dead.

— • —

CHAPTER 43

THE RING

R ustin laid on a soft bed, bigger than he was used to. His breath
was even, deep. Anyone looking in on him, which his uncle had
done twice already, would assume that Rustin was sleeping peacefully.
Craig had not seen, that beneath the blanket, the boy's hands were
clenching and unclenching. He tried to pull himself out of a nightmare, a nightmare where he was blind and unable to protect himself.

You want to have a little fun?

Rustin moaned, his head tossed once, then twice.

You little shit. Want to join in?

His fingers tingled. It was getting harder and harder to breathe.

Bullet in your head. Fun.

Somewhere outside the dream, there was the sound of a shrill
scream that wouldn't stop. A hand brushed back Rustin's bangs.

"Rustin, wake up." The screaming continued. "Rustin." Craig
pulled back the blanket and grasped his hand, squeezing it. "Rustin."

Rustin's eyes popped open. The screaming stopped. For several
moments, all he could do was lay there and gasp, his chest rising and
falling at a fast pace.

"Zack, go to the other room."

Rustin blinked. At first, everything was blurry. He felt the bed shift as Craig stood up. Another moment later, he could hear a faucet running. He blinked again as a damp cloth cooled his hands and then his cheeks.

"Deep breaths, Rustin. You, Zack, and I are in a hotel room. You are safe here." Craig squeezed his hand again. Rustin's breathing slowly came under control. "You alright?"

"Yeah." The response was nothing but a whisper. Rustin coughed and repeated himself louder, "Yes."

"You want something to eat?"

Rustin took another moment to take in his surroundings. The quilt he laid on was a dark rose color, the walls that matched were a shade lighter. There was a TV that hung on the wall; beneath it, was a crackling fireplace. As he tried to clear his head, he took notice of the pulled curtains to his right. Rustin shifted in bed and Craig helped him to his feet.

With Craig's help, Rustin limped past a small bathroom and then through a door that led directly to the open area of the room. "You hungry, Rus? How about a quesadilla?" They headed toward a nook where Zack was playing a game of solitaire.

Reaching out in front of him, Rustin grabbed the table of the nook and slowly swung himself in, right next to Zack. "Sure. Where are we? Where's Dad?

Zack gathered the cards and set them aside as Craig started puttering around in the kitchen. "Craig won't say. All I know, is we zigzagged in the air for six hours, and once we landed I didn't even have time to go to the bathroom, they were pushing me toward some car with shaded windows. We're probably still in San Francisco." Craig said nothing. "See, what did I tell you?"

"You were on that helicopter for only two hours," Craig answered. The microwave beeped, and a moment later he set the plate of steaming food on the table. "And I can assure you, we are not in San Francisco. Eat up, Rus."

Rustin wasn't all that sure he could eat the food in front of him. The quesadilla smelled great. But his stomach seemed to tell him to stay far, far away from the gooey cheese that melted from the tortilla onto the plate.

"Just try a bite, Rustin," his uncle told him.

Rustin picked up a slice of the quesadilla. He took a small bite and chewed for a very long time. He swallowed. Then, after a slight hesitation, he took another bite, stuffing the rest of the wedge into his mouth.

He found Craig standing beside him; the plate pushed away from him. "That's not what I meant. Rus, this isn't about etiquette. If you can't eat this right now, don't." He paused. "Are you done for the moment?" Rustin nodded. "Okay. Now I want both of you in the bedroom. I have some phone calls to make."

Rustin followed Zack back into the bedroom. He laid back on the bed, his legs spread apart. "Dad threatened this cop in the hospital." He saw Zack looking at him, confused.

Please, Rus. I know you're hurting. Damn, my head.

"Something about an attack on me. That's what that guy said." Rustin shook his head and laughed. "I think, if something had really happened, I'd remember it."

"It's not funny, Rustin!" Zack was upset all at once and Rustin couldn't figure out why. "They hurt you. I told Dad it wasn't Bennett, and he doesn't believe me. I saw what they did to you, Rustin."

A soft knock sounded on their door several minutes later. Craig entered. "Hey, you guys. What's going on? Did I hear you say you saw the attack, Zack?"

"He can't laugh about it! It happened to me too." Rustin could see the pain in his brother's eyes. "You told them to stop Rustin, and they didn't stop. They were saying how excited you were cause-cause-"Zack broke off unable to go any further. He took a deep breath and continued, "They called you a bastard and said you needed to be fucked with."

'If you have a problem with that, tough shit. The boy needs to be fucked with first. Rustin shook his head as the words echoed in his ears. Stunned, he shook his head, "I don't underst-"

"You wouldn't tell me where you — "

Both of Zack's hands covered the top of his head. Rustin could tell his brother was still blaming himself for what had happened. But Rustin didn't know how to reassure him. "I can't remember. Damn it, Zack. I can't. I can't. "

Clueless to either of the boys, Craig had watched the volleyball exchange between them. "Wait a minute, slow down. Let's start over." Craig took a breath, confused. "Zack, you saw the attack? Does your dad know?"

Zack didn't answer. "It's not like that," Rustin said. "He knows when things happen." He was looking at his hands, his mind full of shame. He knew Zack would take over. "But I don't remember."

"I was in the bathroom, and I got this headache, I knew it was Rusi. I told Dad he was by the water, but Rus wouldn't-couldn't," Zack corrected himself, "Tell me where he was." He brought his hands down. "It wasn't Bennett, Craig. It was Meyers."

"But Zack, Robert said you were in your room when the cops came over that first night." Craig tried to make all the details that the boys were telling him fit. But all it did was confused him more. "They never saw you. They didn't know you were twins." Craig cleared his throat. "Let's discuss this a little later. How about a game of cards?"

In the living area of the motel room, Rustin watched as Zack reached for the deck of cards and shuffled. Craig spent the rest of the evening directing the boys through different card games, crazy eights, rummy, and Texas hold 'em. Somehow, they even had pizza for dinner. It was eleven when their uncle called the game quits. "All right guys, it's late," Craig said with a glance at the clock. "Zack, I want you to go get dressed for bed. I need to talk to Rustin alone."

Zack left the room and Rustin followed Craig into the kitchen. As he sat down, he watched his uncle began digging through a box Robert had given him at the airport. "What's up?" Rustin watched as peroxide, medical tape, an ointment, and bandages were laid out on the table. "Why did we leave the hospital?"

Craig opened the gauze package and unscrewed the top of the ointment. The man cleared his throat. "I told you before, that subject is not open for discussion. Everyone is trying to keep you boys safe."

Sitting still, Rustin's eyes stared straight ahead as the bandage over his wound was removed. He cringed when the wound was wiped with iodine and again when an ointment was rubbed onto it. A clean bandage was applied. "Do you need a pain pill?" Rustin shook his head. "You need to go back to bed. If you need that medicine in a while, just let me know." Rustin stood up. When the boy looked up, Craig's brow creased. "What's up, Rus? I know I'm not doing this very well. What do you want? Tell me what you need."

"Zack made a naked clay doll." Rustin looked down at his hands. "Why? Was it my fault?"

"Rustin, none of this was your fault. People did this to you, not the other way around." Craig brought Rustin's head up with a finger under the boy's chin. "Don't stress this, okay? Get in bed, and I'll check on you in a little while, okay?"

Rustin made it back to the bedroom and grabbed a clean pair of pajamas. He ignored Zack, who watched him from the bed. In the bathroom, he changed his pants. It was a moment later when he looked in the mirror, and when he did, Rustin saw nothing but a coward in the reflection before him. *What kind of idiot gets drunk and then goes into hiding?* The reflection didn't respond. *What kind of asshole puts himself in that situation?* Rustin remembered something about a six-pack of beer; the reflection still refused to give some sort of answer. He pushed himself away from the sink and against the wall, his knees buckled. Mere seconds passed before he saw a pair of bare feet in front of him. "Please."

Zack knelt in front of his brother. "You're not a coward, Rus. I was the one drinking beer. You did nothing wrong."

He felt like he was losing everything; his dad had sent him away and even Craig couldn't take him seriously anymore. "What's the secret, Zack?" Rustin's voice shook.

"There's no secret, Rus."

Why can't I remember anything? Rustin's heart was pounding in his ears as Zack left. He took concentrated, deep breaths; by the time Zack returned, the panic attack had ceased.

"Here." Rustin stood up and took the small black box Zack handed him. "I had Dad get it. I think it cost over a thousand dollars. He's become somewhat of a pushover lately." Zack took a moment. "Remember that nightmare you used to have when we were little? We were like three, weren't we?" Rustin nodded as Zack stood up and opened the box. He took out a ring, a ring with a jagged line down the center. "There was this bright light you said."

"And when it broke apart, it gushed with blood." Rustin went back into the memory of his terrified three-year-old self. "We gushed with blood, and the bleeding wouldn't stop. You died."

"And you didn't. This time, there won't be any blood." Zack pulled the ring apart, one side decorated with stars, the other side with crescent moons. "We've always come from the same place, Rusi. What's in me, is in you."

Rustin grinned as he took the ring decorated with moons and slipped it on his finger. "Cool."

There was a knock on the door and Craig poked his head in. "Get to bed, you two. What's on your finger, Zack?"

"The better half of the fertilized egg." Zack looked at Rustin who laughed.

Craig gave a small smile. "All right, boys. Get some sleep." He turned off the light and left the room. The door was left slightly ajar.

Rustin turned over. *If Dad loves me, where in the hell is he?* His head gave an intense throb and it took all his control not to scream. He buried his head in the pillow, his muscles tensed, as he waited for the pain to be over. Minutes passed. Rustin got to his feet and staggered into the living space. His hearing seemed hollow. Everything around him seemed like he was stuck in a vortex.

"Rustin?" Craig walked across the room in two strides. Rustin's legs gave out. While one hand went to his hip, another hand came up across his chest. "I've got you. There's no hurry." Craig eased the boy on the couch. "I'm going to grab your meds."

"No." Rustin struggled to get to his feet. His hand came up trying to reach for something to help him, anything at all. He didn't want to take any medicine that was going to make defending himself any harder than it already was. "No. Got to talk to Dad."

Craig took hold of Rustin's hand with his left hand. "Rus, you're really pale, okay. Try to relax." His uncle made him sit down.

Tears came to Rustin's eyes. "I need Dad." The knot in his stomach hit the same time his head lurched. Rustin swallowed back the vomit.

Craig grabbed his cell phone from his back pocket without leaving the boy's side. He dialed. "Robert, it's Craig."

A moment later, the phone was pressed against Rustin's ear. "Dad," his voice cracked. "Dad, where are you?"

"Rusi, calm down."

"I need you. "Rustin's voice cracked and for a moment, he couldn't talk. His chest felt tight and raced. His fingers clenched the phone until his knuckles changed colors.

"I know. Sweetheart, you need to calm down."

"I can't do this!" Rustin's body shook and started to rock back and forth. Craig sat beside him and started rubbing his back in small circles. "I need you, Dad, please."

"Rusi, deep breaths," Craig murmured. "Everything's okay."

"Dad." Again, Rustin's voice cracked. "I love you."

There was a pause. "I love you too, Rustin. Let me talk to Craig."

Rustin pulled away and leaned against the back of the couch. As his uncle took back the phone, he zoned out; sounds and actions became almost indistinguishable. At some point, the phone was hung up. A voice told someone to go to bed. The couch shifted and after a moment or two, a warm hand took his and squeezed it. Rustin blinked. He found Craig in front of him, a look of concern in his green eyes.

"Rustin, take your medicine." Rustin's body still had a bad tremor. Craig put the pill in his mouth. "I know you're scared. I know you feel lost."

Rustin swallowed the pill and then drank from a water bottle Craig handed him. "I can't do this."

"Do what?" Rustin hesitated and then shrugged. "You don't have to do anything. Not tonight." Craig pulled out the deck of cards. "Gin, ten cards. I'll discard."

They had been playing the game most of the day, and when Rustin played, he usually won. But this time, the boy's hands wouldn't stop shaking, he kept dropping his cards. It was how Craig knew Rustin was repeatedly throwing away his good cards. Forty minutes after they started playing, Craig decided enough was enough. With two jacks, a red queen, and a bunch of scattered numbers, he set his cards down. "Gin."

Rustin kind of giggled, the drug taking effect. "Cool."

"Put your feet up. We'll watch something on TV. Give me a minute."

Rustin dragged his feet on to the couch. He half watched as his uncle put the cards away and turned off most of the lights. Craig then came over and covered him with a blanket. It would be the last thing he saw until morning.

CHAPTER 44

FUTURE PLANS

Atlas couldn't wait until they caught Meyers; it was just a matter of time. Since Daniel had got the make and year of the car, an all-points bulletin had been put out. When the authorities had gone to check out all the motels around Colma, they found that Meyers had checked out, under his son's name, the same day the kid had gone to the Carson residence. The authorities had been to the Meyers's home frequently. Mrs. Meyers always answered the door dressed like she had some place fancy to be. She would proclaim her husband's innocence, disgusted with those who came to her door. The boy was never home. Everyone figured if they found the car or the son, they'd find Officer Kevin Meyers and maybe that Nicole bitch, too.

The APB on Meyers did nothing to ease Atlas's mind. The public would be satisfied with this, but Atlas knew how the system worked. There would never be a concentrated effort to find the crooked cop. The authorities would go about their business, and if they come across Meyers, then actions might finally be taken.

Meanwhile, Atlas was trying to get his daughter to go to sleep. After he read her a story, he pulled the blanket up to her chin. "Good night, Brenna." Most nights, she went down without a sound; tonight though, as he left her bedside, she cried. At first, he was worried, he checked to make sure her clothes were dry and that she didn't have a fever. Once everything checked out okay, he kissed her on the forehead. "Good night, Brenna. I'll see you in the morning."

It was eight thirty at night, and Atlas knew Ashley was in the kitchen making all his favorite foods; the scent made his mouth water. As he made his way back down the hall, he groaned. Not that he didn't appreciate her efforts, but Atlas felt the whole situation was out of his control, and he hated it. In the den, he saw the large stack of papers he had gathered from the internet. They told him that victims and their families should know what questions to ask and what questions not to ask. Another stack of notes, thanks to Lechner, had explained rape to him in more detail, the who, the why, the where. But he wasn't sure what to do with it all. It helped to know that Rustin wasn't the only male who had ever been abused sexually. What was he supposed to be doing right now? Should his attention be more focused on what his brother needed, or should he leave that to his father? Was he supposed to be writing some paper on what he learned? Softly, he groaned again.

It didn't take long before Atlas had his head in his hands once more. He was relieved when Ashley called him from the kitchen. Standing up, Atlas washed his hands in the bathroom and then walked into the dining area. The small room was lit with several candles, a white tablecloth covered the table, and a bottle of expensive wine chilled in the center of the table. "It looks wonderful in here, honey." The yummy potent smell of garlic bread wafted throughout the whole room. Atlas watched his wife as she set a plate of dinner rolls on the table. Before he sat down, he leaned over and kissed her. Then he pulled the chair out for her. "You know, this will soon be behind all of us, to a certain extent. I heard Dad say he was thinking about moving Rustin and Zack up to Washington." He served himself some steaming corn, added butter and a little salt before taking a bite.

Ashley served a large portion of lasagna to Atlas. "Are you wanting us to move with them?"

"No. Dad has a contract agreement with the firm. But given the circumstances, they'll probably ask me to take his place. I just hope I passed the Bar." Atlas took a bite of lasagna. "You want to snuggle up with a movie tonight? Terminator?"

Ashley laughed. "We have a little something to discuss first." She took a sip of wine.

"Ut-oh. What did I do this time?"

"This morning, my two-year-old daughter" Ashley's face was dead-pan, "Informed me that she had a 'bagina'." There was a slight pause before she continued. "She also told me, Seannie wouldn't share his 'eenis'."

Atlas couldn't help it as he burst out laughing. "Really?"

"Were you planning on telling me about this vocabulary lesson?" Ashley shook her head. "This fiasco has caused you to lose your movie pick tonight. We're watching 'Dying Young', you know how sexy I think Campbell Scott is." The phone rang, therefore ruining the romantic moment. Ashley got up to answer it. "Hello? Sure, Dad. He's right here."

Atlas wiped his mouth and stood up. Taking the receiver from his wife, he said, "Yeah, Dad. What's going on? ...We'll be right there." He hung up the phone and looked at his beautiful wife. "We have to do the movie later. I think they finally arrested Meyers. Do you want to grab Brenna, or should I?"

"I'll get her. Can you pack the baby bag and put it in the car?"

In the kitchen, Atlas grabbed a bottle and put it in the small back-pack they used to carry the baby's things. He was about to follow his wife into the room to grab a couple of diapers when Ashley came out with Brenna in her arms. The baby looked drunk with sleep; her eyes were opened just enough for her to see her daddy, and her head bobbed. She held her arms out to Atlas who took her in his arms.

"We still need diapers," he told Ashley. Gently he began rubbing the two-year old's back." Shhh. Does Brenna wanna go for a car ride to see Papa?" The little girl's head nodded and then lay against her father's chest. "Good girl."

Minutes ticked by as they fastened Brenna into her car seat and drove to Robert's house. They walked through the front door without hesitation. As Ashley joined Robert and a couple of police officers in the kitchen. Atlas took his daughter, who was once more asleep, into his father's bedroom. He laid her down in the middle of the large mattress, then placed pillows on either side of her small body to prevent her from rolling over onto the floor. With a quick kiss on her cheek, he closed the door behind him.

The kitchen was empty; he followed the sound of voices into the living room. The police were gone. Ashley had moved to the couch. His dad was pacing, holding a cell phone to his ear. "Look, Meyers's been arrested, he's in police custody." Robert could be seen nodding his head. "Yes, that's great. The thing is, several evidence lockers were broken into. The tissue samples, the rectal slides, the clothing, the camera from the hospital. It's all gone. And they still haven't found Nicole."

Atlas groaned loudly; tonight, was going to be a long night.

XXX

Robert

It was turning into a long night. Officer Bennett had come by not long after Robert had gotten off the phone with Craig. Since Bennett had left, Robert had been on the phone with his brother-in-law for almost ten minutes, filling him in on what was going on with the investigation. He could finally ask about his sons. "Did Rustin finally go to sleep?"

"Yes. He fought it, but he's asleep on the couch now. Zack came in toward the end, but I sent him back to bed, and when I checked on him, he was sleeping. Overall, both your boys are fine. Bored, but fine." Craig paused. "I'll admit I am a little worried about them, though. Zack keeps insisting he knows that Meyers's responsible for the attack against Rustin."

"He is, Craig."

"And Rustin said that Zack made a naked clay doll of him."

"He did when Rustin was in the coma."

"Explain, please. And quick, I don't know how much longer I have the room to myself."

"They have this telepathy thing always going on between them. One will interrupt the other, finishing each other's sentences. They always know when the others in pain. I see it as telepathy overlapping. Don't worry about it, the boys do it all the time."

Craig groaned, "You owe me, you know that, right?" A slight pause. "And what's with this ring they both have? Zack's been gloating you spent over a thousand dollars on it. You realized he manipulated you into buying it, right?"

"I found it a relief he could finally manipulate me. Yes, he's up to his old standards, but no, it won't last for very much longer." Robert laughed, "I'll let you go. I'll try to get back with you tomorrow."

"All right, bye." The line went dead.

Putting his phone down, Robert looked at Ashley first and then Atlas. "Your brothers are driving Craig nuts."

"Do you think we have a chance of winning without the evidence?" Robert watched Atlas grasp Ashley's hand and squeeze it gently. "What do you think the defense will do?"

"They'll probably push for an arraignment, and if it goes to trial," Robert sighed, "Then they'll bring it to trial fairly quickly, once they find Nicole. As for the other, I don't know. We still have the hospital records; they'll be able to make us another set of duplicates. And Bennett had a couple of drawings at his desk. I just hope that's enough."

CHAPTER 45

BREAKTHROUGH

Jensen lay in bed, his body tense. *Raised bruises, black and blue* **It's your fault.** Horrified, he drifted off into yet another nightmare. *Some outlined in dark red. The high-pitched cry.* **You should have protected him!** A nightmare filled with guilt and a strong desire to escape. Jensen had tossed and turned then he buried his face into a pillow. *Do you have a girlfriend?* But the need for oxygen became a necessity. **It's too late!** Flinging onto his back, Jensen kicked out. **You worthless piece of shit!** He tried to rid himself of it all *legs spread wide.* **You should have protected him.** But the guilt wouldn't go away. *Pain written all over a* **Bastard.** *Fragile* **asshole.** *Body* **fucker.** Jensen woke up drenched in sweat. It took several moments for him to regain his composure. His mind stopped racing. His heart rate returned to normal. Shadows on the walls went from threatening to non-existent. Yet the word *fucker* continued to echo in his ear.

With a glance at the clock beside his bed, Jensen groaned. It was four-thirty in the morning; he tiptoed downstairs and turned on the TV. The next several hours were spent flipping through the channels. At a quarter 'til seven, he was back upstairs as the morning light filtered into his room, Jensen could no longer ignore the pain in his stomach nor the words and nightmares that still crowded his brain. He went into the kitchen, started the coffee, and pulled out all the ingredients for an omelet. He cracked a couple eggs and stirred in shredded cheese, ham, and avocado before he poured it on the griddle. For a time, all that crossed his mind was the preparation and consumption of a meal that would get him through the morning.

It was after nine when Jensen grabbed a bottle of water from the fridge and took a seat at the counter. He was relieved when he had overheard his father tell his uncle that Meyers had been caught. *Two down, one more to find.* With his mind somewhat focused, he knew it was time for him to make an overdue phone call to his grandparents. He picked up the phone and dialed.

"Hello." A woman's voice was heard.

"Grandma Carson, it's Jensen."

"Yes, hello dear." There was a long-drawn-out silence. Then, "How are you?"

"I'm okay." Jensen took a sip of water before he went on. "I owe you and Grandpa an apology. I shouldn't have blown up like that. I'm sorry."

"Apology accepted," the older woman simpered. "How is Rustin?"

Jensen knew better than to go into details. "He's okay. Can I ask you something?"

"Of course."

"Why did you leave the day after Rus was found?"

Mrs. Carson hesitated. "We felt it best that we let your father deal with things on his own. He was so adamant that Rustin had been, what he believed, was raped. We just wanted him to see the truth for what it was. That's all."

The Truth? "What truth? What are you talking about?"

"Boys cannot be raped," Mrs. Carson answered with confidence. "Obviously, Rustin needed to learn a lesson. Now he'll think twice about hanging out with the wrong crowd and putting himself in dangerous situations."

Jensen had been in enough social science classes to know bull shit when he heard it. "You mean, like girls wearing short skirts late at night?"

"Exactly. Now, I must get off the phone, dear. I need to get ready for brunch, your grandfather's taking me out this morning. Talk to you later." The line went dead.

Jensen hung up the phone and downed the rest of the water. He knew he had done the right thing by apologizing to his grandmother. It was one of the basic rules their dad had taught them; always respect those around you, regardless of how they treat you. If their beliefs differ from yours, it was the same thing. But when people acted so ignorant, even when there are facts that proved the opposite, Jensen had a hard time knowing how to deal with them. Male rape did happen; it's been proven repeatedly. Jensen didn't know the details, but he had seen his brother's battered body. *And how's a guy supposed to protect himself from being raped anyway. It's not something that a person thinks about regularly. Or at all. Hell, I never even thought about it until we found Rus.*

Robert walked into the kitchen. "You need to make a phone call, Jensen."

"Just did. Apology made, I've been forgiven, and you have been accused of not seeing the truth." Robert looked at him puzzled. "Evidently, Rustin needed to be taught a lesson. Do you realize they never saw Rustin? They left right after he was found."

Robert gestured for him to sit down, and Jensen did. "I didn't ask them to come visit to help us deal with Rustin's attack." Jensen looked confused. "I invited them here to keep the house in check, help me keep up with the bills, keep the house clean. That's all. And they did what I needed them to do." Robert paused. "In fact, I'm surprised they stayed as long as they did." Jensen didn't want to insult his grandparents and risk getting into trouble. But he was angrier now than he had been. Robert noticed. "Just say what's on your mind, son."

"I don't get it, we're all supposed to be there for one another, yet they're denying what happened to Rustin." Jensen grabbed a sheet of paper that lay on the table, glanced at it, and slowly tore it apart. "Did you see his body, Dad? Did you see what they did to him? How do we know he's okay now? That he will not die?"

Jensen felt Robert lay a warm hand on his. "Rustin is getting better; he's just going to take some time to heal. He did leave the hospital soon after surgery. But Craig's monitoring him."

Gathering the piles of shredded paper, Jensen threw them in the trash. "Are we really moving to Washington?"

"There's this great place, a two-story cabin on the lake. I'm definitely thinking about it." Robert sighed. "Atlas will be taking my place at the firm if I do decide to take it. You'll be allowed to decide if you want to stay here or come with me and the boys. I recon you'll want to finish your senior year here." Jensen nodded. "Don't worry about what your grandparents think. You don't have to agree with everything they say, but you must respect them, All right?"

"Sure, Dad."

Late that morning, Jensen stepped onto the school grounds dressed in the same clothes he had worn the day before. Only now, the black slacks and navy green shirt were wrinkled. As he entered the school's office, his brain was once more flooded with the images from his nightmares, the horrible, filthy words, and as always, the guilt. That was bad enough, but as he was on his way out the door, he heard the mutterings of nearby students. *Sex. Liked it. Loser.*

He had already exchanged his finished homework for a new stack of papers. As made his way across the quad toward the choir room, he heard Travis call to him. "Back off," Jensen muttered.

Travis, not having heard the response, ran up to him and gave a playful jab on the arm. "How you do-" It was as far as the boy got, Jensen shoved him back hard. "Jen-"

"I said, back off." Jensen's already hazed mind sank further into oblivion, into a tunnel of sorts. His fists bypassed his brain, striking Travis's face and chest blow after blow, as if he were a punching bag, Travis was soon sprawled on the ground, his arms draped over his head to protect himself from further injury. The nightmares from the night before pounded into Jensen's mind's eye until....

"Mr. Carson." *Someone was pulling against Rustin's arm. No, it wasn't Rustin's arm.* "Jensen."

Blinking, Jensen found the tunnel he had been in, vanished. His left fist lay against his best friend's face, he had no recollection of what had happened, how he had got into this; Travis's face was bloodied from the mouth and nose. "Oh, damn."

Several students and a teacher had gotten involved. Jensen allowed himself to be pulled back. Miguel helped Travis to his feet, while Adrian and another student still had a hold on Jensen by the crook of his arms. The principal, Ms. Hernandez, stepped within his line of vision. "Mr. Carson, let's go draw up some explosion papers, shall we?"

"No!" Travis yelled, as blood dripped from his mouth.

"Silence, Mr. Jacobs. You'll come to the office and get some ice for that lip. Then you'll go to class. Everyone else, you're excused." Jensen was released for a short moment, as his schoolmates did as they were instructed. The short woman stood just below Jensen's shoulders, but she still got a firm grip on the back of his neck. "Let's go, Mr. Carson."

With a deep breath and a sense of dread, Jensen made his way into the main office. He tuned out as the principal retold the incident to the secretary and then Ms. Hernandez led him into her personal office. The room was at least twice the size of the offices that principals often had. But this was a private school. The woman's desk sat in the room's corner with the usual computer, phone, and stacks of papers. Several large, potted plants surrounded the area. Jensen was told to sit on a leather love seat on the opposite side of the room.

It's over. My life is totally over. Dad's going to kill me. Jensen had never sat down; he paced, left, right, and back again.

"Jensen!" The voice broke into his thoughts. Jensen looked up. "We're calling your father. You need to sit down." Jensen hesitated. "Sit down."

Jensen sat down. The moment he did, his feet twinged like he was having a spasm. His fingers snapped. *Where will I go? Dad's gonna kick my ass, if he doesn't kick me out of the house. Oh, god.* Several minutes passed. His left leg started to bounce up and down. Jensen looked up again as Ms. Hernandez called his name. "Yes, Ma'am."

"Stop." The principal glared at him, then went back to pounding on her computer keyboard.

Jensen bit back a cry. He leaned forward and buried his wrists in his eyes. *I can't do this anymore. Dad, where are you?*

CHAPTER 46

CARSON PROMISE

Atlas came into his dad's office after he dropped Brenna at Rachael's house. The little girl didn't cry anymore when he left her, and although he knew this was a positive thing, he did miss it. He was busy with last year's cases when his father rushed into the room. His hair tousled, his face an odd mixture of exuberance and, if Atlas was reading the man right, concern. "Dad, you alright?"

After Robert regained his breath, he spoke. "They need me down at the station."

"They found Nicole?"

"Yes."

"But?" Atlas asked. *That's great, isn't it?* His dad didn't answer right away, and it threw Atlas off. He watched as Robert shook his head.

Robert cleared his throat and said, "Your brother got into a fight at school. They're threatening to expel him. I need you to pick him up and take him home. Stay with him, all right?"

On his feet at once, Atlas went to his own car and made his way to his old alma mater. San Francisco University High School had been a great experience for him. He wished he could stop by and visit his old school more often. But when did he have the time?

Atlas walked into the school's office and was greeted by the secretary he had assisted in his senior year. "Mrs. McHale, how are you?"

"Alasdair Carson, how long has it been?"

"Nine years, ma'am."

"You still have your manners!" she exclaimed. "How old were you when you graduated?"

Atlas laughed. "I was twelve." He took a moment and a deep breath. "I was sent to pick up Jensen. Can you point me in the right direction?" Without hesitation, he was led to the principal's office.

He addressed Ms. Hernandez and then looked to find Jensen perched on the edge of the leather couch. The boy's head was bent forward, his hands knotted and wringing in his lap. "Jensen?"

"I hit Travis," Jensen's voice shivered and was no louder than a whisper. "They expelled me."

Atlas watched his younger brother get to his feet and start for the door. Jensen's walk, his demeanor, his actions. Something wasn't right. Something was very wrong. Atlas could see it all too clearly. "No, come sit down. It's time for a bit of Carson Promise." He led Jensen back to the couch and made him sit. He knew that the principal had her eyes on both of them. Atlas continued. "Jensen, do you remember your ninth birthday? I found you in your room, crying. Do you remember why?"

When Jensen brought his head up, Atlas almost looked away; the tension, the sorrow that poured from him was too palpable. "All the kids downstairs had moms," Jensen's voice shook. "I wanted a mom."

"JC, I told you I could never be Mom," Atlas sat beside Jensen, unsure of whether to make physical contact. He hadn't seen Jensen like this, ever. "I told you—"

"Carson Promise."

"That's right." Jensen stood. Atlas grabbed him and again, pulled him back down on the couch. Atlas could see Jensen had shattered as if he were a delicate porcelain egg having been pushed from a five-story drop. The boy sat there, his breathing deep and steady; he tried to hide the jagged edges that were bleeding deeply within. "I promised you would never be alone. Come on, Jensen."

"Oh, damn." Atlas watched as the tears came, his whole body was overcome by them. "Atlas-Atlas, I can't do this. His body was so messed up!" He choked on a sob.

Atlas glimpsed concern from Ms. Hernandez. *What am I supposed to do?* Atlas's face was calm. He laid a hand on his brother's leg. "I know- "Atlas was cut off by his brother whose face was pale; Jensen panted.

"It's all different colors." Jensen gasped.

Something's not right. He tried again. With a slight squeeze to Jensen's leg, Atlas tried his hardest to sound as if this whole situation they were stuck in, Rustin' rape, Jensen's probable expulsion, the separation of their family, was something they could handle, that it was no big deal. Even if it was a lie. "Jensen, come on, relax."

"Is he okay?" Ms. Hernandez was now at the edge of her seat. "Should I call for an ambulance?" The expulsion papers she had just finished printing out were laid on her desk.

The gasping increased. Atlas tried once more. "Jensen, listen to me."

"Atlas, someone had forced sex with my little brother!"

The silence was thunderous. Seconds slipped by unscathed, unnoticed. It was the ring of Atlas's cell phone that brought everyone back to the moment. Atlas pulled his cell phone from his back pocket. Without glancing at the caller ID, he brought the receiver to his ear. "Hello? Yeah, Dad. I'm fine. Jensen's not breathing right." Absentmindedly, he rubbed his little brother's head. "Saint Francis. Alright." He hung up the phone. Atlas cleared his throat as he remembered

Jensen's last outburst. "Our little brother was raped."

"I can't move my hand." Atlas watched Jensen stare at his hand, which was cupped and stiff. Jensen waved his entire arm through the air, trying to shake it off, but the effort was wasted. "Oh, damn."

"Okay. Jensen, it's okay. Can you walk?" Atlas pulled Jensen to his feet and watched as his legs failed to hold him. Atlas knelt and spoke in a quiet tone. "Jay, I'm right here. You're not alone." Jensen tried again, and with his brother's help, his feet steadied. Atlas guided him out the emergency side door of the principal's office.

It took more that several minutes to get to the hospital, too long for Atlas's comfort. Jensen spent the time hunched forward in the passenger's seat, his breathing still ragged. Once they arrived at the hospital though, things picked up. Because of Jensen's age, and the prior phone call from Robert, things picked up. Atlas and Jensen were led into the emergency room with no pretense.

"His name?" Atlas was asked by the intake nurse.

"Jensen, Carson. He's seventeen."

"Are you family? What happened? We need an orderly in here, stat!"

Jensen's legs had buckled again. Atlas caught him before he hit the ground, He was relieved when an orderly rushed in to help him lay Jensen on a bed. The nurse handed a gown to Atlas just as Jensen's out-of-control breathing, ceased. Jensen's eyes grew big. He struggled to sit up but was laid back down.

"Look at me." The woman's voice was soft. The nurse grabbed hold of Jensen's wrist and placed a device on his finger. "Everything's fine. There's nothing you can't handle here," she paused, watching the boy struggle. "Jensen, I need you to take a breath."

Jensen's head sunk lower into the pillow. "I can't-"

"Come on, honey. Breathe from right here." She placed her hand in the center of his chest. "Slow, deep breath..." They all watched Jensen's body tremble. His head jerked back twice. The nurse pulled Jensen up and asked for a bucket. She put the bucket on his lap just as the boy lost control and retched. Vomit hit the bottom of the bucket with a heavy thud. "All my..." Jensen drew a strangled breath. "Fault." The last word ended in a high note of distress before he was overcome with the uncontrollable breathing once more. The bucket was then moved to the floor.

Atlas watched the nurse remove Jensen's tie and loosen his collar. She wiped his face and chin and then had him rinse his mouth out.

A person in blue scrubs from somewhere came up to the nurse and a moment later she handed Jensen a pill of some sort; the boy swallowed it with a small cup of water. As Jensen started gasping again, Atlas wondered how this episode would all end. *Does he need to go to a psych ward like Zack? Is he suicidal? How do I protect him?* "Is he okay? What did you give him?"

"It's called Xanax, it'll help calm him down. He had a panic attack, and he's going to be fine." A doctor came in at the last minute of Atlas's rant. He put a hand on Atlas's arm. "Once his blood pressure goes down, you can take him home." The man gestured to the gown and then left.

A curtain was pulled around the bed and Atlas helped Jensen into a hospital gown. Once he finished, he wasn't sure what he could do to help his brother relax. One idea came to mind, but he discarded it at once; it was something that could embarrass the hell out of both of them. But when no other idea came to him. Atlas went back to the original idea. It was the one thing that had always helped his brother in the past. Atlas sang 'Lean on me'. He breathed in all the wrong places, and his voice cracked three times. But he heard Jensen's breathing slow down; he even gave a half smile.

Finally, Jensen looked up at Atlas, who could see the exhaustion on his little brother's face. "You killed that song."

"You alright?"

"I was supposed to be the big brother." Jensen looked down at his hands, which rested like limp noodles in his lap. "I was supposed to—"

Atlas shook his head. "No. Big brother's my role. Jay, you're only seventeen. This isn't on you. This isn't your fault."

Jensen wasn't buying any of it. Atlas was afraid this conversation would induce another attack. *Was that even possible?* "But Dad needs me."

"Yes, Dad needs you. But not like he has." Atlas watched as a bit of color returned to the boy's face. Jensen's eyes drifted. "Go to sleep, okay? I'll wake you when it's time to leave."

Atlas stayed at his brother's bedside for the next hour. It was a little after two in the afternoon when the nurse checked Jensen's pulse for the last time. "He's ready," the woman said. "Do you want a wheelchair?"

"Please. Jensen." Atlas shook Jensen once and then again, a little harder. Jensen's eyes opened. "Come on. Let's get you ready to go home."

Jensen's body fell forward. Atlas grabbed him before he fell face first into the thin blanket that covered him. "Hungry." The boy moaned as Atlas helped him remove the hospital gown and pull the old t-shirt over his head. Atlas didn't think it was necessary to put the dress shirt back on him. "Sir."

Sir? "Yes, Jensen. I'll get you some food." A wheelchair was brought in. Atlas had Jensen's arm around his neck with the orderly standing close by as a precaution. Jensen's body kind of crumbled into it. "You want a burger, maybe some fries?"

"Hungry." Jensen's eyes rolled.

"All right." Atlas stepped in front of the wheelchair, making sure his feet were resting on the footplate and both hands were in his lap. He still wasn't convinced that Jensen wasn't about to slip to the floor. The sooner they got to the car, the better. But first things first. As he stepped behind the chair again, he looked at the nurse. "How long will he be like this?"

The woman smiled at his concern as she handed Atlas a prescription. "Six to eight hours. Give him another the moment he hyperventilates."

Atlas spent the next half hour running errands. He bought Jensen lunch. Then he filled the prescription. At home in the driveway, he found Jensen had nodded off, french fries had spilled onto the floor of the passenger's side. "Jay, you need to wake up." Atlas tried to arouse his seemingly comatose brother with a shake to his shoulder. He slapped him across the face with a gentle hand. He even raised his voice. The only thing Jensen could muster was a barely audible moan. *Okay. How do I do this?* He removed Jensen's seatbelt and then began the struggle of getting him into the house. The seventeen-year-old had swayed the moment he got to his feet. "Jensen, we're almost there," Atlas told him as they reached the doorway.

"Fall." Jensen's knees shook.

Atlas grabbed Jensen under the arms. "You will not fall. I've got you." Atlas helped Jensen into the guest room, a room with a bed, dresser, and walls painted a light peach. Light shone bright through an open window. As Jensen crawled into the bed, Atlas went over and pulled the blinds shut. "Get some sleep, kid."

"Atlas." Jensen turned over to look at his older brother.

"Not now. You need to rest." He watched Jensen try to pull himself up, he lifted his head from the pillow before Atlas pushed him back down. "What is it?"

"If Dad throws me out..." Atlas struggled to hear his brother speak;

his words were slurred. "Can I live with you?"

It's just the drug talking. "Jay, Dad will not throw you out. He's worried about you." Atlas could see his words weren't helpful. "If Dad kicks you out, you have a place with us, okay?" There was a frantic knocking at the front door. "I'll be right back. Sleep."

Atlas left the bedroom door open a crack. He glanced at the clock as he passed through the living room. He knew who it was before he opened the door. "Travis- "

Jensen's best friend pushed his way inside. Travis' eyes were wide, his hair disheveled. Even more out of place were his bruised jaw and swollen nose. Dried blood was still smeared across his face. "Where is he? Where's Jensen? He can't hit me."

"He's sleeping-

"Sleeping? I'll wake his ass –" Travis was bouncing on the balls of his feet.

"Travis." The boy stopped and looked at Atlas. "He had a panic attack."

"Travis, go home." Both young men turned and found Robert in the doorway. The father's voice was sharp. Always obedient, Travis headed for the door. Atlas watched him swallow and take a deep breath. "Wait, a minute. I'm sorry. Atlas, grab me the peroxide. Son, come with me."

Atlas grabbed the peroxide and went to find Travis and his father seated at the breakfast bar. He handed Robert the brown bottle. As Robert cleaned up the boy's face, Atlas saw it was covered with a look of devastation. "Travis, what's wrong?"

"What's wrong?" Both men heard Travis's high-pitched voice crack. "What's wrong?"

"Travis, calm down." Robert brushed the cotton ball along the boy's cheek.

"Jensen's dead and you want me to calm down?"

Robert glanced at Atlas and then addressed the terrified teenager. "Jensen's going to be fine.

He had an anxiety attack and right now he's sleeping it off."

"Sleeping it off?"

"Where's Jensen now?" Robert asked Atlas.

Atlas told his father everything that had happened. "I put him in the downstairs guest room.

Come on, Travis. I'll give you a ride home." As Atlas guided Travis toward the front door, he heard his father call out to him. Atlas turned back.

"Thank you, son."

Atlas nodded. Then, with a hand on Travis's shoulders, said, "Come on. Let's get you home."

CHAPTER 47

BACK ON TRACK

The next several hours were spent just getting through, just trying to figure out how he was going to address responsibility with his seventeen-year-old son. Robert had screwed up and he knew it. He had Atlas fill him in on what happened at the school and the hospital. He was handed a prescription they had given Jensen and was told when to use it. Robert also spoke with Ms. Hernandez and got Jensen's expulsion revoked. It wasn't difficult.

It was almost six when Robert walked into the guest room and woke Jensen. "Honey, wake up." He pulled the sheets back and leaned Jensen up against him. "Let's go to the bathroom, okay?"

Eyelashes fluttered for several seconds. Blue eyes opened. Jensen fell forward; Robert put an arm around his shoulders. "My fault."

"Shh." Robert practically carried Jensen to the bathroom. As the boy sat on the toilet, the father saw the red in his son's weary eyes. *I've put too much on him. What do I do now?* He remembered Jensen before the attack on Rustin; always with a grin on his face, Jensen had a hard time focusing on subjects that weren't related to music. These days, however, his homework in all subjects were completed and turned in. He submerged himself with the running of *Just the Five of Us*, and he spent every minute that was asked of him with Rustin. "Damn it,"

Robert muttered.

"I'm sorry." A single tear ran down Jensen's exhausted face.

"Honey, not you. It was never you." Robert rubbed the tear away. "Let's get you back to bed." *If the sheets need to be changed later, I'll change them.* Back in the guest room, Robert laid Jensen down. He removed the boy's slacks and then pulled a blanket up to Jensen's chin. He rubbed his son's forehead until the boy's eyes closed. "Sleep well," he said. Robert kissed him on the head before he left the room.

Around eight, Robert called the Jacobs' home. The conversation had gone well. After apologizing for his son's actions, Robert suggested that in a day or two the boys should be forced to deal with what had happened. Both Jacobs' parents agreed.

Robert entered the guest room the next morning and found Jensen sitting at the edge of the bed, his fingers were entangled in his hair. The boy stood and made many apologies and promises, everything from staying in his room for the rest of the year to writing a twenty-page paper on the legal ramifications of assault. Finally, Robert pushed him onto the bed. "Stop."

Jensen fell silent at once; the father could hear the rapid intake of breath that he associated with Rustin's flashbacks. "Jensen, slow down. Deep breaths." Robert watched Jensen's chest rise and fall. "Now, listen to me. This is not your fault."

"Dad, I hit Travis." Tears welled up in Jensen's eyes. "I totally lost it. They expelled me. You're gonna kick me out?"

"Jensen, I love you. You are not going anywhere." Robert sat beside his son. He took a moment to get his thoughts in order. "I called the school. It was agreed that you're under too much stress. You will not be expelled, and you will continue to go to choir practice." Robert paused. "You'll have a tutor once this is all over. Tell me what happened."

"I hit Travis. I failed." Jensen's voice cracked. "I failed Rustin." Robert raised his eyebrows at that but said nothing. "I can't-can't get the bruises out of my head." Jensen paused, then looked up at his father. "He cried, Dad."

"I know he did. Go get dressed. We're going out for breakfast."

"Not Scrappy's, please."

"Not Scrappy's," Robert agreed. "Go on now."

It was twenty minutes later when he went upstairs and knocked on Jensen's bedroom door. He entered without an invitation. Robert found Jensen dressed in black slacks and a red tailored shirt. The task of knotting his tie held him back, it seemed an impossible undertaking. Jensen shook as if he held a block of ice in each hand. "Come here." By the age of ten, all four of his boys could knot a tie with success. Robert wasn't sure if it was the traces of medication or just nerves. It didn't matter. Robert stepped forward and fixed his son's tie and collar. "Where do you want to eat?"

"I'm not hungry." Robert knew he was lying; he could hear the boy's stomach echo from where he stood. "Can I go back to bed?"

"No. How about the Hard Rock Cafe?" Robert knew it was Jensen's favorite restaurant, with its music memorabilia displayed.

"Atlas said they make their meatloaf like Mom's."

"Nobody could beat Lauren's meatloaf." Robert smiled for the first time that morning. "Hard Rock Cafe it is. I need to make a quick call to the office. Why don't you get into the car?" he suggested. Once Jensen was out of earshot, Robert called the Jacobs.

The ride to the restaurant was silent. Once they arrived, they were the first to be seated, in a private corner in the back. "Order anything you want," Robert told Jensen.

"Coffee?" Jensen asked. He pulled a still trembling hand into his lap.

Why is he still shaking? Robert took a moment before he spoke to the server. "Two coffees, decaf. Him, half a cup." The server left. Before Jensen could speak, Robert found the words that had been escaping him since the night before. "I have spent the last couple of months depending on you as if you were an adult. I was wrong, and I apologize. From now on, your responsibilities are your schoolwork and music. Understand?"

"But Dad. Rustin—"

"Rustin is my responsibility, not yours. End of discussion."

The coffee arrived, and after he added a bunch of sugar and crème, Robert watched Jensen's tremor steady. They ordered lunch and before too long, a huge plate filled with a humongous burger and a side of onion rings was set in front of Jensen. While Robert poured a small cup of ranch dressing over his chicken sandwich, Jensen added barbeque sauce and a couple onion rings to his burger. Several minutes passed as they ate in silence. Robert looked up when Jensen put his half-eaten burger on the plate. "Son, what is it?"

"I don't want to break, Dad."

"That's why we're here, just you and me. Tell me." Robert knew that if he didn't push, Jensen would continue to keep everything bottled up. "Talk to me, Jensen."

Robert watched as Jensen tried to get his thoughts in order. Jensen drew a huge breath before he spoke. "It's so ugly."

"What's ugly?" Robert had an idea what was on his son's mind. But he wanted Jensen to voice it. "What's ugly?" he repeated in a soft tone.

"All of it, Dad. What they did to him." Several people turned at Jensen's rising voice. Neither parent nor child paid attention. "Did you see his body?"

"Tell me what you saw." Robert watched Jensen shake his head, his fingers once more entangled in his curls.

"No. No. I will not be weak anymore. I failed you, Dad."

Oh, damn. "Jensen, you did not fail me. Jensen, look at me." Robert watched the boy's head rise; his hands fall from his head onto the table. Jensen's eyes overflowed with pain. "A man's greatest strength in his ability to be weak. He learns what he's capable of handling. Learning that, gives you strength." Robert grabbed both of Jensen's hands. "Now. Tell me what you saw."

Over the next hour, graphic, sometimes foul words poured from Jensen. The once unprocessed emotions came at Robert like a quiet hailstorm. The server would come to refill their drinks; after another half cup of coffee, Robert switched his son to milk. But other than that, he never said a word. Finally, Jensen was quiet. "That was a lot you had on you, son," Robert acknowledged. "Do you feel better?"

"A little." Jensen ate his last onion ring that must have been cold. "Dad? When are the nightmares going to stop?"

"I don't know. But if you have another one, I want you to come get me. All right?" Robert glanced at his watch and then excused himself to go to the restroom. At the front of the restaurant, beyond Jensen's line of vision, Robert bypassed the bathroom. Instead, he went to the lobby area, and broke out into a smile. The Jacobs were there. "Back left corner," he told Travis. "Work it out."

CHAPTER 48

THE VERDICT

On March twenty-eighth, Robert moved the twins into an upscale hotel on Market Street, not even a mile from the Justice Hall. The inside of the hotel was decorated in blue, white and grey, colors that mimicked those found throughout the city's skies, sand, and ocean.

Arriving early, Robert had hoped Rustin and Zack could relax. He took them to the Embarcadero during the day and rented movies in the room in the evenings. Meals were taken on the fifth floor at a restaurant called MKT, which boasted one hundred-and eighty-degree views of the city. In the mornings, they enjoyed lemon ricotta pancakes, French toast with orange maple syrup, and always a blueberry pie smoothie. Dinner was a burger with bacon jam and cheddar for the boys and shell oysters and grilled asparagus for Robert.

The trial itself took two weeks. Craig was there for support, as was Alasdair, Ashley, Keisha, and Nathan. On the defendants' side, Officer Meyers wife was present, as were a few other people.

Gary, the attorney Robert hired, had shown the jury pictures of the crime scene and medical reports which were elaborated by Dr. Todd. Lechner presented research on male rape and his correspondence with Rustin. Randy was there and told the court how Rustin had been found that early morning so many months ago.

When each defendant took the stand, their malice and coy tone had disappeared. They presented themselves as respectable individuals. Their alibis placed Kevin and Nicole at a hospital in Contra Costa County, an hour away San Francisco. Oscar had a receipt that proved he was at the Black Horse London Pub in Cow Hollow and the word of the person who had served him his drinks. Nicole was the last to testify.

April eleventh, six A.M. The moon was still visible, the sky layered burnt orange, a pale yellow, and finally a greyish blue. Robert's phone played an Edwin McCain song. He reached over to turn it off and then decided to let the song play. Instead, he gathered his clothes. Moments later, he stepped into the shower. As he soaped up, rinsed off, dressed and shaved, Robert realized how much he wanted this day to be over with, finished. Win or lose. He still believed, that by the end of the day, those three bastards would be on their way to prison. His children's lives would regain a sense of normalcy.

And normalcy is what they needed right now, because the night before had been ridiculously hard. Jensen, Craig, and Atlas had visited for a few hours. During that time, nobody wanted to eat or play a game of cards, or even watch a movie. It was too quiet.

At nine o'clock, everyone else left to go home. Robert had both boys take a shower and he even ordered them a cup of hot cocoa, hoping it would help them sleep. Instead, Rustin started having nightmares. And not like the nightmares he had when he was with Craig. But nightmares where he couldn't wake up, where his eyes were open, but he couldn't snap out of it. Even Zack couldn't reach him. Robert sent Zack into the living room to watch a movie. But it took Robert three hours to get Rustin to go back to sleep.

Robert rubbed his eyes and then took a comb to his hair. Turning off the light in the bathroom, he exited his room and walked into the room the twins were sharing. He found Zack peeking through the curtain. "Zack." The boy startled and then looked at his dad. "You're safe, you know that, right?" Zack nodded. Robert didn't want to put any more pressure on the boy, but he had to ask. "How do you think Rustin's handling it?"

Zack seemed surprised by the question. He looked at his twin brother who lay curled up in a ball; the bear had fallen to the floor. Zack walked over and picked the stuffed animal up off the floor and tucked it beneath the blankets near Rustin. "Ever since he heard her voice," it was obvious to Robert that Zack was talking about Nicole. "It's like they're all attacking him again. He hears their voices."

"So, he remembers what happened to him?"

"No," Zack shook his head. "It comes to him in flashes, when he screams. But once an attack is over, he remembers nothing." He paused. "I want to help him, but he won't let me. I wish he trusted me.

"You saw the flashes?"

"Still do, all the time." Zack stared off into space. "How do we wish those jerks are in prison? Like Grandma Antonelli did when Aaron killed Mom?"

Robert got up and guided his son to a chair. *I get it.* But just to be sure, he asked, "Is that what's bothering you?" Zack nodded, and Robert cleared his throat. "We don't. We wish there was a better way to protect us and them, because sending them to prison isn't really going to solve the problem, is it?" Zack shook his head. "You and your brother still have to deal with the attack and the defendants will either be attacked in prison or learn skills that will not help them lead a productive life after they're released." Robert leaned over and kissed Zack on top of the head. "Go get ready for the day."

An hour later, Robert had both boys in the car. They could have gone to The Grove, a restaurant within walking distance to the courthouse, but Robert drove Zack and Rustin to Scrappy's. At the door they passed a sign that read *Private Party*. Considering the half dozen phone calls, he and Craig had made two nights before, he wasn't shocked to find the diner with a good-sized crowd.

Tables pushed together were already overflowed with cups of coffee, milk, and juices of various kinds. There were also bottles full of ketchup, sugar pourers, and syrup dispensers. Brenna was sitting on a booster seat, a plate of food in front of her and sticky syrup smeared across her face. "Papa!" she squealed, trying to escape from the table.

Robert gave his granddaughter a wave and then turned from her as Atlas and Ashley redirected her attention. As he turned away, he found Jensen had approached them. He gave his middle son a quick hug. "How are you doing this morning?"

"Good."

"You know you're prepping the concert with Mr. Delaney today, right?"

Jensen nodded. "Then I pick up Natalie and head back to our house." He paused. "Joel's got me taking orders. What do you want?"

"Coffee and a bagel. Zack. Go help your brother with the food."

Robert led Rustin to the end of the table and then greeted everyone who had come. Craig was there, of course, and Keisha and Nathan. The surprise was that Leo and Charlotte had made the drive down the day before.

It wasn't long before all of them were crowded together, eating. Even Joel and the cook Danielle had joined them. Robert watched as Rustin took a bite of his rodeo burger before popping a fry in his mouth. Zack was enjoying his usual combination of oatmeal and onion rings dipped in syrup. As the meal progressed there were discussions about work, school projects, and the need for a vacation.

All too soon, it was twelve fifteen and everybody dispersed. Ashley was taking Brenna home, Jensen and Natalie were headed to school, and the rest of them were headed to the courthouse.

At this time of day, the sun shone brightly and the air was brisk. Robert pulled into the parking lot of 850 Bryant Street and found a spot. The Hall of Justice, where the trial had taken place, was a seven-story high rise that housed three hundred inmates on the top floor.

"Come on, boys." Robert took the keys from the ignition and opened the car door. "One more hour and this will all be over." There was a small crowd waiting by the front door of the Justice Hall. But as he watched, a single person broke away and started walking toward him. His dad, Hal. Robert glanced at his watch. *Twelve-thirty.* He raised his voice. "Craig, take the boys inside." He watched as his brother-in-law guided Rustin and Zack through a set of glass doors. Everyone followed them into the building. Once the doors shut, Robert looked at Hal. "What are you doing here?"

"Your mother and I separated," Hal answered in a gruff voice. He shook his head. "What happened to Rustin, the way we left, it wasn't right. I came to apologize."

Robert opened his mouth to respond but realized his dad wasn't finished. He closed his mouth and gave a nod.

"I was six the first time it happened. And it happened almost every night until I turned ten. It wasn't as bad as what Rustin went through, no head injury, no intercourse. Just touch. And it happened almost every night until I turned ten." Hal paused. He took a quick glance at the Justice Hall and then looked Robert straight in the eye. "The day before my tenth birthday was the last day she ever touched me. She finished at eleven o'clock that night, kissed me on the lips, and disappeared."

A long minute passed. Robert clapped his father on the shoulder. "We're good. Should we go in?"

Going to court was like going to the theatre, and every theatre had the same set up, the same cast of characters. In San Francisco's Hall of Justice, the backdrop was a grey wall adorned with several rectangular brown panels. A silver circular disc, California's seal, hung between two of the panels. Two flags, the Stars and Stripes, and the state bear hung from golden metal poles, situated to the left of where the judge would sit.

Beyond the backdrop was the stage where the performance, for lack of a better word, would take place. The judge, aka the protagonist, would sit elevated at the bench facing everyone, with his side kick, the court reporter not far away. Props included two massive desks facing the judge, the defense seated on the left, the prosecution on the right. More players still included not just a bailiff, but fourteen individuals from all over the city. They sat on the right, in two rows of seven. These people were the twelve chosen jurors, plus two alternates.

Finally, off stage behind a long wooden separation, was where the audience would watch. The audience could include supporters for the defense or the prosecution, media (unless restricted by the judge), or anyone else from the public.

But before the curtains closed on the finale, they had to step into the courtroom one last time. Robert patted Zack's shoulder when the boy looked out at his twin who was still in the hallway. "Let's go sit down, Rustin."

Rustin shook his head. "I don't want to."

Robert watched Zack step forward, his hand raised, his fingers extended. Rustin's hand met his halfway.

It was when the gesture ended that Robert looked at Zack first and then Rustin. "However this ends, tonight we'll be home. Tonight, you'll sleep in your own bed." Robert smiled and then followed both of his sons into the courtroom.

It was one o'clock in the afternoon when five men and nine women, all of them well dressed, filed into the jury box and took their seats. The bailiff was standing by the door. Dressed in a tan shirt, a badge pinned at his chest, he stood straight, his feet planted a foot apart and his hands hung loosely at his sides.

As the door to Judge Tolliver's chambers opened, the room fell silent. A woman in a long black robe came into the courtroom. The door closed, echoing loudly. Judge Tolliver took her place behind the stand. The past two weeks had taken its toll; the judge appeared tired and cross. But Robert set the thought aside. It didn't matter what the judge thought when the jury would be making the decision. "Be seated." Everyone sat down. "Has the jury reached a verdict?"

A woman with a sturdy build and a pair of thick red-rimmed glasses stood, a pile of papers in her hands. "Yes, Your Honor." She had them handed to the bailiff who proceeded to give then to the judge.

Moments after Tolliver flipped through them, she had them handed back to the head juror. "Will the defendants please rise."

The tension in the room was heavy; it was like a stretched-out balloon ready to pop. The head juror cleared her throat as she glanced down at the paper in her hands. "On the charges for Kevin Meyers, we find the defendant guilty of kidnapping in the first degree, with a firearm. We find him not guilty on the charge of accessory to rape. On the charges against Nicole Taylor, we find the defendant guilty of accessory to kidnapping. On the charge of rape in the first degree, we find the defendant guilty. On the charges against Oscar Hernandez, we find the defendant guilty as an accessory to kidnapping in the second degree. We find the defendant guilty of sodomy in the first degree and guilty of rape in the second degree."

"Oscar Hernandez, Nicole Taylor, and Kevin Meyers you will be held at the California Department of Corrections and Rehabilitation in Oakland, California. Sentencing will be in two weeks' time." Judge Tolliver banged her gavel. "Court is adjourned."

As the judge returned to her chambers, several bailiffs came forward, each with a set of handcuffs in hand. It was at this time that Robert felt all the tension just go, like the release of that over-blown balloon. He had to stop himself from jabbing his fist in the air and grinning his teeth out. The worst was finally over.

Robert had stood up and was shaking Gary's hand when he heard a voice nearby. "I will never forget that tight little ass." Robert turned around. He saw Nicole struggling as her hands were pulled behind her back. A smile was plastered across her face. Robert stepped sideways, blocking his son from view.

"Ignore her." Robert looked down at his son who was staring straight ahead. He watched as Rustin didn't even blink. Robert knelt down. "Hey, Rusi, it's over. We get to go home." He was surprised when Lechner came up to them. Robert exchanged a glance with the psychologist and nodded. He took a step back.

"You and I are going to spend a lot of time talking." Lechner put a pair of strong hands on Rustin's shoulders and pulled the boy to his feet. "Look." He turned Rustin to the left where the bailiffs had handcuffed Nicole, Oscar, and Kevin. They were marching the three convicted felons through a dark, heavy door. "You see that? They can't hurt you or anyone else now."

Rustin turned to look at his dad, his expression unsure. "I did that?"

Robert pulled his son against his chest; he kissed the top of Rustin's head. "Yes. Yes, you did."

—·—

CHAPTER 49

WIZARD!

J ensen planned to major in music, but he often wondered if this performance would be the end, not just for him, but for all the students who were to graduate this year. Nothing in the world soothed and excited him so much, all at the same time. The music he would always have until the day he died; nobody could take that away from him. It was the camaraderie of this group of friends that made the music mean so much more.

The seventeen-year-old had spent most of the day preparing for that night's concert. He helped Delaney with various tasks, which had him checking the sound system and setting up the mics and pulling the risers from their dusty home beneath the stage. It also included the stage set up, which always took the longest out of everything that needed to be completed. It had been a long day and it wasn't over yet.

Jensen had begun his morning focused, aware of not just his responsibilities but also of the enchantment early on; the stress of the past several weeks vanished. He enjoyed the quickening of his heartbeat as he entered the room that evening. It shouldn't have affected him so, but he was always blown away by the sensation. Jensen had tried to explain it once to Alasdair, how it was beyond nerves, beyond plain magic. Some might describe it as the old cliché' of the smell of excitement in the air. But what was that? Jensen knew. It was a wizard's stench of bright lights and raw nerves, cascading fears and shrieking yet stable footsteps. The clock was already beckoning at him, *It's almost time, it's almost time.* The lights would dim and a room full of eyes would be focused on him. If his voice cracked, if he missed a note, or if he stumbled a few steps, it was still there, because that was a part of it too, with the stench and the footsteps, and as always, the tingles and jitters. When the evening was over, when the curtains finally closed and they had all gone home, the tingles and jitters would still be there.

Julia came up behind him, her strong yet gentle fingers released the knots in his shoulders. "Do you know how cute you are?"

Jensen turned around with a big smile on his face, he kissed Julia on the lips. "No, tell me." A freshman girl with red curls scurried by, her head in her hands. Concerned, he grabbed the girl by the arm. "What's the matter, Mary-Ana? You having a little stage fright?"

"I can't do this. There's too many people out there! I'm going to screw up, I know I am!" Tears flooded down her pale cheeks.

He smiled and laid a calm hand on her shoulder. "Take a deep breath, Mar. You can do this, I've heard your solo, and you rock."

"The octave's too high."

"Hey, you hit it at practice. Did you hear *Just the Five of Us*?" Mary-Ana nodded. "Travis missed his note twice."

Jensen felt his arm being slugged. He exchanged a grin with Travis who had heard the conversation. "Thanks, Carson."

"Any time, Jacobs." Jensen shook his best friend's hand and then turned his attention back to Mary-Ana. "Don't stress it, you can do this."

"Mar, let's go outside and get you some air." Shrugging out of his dress coat, Jensen draped the cloth over Julia's shoulders. He watched his girlfriend lead Mary-Ana out the door.

Mr. Delaney came up behind him. "Jensen."

Turning around, Jensen said, "Yes, sir?"

"Name the stage rules of performance." The older man stood before him, rubbing his palms together. Everything was on the line tonight. If Jensen couldn't pull off running the concert tonight, it would put next year's group, especially *Just the Five of Us* at risk for not having a student run the program. Whomever ran the program was guaranteed a shoe in for grad school. Therefore, failure tonight was not an option. Not that Jensen was worried.

"Introductions, by first and last name, no nicknames. Keep dialogue short and succinct. And above all else, no personalization. Failure to adhere to the rules will cause detention, demerits and dismissal from the class."

"Well said. You ready to get everyone warmed up?" Jensen nodded. "Okay, I'll be right up front, off to the left, if you have any problems."

"There won't be any problems."

"You have the nights' program?" Jensen nodded. Delaney patted him on the back. "Good luck." The instructor looked at all his students and raised his eyebrows. "Let's not break any legs." Everyone laughed and a moment later, the man was gone.

Clearing his throat, Jensen spoke in a loud clear voice, "Everyone, get in your groups." He stepped back and watched as his fellow singers waded past each other in two different directions, taking places on the risers in the center in the room. Jensen then took a moment as he went outside and called Julia and Mary-Ana back inside. Finally, the movement stopped. Everyone was looking at him. The tension in the room was palpable to the extreme; something had to get them to relax or the whole night would be a disaster. "Sing the scale, forwards, backwards, and hold the last note." Jensen sang with them and then cut out at the end to hear how it sounded. "We can't sing off key, guys.

Delaney will kick my ass." The class laughed. Jensen grinned. "Yawn." The entire yawned, a noise that started at the highest of everyone's range and went to the lowest. He had them go through the scale again. "That's more like it. Chorus, grab your robes, get ready to go on. Everyone else, relax." He grabbed his dress coat from Julia and kissed her before he slipped it on.

With a deep, steady breath, Jensen could feel the adrenaline rush that came with every performance. He walked up the staircase that led from the choir room to backstage. Slowing his stride, he passed the heavy curtains and ambled to the front of the stage. He paused to see where his family was among the audience and found them in the second row off to the right. Jensen cleared his throat and grabbed the microphone stand in front of him with a smile. "It's good to see all the parents and fellow students out there in the audience." He took another breath. It was an attempt to slow the intro down; once it was over, it was over. Forever. "Later tonight you will hear the talented Mary-Ana Carter, Nakia Santini, and Kim Swartz perform solos that will make your spine tingle and your ears crave for more." The audience laughed when Jensen's expression changed to something that looked like he was unsure of himself. He shook his head and laughed. "Let's start tonight off with several pieces from Chorus. Enjoy the evening." Pausing again, he looked at Delaney who gave him a nod. Jensen grinned and backed away from the mic. A moment later he spun around on his heel and walked off stage where members of Chorus were lined up, dressed in long red robes. "Knock 'em dead, guys," he told them.

Back in the room, he prepared Nakia for going on and then sat on the highest riser. It was the first time he had been off his feet in hours. During the next two and a half hours, Jensen kept things on schedule and running smoothly. It wasn't until the last soloist, Mary-Ana, went on stage that he thought about the repercussions of the court verdict, that he thought about what his final words of the evening would be.

Jensen looked around the busy and crowded room. He noticed that half of the group was changing their outfits one last time; Travis was in the back of the room pulling his shirt over his head and Steve was stepping into a pair of black slacks in a corner not that far away. Elizabeth was hidden behind a curtain that had been put up earlier that day; proper British girls did not undress in front of members of the opposite sex. Julia, however, didn't hesitate as she adjusted her long black skirt and then pulled off her top. She replaced it with a yellow blouse. Jensen couldn't help but smile as she adjusted her bra strap before she fastened the last few buttons.

Travis pulled him up to his feet and then slapped him on the back. "One more speech, man."

Jensen clapped his hands to get everyone's attention. "All right everybody, tonight has been awesome. Let's get lined up for the finale. Remember, I make a couple comments, *Just the Five of Us* walks on stage, and as we start the main verse, everyone enters through the back doors." Jensen grinned. His heart raced; his whole body tingled. He felt more alive than he had in a long time. Removing his dress coat, he slipped into his vest. As he looked around, he saw the other guys were ready. "Let's do this."

Jensen followed Steve, Miguel, Travis, and Tyrese into the shadows of the background where five mics had been placed to one side. Jensen grabbed one and then walked to the center of the stage. He paused here for a moment. *I could so screw my GPA right now.* He took a quick glance at his teacher thinking of all the demerits that would soon be on his record if he did not adhere to the school's regulations. Younger classmates looked up to him to do what was right. *What was right?* Jensen's eyes drifted. He recognized Rustin who was sitting in the audience, of his little brother who not too long ago was fighting for his life; the battered body of his little brother had survived. They had all survived. *Fuck the demerits.* "This year hasn't been easy." Jensen let his gaze fall to his youngest brother whose baseball cap did its best to cover the gauze that protected Rustin's head. "Rusi went through hell, we all did. Me, and Rus, and dad, and Zack and Atlas." Jensen's voice cracked. There was a slight rustling in the crowd. He could see Delaney, his face nothing but a shadow in the dim light. He waited a moment and cleared his throat. "I wanted to say thank you, to all of you. Because, we made it. Rusi, you made it." There was another pause from Jensen when the audience began to applaud and cheer. When the audience died off, Jensen grinned. "Usually the lead senior, that would be me," the crowd laughed, "Would sing the intro before *Just the Five of Us* joined in, as the finale to this concert. Tonight, though, we've stepped it up a bit." He looked toward his family. "Rustin, we're glad you're back home."

Jensen stepped into the shadows again as Tyrese approached a mic stand and began beat boxing with a steady rhythm. He watched as Miguel took his mic and began his solo. As he finished and the main verse began, the five of them walked to center stage. He could just barely see the back doors open and two columns of students separate and in absolute silence made their way around the room. *I didn't think it would work. This is outstanding!*

Jensen stepped forward again, mic in hand. He turned and faced Travis. "*Just call on me, brother-   Yeah-*

When you need a hand-

Come on— "Travis hit the note and then went off on a musical tangent, his voice ascended and descended three different octaves, jumping from one range to another and back again. It could only be described as crazy. With the surge bellowing inside of him, Jensen joined in. Travis backed off and allowed Jensen a solo. The crowd was going wild. Jensen finished, nodded at Travis, and brought up his hand and counted *one, two, three.*

When the two of them came in together, the pitch was perfect. *We all need somebody to lean on.* The crowd watched Jensen and Travis exchange handshakes, and then there was nothing but blackness. He could hear a collective gasp go throughout the whole room. Counting off to three in his head, Jensen grabbed the portfolio that he knew was at his feet. Miguel slammed his portfolio on to the stage, quickly followed by Steve and Tyrese. Jensen slammed his portfolio. As Travis slammed his portfolio, drums, trumpet, and saxophones crashed the party, so to speak. The lights came on from one side of the room to the other, revealing a beautiful collage of colors and sound.

With the lights back on, *Just the Five of Us* stepped forward on stage as the entire choral body joined them in the final verse of the song, complete with all the runs they had mastered that afternoon.

As the final note of the song drifted off, the singers were awarded with a standing ovation. Jensen lingered on stage as everyone else filed off. Finally, he walked off, the adrenaline that he had felt coursed through his blood like a burning flame, did not realize that it was over. Back stage, down the steps, and in the choir room, he and Travis were surrounded by their peers.

"What made you do that?" someone asked Travis. "You didn't sing it like that during practice."

"That was outstanding!" cried another voice.

Jensen caught Travis' eye. "It was time," Travis told everyone. "Everything has been about control. Getting it right. Forget that fucking crap."

"Excuse me?" No one had seen Delaney enter the room.

"Music is what it is, sir," Travis went on without apology. "If I had sharped that note instead of getting it right, it may have dropped my grade a bit. It would have been embarrassing. I'm a first tenor, I should have no problem hitting that note. But it wouldn't have been the end of the world." Travis looked at his best friend. "JC, the controls back where it should be. Let it go."

"This summer? On the road?" No one had any clue what they were talking about.

"Yeah." Travis laughed. "On the road."

"Travis, code of conduct violation. Two demerits." Travis nodded. Delaney sat down at the piano and started running his fingers over the keys. "Jensen, a word."

Bringing his hand up to his mouth, Jensen coughed. "Yes, sir." He pulled a stack of sheet music from his backpack and approached his teacher.

"Leadership is earned, Mr. Carson." Delaney took the stack of papers and paused as he laid them on top of the piano.

Action around the classroom ceased. Again, all eyes were on him. *Damn it. I should have kept my big mouth shut. Dad's gonna kill me.*

"You broke every rule tonight. You put everything this program stands for in jeopardy. Give me the school's code of conduct."

Jensen looked his teacher in the eye. "Yes, sir. I did. We live by the code of FLAW, sir." He stood erect, his head high. "We're to treat each other like Family. We respect and protect Life at all costs. We Act, we never stand back and do nothing." Jensen took a deep breath. "And Words, sir. Words have power. We use them wisely."

"Mr. Delaney," Tyrese stepped forward. "He may have broken all stage regulations. But sir, he did follow the code. His words let everyone feel a closure to something that has affected all of us. I wish I had the ba-"Tyrese caught Steve shaking his head discreetly. "Nerve. I wish I had the nerve to step up like he did tonight." Julia, Travis, and Miguel stepped to either side of Tyrese. Others in the classroom were nodding their heads.

Mr. Delaney stood up and took a brief glance around the room. Then, looking at Jensen, he said, "Agreed. Your performance tonight, your running of this group, your ability to pull all of this together, proved your leadership qualities. And that's not even taking your personal life into account. I could expect nothing more. You will pass this class with an A plus, and your college recommendation is already written. Congratulations, Mr. Carson." Jensen's response, a soft audible word of thanks, could not be heard over the applause.

The surrounding crowd broke up. Everyone put their choir robes back into the closets. They gathered schoolbooks that had kept them occupied during the concert, worn backpacks were slung over weary shoulders. "Remember, my house this Saturday. We're going to end this right. Everybody bring something."

He stayed until the room was empty, picking up empty water bottles from the floor. "You ready to go home, Jensen?"

Jensen found his father at the door, surprised by his words. He grinned. "Yes, sir, let's go." Stepping out into the cold air, Jensen let out a whoop. Earth was a billion light years away. It would take most of the night for him to touch back down. Those blasted tingles and jitters wouldn't let him alone. And Jensen wouldn't have it any other way.

CHAPTER 50

A MANILLA ENVELOPE

The next morning, Atlas groaned and opened his eyes. Ashley was awake and staring at him. "Why didn't you wake me?" He leaned over and kissed her, then looked up at the clock on the wall, shocked. "It's after ten."

"I already called Mom and Dad. They're taking Brenna to Schwartz. She'll be home about four." Ashley got out of bed and Atlas followed her to the bathroom. "I signed for an envelope about ten minutes ago. It looks kind of official."

"Later. Since we have the whole day to ourselves, what's on the agenda?"

Ashley lifted her eyebrows suggestively. "Wouldn't you like to know?" Atlas watched her undress and step into the shower. "We'll have dinner at your dad's tonight. Is your uncle still visiting?" she asked, raising her voice over the sound of the water pressure.

"He leaves bright and early tomorrow morning. Mind if I join you?"

"Step right in, baby." Atlas disrobed and stepped into the shower, closing the door behind him. The glass steamed up and the silence that followed was enjoyable.

Sometime later, they were both headed out the door, Atlas had the envelope in one hand and the car keys in the other. "Where to, my queen?" He laughed as Ashley grabbed the keys from his hand and walked past him to the car.

Atlas got into the passenger's seat, put his seat belt on, and leaned back as his wife pulled out of the driveway. It was nice to spend the morning not stressing about anything. As Ashley drove, he recognized the roads they were taking. "Scrappy's?"

She stopped at a light and looked at him. "Is that alright?"

"Perfect." He smiled and kissed her right before the light changed.

At Scrappy's, Joel seated them himself and handed them menus. It wasn't long before Ashley was served a plate with a veggie omelet, hash browns, and a side of fruit. Atlas had ordered a rodeo burger dripping with BBQ sauce and a side of onion rings.

"You didn't open the mail," Ashley said after swallowing a bite. "Are you nervous about the results?"

Atlas shrugged as he picked up an onion ring. "Other stuff on my mind." He was silent as he popped the onion ring in his mouth and then took a sip of iced soda.

Ashley was almost finished with her omelet, but Atlas was not surprised when she waved Joel down and ordered a large brownie, topped with vanilla ice cream, and drizzled in chocolate syrup. He knew soon he would be sent to the store in the middle of the night for potato chips, pickles, and a thick chocolate milk shake.

"What are we supposed to do now?" Ashley asked, taking a sip of her shake.

"What do you mean?"

Ashley set down her glass and carefully wiped her mouth. "I mean, it's over. But it's not really over." Atlas looked at her puzzled. "The case. We won. But your brothers still lost, kind of."

Atlas shook his head. "You can't think of it like that. Losing is always a possibility in court. Whether we won or lost the case, we still have to help Rustin and Zack get through this. It never just goes away." He could see the stress painted across Ashley's face. "We're family, we deal with it together. Always have, always will." Atlas paused and managed a smile. "You're a part of that family, as is Brenna and our future child that you are carrying. So, no more stress. Let's have some fun before we head over to Dad's. What do you want to do?"

Ashley excused herself twice to use the restroom while Atlas waited for and paid the bill. The second time she came back, she announced they were going to the mall.

"Why are we doing this so early?" Atlas asked as they pulled into the parking lot of the mall. "We don't even know the sex of the baby."

"It's a baby, Atlas. Not a socially challenged society." Atlas hid a grin; it was starting already, the attitude, the desire to change the world, the adamancy that her children would be the ones to change all the injustices. "We need a theme." Ashley got out of the car and led Atlas into a large department store. "I picked last time." She grabbed a shopping cart.

Atlas laughed. "Honey, I don't care. What-"

"You don't care?"

"Okay, I do care. I just don't- "Atlas stopped and turned to his wife; he took her by the hands. "Alright. Gender neutral, right?" Ashley nodded. Atlas was slowly remembering how this worked. He started going through all he was being introduced to by his daughter. *There's always Sesame Street. Ashley said that was overdone last time. And Barney's too big, the baby would be terrified. Where she got that idea, I don't know. We just did Winnie the Pooh.* "What about Care Bears? They're gender neutral, aren't they?"

"Care Bears, that's a wonderful idea!" Erica kissed Atlas on the lips and then dragged him through the store.

He piled everything in the cart, the crib sheets, the border, the fabric for a new baby blanket, Care Bear themed, of course. The cart was piled high when she started toward the children's furniture department. "We don't need new furniture, do we? The crib we have in the garage-

"We'll donate that to the crisis nursery. All of it."

The mania of pregnancy. And Dad went through it three times. "All right, honey. Remember, we need to pick up Brenna and head to Dad's soon."

"Brenna?" Ashley was enthralled with the colors and styles of cribs. Her attention refused to be diverted. "Green or yellow. Maybe purple." she continued under her breath.

"Your daughter, remember? Little girl, light brown hair, calls you mommy."

"Oh, uh-huh."

"Never mind. Which one are you looking at?"

Atlas dragged Ashley out of the store before she looked at baby clothes. But as they headed toward the exit, they passed by the woman's clothing section where there was a sale on coats. It took another twenty minutes to direct Ashley out of the store. Finally, with the backseat of the car full of items, they realized a trip home was necessary to unload before they could pick up their daughter.

CHAPTER 51

NEW HOPE AND DREAMS

It was after midnight by the time everyone had settled down for the night. After Jensen's performance, Robert went to the local pizza joint and picked up half a dozen pizzas and the same amount of two liters. They talked about how the weather was clearing up, new movie releases, and other safe topics. The Spencer's went home right before eleven, Hal took the guest room upstairs while Leo and Charlotte took the downstairs suite. Atlas and Ashley went to their home with a promise to return the next morning.

Robert woke Saturday to the wonderful smell of coffee dripping from the percolator. He dressed quickly in jeans and a sweater and ran a comb through his hair. Then he headed downstairs.

He found Jensen at the stove frying sausage; the bacon was already on a plate, covered. Jensen looked up. "Hey, Dad."

Robert stepped forward, shaking his head. He grabbed the spatula from his son's hand. "No. You go to the solarium and play some music. I'll take care of—"

Jensen lifted his eyebrows and smiled. "Dad, it's just breakfast. It's okay. I got this." A timer went off. The teenager paused as he stepped back and pulled on a pair of oven mitts. A minute later, he was inhaling the warm delicious smell of blueberry muffins.

Robert was incredulous. "You made muffins?"

"From a box, Dad. Grandpa Hal and Uncle Leo left to get donuts and stuff." Jensen took a moment to turn off the oven. "Can I invite Julia and Travis over?"

Robert smiled. "Just Julia and Travis. I don't need Steve and your other friends eating us out of house and home."

"We're back!" Leo entered the kitchen with several plastic bags; Robert was happy to see a package of paper plates in one of them. Leo was followed by Hal who carried boxes of donuts and cheese Danish.

It was as Craig swooped in to help carry things that Robert saw a white Cadillac pull into the circular driveway. An older woman opened the passenger side door and stepped out. Robert stepped around everyone and hurried down the stairs. "Patricia Antonelli! What are you doing here?"

"Next time there is a catastrophe like this, I want to hear it from your mouth." The woman had always put anyone of them in line. "Not by two little chirping birds." She glared at Craig and Leo before turning her stern eyes back to Robert. "Do you understand me?"

"Yes, Ma'am." As he went to give her a hug, he saw Rustin taking measured steps down the stairs. Once at the bottom though, he broke into a run and collided with Patricia. Robert was about to reach out and pull his son back, but the woman raised her hand to let him know she was alright. He turned his attention to the top of the stairs where Zack stood watching. "Let's take Grandma's things to her room and we can get you ready to go with Alasdair." Robert paused as his eldest child pulled in behind the Cadillac and the engine quieted. Atlas didn't get out immediately but slid open an envelope, pulling out the contents. He closed his eyes. When he opened them again, Alasdair broke into the biggest smile he had ever seen. Robert cleared his throat. "Let's go, son."

Robert and Zack grabbed a couple bags from the chauffer that had dropped Patricia off. Robert paid him handsomely before heading back to the house. After some rearranging of sleeping quarters, they made it up to Zack's room. "I want you to have a good time up at the cabin. Try to relax, okay?" Robert smiled as Zack began to unceremoniously stuff clothes into a duffle bag. " I remember what you said yesterday. It'll take time for Rustin to realize what happened, to put the pieces together. But he does trust you."

"I know, Dad." He stuffed the sleeve of a hoodie into the bag and then struggled to zip it shut. When he couldn't, he took all of it out and started to fold it.

As Robert went to sit down, his feet slid on a rug at the side of Rustin's bed and revealed a trap door Robert had long forgotten about. Robert knelt and removed the board. Smiling, he sifted through old report cards, a detention slip, and at the very bottom, a book that was withered with time. Robert saw the name on the cover and began flipping through the pages. The pictures were beautiful, framed with just the right amount of light on a perfect background.

"Dad?"

Robert had gone to Rustin's desk. He methodically went over it and found what he wanted; the stack of photos that had been processed from Rustin's old camera. They were all the same, the same beach, the same sunset, only the people in the photos had changed, aged to another time.

"Dad?" Robert could hear the old fear creep into Zack's voice. "What's wrong?"

"Nothing." Robert realized the answer wasn't good enough. "The book Rustin spoke about, the one your Mom put together." Zack came beside him, "I think this is it."

Several minutes passed as the two of them went through the book, page by page. Finally, Robert left Zack alone upstairs to finish packing. He ended up in the kitchen, where he found Patricia and Rustin at the breakfast bar.

Patricia seemed to take her time making her special hot cocoa. She mixed a steaming cup of milk with a spoonful of unsweetened cocoa, a table spoon of sugar, some caramel, and a little sprinkling of cinnamon. She brought it to the table. "How about we go to my room?"

"No." Rustin took a deep breath as he wrapped his hands around the mug. Tears came to his eyes. "I want Mom."

Seconds ticked by. Robert desperately wanted to jump in, but he didn't dare. To prevent himself from making that mistake, he went into the living room where he found Atlas and Ashley hanging their coats by the door. "Papa!" Brenna ran toward Robert who caught her in his arms. "Alasdair." His eldest son looked at him. "Bar Results."

"Passed with flying colors." Atlas grinned and stepped forward to hug his dad, his daughter squashed in between.

"Help!" she cried. The three adults laughed, and Brenna was released from the vice like hug.

Robert then took in the pale pink coat Ashley was wearing; he'd never seen it before. "Someone's been shopping." He paused. *Brand new coat, a grin that never leaves her face.* "So, how far along are you?"

"Six weeks." Ashley looked at Atlas, "Did you tell him?"

Atlas had removed Brenna's jacket and the little girl ran off toward the solarium. "Someone's back there?" Robert nodded. Atlas smiled at Ashley. "Dad always knows. He knew when Mom was pregnant with Jensen. And he knew something was different with the third pregnancy. Call him the Pregnancy Whisperer."

"Robert?" Patricia's head was poking out from the kitchen door. "Rustin needs you."

Robert shooed everyone into the solarium as Rustin shuffled into the room. "How you are doing, Rusi?"

"The place they said they found me. I want to go."

"No. That's out of the question.

"Because it's a lie. I knew it."

Robert grabbed Rustin and led him into the bathroom. "Look in the mirror, son. Look at your head. Do you remember the pain? Because I watched you curl up into a ball and scream. That pain was real. It didn't come out of nowhere." Rustin broke away, and before Robert could grab him, the boy was out the door.

Robert looked for half an hour and was about to call the police. He found Zack sitting on the front porch, rubbing his hands together most aggressively. Robert laid a hand on his son's shoulder. "You alright?"

"Yeah. When are we moving to Washington?"

"I called my real estate agent and canceled the move. Our support system is right here in the city. This is where we belong."

Zack stood up and for the first time in months, he looked Robert in the eyes. "I'm going to take care of Rus."

Of course. Why didn't I ask Zack to begin with? Robert took his time considering and then nodded. "Is he on the property?"

"Yes, sir."

"Call me if you need me. I'll either be in the kitchen or with your Nana. Just make sure you both stay here." Robert watched as Zack nodded and then stood up. His eyes followed as his son went into the backyard, and finally satisfied, Robert went back in doors.

CHAPTER 52

TWINK SPEAK

Robert nodded. "Just make sure you both stay here."

Zack fought hard not to roll his eyes; tonight, was not a good time to express any sarcastic attitude. He had learned this the hard way many times. Instead, he nodded and then headed into the back yard, pulling his tie loose. Damp grass squished beneath his shoes. *The sensor lights will be coming on soon.* He continued past the gated pool to the large sturdy oak tree and his childhood tree house.

It had been a couple years since any of the boys had been up here and it showed. Cobwebs in several corners, an empty soda can was propped on a window ledge, several fast-food wrappers littered the floor. Pokémon cards stained with dust lay scattered on a small table in the corner. An ill bought once bright orange Furby was still stuffed behind a pile of outgrown Halloween costumes, Spiderman, the Hulk, Wolverine. The costumes had been worn during many rounds of capture the princess, aka Natalie. And the Furby? That had been a gift from Grandma and Grandpa Carson to Rustin on his seventh birthday. Posters of Buffy the Vampire Slayer and Michael Jordan were tacked to the wall. In the center of it all were two very patched bean bag chairs.

When Zack had been sitting on the front porch, he had seen Rustin pacing back and forth the cramped space of the tree house. But he found his twin brother stretched back in one of the beanbag chairs, his eyes closed, his breath slow and deliberate.

Rustin sensed Zack across from him and the flash began. *He sees a mirror's reflection, but it doesn't wear purple or green. He doesn't know who it is. The reflection is sitting on a toilet encircled by singing babies.* "Truth or lie?" Rustin asked, opening his eyes.

Sinking down into the green beanbag, Zack looked directly at his twin. "Truth."

A car swerves around a corner, nearly hitting him. And it's clearly Rustin who's staggering with bloodshot eyes; he's wearing a purple hoodie.

"No." The image ceased movement as Zack interrupted. "I told you, Rusi. I was the one who was had a beer and I never got drunk. That stuff was nasty." Zack's cheeks reddened. "I was the one on the toilet.".

Rustin slowly shook his head. The image changed. Zack was now the one with a beer in hand, minus the bloodshot eyes. The memory melts away.

A woman in blue jeans, a red t-shirt, and high-heeled shoes that assault the tile floor with a deafening ring. She walks into a room where someone lays connected to machines that pierce the ears as loudly as the heels. The faces are adult, fuzzy, and unrecognizable. "Truth or lie?"

"Not sure," Zack answered. "Probably a lie, though."

"Why?" Rustin demanded.

"Because, if that was her," talking about Nicole, "Everything else she said was a lie. I know she hurt you. I saw her."

Rustin took a moment, deep breaths to calm his nerves. *Another bed. This one, Rustin, lays in. Natalie's suddenly there, and then there's this bright light that explodes between them.* Zack laughed; he couldn't help it.

"Truth or lie?" Rustin again demanded an answer.

"Lie. Definitely a lie." Zack laughed again.

"It's not funny." Rustin shot up to his feet, towering over Zack.

"OK, I'm sorry." Zack held up placating hands.

Rustin crumbled back into his beanbag chair. The silence between them, that had been a static force filled with scrambled pictures, gradually came into focus. They both breathed easier. "One more," he whispered.

A light flashed through the tree house. Zack went to the small window and found someone had turned on the lantern. The yard flooded with light. He paced the small area as he waited for Rustin to be ready. After a few moments, another sequence begins.

Zack had seen many flashes over the last several months. But this one, this one he hadn't seen before. Zack saw a flash of bare skin, and then hands. Nothing but hands. He recognizes his father's hand, complete with the wedding ring. But the others are all foreign to him. *Large, small, covered in latex, rough with calluses.* The flash stops all at once, as if there isn't anymore. It feels unfinished. But Zack understands without words, without flashes or sounds. "What, you proposing to me? Aren't you supposed to do that on bended knee?" Both Zack and Rustin laughed.

Minutes later, Rustin left Zack in the tree house, something about needing to clean the space so Brenna could use it. Whatever the reason, Rustin was satisfied that he had a few truths; if Zack had gone on describing who the hands belonged to and their part in the crime, Rustin would have known it was all a lie.

In front of the house again, Rustin paced the circumference of the yard. Something was still bothering him, something he had asked his dad about earlier that day. What about Natalie? *I might as well just die.*

Who wants to live with such a coward anyway? A truck pulled in front of the house; a horn honked. He watched Ryan wave and somehow raised his own hand. *So much as for cleaning the tree house.* Rustin rolled his eyes.

Shut up. I do. And so does she. Zack walked past Rustin and punched him lightly on his shoulder. Zack then raised his hand up. Rustin's hand came up and met his in their custom. *You're not a coward, Rusi. You're one of the strongest people I know. Go get the girl, damn it.* Atlas walked past them toward the truck. Zack let his hand drop after a moment before he followed.

As the truck drove away, Rustin paced back and forth, his thoughts chasing one another in a circle. Those that involved the court case, his injuries, and flashes of the attack that seemed more like a nightmare than a true memory. He heard the front door open softly. Rustin stopped pacing. He turned and watched as Natalie approached.

She raised her small hand slightly and appeared to lean forward. But as an afterthought, she pulled back.

I want this, Zack.

Kiss her then. Rustin could see Zack seated in the back of the cab, much like Zack had seen him months ago by the stream, where Rustin had been discarded and left for dead. This time, however, Zack had a ridiculous grin on his face. *Count to three, lean in, and kiss her. Hold on. Let me tell Atlas to turn the car around. I could do it for you.*

No. "Like hell you will." Natalie looked shocked. Rustin grinned, shaking his head. "Not you." Silently, he counted to three and then leaned forward: a soft pair of lips met his halfway.

ABOUT AUTHOR KC WARDELL

Just to get it out of the way since I know it's going to be asked, I'm paralyzed and still following my dreams.

I'm a book hoarder. Hey, I like to read.

I graduated from CSUS with a bachelor's degree in psychology. My focus was school shooters.

Back when I was eighteen, I pulled together a project with the help of family and friends. It was called *Operation Take Heart*. We raised money to buy Christmas gifts for kids locked in Juvenile Hall. I did this for almost ten years.

On the home front, I have a son named AJ and three chihuahua's named Lacey, Brownie, and Milo. They think they rule the house.

I live in Northern California.

Thank you for reading 'Carson Promise'. You can find out more about me, my book(s), and upcoming projects here:

Facebook-Author KC Wardell

Twitter

LinkedIn

Youtube

Hope is Always Within Reach

KC Wardell